MAD COWS
COME BACK TO BITE

Mad Cows Come Back To Bite

A Novel

Benson S. Forbes

ISBN-10: 0615784879
ISBN-13: 978-0615784878

Revised and Republished by
Shari S. Forbes
PO Box 1424
Sherwood, Oregon 97140
2013

1985

Barbados

A toddler is splashing in the surf near Mullins Beach. Suddenly, she begins to shriek in pain. Her mother comes running and scoops her
up. She sees the raised welt that looks like transparent seaweed wrapped around the baby's leg. She races to the house and squeezes
the juice of freshly cut limes on the welt.
She knows this is the only thing that will ease
the searing pain of a jellyfish sting.

The Big Island of Hawaii

It is afternoon. The children at the orphanage are finished with their chores. The nuns are supervising them as they play outside. A small girl named Abigail tugs at Sister Mary Rose's habit and points to the
sky. Sister shields her eyes with her hand and looks up.
"Look, Sister. It's the biggest kite I've ever seen,"
says Abigail just before she dies.

Chapter 1

A RMED MARINES PATROLLED the perimeter of the White House, and workmen hurriedly finished removing spectator stands outside the Capitol as snowflakes began to fall in Washington, D.C. It was the day after Glenn O. Forbes at the age of fifty-four had been sworn in as America's new President. He was the first Independent ever elected to the post.

Inside the White House the new President began his first day in office in the breakfast room clad in a monogrammed silk dressing gown. With him at the linen-swathed table was his wife, the new First Lady Maxine Hoover Forbes, and his trusted friend and recently-appointed chief security advisor General Howard Kingsman.

The Forbes-Kingsman alliance went back to their boyhood days when they grew up together on adjoining farms in Rush County, Kansas. The friendship had continued through the years even though they had taken separate paths after high school. Forbes had gone to Harvard to study law, while Kingsman had opted for a military career and attended the Air Force Academy near Colorado Springs. Later, during Forbes's stint in the Air Force, he and Kingsman had flown missions together during the Gulf War.

During one sortie, Iraqi anti-aircraft fire had brought down their Super Hornet F18 near Kirkuk in northern Iraq. They had ejected from the plane before it crashed and had evaded hostile troops for three days by slogging and crawling through the murky water in a chain of irrigation canals. On the fourth day, they came across some friendly Kurds who hid them out until a special ops unit rescued them two weeks later. Having been declared MIA, presumed dead, they made worldwide news and were given a hero's welcome upon returning to the U.S.

After that, the two followed separate paths again - Kingsman continuing his Air Force career and eventually being promoted to General, Forbes pursuing a political career. Fed up with the tired trite platforms of the major parties, Forbes had chosen always to run as an Independent. This, he believed, enabled him to stand for what he truly believed in and to be an honest representative of the people. Apparently, the people agreed, because they had elected him to every office he had sought - first as Congressman, then Senator from Kansas, and now as President of the United States. Throughout it all, he and Kingsman had remained friends and allies, and now it was only natural that Forbes would want his trusted friend by his side as his top advisor.

Now on his first day in office, Forbes was preparing to tackle his immense new job as he had always prepared - by starting the day with a good, hearty country-style breakfast. As he swallowed his last bite of Black Angus steak and leaned back in his chair, his wife Maxine glanced at her watch and put down the morning edition of *The Washington Post* that she had been reading while sipping her coffee.

"Your inaugural speech has good reviews in *The Post*, Glenn," she said, smiling at him. "So far so good. Do you think you'll be able to carry out all those promises?"

Kingsman looked up from his plate and grinned. Forbes winked at him. "You know me, Max. When I say I'll do something, I do it. This town needs to be held accountable. Too many past Presidents have ignored the real issues and concentrated on catering only to those who contributed to their campaign funds. I at least have always managed to get elected without getting millions from people who wanted something in return. Now it's time to clean up this budget deficit and start spending the taxpayers" money on our own people instead of footing the bill for every other downtrodden country in the world."

Maxine grinned at him. "Well, your refusal to participate in the traditional inaugural celebrations was definitely a start, although I certainly would have liked to do some partying," she said somewhat wistfully.

"You know, the Washington crowd has already given you a nickname - President Scrooge."

This brought a chuckle from Kingsman and Forbes. "I don't give a Kansas rat's ass what they call me as long as I can make a difference in spending priorities," he said. "It doesn't make sense to spend millions on partying at public expense when there are millions living at the poverty level and the elderly can't even afford prescription drugs."

"You're so right, Sweetness," said Maxine, rising from the table and giving the President a peck on the cheek. "Helping the poor and the elderly - especially the undernourished children - is what I want to accomplish, and I'm off to my first meeting to do just that. By the way," she added, pointing at the scant remains on the President's plate, "did you enjoy your first presidential breakfast? Steak rare enough for you, and eggs runny enough?"

Forbes smiled up at her and glanced at Kingsman with a twinkle in his eye. "Sure did, Max. I feel right at home. My brother-in-law raises the best beef in the country, maybe the world, isn't that right, Hank?"

"You've got that right," said Kingsman, putting down his fork and pushing his chair back from the table. "Nothing better than Kansas beef, anywhere, anytime. Thank God, we're not going through what the Brits are with all that Mad Cow and Hoof and Mouth business."

Forbes frowned. "Yes ... this outbreak of Foot and Mouth as the Brits call it seems to be growing into an epidemic. It will be costly for them - having to slaughter all that livestock. We've got to make sure it doesn't happen here. If it did, it would devastate the whole beef industry, and what we don't need right now is another economic crisis. We had our taste of that with the Mad Cow outbreak in Washington State in 2003. Remember?"

Maxine nodded. "Yes. That was terrible, with Japan and others banning importation of our beef and the grocery stores taking all the beef off the shelves. I know how our farmers and ranchers suffered over that. I certainly feel sorry for the Brits."

She glanced at both men who now wore grim expressions as they recalled the first known case of Mad Cow Disease in the U.S. It had been discovered in a dairy cow in Washington State in December of 2003. "Let's change the subject, shall we? Hank, don't you think it's about time you settled down and got married? You surely don't want to spend the rest of your life being a bachelor do you?"

The General grinned at Maxine. They had been through this many times before. "Haven't met anyone who wants to put up with the likes of me," he said. "I'm good for a one-night stand, but when they start getting to know me, they're off like a shot!"

"Ho! You can't tell me that!" scoffed Maxine. "I think it's you who's off like a shot the minute you start to have any kind of feelings. The Big Bad General, the War Hero - tough as nails, but I know better – you're just plain scared!"

Kingsman hung his head in mock humiliation. "You've got my number, lady. Always did," he said meekly. He picked up the titanium briefcase he had placed on the floor by his chair and placed it on his lap. "I promise to mull over my shortcomings and try to do better, but right now I have an urgent matter that needs the President's attention," he said, glancing at his wristwatch.

Maxine took the hint. She leaned down and gave her husband another peck on the cheek. "Ok, I'm off. I'll leave the two of you to presidential matters. See you this evening, darling, and good luck with your first Cabinet meeting."

Forbes squeezed her hand. "And good luck with your meeting. I'll be eager to hear how it went at dinner tonight."

Forbes and Kingsman watched as Maxine walked toward the door. She paused in front of a large oval mirror on the wall near the door, straightened her navy blue suit, adjusted her cream-colored silk blouse collar and smoothed down a few strands of her natural platinum-silver hair. Her hair had turned prematurely gray in her early thirties and she had considered dying it blonde but decided against it after Glenn reminded her that the silver hair lent her youthful face more credibility as the wife of a politician.

When the door closed behind her, Forbes rose from the table and motioned for Hank to follow him to the sitting area close to the fireplace. Hank placed the briefcase on the coffee table between them and sat down on a couch with a grim look on his weathered face. "So, what's up?" inquired Forbes, nodding at the briefcase as he settled into a comfortable leather wing back chair.

"That's what you'll have to find out," said Hank, thumbing the combination lock on the case. "I was told to give this to you - for your eyes only. I don't have a clue what it is, but it does seem ominous."

He opened the case and withdrew a black file folder bound with red ribbons secured by an official-looking black wax seal. Forbes raised his highbrows in curiosity as Hank pushed the file across the coffee table towards him. He hesitated, still looking at Hank.

"Go ahead. You're the only one who can break the seal, Mr. President," said Hank with a wave of his hand.

Still looking at Hank, Forbes reached into his breast pocket and pulled out his reading glasses and put them on. Then, without further delay, he took up the file and briefly examined it before breaking the seal. He quickly untied the ribbons and opened the file. "Project Rattlesnake?" He glanced up at Hank from the title page of the file. "This was not mentioned in any security briefings I had yesterday and earlier this morning - not by the CIA or the National Security Council."

The General shrugged and rubbed his chin somewhat nervously. "And what about the FBI? They're supposed to know everything." The General just shook his head.

Forbes frowned and looked back down at the file. "What is this then, that even our top secret agencies don't know about?" He muttered more to himself than to Hank. He turned the next page and began reading.

As Forbes read, Hank occupied himself with some other paperwork he had in the briefcase. He glanced up at the President occasionally when he heard him utter "Good God!" and "Oh, Hell!" at various intervals. The President didn't look up. He just kept reading until he had finished the twenty pages in the file and without hesitation, he flipped back to the beginning and read through the document again.

At last he put the file down on the coffee table and without saying anything, rose from his chair, stretched and went to the window where he stood for some time gazing distractedly at the snow falling outside. The flakes were thick and swirling now making it difficult to see the traffic on Pennsylvania Avenue.

Finally, he turned and faced Hank who had been watching him and waiting for a response. "You have no idea of the contents of this file?"

Hank shook his head. "No idea at all other than I was told it was urgent that you should see it."

"Where did you get it, Hank?"

"From your predecessor yesterday after you were sworn in. He gave it to me himself when no one was watching, and he told me to give it to you first thing this morning."

"Damn! Project Rattlesnake - it was about to strike and now it's been thrown at my feet, and if we aren't careful, it's going to bite us where no one will suck the poison out!" exclaimed Forbes, running his fingers through his dark hair.

Hank watched him with concern. "What is it, Glenn?"

Forbes looked at him for a moment, considering. Then he strode to the coffee table, picked up the file and shoved it at Hank. "Here. You read it, Hank. I can't deal with it totally alone. At least two of us in this administration will know, but it can't go any further than that, understood?"

Hank nodded. "You know you can trust me, Mr. President," he replied quietly.

"Yes, Hank. I do know that," said Forbes. "That's why I want you in on this. Read the damned thing."

Hank bent his head, examined the title page, turned to the next page and began to read. While he read, Forbes paced about the room for a bit, then stood gazing again out of the window at the flurry of snowflakes. Suddenly, there was a light knock on the door. Forbes glanced at Hank who was totally engrossed in his reading. He went to the door and cracked it open. A boyish face peered in at him. It was Victor Hardwood, his Chief of Staff.

"What is it, Vic?" asked Forbes impatiently, causing the smile to disappear from Hardwood's face.

"Excuse me for interrupting, Mr. President, but you have a cabinet meeting in twenty minutes, and in the meantime there have been calls from various heads of state all demanding to talk to you."

The President glanced over his shoulder and saw that Hank had finished reading the file and had put it back in its folder. He turned back to Hardwood. "Tell the Cabinet to hold their horses, and inform the switchboard that I don't accept telephone calls willy-nilly. Set up a telephone schedule. If there is anyone who wishes to talk to me it will be by appointment only. Otherwise, I'll be spending all my time yacking on the phone."

"Yes, Sir," said Hardwood, puzzled by the President's gruffness. He attempted to peer into the cracked door to see who was with the President, but Forbes quickly closed the door. Forbes returned to his chair across from Hank. "That guy needs to get his head on straight," he muttered as he sat down. "Well, Hank?"

Hank shook his head. "It seems no one anticipated the consequences at the outset. Looks as if it fell through the cracks and nobody took much notice."

"Horse shit!" said Forbes vehemently, startling Hank out of his reverie. "It's a stupid cover-up. Not one of my predecessors had the guts to kill it, and now It's grown into a full-sized rattler ready to strike at any second, and it's been thrown into my bed! You never imagine that when you get yourself elected President that you're going to have to deal with such a thing on your first day in office. This will jeopardize our credibility as a nation, and I can't even imagine the cost that will be incurred in getting this thing ..." He stopped abruptly and drew himself up in his chair.

Hank waited. He knew his friend well enough to know that a plan was about to be announced.

Forbes pointed his finger at Hank. "We need to keep this close. No leaks, no press rumors," he said in his take-command voice. "Hank, we need a good team to resolve this once and for all. It has to be a separate operation without links to the CIA or to any other government agency, and that includes the military. It's been a total fuckup to this point, and we can't afford to have it screwed up even more by anyone who has a vested interest. It must be a civilian enterprise with absolutely no links to this administration except for the two of us."

Hank swallowed hard and nodded in agreement.

"I want you to run it, Hank. You're the only one I can trust," Forbes continued, his eyes boring into Hank's. "Can you do it with absolutely no visibility?"

Hank leaned forward in his chair and struck the file with his closed fist. "You know I can, Mr. President! It will certainly break the monotony of making reports at endless go-nowhere meetings and listening to people who don't know what they are talking about."

"I know what you mean – that's precisely what the President's job is all about. I couldn't have said it better." Forbes smiled and rose to his feet. "Ok, Hank, the job is yours. Get your team together and after that ... well, I suggest you start in the UK, if you know what I mean."

"Certainly do," said Hank with a knowing smile. He quickly put the file back into his briefcase, closed the lock, and attached the briefcase to his belt with a steel chain. He stood at attention and saluted. "Thank you, Mr. President."

Forbes saluted back. "I'll expect to be kept up to date, Hank. If there is anything pressing, use my direct line. Don't use the switchboard. No appointment is necessary in your case. I don't want Hardwood putting you on the official schedule for all the world to see," said Forbes with a grin. He went over and clapped his old friend on the shoulder. "And by the way, Hank, wear civilian clothes the next time we have breakfast. It's too early for me to be suited up."

Hank smiled. "All right, Sir. Whatever you say. You're the Commander in Chief."

Forbes chuckled and clapped his friend on the shoulder again as he walked him to the door. "If there is anything special that you need, let me know, Hank. You have a full load to carry, I'm afraid."

"Don't worry. You can count on me, Mr. President. I'll have something to report by the end of the week," Hank said as he strode rapidly out the door, eager to get on with his mission.

*   *   *

Twenty minutes later the President walked into the Cabinet room dressed informally in a blue polo shirt and beige corduroy jeans. The Cabinet members rose to their feet and applauded as he took his seat at the head of the large conference table.

"Good Morning, Mr. President! We're honored to serve on your Cabinet," exclaimed Secretary of State Charles Robinson, who appeared to have assumed the role of spokesperson for the group.

"Thanks, Charlie, and welcome to all of you on this first day of my administration," said Forbes, motioning for the group to be seated. "We have lots to discuss, so let's save the congratulations and get to work, shall we?"

"Yes, Mr. President," chorused the group. The President opened the file in front of him and turned to the Secretary of State. "Charlie, you're up first. Tell us what's going on with the Brits and the Russians."

Robinson's smile faded. "The fact is, Mr. President, we're not sure. Our analysts can't figure out why Britain and Russia would enter into a mutual military aid agreement - especially Britain, since it is protected by our missile shield."

"Do we have a copy of the agreement? Maybe there is something in the small print that explains it all," asked Forbes.

Robinson's face reddened and he looked down at his hands folded on top of the table. "No, Mr. President. The State Department does not have a copy. All we have is the news article from *The London Times*."

"A news article! Surely the CIA has a copy?" asked the President, turning his attention to Raymond Thomas, the CIA Director, who was seated across the table from Robinson.

"We don't have a copy either," said Thomas, embarrassed. "All we have is *The Times* article, and I know that sounds stupid."

"You're right about that, Ray," said Forbes. "It sounds more than stupid! An organization as big and with the reputation of the CIA doesn't know what's going on between our most trusted ally and the Russians! You'd better get a copy and at the same time get your analysts to come up with reasons for the treaty. How the Brits could make such a radical change in their foreign policy without us knowing is beyond my comprehension!"

The President looked around the table. All the Cabinet members were wearing hangdog expressions and refused to look him in the eye.

"If you know your history, you know it was just this kind of agreement that forced Britain into the First World War - all because of a secret pact involving France and Russia to protect themselves from the Germans," said Forbes in a calmer tone. "So why, gentlemen, after all those cold war years, would Britain now find it necessary to make a pact with the Russians? It just doesn't make sense."

"Possibly it's because Russia is on our potential nuclear target list ..." mused Robinson, somewhat hesitantly.

The President looked at him in disbelief. "Charlie, if you follow that line of thinking, that means if we attacked Russia, Britain would go to their aid and attack us! That's utter bullshit!"

A pall of silence fell over the Cabinet room. Forbes paused, shook his head, and crossed off the first item on the first agenda of his Presidency.

*   *   *

Chapter 2

T HE WORST CONSTITUTIONAL crisis since Edward VIII"s abdication was about to embroil England, and it was on the brink of losing its close relationship with America - an alliance that had been in place since World War II.

The ruling party, headed by Prime Minister Alistair Cain, had lost its majority in the House of Commons because of a no-confidence vote. Despite denials from the Prime Minister and his Cabinet, the vote had been based on an unsubstantiated article in *The London Times* alleging that the government had made a secret pact with Russia.

According to the article, Britain had agreed to go to Russia's aid if it was attacked, and vise versa. The article, however, offered no explanation as to why the government would agree to such a sudden reversal in its foreign policy, nor did it name a source of the information. It had long been supposed there would be no need for a treaty with Russia because of Britain's membership in NATO and its alliance with America. At Prime Minister Cain's directive, MI5 was conducting an expedient investigation to uncover the source of the article.

To make matters worse, a serious outbreak of Foot and Mouth Disease had occurred in Southern England and, on top of that, increasing numbers of people were being hospitalized with symptoms of Mad Cow Disease. Public demonstrations - even riots - in protest of the government's handling of these crises were growing in size and violence and occurring in most of England's major cities.

Following the no-confidence vote in the ruling party, protocol required that the Prime Minister should go to Buckingham Palace and hand in his resignation to the Queen. The Queen would then dismiss Parliament, and a general election would be held to elect a new government.

Against all precedence, however, Prime Minister Cain refused to hand in his resignation, under the pretext that the intermingling of country people with city people in a general election in the midst of the Foot and Mouth crisis would cause the disease to spread out of control.

The drizzle on that Friday morning in January was cold and penetrating. Pedestrians drew up their coat collars and wielded umbrellas against the raw, bitter wind blowing from the Thames. As they scurried along, they noticed the road barrier erected at the entrance of Downing Street. Police officers armed with automatic weapons stood guard at the barricade, while more armed police lined the rooftops and observed the passing crowds below through binoculars.

At mid-morning a line of black chauffeur-driven Bentleys approached the barricade. Before each car was allowed to proceed, police examined identification papers of the passengers and checked them against a visitor's list. Once allowed to pass, the chauffeur drove the short distance to Number Ten along the street lined on both sides by armed police. At the entry to Number Ten, a police officer again checked the passengers" credentials before they were allowed to disembark and go inside. The chauffeur then drove forward some distance and parked making room for the next car in line.

Just as the officer at the barricade had accounted for nearly all the visitors on his list, a sleek black Jaguar pulled up. The smoke-tinted electric window whispered down, and the officer peered into the car noting that the driver was the sole occupant. Unlike the other visitors, this man was dressed in sporty tweeds with a matching snap-down cap and black kid driving gloves. Despite the dark dismal day, he wore expensive designer sunglasses.

"Picture identification, please, Sir."

The driver held out a laminated ID card and removed his sunglasses, looking directly at the officer. The officer observed that the man's jet-black hair, piercing blue eyes, and strongly etched facial features matched those on the picture ID. He turned away and typed in the name on a palm-sized computer. After a few seconds, a message flashed on the screen. The officer promptly turned back to the driver and handed him his ID card. "Sorry, Mr. Fleet. No admittance. Please turn around and leave."

The driver shook his head and with a lazy smile held out the ID card again. "I'm afraid that's impossible officer. I received a telephone call early this morning from the Prime Minister's secretary, and I am expected for an appointment. Please check again."

"Most unusual," uttered the officer, looking at the card again. "Your name is not on the visitors" list. What is your business at Number Ten, Mr. Fleet?" he inquired, putting on his sternest look.

"Diplomatic," said Fleet with a nonchalant shrug of his shoulders.

Still watching Fleet, the officer brought the lapel of his uniform up to his mouth and spoke into a tiny microphone clipped to it. "Phillips here. I have a Mr. Julian Fleet who claims to have an appointment at Number Ten this morning. He says his appointment was made through the Prime Minister's secretary, but he isn't on the list. His identification is in order."

While he waited for a response, Officer Phillips stared curiously at Fleet who returned his gaze unabashedly. After a short while, a muted voice came through the tiny speaker on Phillips's lapel. "Officer Phillips, we have confirmed the appointment. Let Mr. Fleet pass."

"Right," said Phillips into the microphone. "Should I make a notation on the computer?"

"No!" responded the voice in an adamant tone. "Mr. Fleet is on *unofficial* business."

Phillips raised his eyebrow as he returned the ID card to Fleet and stepped back from the car door. "Sorry for the inconvenience, Sir, but your name wasn't on the official list."

Fleet grinned good-naturedly at him and waved a hand as the barricade lifted. He rolled up the window and the Jaguar continued up the street to Number Ten as a puzzled Phillips stared after it.

*　　*　　*

Inside the Cabinet Room at Number Ten Ministers retrieved folders from worn leather satchels, seated themselves around a long oblong table and sat fidgeting and shooting nervous glances at each other.

They all drew themselves up to attention when precisely at eleven o'clock Prime Minister Alistair Cain walked briskly into the room and seated himself halfway along the table. He quickly glanced around and then down at the agenda before him. "Now, gentlemen, it's business as usual," he pronounced abruptly. "You are first on the agenda, Mr. Atkins," he said, looking at the Minister of Agriculture. "How are we progressing in containing the Foot and Mouth?"

Atkins's face reddened slightly as he looked down at his folder and cleared his throat. "Not good news I'm afraid, Prime Minister. The number of animals diagnosed with the disease has increased, and as of this morning there were fifty new cases reported in Hampshire. Counties in the South of England are the most affected. We have quarantined Kent, Sussex and Hampshire and have banned the transportation of both live and dead animals. As of nine o'clock this morning 807,600 animals had been destroyed, and the supply of red meat is becoming critical. All that's really left for the consumer is pork and poultry, and there will soon be a shortage of those."

"How many sheep and how many cattle have been affected, Minister?"

Atkins swallowed hard and glanced down at the opened folder again. "Out of the 807,600 animals infected with Foot and Mouth, 12.5 percent are sheep, one percent are pigs, and the rest are cattle," he read.

"Give me the actual number of cattle infected, Minister! I'm not a human calculator!" exclaimed the Prime Minister in exasperation.

"Six hundred ninety-eight thousand, five hundred seventy-four," piped up John Bartlestone, the Minister of Defense, before Atkins could respond.

"Thank you, Mr. Bartlestone," said Cain. He frowned at Atkins registering his displeasure and turned to the Minister of Health at the far end of the table. "Mr. Strong, how many people do we believe have contracted Mad Cow? Give me numbers, not percentages."

Hubert Strong shuffled the papers in his folder, pulled out a report and peered at it. "Twelve thousand nine hundred and seventeen, Prime Minister."

A collective gasp was heard around the room.

"Including one hundred and twenty-six reported only yesterday," he added.

Cain turned back to Atkins. "Was Mad Cow found in any of the cattle that were destroyed for Foot and Mouth, Minister?"

Atkins shook his head. "None so far, Prime Minister."

Cain paused for a moment, frowning. He looked up at Strong. "How are your Ministries services coping, Mr. Strong?"

Strong shook his head. "We are stretched to the limit. All hospital wards in Leicester, Nottingham and surrounding towns are full, and we are now converting unused barracks at military bases."

The Prime Minister looked at the others seated around the table. All faces wore grim expressions. He turned back to Strong. "Is there a cure for Mad Cow in humans?"

"There is no known cure for Mad Cow, Prime Minister," replied Strong shaking his head miserably. "We're doing all that we possibly can, but no breakthroughs yet."

"What about Foot and Mouth - is there a vaccine for that, Mr. Atkins?" asked Cain gracing the red-faced Minister of Agriculture with his penetrating glare.

"The Americans have sent us samples that they think will work on this particular strain. We are testing it now, but I'm afraid it will take six weeks to know the results."

Silence fell over the room again as the cabinet ministers glanced nervously at each other and waited for the Prime Minister's response. Cain sat back in his chair and rubbed his chin as he digested this grim news. At last he drew himself up and banged his fist on the table. "We are at war, gentlemen!" he declared passionately. "We must do all we can to defeat these diseases; otherwise, this country will be devastated!" He paused and looked around the room at the solemn faces. "The first priority is to contain the Foot and Mouth. This must be *the* top priority of each Ministry."

Atkins was the first to respond. "I believe we have enough resources, Prime Minister. The police and the army are assisting in setting up roadblocks. All vehicles and people go through disinfectant before they are allowed to leave contaminated areas and there is a complete ban on cattle markets throughout Great Britain."

"Then why are new outbreaks occurring in Hampshire, Minister?"

Atkins shrugged his shoulders. "Despite our extraordinary precautions and measures we are taking, the new outbreaks are occurring in what we deemed to be disease-free areas."

"Are you suggesting, Mr. Atkins, that foul play is afoot?" asked the Prime Minister, raising his eyebrows.

Atkins shrugged his shoulders again, and the Minister of Defense spoke up. "We can't be sure of that as yet, but we are conducting a full investigation."

"Be sure that you do," said Cain, waving his hand. "We need to get to the bottom of this quickly. Otherwise, the demonstrations and unemployment will intensify, and we don't want the general public to lose confidence in us, now do we?"

The Cabinet members looked uncomfortable, each remembering all too well the recent no-confidence vote in Parliament. The Prime Minister turned his attention back to the Minister of Health. "What are your plans to contain Mad Cow if it is caused by eating contaminated meat?"

"All meat intended for human consumption is inspected, and, as an extra precaution, we have banned the sales of meat on the bone."

"Is there a test for Mad Cow, Minister?"

"Not at this time, Prime Minister. It is diagnosed by symptoms only. The disease can only be confirmed by doing an autopsy on the brain after death."

A pall fell over the room.

"One has to be dead, Minister?" asked Cain in a low tone. "To confirm the disease?"

"Yes, Prime Minister, the only way at present is to dissect the brain."

"Listen carefully, Minister. All possible scientific technology must be employed to find a cure and a better way of diagnosing it, as well as finding out why so many people are contracting the disease. It's up to you, Mr. Strong, as Minister of Health, to direct this effort, and spare no expense."

"Here! Here!" cried the Cabinet members in unison.

The Prime Minister nodded in appreciation of their response, and after dismissing the Ministers of Agriculture and Health to prepare a joint news release at one o'clock, he turned to the Chancellor of the Exchequer.

"Time now for your report, Mr. Nelson. Give us the bad news about the economy."

"Yes, Sir. The news is indeed not good," said Nelson. "The direct cost for the impact of Foot and Mouth on the farming sector, so far, is three billion. Additional cost for the Ministry of Health is two billion, and the loss in tax revenues is devastating. We will need to borrow vast sums to keep the government operating."

"What about unemployment? What are the numbers?" asked the Prime Minister with a sigh.

"Not good, Prime Minister," said Nelson, shaking his head, and holding up a document. "I have the latest numbers here. Since the first outbreak of Foot and Mouth unemployment has gone up to ten and one-half percent." Glancing at the Prime Minister's glowering frown, he hastily added. "You can be assured that unemployment benefits are being given top priority, even though the Treasury has only enough resources to last six months unless taxes are increased."

The Prime Minister halfway rose from his seat and leaned across the table. "Nonsense! We cannot possibly raise taxes at this time! The public would tar and feather us! We must find other means of raising revenue. What do you propose?"

"The only alternative is to go to the Swiss bankers with cup in hand. I can think of no other option," said Nelson hesitantly.

"We are not beggars, either!" exploded Cain. "You know the Swiss will want their pound of flesh, and I cannot condone that."

As the other Cabinet members fidgeted under the Prime Minister's fierce outburst, Chancellor Nelson looked down at the table. "Very well, Sir," he muttered. "I will put the feelers out, but we will pay dearly with anyone. In circumstances such as these, even the poorest nations have the advantage."

"Then, by God, it's time we called in our loans, Mr. Nelson!" roared Cain, banging on the table. "You know as well as I do that Great Britain has always been generous in assisting developing countries, and now they need to reciprocate - especially those who have more gold reserves than we do."

Nelson nodded miserably, still looking down at the table.

"Mr. Wheatly! What plans do you have for containing the demonstrations? We certainly do not want to see any violence," said the Prime Minister, abruptly turning to the Home Secretary.

Wheatly started at this sudden shift of focus to himself. He cleared his throat nervously. "Er ... ah, yes. We estimate there will be about half a million demonstrators this weekend in Westminster and Trafalgar areas. The Metropolitan Police have canceled all leave and they are bringing in additional police from the home counties. After seven o'' clock tonight, all roads to Trafalgar Square and Westminster will be barricaded and all underground stations in the area will be closed."

"Excellent, Home Secretary," said Cain with the hint of a smile, and Mr. Wheatly visibly relaxed. "This policy of containment sounds like a good idea. Any other precautions?"

"Yes, Prime Minister. We have installed an additional three thousand security cameras throughout the area."

"Any intelligence on the world trade dissidents? Seems it would be an excellent opportunity for them to infiltrate the crowd and raise havoc."

"Nothing concrete, but we are on our toes."

"Well, be sure to plan for all contingencies, Mr. Wheatly. We don't want any surprises," said the Prime Minister. He glanced at the Victorian clock hanging on the wall at the far end of the conference table. "Well, gentlemen, it appears we can only wait for this meat shortage to take its course." The hint of a smile tugged at the corners of his mouth. "I dare say Mrs. Cain is not in the best of moods these days - nothing but tinned corned beef. It does not do well for Sunday dinner, you see."

The Ministers relaxed slightly, chuckling at the Prime Minister's subtle attempt at humor. Their smiles soon disappeared, however, when Cain suddenly rapped the table with his fist. "Back to the agenda," he said. "I have something important to say so listen carefully. This Prime Minister and you, the Cabinet, are in full agreement. This government lost its majority because of an unfounded newspaper article. The article is a lie. There is no alleged treaty with Russia. Does anyone here have doubts? If so, he should say so now." Cain looked slowly around the table from Minister to Minister.

"I do not have doubts, but there have been a number of inquiries from our allies, particularly from the Americans. It is difficult to convince them that an article printed in such a prestigious paper as *The London Times* has no basis in fact," said Sir Albert Rid, the Foreign Minister.

"I'm aware of that, Minister. Remember that it's a new administration over there, and it is natural that they would be highly suspicious. I am scheduled for my first teleconference with President Forbes later today, and I will attempt to clarify matters with him. As you are aware, I have directed MI5 to conduct an investigation into the source of that piece in *The Times*, and we should soon have an answer. Meanwhile, we must continue to maintain a united front in denying that there is anything to this alleged treaty. Again, if there is anyone here who doubts this, he should speak up now and immediately tender his resignation."

The Cabinet room remained silent as Cain again waited for a response. Finally, after hearing none, he spoke again in a subdued tone. "That concludes this meeting, then, and remember what is said here, stays here. Any leaks will be investigated and the one responsible will be held accountable. Do you understand?"

Ministers either nodded or murmured their acknowledgment as they quickly packed their briefcases. The Prime Minister stood up and nodded at each Minister as he left the room. When the last Minister had departed, he motioned to his private secretary. "Ask Lord Davenville to come in now," he said, smoothing back the thick, springy hair on both sides of his head.

On his way to the sitting area near a fireplace, Cain paused by a mirror to check for any signs of perspiration on his forehead. There were none. He stood back slightly and took in a larger view of himself. In his post-fifty years, people had begun remarking on his resemblance to Rex Harrison, but he couldn't see it. Probably, he didn't want to see it, because he had always loathed Harrison and generally thought of most male actors as twits, with the possible exception of Michael Caine. But then, perhaps that was because of the name which was the same as his except with an "e" on the end. This little episode of woolgathering came to an abrupt end when his secretary opened the door and announced, "Lord Davenville, Prime Minister."

Cain quickly turned from the mirror and stepped forward to greet the tall, distinguished-looking gentleman who strode into the room. Lord John Russell Davenville was the current Davenville serving on the Queen"s Privy Council. There had been a Davenville on the Privy Council ever since 1910 when King George V had appointed his great-grandfather Lord Alfred Davenville to the post.

"My Lord, it's a pleasure to see you. I trust you were not kept waiting too long," said Cain, shaking Lord Davenville's hand.

"Alistair," said Davenville, acknowledging the greeting. "Not at all. In fact, I just arrived from a meeting with the Queen at Buckingham. Let's dispense with the formalities, shall we? Call me John. After all, we're old friends and this is an informal conversation just between the two of us."

"Right you are, John. And how is Her Majesty?" asked Cain, motioning Davenville toward an overstuffed armchair near the fireplace.

"Her Majesty is in good health and sharp as a tack, despite her age," said Davenville as he took a seat. "I daresay she takes after her mum. At the rate she's going, our Prince Charlie may never have the opportunity to be King."

Cain grinned as he sat down opposite Davenville and crossed his legs. "Such a pity after spending a lifetime in training. Spot of sherry?"

"That would be pleasant," said Davenville.

Cain poured Harvey's Bristol Cream from a cut-glass decanter into two small liqueur glasses, and handed one to Davenville. "Your health," he said, raising his glass.

"Cheers," said Davenville, raising his glass.

Each took a small sip of the rich amber liquid. "And now, down to our business at hand," said Cain. "What is Her Majesty's view of the current crisis in the government, and how will the Privy Council advise her?"

"As you know, when a ruling party has been defeated, precedent requires that the monarch dismiss Parliament so that a new government can be elected. Her Majesty is somewhat perplexed that you have not appeared to tender your resignation as is the usual protocol in such matters. She is expecting to follow precedent. Royalty is not in the business of breaking tradition, as I'm sure you are well aware," said Davenville, with an elegant wave of his hand.

"Unless you think of Henry VIII," said Cain, eliciting a chuckle from Davenville. "Seriously, wouldn't Her Majesty consider breaking tradition if there were a very good reason for it - a reason that is in the best interests of the country as a whole?"

"Her Majesty is certainly willing to consider all arguments and generally heeds the advice of the Privy Council before proceeding on any weighty matters. Let me hear your arguments, and I will take them up with the Council. If the Council concurs, then we will advise the Queen accordingly," said Davenville, reaching for his glass of sherry.

"First and foremost, the vote of no-confidence in my party was based on an unfounded allegation in *The London Times*. My Cabinet members and I have consistently and adamantly insisted that there is no truth to it - no treaty with Russia whatsoever. I have ordered MI5 to uncover the source of that article, and as soon as that happens, I can assure you that the vote will be reconsidered," said Cain, leaning forward in his chair.

"Be that as it may, Alistair, the fact remains that the vote did occur, and the precedent is to elect a new government, regardless of the circumstances behind the vote," said Davenville, again waving his hand.

"Then perhaps the Queen would be moved by the fact that holding a general election at this particular time would have a devastating impact on the entire country," said Cain.

"How is that exactly?" inquired Davenville, raising an eyebrow.

Cain leaned even further forward in his chair and stabbed a finger into the air for emphasis. "It would cause Foot and Mouth to spread all over the Kingdom, that's how. Just think - all those people traveling into the polling places and then back again. It's already spread to another county in the south despite the quarantine efforts and the huge numbers of livestock we've had to slaughter."

"Yes," said Davenville. "I see what you mean. I believe that is a convincing enough argument for the Privy Council to advise Her Majesty to at least delay the procedure. I will take it to the Council this afternoon. Mind you, I cannot promise that I can get them to agree to forego the election altogether - only to delay it until the Foot and Mouth crisis has passed." He rose to his feet, and Cain did likewise.

"Thank you, John. The delay will certainly help," said Cain with a smile. "Regarding the shortage of meat, perhaps you could also suggest a couple of other ways in which Her Majesty could help ..."

Davenville chuckled. "While the iron is hot, eh? All right, Alistair, out with it."

"Well, perhaps she could use her influence on the French to get them to stop blocking our efforts to lift the restrictions on importing meat from countries outside the European Union during this crisis. The Americans have offered to ship beef to us, but their hands are tied because of the EU restrictions."

"I'm sure Her Majesty would be most happy to use any influence she can on the French, but whether the French will be influenced by anything other than their own self interest is another matter altogether," said Davenville. "Is there anything else?"

"Just one more thing. It might be viewed as a splendid gesture if the Royals - Her Majesty and the Prince of Wales - were to donate meat from their large herds to those in greatest need. Royalty doing its share, that type of thing, what?"

Davenville gave him an amused smile. "I'm sure there will be no problem whatsoever with that particular suggestion. I must be off now. You'll have an answer later today as to how all this is received by the Privy Council."

As Cain accompanied Davenville to the door, he smiled at his old friend. "Thanks, John. You don't know how much it means to me to have a friend in high places."

"Sometimes, we need all the friends we can get," said Davenville, pausing before the door. "Rest assured, I'll help all I can so long as the good of the Kingdom is at stake."

Shortly after Davenville had exited, Cain again summoned his secretary on an intercom. "It's time for Mr. Fleet," he said.

"Yes, Prime Minister. He is waiting," replied the secretary. Cain stretched his arms and returned to the fireplace smiling to himself. So far, so good, he thought. The door opened, and Julian Fleet strolled in.

"By Jove, Julian, if you aren't the picture for the fashion plates!" exclaimed Cain, a huge grin spreading across his face.

"Oh, do you like it, Prime Minister? Have to keep up appearances you know." Fleet put a hand on his hip and executed a 180-degree turn, showing off his tweeds. At the end of the turn, he struck a pose, and looked at Cain with a haughty expression.

Cain burst out laughing. Fleet grinned, relaxed his stance, strolled casually over to the fireplace and unceremoniously flopped down in the overstuffed chair. "And a dismal good afternoon to you, Prime Minister," he said.

"By God, James Bond had nothing on you, my fine-feathered friend," remarked Cain as he took a seat across from Fleet.

"Not surprising as he was my role model," said Julian.

"Yes, well I hope his instruction serves you well in the upcoming mission. Do you now have full knowledge of the problem and the task at hand that we discussed last week?" asked Cain, growing serious.

"Yes, Prime Minister. I believe I have full understanding after doing the bit of research you mentioned."

"You must be sure, Julian. The problem must be resolved as quickly as possible. Otherwise, calamity will beset us all."

"Yes, Prime Minister. I am fully aware of the urgency and the consequences if the operation fails."

"There is so much at stake, Julian. The operation absolutely must not be traced back to this office. For that reason, you cannot use the normal resources, you understand. You have free rein to use people of your own choosing, but under no circumstances use anyone who has ties to any of the Ministries involved."

Julian nodded. "Of course, Prime Minister. That goes without saying, but what about the Americans?"

Cain frowned. "I'll leave that up to you, Julian. You're the expert here. Just be sure to use people you can trust. The Forbes administration is just getting started, and they may try to throw their weight around a bit at the outset."

"That is to be expected," said Julian, "but from what I've learned about this Forbes fellow, I'm convinced he will do what is necessary."

"I have my first conference with him this afternoon, and of course I will not broach the topic. I'll just let you get on with it. I expect I'll be discussing the Foot and Mouth situation. You know, the Americans have offered to ship meat to us until the disease can be contained. If it weren't for the bloody French, we'd be eating Kansas beef right now."

"Kansas beef?" Julian laughed. "Where is Kansas?"

"Somewhere near Texas, I believe," said Cain with a grin. "All I know is Forbes was born there. Anyway, we must not dally," he said looking at the clock. "Is there anything else?"

"Short of cash, that's all."

"How much this time, Julian?"

"Fifty-five thousand," said Julian in a low voice, glancing over his shoulder at the closed door.

Cain raised an eyebrow. "Is that for bills outstanding, or is it for the operation?"

"Bills outstanding - mainly the hotel suite, which is quite costly."

"Can't you cut down your expenditures, Julian? They seem excessive," said Cain.

"I have cut them down to the minimum, but you must remember the role I'm expected to play, and that is expensive."

"I do understand," said Cain with a sigh. "I'll see to it that a substantial amount is deposited in the account today. I don't want to impede your progress in the task at hand."

"Thank you, Prime Minister." Julian reached for his hat.

"Where in the dickens did you buy that?" asked Cain, pointing at the hat.

"From Tanners on Saville Row."

"I'm paying for that?" Cain asked with a snort.

"The cost of keeping up appearances, Prime Minister."

There was a soft tap on the door. Cain stopped in mid-chuckle and put a finger to his lip. "What is it?" he called out, looking at Fleet.

The door opened and the private secretary looked into the room. "Sorry to interrupt, Prime Minister, but the President of the United States will be calling in five minutes."

"All right, then. I'm on my way. It was good to see you, Julian. Do keep me abreast of your endeavors, won't you?" Cain winked at Julian as he stood up. "I must not keep the new President waiting."

Julian nodded and watched as Cain walked out of the room. Then he went to the mirror and put on his cap, adjusting it as he tilted his head at various angles. Then he pulled his sunglasses out of his breast pocket and put them on. Satisfied that his appearance matched his role, he walked out of the Cabinet Room. He paused at the front desk to lean over and say something to the pretty young receptionist that left her blushing as he strode jauntily out of Number Ten Downing Street.

*   *   *

In his private office, Prime Minister Cain sat behind his desk looking expectantly at the video screen that covered the wall opposite him. A few seconds later the screen flickered and President Forbes appeared sitting behind his desk in the Oval Office.

"Good afternoon, Mr. President, and congratulations again on your election," opened Cain, being careful to look directly into the microcamera mounted above the screen.

"Good morning, Prime Minister, or I should say, good afternoon there," said Forbes with a pleasant smile. "I hope I'm not interrupting anything important?"

"Just a great deal of foot in mouth," said Cain with a grin.

His attempt at humor was not lost on Forbes. "Well, at least that's better than 'hoof in mouth,' as we call it over here."

As the two men chuckled and relaxed slightly, Cain was thinking that he detected a slight nasal twang in the President's speech, and he wondered if that was a Kansas accent.

Forbes's face grew serious as he leaned forward with his hands clasped on the desk in front of him. "I understand the Foot and Mouth outbreak is taking its toll, and that, aside from the impact on your agricultural economy, you're suffering a severe shortage of meat. I want you to know that America stands ready to ship ample supplies of beef to tide you over through this outbreak."

"I know of your offer, Mr. President, and it is very much appreciated. We would certainly take you up on it at this very moment, but as I'm sure you're aware, the European Union has strict import limitations. We have been attempting to get the EU to lift the restrictions for Britain in this case, but the French have vetoed the proposal and refuse to budge so far despite all our diplomatic efforts. France can be very obstinate, you know."

Forbes nodded sympathetically. "How well I know, Prime Minister. America still has not forgotten, nor, in many quarters, forgiven France's stance over Iraq in 2003. Unfortunately, this particular situation is a European matter in which America has no say."

"We are continuing to work on the matter through all our diplomatic channels," said Cain. "We hope France will see the light before matters become too devastating. I thank you most sincerely for the offer, and I hope we will yet be able to take you up on it."

"The United States always stands ready to assist an ally," said Forbes. "We remember all too well what happened to our agricultural economy back in 2003 when we had that incident of Mad Cow appearing in Washington. Is there any other way we can help?"

Cain cleared his throat. "Now that you mention it, there are no restrictions on financial aid ... our coffers are running rather short at the moment."

Forbes remained poker-faced, but Cain thought he saw a slight flickering of the eyelids. "At the moment, I am not prepared to offer monetary assistance, Prime Minister. I have promised the American people to balance the budget, pay off the deficit, and to spend taxpayers" dollars at home. This is not to say that I won't take it up with my Cabinet and my budget people, but I can't promise anything at this time - especially not so early in my administration."

Cain sighed. "Well, I do understand your position after all those years of assisting other countries in achieving their freedom and fighting terrorism. We, of course, were always right by your side."

"That is true," said Forbes nodding. "America has had no greater or more trusted ally than Great Britain ever since World War II. And that brings me to another topic ..."

Here it comes, Cain thought, bracing himself for the inevitable question.

Forbes picked up a newspaper from his desk and held it up. "We are obviously concerned about this article that appeared in *The London Times* stating that you have entered into a mutual aid treaty with Russia."

"That article is unsubstantiated, and there is no truth to it," said Cain. "There is no treaty with Russia."

"I would like to take you at your word, Prime Minister, but you must understand my difficulty in convincing my administration that there is nothing to the article when members of your own Parliament have taken a no-confidence vote in your party because of this very issue. Where is the proof that there is no such treaty? Surely, a paper as prestigious as *The London Times* would not print something that had no basis in fact," said Forbes.

"That is precisely the problem I am facing," said Cain trying to remain calm. "*The Times* cited no basis for the article, and it has refused to reveal any source. My government is employing all its resources to uncover the source, and I am confident the issue will soon be laid to rest and the no-confidence vote will be reconsidered. Again, I repeat, there is no treaty with Russia."

"I have to admit it's difficult to imagine that Great Britain would do such a thing, considering your alliance with us, and the fact that you are protected by your membership in NATO as well as our Missile Shield. Of course, you know that if it were true, America would have no other option than to withdraw the Missile Shield?" asked Forbes.

Cain's face reddened, and he waved his hand at the camera. "The Missile Shield doesn't do us a great deal of good, does it, if a missile fired from Europe can reach us in a scant three minutes."

The two men stared stonily at each other for a few seconds, and then Cain collected himself. "At any rate," he began, "all I can do is repeat that there is no treaty with Russia and that Great Britain has no desire to jeopardize its alliance with America. I ask for your patience in this matter and assure you I'll soon have proof that the *Times* article is totally unfounded."

Forbes again held up *The Times* and slowly and deliberately placed it on the side of his desk. "All right, Prime Minister. The U.S. has no desire of damaging our relationship, either. I'm willing to take you at your word and play the waiting game with you until the truth comes out ... one way or the other. Let's just hope it's soon."

"Thank you, Mr. President. I assure you that every measure is being taken to uncover the source of that article as quickly as possible.

There's a great deal at stake here." Cain put on his most sincere look for the camera.

Forbes stared back at him for a second, then his mouth twitched. "Speaking of „steak," how about if I send you a box of Black Angus T-bones? No quotas on gifts from one friend to another is there?"

Cain laughed. "Not at all! But if my countrymen found out, they might be tempted to reinstate that quaint old English custom of drawing and quartering."

"Ok, I don't want to cause you any more problems," said Forbes with a chuckle. "I'll hold the hounds at bay until I hear from you."

"Thank you, Mr. President. I promise you'll be hearing from me soon. Here's to a long and continued British-American alliance."

"Ditto, Prime Minister. Don't be a stranger, now, y'hear," said Forbes with a grin.

The screen went blank leaving Cain sitting there shaking his head and smiling to himself. He glanced at the clock. Time for the next order of business.

*   *   *

Chapter 3

G EORGE GOATER, THE third assistant to the head of the European Policy Section at the Foreign Office, was busy cleaning out his desk. He had been given three months' notice of his coming forced retirement by the department's administration division. Having been a civil servant since graduating from Cambridge University, he knew his middle age would prevent him from getting another job with the same prestige as the position he had held at the ministry. Having acquiesced to this fact, he was looking forward to the peace and quiet of the country where he could potter in the garden and dabble at writing.

"Well, George, you're retiring at the right time. This treaty business is going to stir things up," said Adam Freeman, his office associate. Adam was leaning back in his swivel chair, feet propped on his desk, reading *The London Times*. "How did *The Times* find out about it? None of us were involved. The Foreign Minister did not have it reviewed by the European Policy Council nor was it evaluated for reaction from America."

"Haven't read about it, Adam," muttered George as he emptied the contents of a desk drawer into a wastebasket. "I could care less. After today, I'll be in the country smelling the roses. No more policy decisions for me. I'll leave that to the bright young lad who'll be my replacement."

"It says here," continued Adam, "the treaty is a mutual aid pact between us and Russia. We'd go to each other"s aid if we're attacked."

"Attacked by whom?" George pulled out another drawer. "Didn't think we had any enemies. Russia certainly has. China and America for sure, and to be honest Adam, it doesn't seem logical. Nothing to be gained by it. I'm just pleased to get away from it and leave it to you to sort things out."

"Must piss the Americans off. Must have caused a diplomatic nightmare for our Embassy in Washington," Adam persisted. "It was an underhanded trick, if you ask me ..." He swung his legs off the desk and plucked a sheet of paper from his in-box, scanned it, then crumpled it into a wad and pitched it at the wastebasket. "It's strange, George. Why would the Prime Minister enter into such an agreement?"

George sighed. "I have no idea, Adam, and I don't really care. All I want to do is get out of here and let people like you worry about it. No sense having an opinion anyway as it won't change anything." He peered into the wastebasket and picked out a couple of pens to add to his cardboard box of personal items.

"I'm sure there is more to this than what's being reported," said Adam, leaning back in his chair again and clasping his hands behind his head. "There must be a valid reason. *The Times* would not publish something that is not true."

"I've heard enough, Adam. I'm off," said George. He pulled out his desk drawers once again to make sure he hadn't missed anything. Satisfied that he had collected all that he wanted to take with him, he closed the last box.

"Don't see why the Americans should be upset," continued Adam. "They are the strongest military power and their nuclear arsenal is second to none. And as far as Russia and ourselves are concerned, America will not be attacked."

"It's all hypothetical, and I leave you to it. Ta ta." George stacked the three boxes one on top of the other, picked them up and anchored them with his chin. He had made it to the door and was attempting to use his toe to open it, when Adam suddenly sat up in his chair.

"What? You're off, then? Already?" He sprang up from his chair and went across the room to open the door for the struggling George. "All these years together, and I didn't even have the chance to say good-bye. I'd shake your hand, but I can see you've got your hands full."

George chuckled. "Goodbye, Adam. Hope you get on with my replacement."

"Goodbye, George. Be sure to look me up when you come up to London," said Adam as he watched George wrestle the boxes to the lift. George propped the boxes against the wall to free his right hand to press the "down" button.

When George emerged from the lift on the ground floor lobby of the Foreign Office, the security guard Stan Straw looked up from the newspaper he was reading. "You're off then, George?" he asked, not bothering to get up from his seat behind the lobby desk.

"Yes, I've cleared everything out and am off to a life of peace and quiet in the country."

"Well, don't forget about your retirement party tonight at the Savoy," said Stan. "I've been looking forward to that all week."

"How could I forget? I've been reminded all day," said George with a grin as he tried to see around the boxes for a place to set them down.

"Bringing a girlfriend?" asked Stan as he put down his newspaper and stood up behind the desk.

"Nah, I've had enough of women for a while. After thirty years of marriage and a divorce, I'd rather have a belly full of champagne. At least you can be sure of that sticking with you until the next morning!"

"Poor George. Such a pity not having a lady friend to help you celebrate your retirement. Here, let me help you with those boxes," said a feminine voice behind him.

George turned to see an attractive slender redhead walking toward him from the ladies" loo. His face lit up in a broad smile. Sherry Davenport was the secretary to his boss, the Director of European Policy. He found her much to his liking and had had yearnings ever since his divorce - even before the divorce, if the truth were known.

George was suddenly speechless as Sherry helped him place the three small cardboard boxes on the desk in front of Stan for inspection. He finally found his voice.

"Thank you very much, Miss Davenport," he said, brushing off his suit jacket and adjusting his tie as he looked up at her. She was slightly taller than he was, and he also found that immensely attractive for reasons he could not explain.

She smiled at him and said, "Think nothing of it, George, and now that we're no longer on formal office terms, just call me Sherry."

"Is this all you have to show for thirty years of work?" asked Stan as he completed his inspection and closed the last box.

"The way the cutbacks are going, when we retire, we'll be lucky to walk out of here with a pair of shoes, Stan," said Sherry, winking at George and nudging him with her elbow.

"Well, George, I certainly didn't see any top secret documents or nicked Foreign Office property, so you're free to go," said Stan.

George glanced at his wristwatch. "Yes, I must be off before the rush sets in. I have to rent a tuxedo for the party."

"See you there, George," said Stan as he stacked the boxes in George's outstretched hands. "Mind you get a taxi and don't try to take the underground. I just heard all the underground stations in the area around the Savoy will be closed at seven tonight because of the demonstrations. They're expecting thousands to show up, and the police are taking extra security measures in case of riots."

"What about the Savoy?" asked Sherry. "Do you think that will be closed?"

"Oh, not likely," said Stan. "The Savoy's never been closed in my memory, and I'm sure a few hundred thousand hooligans won't cause that to happen."

"Good," said George. "I'll just be off then."

"Good luck, George, and congratulations on your retirement. I'll see you tonight at the party," said Sherry as she held the door open for him. "Perhaps when you come up to London in future, we could have lunch."

She gave him a beautiful smile, and George felt a tingle run up his spine. "I"ve got your number, Sherry," he said as he stumbled out the door. It was the first time she had ever indicated an interest in him.

*   *   *

The next morning George regained consciousness at the sound of a thunderous drumming. At first he thought it was rain drumming against a window pane until he realized it was inside his head. And not only in his head, he soon discovered. Every pulse of his heart sent a loud, painful reverberation throughout his entire body as if someone was slowly and deliberately striking a huge gong. He tried to crack open his eyes, but his eyelids felt as if they were glued shut with a layer of sealing wax. He brought one hand up and slowly rubbed his eyelids. When he was finally able to open his eyes, he was staring straight up at an intricately molded ceiling, and out of the corner of his eyes, he caught a glimpse of plush purple velvet drapery. He seemed to be lying flat on his back in the center of a vast bed, and he had no idea where he was.

George closed his eyes again. He'd had many hangovers before, but it now appeared he had the mother of them all. His brain seemed to shriek in protest as if someone were stripping the gears when he tried to think. Finally, it creaked into action and he had a fuzzy recollection of his retirement party at the Savoy - a sea of faces, endless upraised glasses and the consumption of vast quantities of champagne. Beyond that, he remembered nothing. He could only surmise that he had blacked out and someone had put him to bed somewhere.

As he lay there trying to remember, he raised a hand to his face and felt the sharp bristles of overnight beard growth. He checked out his lips. They were dry and cracked. He tried to lick them with his tongue, but soon discovered his tongue was a hard dry piece of cardboard - a strange phenomenon that always occurred when he drank any kind of wine. Each tooth wore an Angora sweater, and the taste in his mouth was too horrible for gentlemanly description.

He moved his hand down. At shoulder level, he encountered satin material - a sheet drawn up over him. Slowly, he ran his hand down below the sheet and was startled to discover that he was stark naked. Then he felt something else - flesh that did not belong to him. George froze and his eyes flew open. He turned his head fractionally to the right. There, up against his right shoulder, rising above the purple satin sheet, was a bare black shoulder and the back of a head covered with a short curly mop of jet-black hair. Tattooed on the upper part of the shoulder blade was a symbol of some sort and the word "Yin."

Catching his breath, George quickly looked the other way, and he gasped involuntarily at the sight of another naked shoulder up against his left side. This shoulder was nearly alabaster white, and long, straight whitish-blonde hair reached down to the sheet level. This shoulder bore a tattoo of the same symbol, but with the word "Yang" etched above it.

George's head snapped back to center. He stared up at the ceiling again, barely daring to breathe. He lay rigidly trying to remember, but nothing came to him. Now he was vividly aware of a body pressed up against him on each side. "What is this? A bloody sandwich?" he thought, not realizing that he had murmured out loud.

There was a stirring on his left, and a feminine face peered down at him. "Well, look who's awake," said the blonde. She leaned across him to shake the black shoulder on his right, and as she did so, her naked breasts nearly grazed his lips. George's eyes snapped shut. "Come on, Yin. He"s awake. Time to go to work."

Now he felt movement on his right and another presence above him. "Thought you said he's awake. His eyes are closed," said a husky voice. George was afraid to open his eyes.

"Oh, he's awake all right, just playing cat and mouse, I expect."

"Well, we know how to wake him up, don't we?" said the husky

voice, and George felt the sheet being lifted.

He shot straight up to a sitting position clasping the sheet up to his neck. "What is this? Who the bloody hell are you?" he cried out in alarm. He averted his eyes from the blonde, who was wearing nothing, and focused on the black lady who at least was wearing a sequined black bikini.

"I'm Yin and that's Yang," said the black lady in her husky voice. "You don't remember anything?" She raised her eyebrows and rolled her eyes.

"All I remember is drinking a lot of champagne at my retirement party," said George putting a hand to his head.

"Such a pity," said the blonde. George glanced at her and quickly averted his eyes again when he saw that she was absent-mindedly running a hand over one of her naked breasts. "You certainly seemed to be having a very good time indeed."

"Your work mates would be disappointed," said Yin. "They came up with the money to pay for our services, you see. They were going to procure the services of one of our associates for half the price, but when they found out about us, they passed the hat and came up with the money to hire us. They thought it would be more fun for you to have a full range of experiences, you see."

"Bloody hell, a full range of experiences? At my age, I'm lucky just to have a basic experience, especially after all that champagne," said George shaking his head.

"Oh, you had no problem there," said Yang. "Provisions were made, you see. You had 400 milligrams of sildenafil slipped into your champagne."

"Sildenafil? What's that?" asked George, growing redder by the minute.

"The most common brand name is Viagra," said Yin, with a chuckle.

"Oh, I have heard of that," said George. "Never had occasion to try it, though. Always thought it was a marketing gimmick."

"It worked splendidly," said Yang. "You kept us busy."

"Well, I can't remember anything," said George trying to recollect his potency.

"Do you remember seeing any colors?" asked Yin. "It's a common effect."

George looked up at the ceiling, noticing again the heavy velvet draperies that seemed to surround the bed. "Come to think of it, I remember the color purple. Must be those drapes. Where am I, anyway?" asked George, still struggling to remember.

"Room 457 at the Savoy," said Yin. "And very nice too."

"The Savoy! That's bloody expensive for an ex-civil servant!" exclaimed George with a grimace.

"It's part of the package," said Yang. "A pity you don't remember. If you'd like a repeat performance, we have just enough time before checkout. The cost is a thousand pounds."

"A thousand pounds!" gasped George. "No, no, I couldn't afford that even if I wanted to."

"Actually, a thousand is quite worth it for what you get with our full range of experiences package," said Yin. "We have no problem getting clients, and most of them come back for more. In fact, we have another engagement this afternoon."

"What exactly is this `full range of experiences" business?" asked George, trying to imagine. "Does that mean the cost of the room and the drug are included?"

Yang giggled. "That plus a full range of sexual experiences!"

"Yes. You see that's why we bill ourselves as Yin and Yang. You've heard of the Chinese symbol?" asked Yin, pointing to the tattoo on her shoulder.

George frowned. "Vaguely. Doesn't it have something to do with opposites?"

"That's right," said Yang, sitting up on her knees directly in front of him. "It has to do with the balance of opposites in nature."

Yin also rose to her knees in front of him. "That's right. For example, I am Yin. I am the moon."

"And I am Yang. I am the sun," said Yang pointing at herself.

"I am darkness," said Yin pointing at herself.

"I am light," said Yang. "And I am summer."

"I am winter," said Yin. She glanced at Yang with a mischievous grin.

"I am feminine," said Yang, with a sideways glance at Yin.

"And I am masculine!" said Yin, pulling down the bottom of her bikini to illustrate.

"Oh, bloody hell!" cried George, pulling up the sheet and covering his eyes in embarrassment. Gales of laughter filled the room. Despite several strong tugs on the sheet, George clutched it tight and refused to come out. He lay there rigidly, feeling a great deal of movement in the bed around him.

"All right, you can come out now, George," said Yang. "We're decent at the moment. We have to leave soon in order to have time for breakfast before meeting our next client."

George slowly pulled the sheet down just below his eyes and saw that Yang was now wearing a skimpy bra and a thong. Yin was standing by the bed in his or her bikini.

"We'll just use the loo quickly and be gone. You have an hour to collect yourself before checkout time at noon," said Yin.

The two scooped up clothes from the floor on either side of the bed as George watched speechlessly from beneath the sheet. After they had disappeared through a door on the far side of the room, he sat up in bed and looked about at his surroundings.

Strewn across the floor on his right was his rumpled tuxedo and underwear. Keeping his eye on the door at the far side of the room, he quickly popped out of bed and put on his underwear and then popped back into the bed and drew up the sheet again. Looking about, he noticed a television screen built into a dark-wood cabinet to the right of the bed. He found a remote control on the bedside table and turned on the telly.

He surfed the channels until he found a news station and turned up the volume in order to hear the newscaster over the sound of the shower emanating from behind the closed door.

"Last night's Westminster riots are the worst in living memory with 1,800 arrested and an estimated ten million pounds in property damage," the commentator was saying, with a stern look on his face. The station cut to a tape of police wearing riot gear and confronting demonstrators, and then a scene of scuffling teenagers. The view then shifted to show police forcing a crowd back with water cannons.

The scene shifted back to the studio and the news commentator. "In a statement early this morning Home Secretary Wallace Wheatly vowed to deal severely with the hooligans who started the riots, claiming the demonstrations were peaceful until a few troublemakers infiltrated the crowd."

George clicked off the telly and put a hand on his throbbing forehead. "I will be pleased to get away from this lot to the peace and tranquility of the country," he muttered.

"Well, ta ta, Darling," said Yang, emerging from the bathroom door, dressed in a white mini-skirt and clinging low-cut white jersey top that showed her cleavage. "We'll just leave our card here on the dresser in the event that you would like another engagement. We haven't had so much fun since the French President was in town."

"The French President!" gasped George. "You mean he was a customer, too?"

"We have all sorts of clients, Darling," said Yin, following Yang into the room. She-he was wearing a simple black clingy dress that ended mid-thigh. She propped one leg on a nearby chair and bent over to buckle an ankle strap on her three-inch stiletto-heeled black satin shoes. "You would be surprised at some of them," she said with a grin as she stood up. George estimated she was well over six feet tall with the shoes on.

"Remember, if you want the same again it will cost you a thousand," said Yang, as she placed a card on the table next to the television.

George shook his head. "I can't afford that now that I'm retired. Besides I can't remember anything about it."

"Next time, we could throw in some memories," said Yin, pulling a micro video recorder out of her handbag and holding it up for George to see. "This is the latest from Japan. Records up to twelve hours and has night vision too. There would be no problem. The disc would be yours and included in the fee."

George gulped. "What about last night? Did you record that?" he asked.

"Oh, no, Darling," said Yang motioning at Yin to put the camera away. "Recordings are only made at the request of the customer. It would be bad for business otherwise."

"I see," mumbled George. "Thanks just the same, but I don't believe I'll be seeking your services again on my own."

"Well, ta ta, then. Remember you have until noon to leave the room."

George gave a feeble wave as the two left the room. As soon as the door closed behind them, he quickly got up and nearly ran to the loo.

*   *   *

Chapter 4

G EORGE REACHED THE lobby of the Savoy breathing a sigh of relief that he had not run into anyone he knew. He looked about in amazement. Hundreds of people in rumpled clothes were lying or sitting on makeshift beds on the floor.

"What's going on?" George asked a porter who was standing just outside the lift.

"The riots last night, Sir. The police herded people in here for safety. At last count, there were four hundred."

"Is it safe to leave the hotel now?" asked George, raising his voice to be heard above the din of hundreds of conversations taking place among the accidental hotel guests.

"At present, we are still waiting for the all-clear from the police," replied the porter, shaking his head. "It may be a while. I suggest you go to the American Bar upstairs for a drink. You'll be more comfortable there, and you are certainly dressed for the part."

George blushed slightly, realizing that the porter had been appraising his somewhat crumpled tuxedo. He nodded at the porter and threaded his way through the people in the lobby toward the flight of stairs that led to the American Bar on the second floor.

The bar was packed. It appeared there was standing room only, but after squeezing his way through the patrons, George spied an open stool at the cocktail counter. He managed to commandeer it before anyone else discovered the vacancy. He had just sat down and had pulled a twenty-pound note from his pocket, when he heard a familiar voice.

"Hello George. You were lucky to have a room for the night. I had to sleep on the floor in the lobby."

George spun around on his stool to see Stan, the guard at the Foreign Office, smiling down at him.

"What will it be?" asked a harried barman, trying not to sound impatient.

"Two pints of bitter," said George without hesitation, laying the twenty-pound note on the counter. The barman quickly placed the order on the counter before him. "Here you are, Stan," said George, passing one of the pints to Stan.

"Cheers," said Stan, raising the glass to his mouth. "Must have been quite a riot last night. The police cordoned off everything from the Tower Bridge to Westminster. Nobody let in, nobody let out."

"What caused the riot? According to what I heard on the news this morning, a few hooligans started it all." George took a sip of the bitter.

"Poppycock! It was those World Trade Dissidents fighting each other. One lot is more radical than the other is. Every time they demonstrate, there's violence. Brings more publicity to their cause."

"The news made no mention of that," said George. "In fact, no reason was given for the demonstrations."

"What do you expect, George? The Government doesn't want us to know how deep the Foot and Mouth crisis is."

"I see you are alive and well after last night," said a feminine voice that sent a little thrill up George's spine. He and Stan looked around to see Sherry Davenport squeezing through the crowd toward them.

"What a nice surprise, Sherry," said George as he got up and offered her the counter stool. "I didn't expect to see you this morning. Did you get stuck here at the hotel as well?"

"I was lucky," said Sherry with a smile as she sat down. "I had booked a room because I didn't want to be caught up in the demonstrations. So, how are you this morning, George? The last I saw of you last night you were feeling no pain and had a lady on each arm."

George reddened. "As for this morning, I have a bloody hangover, but the bitter is helping - hair of the dog, I suppose. As for last night, I remember nothing."

"I know what you mean about a hangover. The champagne was

wonderful going down, but it's certainly not treating me well today," said Sherry. "The best remedy for me is a Bloody Mary."

"Well, at least you didn't end up sleeping on the floor in the lobby, like the rest of us," said Stan as George summoned the barman.

Just as Sherry's Bloody Mary arrived and George reached into his pocket to extract another twenty-pound note, a shrill ringing emanated from inside his tuxedo jacket. "Damn nuisance," muttered George, as he placed the note on the counter with one hand and withdrew a cell phone from an inside breast pocket with the other hand. "I won't be able to hear over this din."

"You're right, George. There is a phone privacy dome just outside the men's room to the right," said Stan, pointing toward the left side of the cocktail counter.

George squeezed through the crowd to the privacy dome and he dialed a coded number into his videophone.

After a few moments a man's face appeared on the small flat screen. George squinted at the screen, not recognizing the middle-aged face with a receding gray hairline.

"What can I do for you?" asked George, puzzled.

"Hello, George. My name is Gregory. I must meet with you right away on a very important matter."

"Important matter?" asked George, straining to see if he could ascertain the caller's location, but the man appeared to be standing up against a brick wall, and all he could see was his face.

"Yes, George," said the caller. "It's most important that I see you. I must talk to you about a sensitive matter concerning the Foreign Office."

"I don't work there anymore. I suggest you talk to the Foreign Secretary," George replied grumpily.

"I have something to show you, George," said the caller as if he hadn't heard George's comment. The screen flickered, and suddenly George was viewing a moving picture of himself lying on a bed with a ridiculous grin on his face as a naked Yin and a naked Yang undressed him. George's mouth fell open.

Suddenly, the video disappeared and the caller's face confronted him again. "That would be very bad publicity for the Foreign Office, George," said the caller in a low, conspiratorial tone. "The tabloids would have a hay-day, especially, if it became know that petty cash from the Foreign Office was used to procure the services of the ah ... ladies." The Foreign Office would have no option but to make some heads roll and cut off a certain retiree's pension, don't you think?"

"Enough, enough," said George, covering his eyes with one hand and hanging his throbbing head. "Where do you want to meet?"

"At the Florence Nightingale Museum on Bridge Road across Westminster Bridge," said the caller briskly and hung up.

George stood totally rigid inside the dome, staring at the now-blank screen. "Have you finished, Sir? I have an urgent call to make," said a gentleman dressed in a military officer's uniform who was looking in at George through the clear plastic.

George stared at the officer and the officer stared back at him.

"Are you all right, Sir?" asked the officer. "You seem quite pale and out of breath."

George suddenly shrugged his shoulders and ducked out of the privacy dome past the startled officer. He looked into the bar and saw that Stan and Sherry had their backs to him. He hesitated for a second and then rapidly made his way to the cloakroom on the lobby level to retrieve his trench coat and a duffel bag containing his street clothes.

After donning the trench coat, he walked to the main entrance and confronted the constable who was standing guard there. "I must leave," said George, in as business-like a tone as he could muster. "I have to get to an important Foreign Office meeting."

"Identification please, Sir," responded the constable, holding out his hand.

George reached into his inside coat pocket and brought out his wallet. He flipped it open and showed the constable his F.O. card.

"Where do you have to go, Sir?" asked the constable as he leaned forward to examine the card.

"Bridge Road on the other side of Westminster Bridge," answered George.

"Your colleagues left earlier, Sir. They had a police escort to another place. Are you sure you want to go to Westminster Bridge?" asked the constable.

"Yes, yes, Westminster Bridge," repeated George impatiently.

"It would be quicker to cut through to the Embankment, Sir. Charring Cross Road is blocked in both directions and no pedestrians are allowed through. Use the hotel emergency door at the rear of the restaurant," said the constable. He placed a finger under his right-front lapel and pointed a micro-camcorder at George. "Foreign Office gent will be using Embankment emergency door," he murmured in a low voice.

George nodded at the constable and walked back through the hotel lobby, down some steps, and into the restaurant, where he saw the exit door at the far right side with another policeman stationed outside.

The smell of burning rubber and tear gas fumes greeted George as he stepped onto the flagstone paving outside the hotel. He looked towards the Thames; thick black smoke hovered over the water. The clanging of fire engines and the pulsating screams of police sirens assaulted his ears. The smells and sounds evoked memories of the IRA bombings in the 1990s. He quickened his pace. After a short distance, he could see cars still ablaze on Waterloo Bridge, while towing lorries and flat bed recovery vehicles waited in turn to help clear the bridge.

George pressed on until he reached Westminster Bridge. There the scene was similar, but more intense with more burning cars and even the skeleton of a burnt out double-decker bus.

George paused to survey the damage before climbing the steps to the road.

"You can't go that way, Sir," said the policeman standing guard at the top of the steps. He was wearing a florescent orange-colored waistcoat. "It's not safe at present. We're expecting a few more petrol explosions."

"I must get to the other side. I'm on official Foreign Office business," said George, trying to sound official.

"Your name, Sir?" asked the policeman. "And where did you come from?"

"George Goater. I spent the night at the Savoy."

"George Goater, Foreign Office employee, spent last night at the Savoy Hotel," whispered the policeman in the direction of his right-front lapel.

Within a few seconds George heard a faint whispered response.

"All right, Sir. Just wait until that lorry gets out of the way," said the policeman, pointing at a towing operator attaching a steel cable to a burnt out car. "When I give you the go-ahead, keep as close to the side as you can, and quickly does it."

George nodded his understanding, and they watched as the operator climbed into the cab and revved the engine. The lorry's wheels spun on the oily road and plumes of blue smoke bellowed into the air. Then the tires found a grip, and the skeleton of the car slowly moved forward emitting a loud metallic clanking sound. The tireless rims of the car gouged deep grooves into the roadway as it passed.

"Now, Sir." The policeman motioned for George to cross the yellow ribbon barrier.

George lifted his trench coat over his head and dashed through the black smoke and flames that engulfed the roadway. When he reached the other side another policeman met him.

"Got through all right, Sir? You'd better wipe the soot off your face before you attend your meeting."

George pulled his trench coat back down on his shoulders and wiped his face with a handkerchief.

"Much better, Sir," said the policeman, peering at George's face with a grin. "Bridge Road is down to the right."

"My word, Constable, you're very efficient," said George. "You know my destination and you know about my meeting."

"Yes, Sir. Not much happens without the police knowing. It's this technology," said the policeman fingering his right lapel.

"Being so, then what is my meeting about?" asked George.

"Oh, I don't know that, Sir. We only monitor pedestrians, and besides, it would be against the law to know any more as it would be an invasion of privacy."

"Right you are, Constable," said George with a grin as he resumed his walk toward Bridge Road.

After five minutes George finally reached the Florence Nightingale Museum. He looked around to see if anyone was waiting there, but the area was deserted. He set his duffel bag down and shifted from foot to foot and paced around. Still no one appeared.

After lingering in front of the museum for what seemed a long time, George walked back to the main road. Looking back towards the bridge he saw the policeman and eight flat-bed lorries queuing to remove cars. He looked in the opposite direction and shook his head; there was no sign of anyone.

George brought the lapels of his trench coat together. A cold damp wind had come up and now it began to drizzle.

"Do you want a ride?" called out a driver from a flat-bed lorry that stopped on the road in front of him. "It must be bloody cold just standing around."

George looked at the burnt-out Rolls Royce on the flat bed and then at the driver.

"I have a nice porn video," said the driver, with a leering grin that exposed two jagged broken front teeth.

George's eyes bulged and he could feel his face grow hot.

The driver laughed. "That's right, George. Hurry up and jump in." He nodded his head toward the passenger door.

George climbed in and the driver revved the engine. The gearbox protested loudly as he changed gears.

George looked closely at the driver. It was not the face he had seen on the videophone. "Where are we going?" he asked nervously. The vibration of the lorry added a stutter to his speech.

"Have to take this load to Gravesend," yelled the driver over the din of the engine. "Going to dump this load at a scrap yard. Just sit tight. It will take a while."

"This is all very strange," said George with a frown.

"They thought it better this way," yelled the driver. "The police can track anyone with those damned cameras. Using the lorry was a bloody good idea."

"Who are *they*?" asked George.

The driver revved the engine again and changed gear, ignoring his question.

George sat staring out of the windscreen without speaking. It was impossible to try to hold a conversation with the driver over the noise of the engine. The vibration was causing his head to throb again and he wished he had another pint of bitter. As the lorry made its way out of the Westminster area, George noted that the black smoke and smells of burning rubber had subsided. He saw people on the pavement going about their normal Saturday morning business. His eyelids began to droop, his chin dropped down on his chest, and he slept.

*   *   *

"Wake up George!" The lorry driver reached over with one hand and roughly shook George's shoulder.

George came to with a start and discovered he had a crick in his neck. He looked out the windscreen and saw that they were driving down a muddy lane towards a huge sign that read *Acre Metals - Scrap Metal Merchants.* "Are we there?" he asked.

The driver did not respond. He stopped outside a corrugated steel shed where an unshaven man dressed in overalls and holding a clipboard waited.

"This is where you get out, George," said the driver as he rolled down the window and spoke to the man with the clipboard. "How are you, Tom? I have a Roller for you."

As George hesitantly opened the door and climbed out, another man appeared at the entrance to the shed. George immediately recognized him as the man he had seen on the videophone. Before he had a chance to close the lorry door, two burly looking men burst from the shed and grabbed him by both arms and dragged him inside the shed.

The first man closed the door and turned to him. "Well, George, I'm pleased you kept the appointment. My name is Gregory, remember?"

George nodded. "I don't understand why you took all the trouble to get me here. The whole matter could have been handled in a more gentlemanly way."

Gregory grinned and motioned to the two men to free George's arms. The men backed away and George rubbed his left shoulder with his right hand. "No need for the heavy stuff. I suffer enough from bursitis without all that."

"Follow me, George. There are some people you must meet." Gregory turned on his heel and headed for the back of the shed. George followed, glancing apprehensively at the surroundings. The two burly men trailed along behind him. They came into an open yard at the rear of the shed where an enormous machine was breaking cars into small chunks. The noise was deafening. George covered his ears with his hands. Gregory just grinned and shook his head, motioning for George to continue following him.

They wound their way through the maze of the scrap yard. When they reached the perimeter, Gregory stopped and pointed to a black American-made limousine parked beside a large heap of wrecked cars. George continued on his own toward the limo, glancing back at Gregory and the two burly men who stood watching.

As he approached the vehicle, the driver's door opened and a man wearing a chauffeur's garb stepped out and stood stiffly at attention with his hand on the rear door handle. When George reached the car, the chauffeur opened the door and stood back for George to enter.

"What's all this about?" said George indignantly as he climbed into the limo and sat down on a supple leather seat that ran across the back of the car. He could make out nothing in the dim light other than that he appeared to be in a sort of living room. He had never been in a limousine before.

"Pleased to meet you, George," said a soft male voice with an American accent. The voice came from somewhere towards the front of the car. As George's eyes adjusted to the dim light, he became aware that he was seated on the back seat facing a long couch-like seat that ran up the left-hand side of the vehicle and curved around the back of the driver's compartment. Along the right side of the car was a highly polished wood cabinet. Two men were seated on the couch, one at the far end facing him, and the other on the left side facing the cabinet.

"You seem to know who I am, but who are you?" asked George.

"My name is Chester Abrams and this is Sylvester Monroe," said the man at the front of the car, waving his hand in the direction of the person seated on the left.

George tried to make out their features. The man on the left seemed familiar, but he couldn't think why. "Your names mean nothing to me. What's the meaning of this?"

"Have no fear, George. We are friends," continued the man named Abrams. "We have contacted you on a matter of extreme importance, as the United Kingdom is on the brink of a civil war, and you can help prevent it."

George's mouth dropped open in surprise. "Utter nonsense. This country is run on democratic principles. We have a Parliament and a Queen. A civil war is out of the question. All disputes are resolved in a courteous and honorable way."

"There you have it, George. You have a monarch and a Parliament. In the current situation, if the Prime Minister does not want do what the Queen asks, what will happen? Remember the Queen is Commander in Chief of all of Great Britain's armed forces."

"You're not suggesting the Queen would forcefully remove a legally elected Government?"

"It's a possibility, George."

George looked at the man named Monroe, who had spoken for the first time. The sound of his voice jogged his memory, and now he knew why he had seemed familiar.

"So, why is the trade attaché at the American Embassy interested in Britain's internal affairs?" he asked with a modicum of sarcasm. "Great Britain is not the same as America where your President can stick his finger at whomever he wishes, as he is the Commander in Chief. He does not need approval, even if it means war."

Monroe put a hand up. "Calm down, George. All we are saying is that if the Prime Minister and the Queen do not resolve the problem soon, then ..."

"Great Britain would lose allies and friends throughout the world," said Abrams, finishing the sentence, and drawing George's attention back to him.

"Well, you've got it wrong about the Queen. In her situation, the title of Commander in Chief is in reality only a ceremonial one. She does not command the military in war time."

Monroe waved his hand impatiently. "Yes, yes, George, we know. We know the Prime Minister has a Minister of Defense whose ministry is in charge of the armed forces."

"Well, I can't help you in any case," said George. "I've just retired and I don't want anything to do with such matters. Anyway, you could find a better candidate who is in a higher position at the Foreign Office than I was. I for one believe it is ridiculous to think the Queen and the Prime Minister will not resolve the crisis in an honorable way. That they would resort to arms is ridiculous."

"Think about your pension, George," said Monroe quietly. "If your little episode at the Savoy became known, your pension might be taken away from you. After all, the incident occurred before midnight and technically you were still on the Foreign Office payroll."

"So it *is* blackmail," said George heatedly. "I thought as much! Either I do as you say, or I lose my pension for which I have worked thirty years!"

"Oh, I wouldn't call it blackmail, George," said Monroe in an even softer voice. "I'm sure you would do it because you are an honorable man and for the sake of your country."

George opened his mouth to rebut, but was interrupted by the bleeping of his cell phone. George pressed a button and put the phone to his ear, still glowering at Monroe. Then a puzzled, worried expression clouded his face. "I have an incoming priority call from my ex-wife," he said, raising his eyebrows.

"You can take it there," said Monroe pointing at a display mounted on the end of the wooden panel facing George. Almost instantaneously, the screen displayed the words, *Access by your personal identification number.*

George nervously punched in the code, and suddenly there was his ex-wife Geraldine wiping her eyes with a handkerchief.

"George, at last! I've been trying to call you since first thing this morning. There was no answer at your regular number, so I had to get clearance to use your Foreign Office network."

"What's the matter, Geraldine? Are you all right?" asked George, glancing at Monroe and Chester who were watching him.

"It's your father, George. He had a heart attack this morning. You'd best get to Bridgefield Hospital."

"Heart attack? What?" George yelled, forgetting his surroundings.

"Yes, George, your father is in hospital. I'm there now. The police called me as they couldn't find you, so you'd best get here quick."

"You're at the hospital?"

"Yes, George, that's right. Are you hard of hearing or drunk again or what?" said Geraldine impatiently.

"Dad - is he all right?"

"He's still in the intensive care unit. Get here immediately. I've done all I can. I have to leave for an appointment now."

She disconnected and the screen went dark. George slumped back into the car seat in a state of shock.

"Sorry to hear about your father, George," said Abrams in a soothing voice.

"Yes ... I must get to Bridgefield Hospital right away ..."

Abrams pressed a button and the glass panel behind the chauffeur's compartment slid open with a whisper. Abrams said a few words to the chauffeur in a low voice, and without delay, the glass panel slid shut and the chauffeur started the car.

George sat looking out the heavily tinted window in a daze as the limousine pulled out of a back gate of the scrap yard and sped down a road leading to a motorway that would take them to Bridgefield.

As the car turned on to the motorway, Monroe broke the silence in the passengers" compartment. "We're sorry to hear about your father," he said in his most compassionate tone. "Briggs up there will get us to Bridgefield in record time. Meanwhile, you look as though you could use a drink. Name your poison." He nodded at the bar. "We have about anything you would want."

"Two fingers of whiskey, neat?" asked George, perking up slightly.

"Haig, Black Label?"

"Yes, please."

"Two fingers of Haig it is, then," said Monroe, reaching for a heavy cut-glass decanter. He measured two generous fingers of the deep amber liquid into a fancy crystal glass and handed it to George.

"How old is your father?" inquired Abrams after George had taken a sip of the whiskey and relaxed slightly in his seat.

"Seventy-five. He was very healthy for his age. He keeps active on the farm and hasn't been ill for years. It's quite a surprise to hear that he would have a heart attack," said George, contemplating the glass in his hand.

"And your mother?" asked Abrams.

"Mum died two years ago of cancer," said George with a slight quiver in his voice. He took another quick sip of the whiskey.

"What about your ex-wife. How do you get along with her?" asked Monroe.

"Strained, to say the least, since our divorce last year," said George with a frown. "It seems when things go wrong everything follows suit. First Mum, then the divorce, and now Dad."

"I know what you mean," said Monroe with a sympathetic shake of his head. "My wife ran off with a shoe salesman, and now they both live off my alimony payments."

"I know how that feels, too. My ex-wife will get half of my pension. I don't understand why. She has never worked in her life. It's bloody unfair," said George bitterly.

"Speaking of your pension," said Monroe. "I don't want to remind you again, but your pension will be in jeopardy if it comes out about your little party last night."

"Why don't you blackmail someone else?" said George rising up angrily in his seat and sloshing a bit of the whiskey onto his trousers. "There are much bigger fish at the Ministry."

"Yes, George, there are, but it takes a small fish to catch a big one, and you are a minnow."

"I don't know what you want. This is ridiculous. Why pick on me?" George looked down into his glass sorrowfully.

"We're not picking on you, George. You happened to be in the wrong place at the right time, or vice versa," said Monroe. "You know, there are always interesting things going on at the Savoy, especially late at night or early in the morning."

"How do you get away with video-taping in the rooms? That's illegal. Does the management know?" asked George, his face reddening. "I suspect they don't. You Americans think you can do as you please. Sod the pension! I'm going to inform Special Branch and they will pass the word along to our counter intelligence service."

"That would do you no good, George. Perhaps they condone our operation at the Savoy," said Abrams. "We do share, you know. America's interests are the same as Great Britain's."

"Then why is it that MI5 is not recruiting me?" asked George. "Rather than you?"

"There are sometimes ultra-sensitive matters that must be kept out of the mainstream, George. That is why you are in this car. The current situation calls for special handling," said Monroe, leaning forward in his seat.

"Whose side are you on? Are you for the Government or the Queen? It sounds as if you have to make a choice," said George. "If it were me, I would sit back and see what happens. You Americans seem to get excited by any small frou-frou."

"Frou-frou. In Heaven's name, what does that mean?" asked Monroe raising his eyebrows.

"You lot use dump trucks and we Brits use wheelbarrows," said George with a chuckle. Monroe and Abrams looked at each other and shrugged their shoulders.

"We are not asking for much, George. All we want is for you to dig around a little and keep your ear to the ground, that sort of thing." said Monroe. "That's all."

"Dig around for what?" asked George curiously.

"We don't know yet, but we will let you know. You also know your way around London and you will know where to look better than we would," said Monroe. "To us Americans looking for something in London would be like looking for the proverbial needle in the hay stack."

"It's a strange request," said George. "You want me to look for something but you don't know what. Sounds like you're playing a game."

"Oh, It's no game, George. You can be assured of that. There are very good reasons for it, but we are not in a position to let you know what those reasons are," said Monroe, looking at George intensely. George fidgeted in his seat and gulped down the last of his whiskey.

"Road barrier ahead," called out the chauffeur over the intercom. The car began to slow.

A policeman motioned for the car to stop and another policeman came over to the driver's side window. The officer looked inside, smiling pleasantly, and motioned to the chauffeur to open the window.

"Where have you gentlemen come from?" asked the policeman, peering into the car.

"London," replied the driver.

"And where are you going?" asked the policeman looking at the three passengers in the back.

"Bridgefield Hospital," replied George. "My father has had a heart attack."

"Bridgefield is cordoned off because of Foot and Mouth," responded the policeman shaking his head.

"Must get through," called out Monroe, emphasizing his strong American accent.

The policeman looked at them again and gave a brief smile.

"You must drive through the disinfectant," he directed, pointing to a shallow ditch across the road filled with a white liquid. "And stay in the car."

The chauffeur slowly drove the car through the ditch, and the smell of disinfectant impregnated the inside of the car.

"Smells like a men's toilet in here," said Monroe wrinkling his nose.

"And how is that?" asked George. "My toilet doesn't smell ... but I'm British, you see."

Monroe and Abrams looked curiously at George. He grinned slightly and they realized he was making a joke. Laughter filled the car as another policeman motioned for them to stop. The chauffeur stopped the car and rolled down the window.

"This is your travel permit," said the policeman handing the driver a piece of paper. "Keep on the main road, and don't get out of the car."

"Thank you, officer," said the driver as he started to slowly drive on.

"This Foot and Mouth, as you call it, must be serious," said Abrams. "It reminds me of an incident back in the states when a biological weapon experiment went wrong. It took many months to dissipate."

"Very few people were affected," interjected Monroe quickly, cutting Abrams off.

"Foot and Mouth and Mad Cow Disease could be classified as such," said George as he surveyed the bleak countryside. "They could be used as biological weapons."

"Yes, George," said Monroe. "In the wrong hands, both diseases could be used not only to decimate the population, but also to create economic chaos - especially in a country's agricultural economy."

Monroe glanced at Abrams before continuing, and then he looked back at George. "It would also give troublemakers an opportunity to stir things up. Any group with a grievance could take advantage of the situation."

George didn't comment. Being a civil servant, he wasn't used to expressing an opinion on such issues.

Monroe and Abrams fell silent; they left George to mull over what they had said.

After several more kilometers, another policeman standing at another road barrier flagged down the car.

"This is as far as we go," said Monroe when the car stopped. "You can find your own way to Bridgefield Hospital. We have to get back to London. Now, George, remember our offer. Give it some thought, and we'll contact you again in a few days."

George muttered something inaudible as he pushed the door open and climbed out of the car. Monroe motioned to the driver to turn the car around, and George stood watching as the chauffeur executed a U-turn and drove back in the same direction as they had come.

*　　*　　*

Chapter 5

A S GEORGE STOOD watching the limousine drive away, a ruddy-faced policeman suddenly appeared at his side. "Your friends have left you stranded," he said. He looked George over from head to toe. "Where are you wanting to go dressed like that?"

George looked down and realized he had left his trench coat unbuttoned, exposing the crumpled tuxedo he was still wearing. "I had a retirement party last night," he mumbled.

The officer grinned. "You're not trying to get to another party, I hope."

"No," said George rubbing his unshaven face self-consciously. "I have to get to Bridgefield Hospital. My father had a heart attack."

The officer's grin disappeared. "It's a long walk, Sir. There is a shuttle bus that can take you there." He looked at his watch. "It should be here in about ten minutes."

The policeman pointed at a shallow pan filled with a murky white liquid. "You'll need to disinfect your shoes, Sir, and remember to keep away from any animals."

George nodded and walked through the disinfectant. Then he walked a short distance to the bus stop. After a few minutes an elderly woman carrying a shopping basket joined him. George smiled absentmindedly at her as she walked up.

She immediately began to prattle on. "It's a terrible thing to have all these fine animals slaughtered. The country is in a mess, what with the Foot and Mouth and Mad Cow and the Prime Minister refusing to resign." She clucked her tongue indignantly. "Surely something can be done. I remember well the Foot and Mouth outbreak many years ago. It took ages to get it under control. It must have been brought into the country from outside. We should never have joined the common market. There aren't any controls anymore."

"It is a problem for everyone," murmured George. He looked at his watch and then up the road to see if the shuttle was anywhere in sight.

"What about us elderly?" the woman went on. "We have difficulty in making ends meet, the price of food goes up every day, and the shopkeepers are gouging us. The wealthy care only about themselves, and they are the ones making all the money. Something needs to be done about it."

"I'm retired, and I know what you mean," said George. "Here comes the bus," he added, relieved to put an end to the conversation.

The light blue shuttle bus stopped at the barrier and let a number of passengers off. Then it made a U-turn and pulled up to where George and the old woman were standing. George stood back to let the woman on first, and then he followed up the step.

"Bridgefield Hospital," he said as he walked past the bus driver.

The driver looked in the rear view mirror, and when he was satisfied that his two passengers were settled in their seats, he revved the engine, put the transmission into gear and slowly moved forward. As he pulled into the lane on the road, he changed gears again and the bus picked up speed.

Twenty minutes later the bus stopped outside the entrance to Bridgefield Hospital. George got off the bus rubbing his eyes and shaking his head. If it hadn't been for the bus driver waking him up, he would have missed the stop.

George looked up at the hospital; nothing had changed since he was there to see his mother. He climbed the steps and walked through the swinging entrance doors. Knowing the visiting procedure, he went to a computer and entered his father's name. The computer screen instantly gave his father's room number and his father's doctor's name. From the menu George clicked *Visitors Today*, and the names of his ex-wife and the doctor appeared. George went to the menu again and clicked on *Present Visitors*. His ex-wife's name appeared.

"Damn! She is still here," George grumbled to himself as he punched in his name on the keyboard.

When the lift reached the third floor George took a deep breath and got off. He looked at the room signs and then walked briskly to his father's room. He was about to enter when he heard his ex-wife's voice. He hesitated at the door listening.

"That damned George, out drinking again last night, I bet. Got drunk and had to stay in an expensive hotel. He is so disgusting."

The room was quiet for a second and then she continued.

"The silly old fool! After all those years at the Ministry, and all he has to show for it is a paltry pension. It was my best day's work when I divorced him!"

George suddenly felt nauseated, an effect his ex-wife's voice often had on him. How dare she vent her loathing for him to his sick father! He took a deep breath and strode into the room.

"Well, I see you managed to find the time to come and see your father!" said Geraldine in a demeaning tone the instant she saw George come into the room. "I've been here since eight this morning. If you'd stayed home last night instead of being out boozing, the police would have known where to contact you!"

George swallowed hard and tried to ignore her as he looked at his father. He sucked in his breath as he observed the oxygen mask that completely covered his father's face, and the many plastic tubes attached to intravenous drip bottles that hung on stainless steel stands on either side of the bed. He saw that his father's head had been shaved and that pads with electrical wires were attached to his skull.

"What does the doctor say?" asked George gulping.

Geraldine sneered. "You stupid fool, can't you see that your father is in critical condition? You don't need a doctor to tell you that!"

"What happened?" asked George as he tried not to let her goading get to him.

"He had a heart attack. I told you that earlier while you were gallivanting around London."

"Dad was fit as a fiddle," said George still looking at his father. "Something dreadful must have caused the heart attack."

"You idiot. You would have known what caused it if you had looked after your father properly."

"What are you talking about?" asked George looking at Geraldine for the first time. He was mildly surprised to see that she had dyed her hair blonde and noted that it had done nothing to soften the hardness around her eyes and mouth.

"Your father's Black Angus had to be destroyed because they had Foot and Mouth. If you'd been a better son, it wouldn't have happened. Your father is too old to take care of all those cattle by himself."

George clenched his fists and his jaw. "You bloody bitch! That is a wicked thing to say. You know I've always done my best for Dad!" he shouted, no longer able to contain his temper.

"Yes, I can see what your „best" is. Just look at you! You're still wearing a penguin suit, and it looks like you spent the night in a gutter. At least you could have worn something decent and shaved before visiting your poor sick father!"

"You bloody cow!" yelled George. "I pity the man you're with now."

"At least he is a man, not a wimp like you! How I put up with a wilted turd like you for all those years, I will never know!" she yelled back.

"Go back to your society friends! We don't need you here, you bitch!" George's face had turned purple with anger.

"I will tell Clarence about this and how horrible you are to me!" she screamed.

"Clarence? Who the hell is Clarence?"

"Clarence is my new man, that's who, and he's ten times the man you ever were, you ..."

"Is everything all right in there?" A man's voice interrupted from outside the door.

George was staring at Geraldine and raised his hand when he saw her lips forming the word "bastard!"

"This is Doctor Stevenson. May I come in?" asked the voice.

"Please do," called out George as he continued to glare at Geraldine.

The doctor came into the room and looked warily from one to the other as he walked over to the patient's bedside. He examined the vital signs on a bank of monitors, made a few notations on a clipboard he carried, and returned to where George and Geraldine were standing.

"I'm Doctor Stevenson," he said extending his hand to George.

"George Goater," said George as he shook the doctor's hand.

"How do you do? You must be Mr. Goater's son," said the doctor with a smile. "I have already had the pleasure of meeting Mrs. Goater."

"What is the situation with my dad? Is he going to be all right?" asked George anxiously.

The doctor put up a hand and turned to Geraldine. "Mrs. Goater, now that the next of kin is here, I must ask you to leave so that I can discuss the patient's condition with him. Because you are no longer a close relative, I'm afraid you are not privileged to hear a discussion of Mr. Goater's condition. I'm sure you understand," he said, smiling pleasantly at Geraldine.

"He was my father-in-law, and I was the first one to be with him, and now you are telling me to leave?" asked Geraldine, her face turning red with anger.

The doctor's smile faded. "I'm sorry, Mrs. Goater, but that's the way it is, I'm afraid. Rules are rules, after all," he said.

Geraldine stared at the doctor for a moment, then grabbed her handbag and walked hastily out of the room. The doctor walked quietly to the door and closed it behind her.

"Sorry, old chap, but rules are rules," said the doctor as he walked back to George.

"No need to be sorry, Doctor. I am pleased you told her to leave. My ex-wife and I are not exactly on friendly terms, you see," said George.

"So I gathered from overhearing your ah ... tiff when I was at the door," said the doctor with a smile. Then his face turned serious. "Please sit down, Mr. Goater. I have a matter to discuss with you."

George's legs wobbled and he all but fell into the chair. He tried to compose himself for the doctor's assessment.

Doctor Stevenson picked up the patient's chart and glanced at it. "Your father appears to have had a heart attack," he said slowly, "but we can't be sure. We are currently doing further tests to find out for sure what it could be. Now, I don't want to alarm you, but like every other patient who has similar symptoms, we are required to check for the possibility of Creutzfeldt-Jakob Disease - Mad Cow Disease."

George gulped. "Is Dad getting better?"

"It's too early to say," said the doctor shaking his head. "He's only been here since this morning."

"I can't understand it!" exclaimed George, his face turning pale. "I spoke to Dad on Thursday night and he said he felt fine."

"Whatever he has, it came on very rapidly, possibly caused by the shock of discovering his cattle had to be destroyed," said the doctor frowning.

"What about the farm? Is it safe there?" asked George.

"It is my understanding that even though the farm is under quarantine, you will be allowed in. Brace yourself, as the cattle are still being destroyed because they had Foot and Mouth."

George put his hands over his face.

"There's nothing you can do, Mr. Goater," said the doctor kindly. It's best for you to get some rest. I will call you at the farm when there is anything new to report."

George stood up and walked over to his father's bed. He reached out a hand.

"No! Don't disturb him! He needs all the rest he can get, Mr. Goater," warned the doctor.

"Get well, Dad. Get well soon," whispered George. He gazed down at his unconscious father for a moment and then turned to leave.

"There is one other thing, Mr. Goater," said the doctor. "I would prefer for the time being that you tell people your father had a heart attack."

George nodded and left the room feeling depressed. He left the hospital and walked to the main road intending to get a taxi to take him to the farm. It grew dark while he waited for what seemed to be hours. He finally gave up and started to walk.

When he came to a junction he stopped to see if the road was clear before crossing it. Looking to his right he saw a large black Bentley coming towards him. He waited for the car to pass, but instead the Bentley pulled up to the curb next to him. George looked into the car to see who was driving and recognized the driver immediately, but before he had time to acknowledge him the window rolled down.

"Hello, George. You look out of place in that tuxedo," said the driver with a grin. "Where have you been?"

"Just came from the hospital. My dad had a heart attack this morning."

"Sorry to hear that, George. Can I give you a lift?"

"Really nice of you, Martin, but I need to get to my father's farm," said George. He looked down and saw that his trench coat was open revealing the crumpled tuxedo. He began to button it.

"There are no trains or buses running, and taxis are few tonight," said Martin leaning over to look at George out of the window. "This Foot and Mouth outbreak is wreaking havoc with the transportation. I would be pleased to drive you to the farm."

"I wouldn't want to impose on you, Martin. It's Saturday night and I'm sure you have better things to do," said George with a wave of his hand.

"Nonsense! Jump in George, and stop wasting time trying to talk me out of it."

"This is awfully good of you, Martin. I will take you up on your offer then," said George as he quickly climbed in and buckled himself into the passenger's seat.

Martin glanced out of the rear view mirror, put the car into gear and pulled away from the curb. "It's a bloody shame, George. Your father was such a fit man. I just hope he will soon be on his feet again. You know, they can pull you through a heart attack if they can treat you in time."

George nodded. "He has good care," he said.

"I heard about his cattle. Such a damned shame! Your father thought the world of that lot."

"Yes, and they were all pure-bred registered Black Angus. They think the shock of finding out the herd had to be destroyed is what brought on Dad's heart attack."

Martin looked sideways at George and grinned as he turned left off the main road. "I say! It must have been a great party. You're still wearing your tux," he said with a chuckle.

"It was my retirement party, and I had to stay at the Savoy Hotel all night because of the riots. Couldn't leave until late this morning. Then I came directly to the hospital when I got the word about Dad, and I haven't had a chance to change," explained George, nodding at the duffel bag he had deposited on the floor.

"You're retired? You don't look old enough," said Martin. "You lucky sod."

"Luck had nothing to do with it. I was forced to retire. They called it reorganization, but I believe what they really wanted to do was to reduce costs by getting rid of me and hiring a younger man at a lower pay scale."

"It happens all the time, George. When people get over the age of fifty, the attitude is that they become inefficient."

George ignored the comment and focused on the road ahead.

"I don't know what the country is coming to," said Martin after a lull in the conversation. "First the Queen tries to dissolve Parliament, and now new outbreaks of Foot and Mouth are occurring everywhere."

"I can't understand it either. The first outbreak occurred three months ago and now it seems as if it is everywhere."

"There are many rumors floating about as to what caused it," continued Martin. "Some say it was caused by Chinese restaurants importing meat from China, and others say it was caused by the French in retaliation for our treatment of political refugees."

"I don't like the French," said George, "They have always been a thorn in our side. They always take advantage of our misfortune."

"I don't know much about that, George, but you should know, working at the Foreign Office and all."

"Well, the French are standing in our way right now. They won't let us import red meat from America or from the Commonwealth. Surely you know about that!"

"Yes, I've read about that, George. All I can say is that they are business people, just like us. They know that importing meat only from Europe is more expensive and they have a lot of cattle to sell."

"Maybe they do, but we should be able to buy our meat from anywhere we want."

"Well, you can buy tins of Argentine corned beef at Safeway and tins of Spam from America," said Martin with a snicker.

"Quite right. You win that one, Martin," said George with a chuckle. "You should be a politician instead of a car salesman."

"Politicians don't own Bentleys, George. They are only driven around in them."

"Part of their prestige. Makes them feel important, you know," said George.

"That's why I'm driving one," said Martin slowing down to negotiate a curve. "Some men at my age go for younger women, but I prefer two hundred horsepower under the hood. That way I can put my foot down any time I please."

"Is that why you never married?"

"You betcha'! With a car like this, women are easy to come by."

"Well, I've had enough of women for a while, Martin. My ex-wife has put me off them," said George with a sour expression.

"Have you spoken to her lately?"

"Oh, yes. She was at the hospital and caused a bloody row. Thank God, the doctor told her to clear off."

"It won't be long now," said Martin, pointing to a road sign that said they were two kilometers from Wadhurst. "Oh, my God, George! Can you see that? Looks like a huge fire in the distance."

George squinted at the reddish-orange blaze lighting up the horizon. "It looks like it's close to the farm. What in hell's name is burning to cause a smoke like that?"

Martin increased speed and within a minute or two they could see the fire in a field close to the farmhouse. As they drove into the driveway they saw a roadblock manned by policemen wearing florescent jackets. The light from the fire reflecting on the jackets cast a sinister, eerie glow.

"You can go no further," called out one of the policemen who seemed to be in charge. "This farm is restricted because of Foot and Mouth. No one is allowed in except by special permission."

George rolled down the window on his side and announced, "My name is George Goater, and my father lives here." He handed his ID to the officer.

"Just a moment, Sir," said the policeman holding a mobile telephone close to his mouth." I just have to confirm that."

George heard the policeman explain the circumstances. Then after a short silence the officer looked at him and nodded his head. "You can drop him here, Sir," he said to Martin as he shone his flashlight into the car.

George collected his duffel bag and got out of the car. He looked back in the window and thanked Martin for the lift. Martin nodded and drove the Bentley in reverse until he reached the end of the driveway. Then he turned and drove back towards Bridgefield.

As George approached the road barrier another policeman swung it open. Suddenly, the wind changed direction and smoke from the fire engulfed him.

"Better wear one of these!" called out a policeman rushing towards him. "It will prevent you from breathing in the smoke." He handed George a surgical mask, but it was too late. George was already coughing and wheezing. The smell and taste of burning flesh filled his lungs and mouth. Then the wind changed direction again and the smoke lifted.

"It's horrible to see all those animals being destroyed," said George, coughing and looking at the burning carcasses.

"It's the only way to dispose of them, Sir," said the policeman. "It's a damned rotten shame."

George walked on up the driveway to the farmhouse. As he opened the gate that gave access to the house, the front door flew open, and a woman wearing a blue florescent rain jacket stepped out. George was so surprised that all he could do was stand there, one hand on the gate handle, his mouth open, staring at her.

"Mr. Goater?" she said.

"Yes," said George hesitantly. "Who wants to know?"

"Mr. Goater, my name is Peggy Valentine, and I work for the Ministries of Health and Agriculture," she said walking toward him with her hand out.

As George shook her hand, he noticed that she had blonde hair and blue eyes and appeared to be in her late thirties. She had a professional air about her.

"Pleased to meet you, Ms. Valentine. Please forgive my rudeness, but this has been a most traumatic day, what with my father having a heart attack and then seeing his cattle being destroyed, and ..." George hesitated.

The woman smiled kindly at him. "Think nothing of it, Mr. Goater. I certainly understand how you must feel, and I assure you we're trying to get to the bottom of it. That is why I'm here. I've been assigned to discover the source of the disease." She paused and looked closely at him, then took him by the arm. "Oh, dear, you must be exhausted. Come, let's go inside away from this stench and have a nice cup of tea," she said.

George allowed himself to be led into the farmhouse and through a short corridor into the kitchen. He tossed his duffel bag on the floor near a coat tree and sat down at the kitchen table.

"I hope you don't mind. I've rather taken over your father's kitchen," said Peggy as she pulled out a chair and sat down across from him.

George smiled at her. "Think nothing of it, Ms. Valentine."

"Would you like some tea and a biscuit?" she asked as she picked up his dad's ancient chipped teapot.

George nodded gratefully. "Yes, thank you. It will help to get rid of this awful taste in my mouth." He watched her pour tea into two mismatched china cups. "Are you a veterinarian?" he asked.

Peggy raised an eyebrow as she handed George's cup of tea to him across the table. "No, Mr. Goater. I am an epidemiologist. I specialize in contagious diseases. My job is to find out where they come from so the source can be eliminated. If we can't determine the source of the disease, the outbreaks will continue."

"How interesting, Ms. Valentine. You're a detective of sorts, then?" said George as he selected a biscuit from the plate Peggy had extended to him.

"That's right. Only instead of finding the perpetrator of a crime, I find the perpetrator of a contagious disease." Peggy lifted her teacup and gently blew into it before taking a sip.

George dipped his biscuit into his tea and took a bite. Then he took a sip of tea.

"You make a nice cup of tea, Ms. Valentine," said George. He smiled at Peggy.

"Oh, please, let's not stand on formalities here," said Peggy with a smile and a wave of her hand. "Why don't you call me Peggy, and I'll call you George? It's likely I'll be spending some time working here, and I'd like to be on a more friendly, informal basis."

"Very well, Peggy. I like that idea," said George, relaxing and feeling at ease.

"Now, I must ask you some questions, George. Do you feel up to it?" George nodded and smiled at her.

"Let's see," she said, looking down at a notepad and picking up a pen. "Has your father been more than fifty kilometers from the farm recently, George?" she asked.

"Not recently that I know of, but he did go to Barbados last year."

Peggy made a notation on the pad and looked up at him again. "Have you eaten any meals here within the last thirty days?"

George thought for a moment. "Yes, I have, Peggy. To the best of my recollection, I had four Sunday dinners and four breakfasts here last month."

"Mmmm hmmm," said Peggy as she made another notation. "Did the meals include meat - either hot or cold?"

"Yes, the dinners were all roast beef, and the breakfasts consisted of sausage, bacon and fried eggs."

Peggy wrote down George's answer and looked back up at him. "Where did the meat come from?"

"Safeway in Bridgefield," said George. "I generally buy it on the way down from London and fix it for myself. Dad, you see, is a vegetarian and doesn't eat meat."

"Doesn't eat meat? That seems odd what with him raising a herd of cattle and all," remarked Peggy, raising an eyebrow as she lifted the teacup to her mouth.

"Oh, he raises the Black Angus for show and for breeding purposes," explained George. "He couldn't bear to kill one. They are like children to him."

Peggy looked at him as she held her teacup in both hands, elbows on the table. "Are you cold, George?" she asked.

"No, why?" said George, raising his eyebrows in surprise.

"Just wondering why you've still got your coat on, that's all," said Peggy with a smile.

"Oh, that," said George glancing down at his buttoned trench coat. "I've been wearing it all day because I never had a chance to change clothes." He walked over to the clothes tree, took off his coat and hung it up.

Peggy laughed when she saw the tuxedo. "Have you been to a fancy dress party, or what?" she asked. "I haven't seen anyone wearing a tuxedo like that since I saw that James Bond movie - *Casino Royale*, I think it was."

"I've been wearing the stupid thing since last night. Rented it for my retirement party at the Savoy in London," said George, holding out his arms and looking down at the crumpled tuxedo.

"Retirement party?" said Peggy. "You look too young to be retired. Where did you work?"

"It's a long story that I'd rather not go into right now," said George. He sat back down at the table. "I worked for the Foreign Office for many years."

"Well, I've worked for the government for twenty years and still have many years to go before I can even consider retiring. So, what are you going to do now that you're retired?"

"I was going to move here and keep Dad company," said George with a wistful frown. "I love the countryside. Wanted to do a bit of writing and potter about with gardening. It beats the pollution and the crowds in London."

"And what about Mrs. Goater? Is she enthusiastic about moving?" Peggy continued to scribble on her notepad.

"There is a Mrs. Goater, but she is no longer married to me. She divorced me last year after thirty years of marriage. She decided that being married to a low-level civil servant was not what she wanted. Now she is living with a man who works for the Diplomatic Corps. She likes the high life - embassy parties, Ascot, Wimbledon, that type of thing."

"I shouldn't have asked you that, George. I didn't mean to pry," said Peggy. She leaned forward in her seat and looked intensely at him. "Let's get back to the issue at hand. You spoke to the doctor about your father's condition?"

George nodded.

"What did the doctor say?"

"He said Dad had a heart attack."

Peggy glanced over her shoulder as if making sure there was no one to overhear them. She looked back at George, and said in a low voice, "Did he tell you there is the possibility that he has something else - even Mad Cow?"

George's mouth dropped open. "Yes, but how did you ... ?

"I'm with the Ministry of Health, remember? My job is to find the source of the Foot and Mouth outbreak here, and as a precautionary measure, I need to rule out the possibility of another case of Mad Cow in the area. Don't worry," she said quickly noticing George's obvious discomfort. "I won't tell anyone. It's a secret between you, the doctor, and me. Besides, he may not have Mad Cow at all, and perhaps I can verify that. So far I have learned from what you have told me that if he does have Mad Cow, he didn't get it in the most common way, which is eating contaminated meat."

George sat up in his chair. "Yes, I see what you mean - because he is a vegetarian. I should have thought of that when the doctor told me how the disease is usually contracted. Does this mean he doesn't have it?" asked George, hope registering in his voice.

"Ms. Valentine," called out a policeman who was rapping on the kitchen window.

"What is it, Constable?" asked Peggy as she opened the window.

"Will Mr. Goater be spending the night? If so, we need to get some groceries. All the food in the house has been taken to be analyzed."

"You're quite right, Constable." Peggy looked back over her shoulder and smiled at George. "Yes, Mr. Goater is staying. Let's see – we'll need some bacon, sausages, eggs, mushrooms and tomatoes. Oh, and just in case, the makings of a roast chicken dinner for tomorrow as well."

"Will that be all?" asked the constable.

"What about tonight? I haven't eaten all day," said George.

"Oh, I didn't think of that," said Peggy. She turned back to the window. "Constable, can you bring us fish and chips for tonight?" she asked.

"Of course," said the officer. "I"m going to Safeway in Bridgefield for the groceries, and I'll stop at Sawyer's on the way back to pick up fish and chips. Should be back in about an hour."

Peggy closed the window after the constable departed and returned to the table. "Now then, George, let's get back to the questions. Has your father purchased any cattle recently?"

George sat back and scratched his chin. "No... the last one he bought was about three years ago - a bull for breeding purposes."

"Have the cattle been off the farm in the last thirty days?"

"No, Dad just moves them around from pasture to pasture, but not off the farm."

"Is there a possibility that any of the herd came into contact with animals from other farms? Also, were people from other areas allowed to come in close proximity to the herd?"

"I don't know about that, but Dad keeps lists of those sorts of things in the cattle shed. He likes to keep records just in case he forgets names." George yawned, and his eyelids drooped. It had been a long day.

"I think that's enough questioning for now, George. Perhaps you would like to freshen up and change clothes before the fish and chips arrive?" said Peggy, noticing George fighting to keep his eyes open.

"Yes, that's a great idea. Luckily, I have some clothes here, and I have my own bedroom and bathroom."

"I'll let you know when the fish and chips arrive, so off with you. I have to do some paperwork now about our little interview," said Peggy, shooing him out of the room.

George went to his bedroom and selected a change of clothes from the closet and laid them on the bed. Then he stripped everything off and went into the bathroom to shower and shave. In about half an hour, he emerged feeling refreshed. After he had dressed in casual khaki trousers and a chocolate-colored knit shirt, he picked up the tuxedo, which he had left lying on the floor. As he was folding the tuxedo to put into a plastic bag, he heard a metallic clinking sound, and he looked down at the hardwood floor. He didn't see anything, so he knelt on the floor and felt around, sure that he had heard something drop. Finally, he saw a small button-sized object lying close to the bedpost. He reached over, picked it up and took it over to the bedside lamp to examine it more closely. He gasped involuntarily when he saw that it appeared to be a micro-transmitter.

"How did that come to be here?" he muttered.

George sat on the bed holding the transmitter. Then he suddenly turned and placed it in a drawer in the headboard of the bed. As he closed the drawer, he mulled over this latest development. There were two possibilities, he thought. Either the transmitter was already here and had fallen to the floor, or he had somehow brought it in with him. He sat on the bed and absent-mindedly scratched his chin. If he had brought it in, it must have been planted on him. He immediately thought of Yin and Yang and then of the two Americans in the limousine.

He lay back on the bed with his arms behind his head, looking at the ceiling and pondering this. He was soon fast asleep.

"George, are you awake?" A feminine voice interrupted his dream that had something to do with opposites and black and white and a scrap yard. "The fish and chips are ready. You'd better eat them before they get cold," continued the voice, accompanied by a rapping on the door.

"I'll be right there," said George groggily. He sat up slowly on the bed trying to remember where he was and who was calling him.

"We also have some nice bread rolls," said the voice, and George remembered. "Peggy Valentine," he thought.

Aloud he said, "OK, I'll be right there!" as he rose from the bed. When he stood up, the drawer in the headboard caught his eye, and he shook his head, still puzzled.

"Are you all right, George?" called out Peggy again, softly knocking on the door.

George opened the door and gave her a big smile.

"Did you fall asleep?" asked Peggy with a sly grin. "You did look a little haggard when you arrived."

"I feel much better now," said George as he followed Peggy into the kitchen. "The shower and the nap have livened me up, and I"m looking forward to those fish and chips. Feel as if I could eat an elephant."

They both sat down at the table, and George smiled as he noticed the neatly laid table. "You've certainly made yourself at home, Peggy.

Dad and I never bothered too much. We just filled our own plates and sat down - usually in front of the telly."

"I hope you don't mind my forwardness, George. I am in the habit of taking charge of things."

"On the contrary, Peggy. I"m enjoying this. It's been a long time since anyone around here cared enough to take the time to set the table."

Peggy stood up and went to the oven. "I just warmed them up a bit," Peggy explained as she used the hot pads to retrieve the two packages of fish and chips. "I can't stand cold chips," she added.

"I'm the same," said George. "Never did like cold greasy things."

"Hot greasy things more to your liking?" asked Peggy with a snicker, as she opened the packages.

George was silent for a moment, not quite knowing what she meant. As Peggy put the fish and chips on plates, she looked over at him with a sly grin.

George laughed. "Oh, I see what you mean," he said. "I didn't intend it to be taken that way. You must think I'm a dirty old man."

"No, not at all," said Peggy. "I'm no prude. I like an off-colored joke now and then. Lightens up the mood, don't you think?"

She put the plates on the table and sat down.

"Yes, I suppose you are right." George looked down at his plate, embarrassed to look at Peggy.

"So, tell me George. What kinds of hot greasy things do you like?" she asked.

George's mouth fell open when he looked up and saw that she was holding a chip up above her mouth with her fingers and sucking on the end of it, her eyes never leaving him. At last she popped the chip into her mouth and chewed it slowly.

"Well, George? Do you, for example, like hot greasy hands? Or how about toes? Or lips? Or oysters?" She grinned at him across the table as she picked up the vinegar bottle and sprinkled vinegar on her fish.

George finally found his voice. "Oysters?" he asked. "What's oysters got to do with it?"

"Oh, that's for me to know and for you to find out," said Peggy in a teasing tone that caused George to blush.

George laughed nervously. "Well, I certainly wouldn't care for greasy oysters in any case, and I prefer them hot rather than cold," he said, not really understanding where this was all leading.

Peggy burst out laughing. "Oh, I do like a man who can laugh and joke about things and not be hung up," she said.

"That's right," said George with another nervous laugh. He still couldn't get the meaning of what she said. He decided to change the subject. "How long do you think you'll be assigned to this farm, Peggy?" he asked.

Peggy smiled mysteriously. "Oh, for as long as it takes, I expect."

George shook his head and concentrated on eating his fish and chips. When they had finished, Peggy gathered the plates and dishes and put them in the dishwasher.

"I can't stand having dirty dishes lying about in the sink," she remarked. "They should be washed right away. Too many illnesses are caused by improperly washed dishes and utensils, you know."

George pushed his chair back from the table. "Thanks, Peggy. That was a treat."

"Oh, you're quite welcome. Do you like wine, George? I have a nice bottle of Merlot. I generally bring several bottles on these assignments. I've found that drinking wine is a good way to get rid of that awful taste of burning animal hides."

"Yes, indeed," said George perking up. "I enjoy a glass of wine now and then. Why don't we go into the front room and have it?"

"That sounds lovely, but I mustn't stay too long," said Peggy. "I need to get a ride to the Inn when the shift changes at ten." She opened a bag and pulled out a bottle of wine. As she opened the bottle, George got two crystal wineglasses from a sideboard, and they went to the front room.

After they were settled on the settee with full glasses of wine, George looked questioningly at Peggy. "Do you have any ideas about what caused this outbreak of Foot and Mouth?" he asked.

"Not yet," said Peggy shaking her head and looking down into her wineglass. "I should have some results on the Foot and Mouth in the morning."

George nodded and took a long sip of the wine. "That is quite good, Peggy," he said. "By the way, do you normally provide food, drink and entertainment as part of your job?" George held up his wineglass and grinned at Peggy.

Peggy smiled. "It depends. If I enjoy the person's company, I do. Country living can be lonely, and it's a terrible blow to learn one's livestock must be slaughtered. I do my best to cheer things up. The government doesn't have feelings. It's the people who work for the government who make the difference. My supervisor could care less. He can't be bothered with the emotional toll – he's just interested in the cold facts. He acts more like a tax collector than someone who works for the Health Ministry."

"Well, Peggy, you are doing a bang-up job here, and I'm very grateful. I've worked in civil service and you are absolutely right. It all boils down to numbers to them. They have no concern for the human side of things."

"At least we agree on that, George," said Peggy. She took a sip of wine and looked thoughtfully at George. "How long has your father had this herd of Black Angus?" she asked.

"Since before his retirement from the Commonwealth Office."

"Another civil servant - how interesting. What did he do there?"

George frowned. "I can't be sure. He never said much about it, but he did a lot of traveling. In fact, he was gone most of the time. Mum used to complain about that."

"He must have been retired for many years," said Peggy.

"Yes. He retired when he was sixty-five, so that makes it ten years this spring."

Peggy thought for a moment, but said nothing. Then she finished her wine and put the glass down on the coffee table. "Well, I must leave now. Otherwise, I will have to stay the night."

She stood up, and George took the cue and got to his feet as well. "You can stay if you like. There is an extra bedroom with its own bathroom," said George with a smile. "I'm sure you would be very comfortable."

"Perhaps another time, George, but tonight I have to get back to the Inn. I have my laptop and portable diagnostic lab there, and besides I need to bring my car back here in the morning."

"I will walk you to the barrier then," said George as he walked with Peggy back into the kitchen and watched her put on her florescent jacket.

"Thank you, but it would be better for you to stay in the house and keep away from the smoke. Otherwise, you'll be coughing all night."

George followed her to the kitchen door and opened it for her. The light of the fire still painted the farm buildings a sickening reddish-orange color.

"It will take until morning for the fire to die down," said Peggy. "Stay inside, keep the windows closed and try to get a good night's sleep. I'll be back around six to fix breakfast."

"I will be up and waiting. A good breakfast is just the incentive I need to get up early," said George. He watched Peggy walk out of the gate, and then he closed the door and went to bed.

*   *   *

Chapter 6

W HEN GEORGE AWOKE the next morning, he looked out of the bedroom window and saw that it was still dark and that there was still a faint glow from the fire. He stood looking out the window for a moment before he dressed. He had just finished buttoning his flannel shirt when he heard a knock on the front door, and he hurried to answer it.

"Good morning, George," said Peggy in a cheerful voice the moment the door opened. "It will be a much better day today. The weather bureau is forecasting sunshine."

George smiled and reached out to take a small aluminum suitcase that she was carrying. "Goodness, this case is heavy," he said as he placed it on a side table in the kitchen. "What do you have inside?"

"That's my portable diagnostic lab. When I hook it up to this computer, I'll have instant access to Bletchley Center," said Peggy. She was busy unpacking her laptop computer and setting it up on the kitchen table.

"Bletchley? Never heard of that before. What is it?"

"It's the data center for the Ministries of Health and Agriculture. All known diseases in humans and animals are on file there. All I have to do is put a saliva sample into the analyzer, and the result goes directly to Bletchley. If the saliva contains any virus, Bletchley will tell me what it is," Peggy explained as she hooked the laptop up to the telephone line in the kitchen. "But enough of that. I'll cook breakfast while you shave."

"Interesting," said George, still looking at Peggy's equipment. Then he looked up at her and grinned. "Did you say breakfast? I can shave very fast, you know."

The smell of frying eggs and bacon soon filled the farmhouse. George wiped the last of the shaving cream off his face, took a final look in the mirror, and hurried back into the kitchen.

"I'm really looking forward to breakfast," announced George as he walked into the kitchen just in time to see Peggy removing a fried egg from the pan with a spatula. "It's been a long time since anyone cooked breakfast for me."

"It's the first time in a year for me," said Peggy. "I normally don't cook breakfast for myself."

"You live by yourself?" asked George. "Aren't you married?"

"No, never have been. Put my career first, and then it was too late. By the time I got around to thinking about it, all the nice men were taken," said Peggy as she forked the final piece of bacon onto a plate. "Sometimes I wonder if I made the right decision - maybe I should have concentrated on finding a husband."

"Don't worry, Peggy. If it's going to happen, it will. It's no good thinking about the past. There is still plenty of time. The right one may show up unexpectedly."

"What a positive thing to say, George. What about you? Do you think you will ever get married again?" asked Peggy as they both sat down at the table.

"Just like I told you, Peggy, I'm not ruling anything out. You never know. Someone may pop up out of the blue when you're least expecting it." George grinned and stabbed a piece of bacon with his fork.

Peggy smiled across the table at him. "Perhaps we should form an alliance and look together, or we can advertise ourselves on the Internet. I've heard of people who have met that way."

"Not for me, Peggy," said George shaking his head. "I'm leery of meeting anyone that way. You hear too many stories about that. I'd rather meet someone on a train."

After they had finished, George cleared the table and put the dirty dishes in the dishwasher while Peggy finished setting up her gear.

"I expect you want to be alone so you can do your work," said George. "You must have plenty of analyzing to do. I would not like to be in your way."

"Oh, you can stay, George. Sit down and I'll give you a

demonstration. You'll find it interesting," said Peggy. She booted up the computer. "Now you'll soon see how the diagnostic system works."

George pulled up a chair and sat down close to Peggy. The computer screen prompted for a password and Peggy quickly typed it in. Then a numbered list appeared. Peggy clicked on *Field Data Entry*. The portable analyzer made a humming sound, and a message on the computer screen directed her to put in a sample.

Peggy reached over to a small metal box and withdrew two sealed glass tubes. "These vacuum vials contain saliva from your dad's cattle," she explained. "All I have to do is place a vial into the analyzer - like so - and press the „Alt" key on the computer keyboard."

George watched intently as the analyzer buzzed and the green light of a laser beam appeared. Almost instantaneously a graph appeared on the computer screen.

"What do have we here?" said Peggy, leaning forward to look at the graph. "It's Foot and Mouth all right, but ..." She paused as she looked more closely at the screen. "Well, I never! The molecular structure is different than the last major outbreak of Foot and Mouth," she exclaimed.

"A different molecular structure ... What does that mean?" asked George, looking at the screen and trying to determine how Peggy had reached that conclusion by examining the graph. The graph made no sense to him.

"All the past Foot and Mouth outbreaks in England have been caused by the same virus, which originated in Europe. This Foot and Mouth is the same type that caused the outbreak in Venezuela two years ago. It's a South American variety. I wonder how it got here," said Peggy pointing to a waveform on the graph.

George frowned. He could make absolutely no sense out of the data displayed on the monitor. "Can Foot and Mouth affect all animals?" he asked, leaning back in his chair. "I seem to remember that during that outbreak sixteen years ago that millions of animals were destroyed, and it took nearly a year to contain the disease."

"Only hoofed animals – that's why the Americans call it Hoof and Mouth - but ..." Peggy hesitated as she scrolled down through the data displayed on the screen. "There is the possibility that this virus might infect other species of animals as well. I can't be sure right now. I'll have to check many more types of animals." Peggy leaned back in her chair, crossed her arms and continued to stare at the monitor screen.

"Surely the powers that be must have come to the same conclusion as you, Peg. Surely they are aware of this different variety and are just as concerned as you," said George.

"Not necessarily. The ministries are full of administrators, just as they were in the other outbreak. They have knowledge but no wisdom," she said scornfully. "My manager will pass my results on to his manager and so on until somebody with some gumption will finally do something. By then it may be too late to prevent a disaster."

"I know what you mean. The pencil pushers and bean counters don't want to ruffle anyone's feathers or say anything for fear of causing a panic."

"It has the horrid potential of ruining our cattle industry for years to come, George," said Peggy. "If this analysis is ignored, it could even cause the downfall of the Government, because when it all comes out at some point, someone will most certainly accuse the government of a cover-up."

"Perhaps they already know and don't want to cause unnecessary alarm," suggested George.

"I don't know about that, George, but I do know if I were the minister in charge, alarm bells would be sounding, and I'd be taking drastic measures."

"Are you sure, Peg, that it's not the same virus as in the past outbreaks? Perhaps the analyzer made a mistake ..."

"Yes, George, I am absolutely sure because I calibrated the analyzer with a known sample before starting. There is no mistake. The results are accurate - your dad's cattle are infected with the same virus as the one in Venezuela."

"That is very strange then, Peg."

Peggy nodded. "Yes, and the farmers will certainly accuse the Minister of Agriculture of a cover-up."

"You know, Peggy, I heard many rumors at the Foreign Office that the Government kept the last outbreaks a secret because they thought the disease could be contained before it could spread any further than the area where it began."

"Well, that policy certainly backfired on them, didn't it? In the end, they cordoned off all the counties and went on a mass killing spree. I just hope this time the Government will let the experts handle the problem and not let it become a political issue."

Peggy sat up in her chair and tapped *F1* on the keyboard. The graph appeared again, and she traced the peaks and valleys with her finger. "Why has this strain suddenly appeared in the South of England? Now that is a mystery."

"It does seem strange," said George. He looked closely at the graph again, but he still couldn't make any sense of it.

Peggy leaned forward with one elbow on the table and propped her chin in her hand as she continued to stare at the chart. "Well, you see, George, if the data is correct (which it is), that means this South American virus has suddenly popped up in England after being contained two years ago in Venezuela. And that is not possible because, according to standard virus theory, a virus cannot survive unless it has a live host. How on earth it managed to survive and show up here is beyond me."

"Maybe it was passed on to the next generation of animals through the genes and somehow an animal was brought here from South America," speculated George.

Peggy shook her head again. "No, George. That's out of the question because all the animals that were infected were destroyed. Even animals that weren't infected were destroyed if they were within a ten-kilometer radius of an outbreak." She leaned back in her chair again, frowning. Then her mouth curved upward in a slight smile. "This is going to be an exciting project, not like the regular work," she said. "This will require a lot of research and investigation, and that's the part of my job that I really like."

"Can we find out about Dad now?" asked George, with a worried frown. "Does he have Mad Cow Disease, or is it something else? I believe you told me that you have a sample of his saliva from his doctor?"

"Right you are, George. We'll take a look at that now ... if you're sure you're up to it," said Peggy, looking with concern at George.

George swallowed hard and nodded his head slowly. "I guess I'm as up for it as I'll ever be," he said with a slight quaver in his voice. "The sooner we know what he has, the sooner he can be treated for it ... if, in fact, there is a treatment."

"All right, then, George. I just need to save the results for the Foot and Mouth," said Peggy as she clicked on *Save,* and then returned to the main menu. Next she removed the vial from the analyzer and returned it to the metal box. She opened another metal box and retrieved another vial with the word *Goater* written in green ink along its length. She inserted it into the analyzer, and looked back at the computer monitor where another graph had appeared.

"There you are, George," she said, pointing at the graph. "This is your dad's saliva sample." She looked closer at the graph and gasped. "Oh, my God, George, your dad does have Mad Cow! And it's not the regular variety either."

"Oh, my God!" said George. He put his hand up over his mouth and blinked back the tears that had started in his eyes.

"There's something very peculiar about this strain," said Peggy as she continued to examine the graph. "It has a perfect wave pattern. Look here and here, George. There are no irregularities, just straight lines to the top and to the bottom of each peak, and it repeats precisely, as if the waveforms have been duplicated. This is too precise to be molecular rejuvenation."

George looked at the graph where Peggy was pointing. "Yes, I see that, Peggy," he said, his voice quavering. "It's as if the lines were drawn with a pencil against a straight edge."

Peggy did not respond as she continued to concentrate on the screen. "Great chicken eggs!" she suddenly shouted. "The virus has been genetically engineered. That's the only explanation for it. That's the reason the spectral output is so damned perfect – it's man-made!"

"What?" cried George. "A man-made virus?"

"No doubt about it. The wave form is too perfect to be otherwise."

"Why in heaven's name would somebody want to make a Mad Cow virus? What a weird thing to do."

"I don't understand it either, George, but these things do happen. Every time there are large outbreaks of any type of illness, conspiracy rumors abound. I've heard them all, from terrorists to unfriendly governments, but up until now, it's always turned out that the illness was caused by a normal virus."

"I've heard those rumors, too," said George. "In fact I even had a theory of my own that the drug companies were behind it so they could make a fortune selling a cure."

"Anything is possible, George, but I'm worried about your dad."

"So am I. Is there a cure for this strain, especially if it's man-made?"

"I don't know, George, I really don't, but Bletchley will give it top priority when I send this."

Peggy returned to the main menu and quickly typed in a note as George looked anxiously over her shoulder. *Urgent. Confidential. Genetically engineered Mad Cow virus outbreak. Need Priority One.* Peggy clicked on *Send*, and the *Instant Messages* window popped up with the word *Received* appearing on it.

"Isn't technology marvelous?" said Peggy. "I'm so pleased the ministries got together and established one safe network. It saves a lot of red tape and fiddling around, and now we should be getting a response very soon."

"Now will Bletchley work on a cure for Dad's disease?" asked George, excited by Peggy's enthusiasm.

"Just a minute, George. I have to check something out," said Peggy as she tapped on the computer keyboard again. "Aha! The DNA confirms that the sample came from William L. Goater. That is your father?"

"Yes, that's my dad, but DNA!" said George surprised. "How in heaven's name would the computer know that?"

"The DNA data bank was established many years ago. Each time a doctor took a blood sample from a patient, the patient's DNA was automatically added to the bank."

George's eyes lit up. "I've heard of that. I remember the flap when they first introduced it many years ago. People thought it would be a violation of civil rights or privacy or something."

"It's not really a violation, George, when you think about it. All doctors" medical files are confidential and kept in centralized data banks. The DNA is simply gleaned from the files and is kept separate from other personal information."

"I guess that's right," agreed George as he looked at the data on the screen.

"Well, now that we have confirmed it is your father, I'll check his medical file," said Peggy, quickly turning her attention back to the computer and tapping on the keyboard.

"Heavens!" exclaimed George when he saw his father's medical history appear on the screen. "First DNA and now his medical information. It seems as if this type of information could get into the wrong hands and be used by insurance companies and the like."

"Relax, George. Only authorized people can get access to it. It's just like online banking."

"Maybe so," said George hesitantly, "but I still don't understand why they would have centralized records."

"Like I said, the Ministry of Health has control of medical records," said Peggy impatiently. "They use them for cost analysis. For one thing, it makes it easy for them to keep track of drug use so they can bargain with the drug companies to reduce costs. Also the data helps to define areas where there are pockets of major diseases."

"Bargaining with drug companies?" said George, wrinkling his forehead. "I've never heard of that before."

Peggy shrugged her shoulders. "It's just one of those secret arrangements to induce drug companies to keep costs down. Using the data in the medical records, the Health Ministry can place bulk orders for drugs, which to me is not a bad idea." She smiled at George.

"It must be a nightmare keeping the records up to date," persisted George, as he stared at his father's information on the computer screen.

"Not really, George," said Peggy with another shrug of her shoulders. "The same day you go to a doctor, his diagnosis is entered into the data bank, so the information is very much under control and constantly updated." Peggy looked back at the screen. "I see your father has had all the normal vaccinations as well as those needed for travel."

George nodded. "Yes, he's a stickler for that."

Peggy looked up from the computer screen at George. "You know, I think it would be a good idea to test you, not that you need to be worried. I'm sure you don't have a virus because it would have shown up by now. If we run a saliva test on you, you can tell me if the data is accurate."

"Well I just had a physical before I retired. It was Foreign Office policy. I was hoping they would find something so I could get more pension, but they gave me a clean bill of health," said George with a grin.

Peggy smiled at his little joke. "Be that as it may, George, I want to test you all the same." She pulled out a drawer in the portable analyzer and selected a long clear plastic tube wrapped in cellophane. As Peggy removed the cellophane wrapper, she noticed George looking at the tube with apprehension. "Don't worry. I've done this thousands of times and it won't hurt," she reassured him.

"Where are you going to put that?" asked George with a wry smile when she had removed the wrapping and held the long tube up to the light.

Peggy laughed. "In your mouth, George, but there are other places I could get a sample." She looked at George meaningfully.

He grinned. "In the mouth please ..." he started to say, but before he could finish, Peggy popped one end of the plastic tube into his mouth and began to squeeze a plastic diaphragm that she had attached to the other end of the tube. "Just relax, George. This will only take a second," she said.

George felt a sucking sensation under his tongue, and when he closed his lips around the tube, the sensation increased.

"That will be enough," said Peggy as she pulled the tube out of his mouth. "My, George, it looks as if you enjoyed that," she teased, seeing the expression on his face.

"I never had anyone suck out my mouth before. I rather liked it," said George with a grin.

Peggy laughed. "It's nothing new, George. Dentists do it all the time."

"Well, I certainly wouldn't let a dentist do it to me," George grinned even wider, enjoying this little repartee.

Peggy smiled and then grew serious. "Now then, let's see what we can find out about you."

George's smile faded as he watched Peggy place his saliva sample into a small glass vial and load it into the analyzer. George and Peggy both looked at the computer screen in anticipation, and sure enough, a graph appeared.

"No Mad Cow, but there is Sildenafil," said Peggy pointing at the graph. As usual, George could not make heads nor tails of the graph.

"Oh, my God!" cried George, clapping a hand to his brow and turning bright red. Peggy giggled. "It's just a trace. You must have used it within the last forty-eight to seventy-two hours. Do you find the need to use Viagra often?"

"No, no! I didn't even know I had it ... I never had it before ... that is ..." said George, tripping all over his words.

"Well, did it work for you?" asked Peggy.

"I don't know ... I can't remember."

"My, my," Peggy said with a grin. "Can't remember. Must have been some party." She turned back to the computer screen. "Now for your medical record, George."

George looked at the screen with apprehension. He saw the data appear, and he leaned forward to read over Peggy's shoulder.

"Hmmm, George, you certainly have a varied medical history - from pneumonia as a child to ..." Peggy stopped.

"What!" George yelled, as his eyes came to rest on the information Peggy was looking at. "I never in my life had a venereal disease! That's a mistake! Why on earth would it say that?"

"No need to feel embarrassed," Peggy said in a soothing tone. "I've got a varied history too."

"Believe me, Peggy. It isn't true."

"No matter, George. It's just a minor thing. No good getting upset about it. Let's look at the rest of the data. If you see anything else wrong, bring it to my attention."

George scanned the information carefully, pausing several times to think.

"I see you've had all the necessary vaccinations, but you need to get a booster shot for pneumonia," remarked Peggy.

"Well, the rest of the data looks correct, except for that venereal thing," said George.

Peggy turned off the computer and removed the saliva sample from the analyzer. "We'll throw this away," she said. "There's no need for us to keep it, unless you want to save it as a souvenir?"

"A souvenir, nah! Throw the damned thing away. I'm still bothered by that venereal thing," George groused.

"Oh, come on, George. You don't have it now, so stop worrying about it. If it gives you any comfort, I've had a dose of it too. I didn't get it the normal way, though, I should add. I caught it by sharing a lady's toy. My girlfriend and I were intent on our careers, but having a need, we fooled around together. She didn't tell me she was also messing around with men," said Peggy, shaking her head.

George's mouth fell open. "You are a lesbian? I wouldn't have believed that."

Peggy waved her hand in front of him. "Oh, no, George, I'm not a lesbian. It was just one of those things we do when we're young and inexperienced. We were just experimenting, that's all. Being an open person, I'm not embarrassed about it, so now you know."

George could not look her in the eye and he had turned red. "Well, I didn't experiment like that, Peggy. I gained my experience in the normal way."

"Whatever 'normal' means," said Peggy with a snort.

"Does the analyzer only work with saliva?" asked George quickly.

Peggy grinned to herself. "No, George. It works with pretty much anything, but it's easier to get results from fluids. Hard samples take a little longer."

"I know what you mean about that, Peggy," said George with a knowing grin. "That's more within my experience range."

Peggy laughed and got up from the table. "You seem in much better spirits now, George. So while I am collecting more samples, keep busy, but remember to stay in the house. I will get my people to do a line search to see if there are other infected animals in the area. I'm very concerned about hedgehogs and rats because they can spread the disease very easily." She put her arms above her head and stretched to loosen her back muscles. "We must stop the wild animal migrations; otherwise, this strain of virus will spread. The wild animals might also give us a clue as to how this virus got here. It's quite a mystery, George, and I'm anxious to get to the bottom of it."

"Can I help?" asked George. "There must be something I can do."

Peggy thought for a moment as she put on her all-weather jacket.

"You said your father did a lot of traveling when he worked for the ministry. Perhaps you could find out where he went. If you can find his passport, that would be a good start," she said. "You're the only one who can do that. It would not be legal for me to look for it without a search warrant, and besides, you know better than I do where to look."

"But you looked at his medical files, and I thought that was illegal," George reminded her.

"Yes, George, but that was different. Look all you can while I'm gone, but don't try and get into my computer," said Peggy. She laughed as she closed the kitchen door behind her.

George returned to his bedroom, still shaking his head and wondering how that venereal disease business had gotten on his medical record. He closed the door to the bedroom and turned around. The first thing he saw was the drawer in the headboard. He stared at it for a moment, and then he looked over at the plastic bag containing the tuxedo.

After a moment, George went over, picked up the bag and removed the tuxedo. He unfolded it and laid it out on the bed. First he examined the jacket carefully with his hands, and, finding nothing, he did the same with the trousers. Once again he found nothing except Yin and Yang's card in one of the pockets. He looked at it for a moment, blushed and shook his head, and then tore it into bits and deposited it in the wastebasket.

He stood looking at the tuxedo for a moment, and then picked up the jacket and went into the bathroom and quietly closed the door. He found a pair of scissors in a drawer of the cabinet and carefully cut a small hole behind the right lapel of the jacket.

He carried the jacket back into the bedroom and laid it on the bed again. Then, he opened the drawer in the headboard and stood contemplating the micro-transmitter he had found on the floor the previous day.

The bedside telephone rang and startled him. He quickly closed the drawer and picked up the phone, holding one hand over his pounding heart.

"Is that you George?" said a familiar shrill voice through the receiver.

"Who else would it be," he answered rudely, scowling at the sound of Geraldine's voice.

"Why aren't you at the hospital, George, instead of being in bed? How can you lay around when your father is in hospital?"

"None of your bloody business," retorted George. "You're not a member of this family any more, and you have no right to be calling here."

"Of course I have the right. You are incapable of doing anything right unless it involves being lazy and inconsiderate. You're a mastermind at that. You never gave me any consideration the whole time we were married, and now you are treating your father the same way."

George planted a fist on his waist, his face beginning to redden in anger. "Sod off, Geraldine! We can manage without you," he shouted into the phone.

"How dare you, George. If it weren't for me, your dad would be lying there dead instead of being in hospital. You had no consideration for your dad while you were out carousing, did you? Your behavior is despicable."

"Piss off!" yelled George and he started to slam the phone down, but it went silent. "Thank God," he muttered. Then he heard a muffled sound as if someone was holding a hand over the receiver.

"Mr. Goater?" said a male voice.

"Yes?" said George cautiously.

"Mr. Goater, this is Constable James at the barrier. Will you allow Mrs. Goater access?"

George started to say "No!" but his eye fell on the tuxedo lying on the bed, and he hesitated. He looked over at the drawer in the headboard.

"Mr. Goater?" asked the constable.

"Yes, she may come up to the house on the condition that she will have to leave when I say so," he said slowly.

George heard the officer relay the message to Geraldine.

"Mrs. Goater agrees," said the officer.

"She can say that, but I don't trust her. I may need your assistance, Constable, if she refuses to leave when I ask her to," said George.

"Right you are, Mr. Goater. I'll escort Mrs. Goater up to the house and wait outside the door until she leaves."

"Thank you, Constable. That would be very much appreciated," said George and hung up the phone. Then he quickly went to the drawer, retrieved the transmitter, and inserted it into the hole he had made in the lapel of the tuxedo. Then he grabbed the plastic bag and hurriedly stuffed the tuxedo inside.

"So she wants to be involved in my business, eh? Well, this ought to do the trick," George said in a low voice smiling to himself. He picked up the plastic bag and carried it to the kitchen where he sat down to wait.

Before long, he heard footsteps crunching on the gravel path that lead to the door. The kitchen door suddenly flew open, and Geraldine burst into the room without knocking. "There you are, you lazy sod! Haven't you got anything else to do than just sit around."

"I like your orange outfit," George remarked, determined not to let her get his goat. He laughed and pointed at the protective suit she was required to wear in a quarantined area. "That florescent color suits you well - much better than those expensive designer clothes you buy."

"Don't get sarcastic with me," she said slamming the door. "It's about time you pulled yourself together. You were forced to retire because of your uselessness, and now you think you can live on half of that paltry ministry pension."

"Speaking of pensions, if it weren't for me, you wouldn't have one. You never did a hard day's work in your life," said George, his temper rising despite his resolve to remain calm. "So what do you want here?"

"I'm just checking to make sure you're not stealing your dad's things while he is in hospital. Knowing you, you would pawn the lot."

"That does it!" yelled George. "You're just here to snoop around and stick your nose into things that are none of your business." He made a show out of running his hand over the plastic tuxedo bag that he had placed on the table.

"What's in that plastic bag?" asked Geraldine.

George grinned. "None of your business."

Geraldine immediately went over to the table and examined the bag. "You still have this?" she shouted. "It should be returned today. Better get it back or you'll be charged another day. You have no sense of money. You think it grows on trees!"

"Then you must have an entire orchard," retorted George. "You picked my tree for thirty years, and it's about time you grew your own money."

"Well, if you don't have the gumption to return this suit, I will. As it happens, I am going up to London this afternoon. And for my effort, I will keep your deposit," she sniffed.

"What's the matter? Your half of my paltry pension not enough for you? Well, the deposit should be enough to buy you a new set of knickers. I'm sure you need clean ones," said George with another evil grin.

Geraldine held the tuxedo bag up to her nose and sniffed. "This tuxedo stinks - smells like sweaty old trollops." She glared at him. "So that's what you were doing - having your weird sexual fantasies satisfied by some cheap old floozy!"

George threw his hands up in the air. "I've had enough of you for one day. It's time for you to leave, and if you don't, I will call the constable and he will drag you out."

Geraldine glared at George and stamped her foot on the floor. Before she had time to say anything there was a knock on the door.

"It's me, Peggy. Can I come in?"

"Certainly, Peggy," said George raising his voice to be heard. "It's only Mrs. Goater in here, and she is just leaving."

Geraldine scowled at George and then at Peggy when she stepped into the room. "Who is this? One of your floozies, I suppose."

""Who is this rude person?" asked Peggy, ignoring Geraldine and looking at George. "I could hear her yelling clear out in the pasture."

"This is my ex-wife," said George. He could see Geraldine fuming out of the corner of his eye as he watched Peggy take off her coat and hang it up.

"Oh, don't mind me. I'm leaving, so you can get on with your perverted acts!"

"That's enough! Constable, it's time!" yelled George in order to be heard through the door.

"Right you are, Mr. Goater," said the constable as he opened the door and stepped into the room. "Mrs. Goater, it's time to leave," he said as he took Geraldine by the arm and began to lead her from the room. She had the plastic tuxedo bag in her free hand.

When they reached the door, Geraldine looked back over her shoulder. "Don't think you've heard the last of this, George!" she said in a harsh voice.

"Spare me," said George, getting in the last word as the door closed.

"Well, that was certainly pleasant," murmured Peggy after a moment of stunned silence.

"Yes, wasn't it though? I apologize for any embarrassment she caused you Peggy," said George.

"Think nothing of it, George. It's not your fault. It's frightening to think of all those years you lived with that," said Peggy sympathetically. "I know. How about a nice cup of tea to calm our nerves?"

"Thanks, Peggy. I would appreciate it. There's nothing like a spot of tea to soothe the nerves," said George.

"I'll just put the kettle on and while it's boiling I'll check my email to see if we have any news from the ministries. Do you want to join me? I'm sure you're interested in what they have to say."

"Yes, I would be interested," said George. He pulled up a chair next to Peggy's in front of the computer and waited for her. She put the kettle on to boil and then sat down in front of the computer and booted it up. After she had entered her password to get access to the computer, she went to her email box.

"Look at this, George," Peggy said as she read the first message. "The Ministry is going to get the Army to help with the slaughter. All animals within a three-mile radius of an outbreak must be culled. This will devastate the farmers."

"That is bad news," commiserated George. He looked at Peggy as she went back to the list of emails she had received. "Is there any news of Mad Cow - any more with symptoms of the virus my dad has, or any antidote for it?"

"No cure yet, George. That will take a little time. The good news is there are no other cases with symptoms of Mad Cow at this point."

"What about Foot and Mouth? Has it shown up anywhere else?"

Peggy shook her head. "None reported."

She clicked on a link in the menu, and a map of the area came up on the screen. "Let me see, we are here," she said placing the cursor near Wadhurst. "Now, if we enter in the three-mile radius ... Bingo! This is the area under quarantine." The area around his father's farm had turned red, depicting the three-mile radius.

"My word," said George. "So many farms will be affected including Lord Bonderbrook's estate." He pointed to a spot inside the red area.

Peggy looked at him with a slight frown. "Lord Bonderbrook? Isn't he Britain's representative at the European Commission?"

"Indeed he is," said George.

"Tell me, George, what sort of animals are on the Bonderbrook estate?" asked Peggy.

"Lord Bonderbrook breeds racehorses, and there is a park with deer and other game - mostly birds: grouse, pheasant, that type of thing."

"That's a start. I'd better have a look around the estate before the Army shows up because they are under orders to slaughter everything within the culling area." The teakettle began to whistle, and Peggy got up to make the tea.

When she and George were both settled at the table with their cups of steaming tea, she blew on her tea, took a small sip, and looked over at George. "What sort of horses did you say the Lord breeds?"

"Thoroughbreds for racing mostly, and he does his own training, too."

"Any winners?" asked Peggy with a smile. "I fancy a bet now and again."

"Oh, yes, he has had many winners. The most famous one is Sunset, the winner of the Grand National five years ago."

"It will be a pity to see those horses slaughtered," said Peggy with a sad expression. "I assume the Lord's horses are heavily insured - not to say that the compensation could even come close to replacing a Grand National winner."

"Yes, it's a sad thing - just like Dad's prized Black Angus," said George, looking forlornly down into his teacup.

"Well, I must get to work," announced Peggy abruptly. She looked at her watch and hurriedly drank the rest of her tea.

"Me, too," said George. "I still have to find Dad's passport."

*   *   *

Chapter 7

A FTER PEGGY LEFT, George stood in the kitchen thinking for a moment and then decided to begin his search in his father's office. When George entered the small office located off the hallway that led to the bedrooms, he stopped and looked around. He smiled and shook his head. The office was so like his dad, he thought - organized from top to bottom, nothing out of place. The desktop was clear of any clutter, and the books on the bookshelves were organized by size and indexed by subject. CDs were neatly stored in an index file beside the computer.

He opened a file cabinet and rummaged through the files until he came to the letter *P*. He pulled the file and sat down at the desk to look at the contents. No passport. He put the file back and went back to the letter *A*. He pulled that file and sat down again to look through it. He saw that the letter *A* primarily stood for *Angus* with each bull filed by name. Each of those files had sub-files where his father kept exact records on each animal. George continued looking through the file, not really knowing what he was looking for. He put the file back in its drawer and pushed the drawer back into the cabinet.

He decided to search in his father's bedroom. Again, as he stood in the doorway and surveyed the room, he couldn't help but smile. The room was neat and tidy and the bed was carefully made. Looking at the bed, George's smile faded. If his dad had taken ill suddenly, why would the bed be made? Still puzzled, George opened a large clothes closet. Here the clothes were neatly organized according to the order in which his father put on his clothes - shirts, trousers, ties, shoes, jackets and topcoats. Underwear and socks were in a chest of drawers close to the bathroom door.

George surveyed the neatly arranged clothes and then looked up at the storage shelf above the clothes. Cases and boxes bore labels identifying their contents. George read the labels and then reached up and selected a brown leather case labeled *Travel*. He put the case on the bed, unclipped the locks and looked inside. The case contained a number of large brown envelopes, each with a year written in black marker on the outside.

George found the envelope for the year his father had gone to Barbados. He opened it and emptied the contents onto the bed. He examined each brochure and receipt carefully before placing it back into the envelope. Then he picked up a bill from The Veterinarian Association of Barbados and frowned. What did it mean, he wondered, as he read the bill: *"Fee for specimen withdrawal: $560. Please use this document as authorization to take two samples marked Indigo One and Indigo Two out of the country."*

George read the bill a second time and the word *specimen* jumped out at him. He knew his father had artificially inseminated his cows to improve the breed, but why would he bring back semen from Barbados? He frowned. It should be the other way around. It was well known that Barbados breeders maintained purebred Black Angus status by acquiring semen from Britain.

He put the bill aside and rummaged through the remaining papers. Amongst these he saw a standard-sized white envelope with the Official Barbadian Government Crest stamped on the left hand corner and addressed to his father. He quickly opened the flap and pulled out a letter.

Dear Mr. Goater:

    The Government of Barbados is thankful to you for assisting us in a very delicate matter. Please use this letter if you need cooperation from our agencies.

        Sincerely,

    The Right Honorable Owen Haynes

    Prime Minister of Barbados

George shook his head and smiled. He thought his dad had retired, but this letter indicated he was still dabbling in diplomatic work - probably to supplement his income, George surmised.

George folded the letter and the veterinary bill and put them into his pocket. He went through the rest of the papers in the envelope. Not finding anything else of significance, he put everything back into the case the way he had found it and returned it to the shelf.

He was about to reach for a cardboard box labeled *Consultations* when his cell phone began to bleep. He pulled it from his pocket and whispered his identification number into the receiver. He waited for the dispatcher's voice but instead got a recorded message: "This is Foreign Office Communications. Your cell system has been deactivated and is now on the Orange Network."

"Bugger!" muttered George looking at the cell phone. "Now I have to pay for the bloody thing." He put the phone back in his pocket and thought for a moment. Then he went back to his father's office, sat down at the computer and booted it up.

He signed on to his father's Internet access as a guest and then entered his own password. His list of email messages came up. There were twenty-one, but after he had deleted all the junk mail, he was left with only two messages from people he knew. He double-clicked on the first message, and a video of Adam Freeman appeared on the screen. "Hello, Old Chap. Hope you survived the retirement party and enjoyed your surprise," he said with a wink. "Just wanted to wish you a happy retirement, and to remind you that you now have to pay a monthly charge for your mobile phone as it is no longer on the F.O. Network. Well, Cheerio. Look me up when you are in London." The video stopped and George deleted this message and went to the next one.

He sat back in his chair and smiled broadly when Sherry Davenport's smiling face appeared on the screen. "Hello, George," she began in her soft whispery voice that set his heart racing. "We didn't know what happened to you at the Savoy. The last we saw of you, you were headed in the direction of the men's toilet. I hope you didn't get flushed away," she said with a small laugh. Her eyes sparkled. "George, please keep in contact, and don't forget that we have a luncheon date the next time you're in London."

George saved the message and ran it again. He was about to repeat it one more time when he heard the kitchen door open. He quickly logged off and shut down the computer.

When he entered the kitchen, Peggy was at the table booting up her computer. She looked up at him and George could tell she was excited about something. "I have some saliva samples from some rats and from Lord Bonderbrook's horses. I just have to analyze them to find out if they have the virus."

"Can I watch?" asked George.

Peggy grinned at him. "Now, now George. That depends on what you have in mind. Are you by any chance a voyeur?"

George laughed good-naturedly. "There you go again, Peggy. What I wanted to do was watch your computer, but I might be interested in looking at something else later on."

"We'll see about that," said Peggy with another grin. "Come on, sit down," she said as she saw the monitor prompting her to put the first sample into the analyzer.

As George sat down next to her, he saw the green laser beam flashing, and then the graph appeared on the monitor screen.

"Hmmm. This sample comes from a common brown farm rat that is a shirt-tail relative of the London wharf rat," said Peggy peering at the screen. "Now let's check for Foot and Mouth virus."

She tapped the F1 key on the keyboard and another graph appeared with a distinctive waveform.

"Good news, George. No virus. This waveform is just the regular rat pattern," said Peggy changing samples in the analyzer. Again the laser beam flashed and a wave pattern appeared.

"By jingle, George, there is a virus in the horse saliva sample!" exclaimed Peggy. "Now I need to see if it's the same virus that infected your father's cattle."

Peggy's fingers raced on the keyboard. Two waveforms appeared on the screen, one overlaying the other. They matched perfectly.

"Oh, my God, George. Lord Bonderbrook's horses are carrying the same Foot and Mouth virus as the cattle. It's that same strain from South America!" cried Peggy. "Even though the disease is not fatal to horses, they can carry it, and they will have to be destroyed."

"What about the deer? Did you get samples from them?"

"I have to wait for the police to bring some tranquilizer guns in order to get samples from the deer. The fire has made them spooky," she said, still gazing at the waveforms on the screen.

"Is it possible for you to the track the lineage of animals?" asked George.

"Certainly, George," said Peggy. "Since the thoroughbred scandal three years ago, all horses have their DNA on file together with the names of their owners. Here, I'll show you." Peggy rapidly typed in more information on the keyboard and pointed at the screen. "There, George. This is a sample of one of the Lord's horses. The data tracks the horse until it dies. If you want to know the particulars of the horse you just point the cursor and click."

"Look at the foal," said George, noticing it was the youngest horse on the list.

Peggy pointed at the name and clicked the mouse.

"There you are, George. Here's the DNA profile. Sally May is out of April Storm. Both the foal and the dam belong to Lord Bonderbrook. Why are you interested in the lineage?"

"I'm just curious Peggy. I thought there might be the possibility that the virus was transmitted through insemination."

"Well, that is possible, George, but the DNA suggests ..." Peggy paused for a moment and examined the screen more closely. "That's strange. There appears to be missing data. There is nothing about the sire."

"Is that important?" asked George without thinking.

Peggy looked at him with a raised eyebrow. "Of course, it is, George. What do you think?"

"Can't you find the sire? I thought you could find anything by pushing a button. The data bank seems to know everything," said George lamely.

"There are limits, George, if no data was entered," said Peggy.

"Do you think the horses got the virus from Dad's cattle?" asked George, changing the subject.

"I can't be sure, George. It could be the other way around. I will have to take more samples from the Lord's horses. Possibly, samples of DNA from the horses would offer a clue as well."

"Are you going to tell the Lord the bad news?"

Peggy thought for a moment. "No, I'll leave that to a higher level official. I will pass this up the line right away. When I went to the estate, Lord Bonderbrook was not at home. The stable lad said he was in Brussels and can't be reached."

"I've met him," said George. "He is very domineering and obstinate, and he likes to throw his weight around. I suppose those are good traits to have if you're dealing with all those Europeans."

Peggy nodded her head and quickly sent an email to her supervisor. "That should do it. Perhaps someone in a high position will be able to find out how to contact Lord Bonderbrook." She looked at George questioningly. "By the way, did you find your dad's passport? It would be helpful to know where your father has been."

George shook his head and pursed his lips. "No luck yet, but I'm still looking. When Mum was alive she used to hide things up for safekeeping."

"What do you mean? Why would she do that?"

"She suffered from dementia and got it into her head that people were stealing things, so she'd hide them up and couldn't remember where she had put them. Then she would accuse Dad or me of taking them. Dad had to have a lot of patience to deal with all that."

"I know what you mean. My father has dementia, and he's always going to the bank and demanding to see his money so he can count it," said Peggy with a chuckle. "It drives the bank manager bonkers."

"Possibly that's why I can't find the passport. Maybe Dad has hidden it up somewhere," said George.

"Well, I'll leave you to do the hunting while I get back to my job. The Army has arrived and surrounded the area, and before they start slaughtering haphazardly, I'd better be out there. I'll be back later to make some tea," said Peggy as she turned off the computer and the analyzer. She donned her jacket and went out the kitchen door.

"Now, where would Dad have hidden it?" George asked himself as he gazed around the kitchen. He went over and opened all the cabinets, but most of them were empty. Peggy had taken all the food items, even those that were tinned or boxed, to be analyzed. He looked at the hanging saucepans and other cooking utensils above the cooker, and then at the display of Chinese Willow dishes in the china cabinet. Instinct told him to look inside the cabinet.

He opened each drawer, examined the contents thoroughly and closed it again. He got on his knees and opened the lower doors. He peered inside. There was the rest of the dinnerware neatly stacked on the two shelves, and there was something else behind a stack of plates in the corner. He grinned and reached in to pull it out. It was a full unopened bottle of Johnny Walker Black Label. He heard a crash. "Bugger!" he exclaimed as he saw that he had broken a plate in his haste to retrieve the bottle. As he was picking up the shards of the plate, he happened to look up and notice the wooden liners that supported the drawers.

He stood up and pulled the right-hand drawer completely out and stooped over to look into the cavity. "Aha, there's something there," he said out loud. He reached in with his hand, but the height of the space made it difficult to get his entire hand completely to the back. He shoved his hand in as far as he could and then with his index and middle finger managed to pinch something between them and pull it out. It was a passport. George smiled broadly. "So that's where he hid it," he said.

He went over to the kitchen table and sat down to look through the passport. He saw a Barbados stamp dated a year ago when he knew his father had gone to Barbados. Suddenly he frowned and sat back in his chair. Then he pulled the letter and the veterinarian's bill from his pocket and opened them up. He looked at the dates on the letter and the bill, and then looked through the entire passport again. "That's strange," he murmured. There was no Barbados stamp matching the date on the bill and the letter when his father had obviously been in Barbados. He folded the letter and the bill and put them back in his pocket and sat mulling over this latest puzzle.

He looked over at the china cabinet for a moment, and then he abruptly got up from the table, went over to the china cabinet and pulled the left-hand drawer completely out. When he looked in the cavity, sure enough, he saw something in there. Once again, he shoved his hand in as far as it would go, and by using two fingers he was able to extract a plastic box the size of a cigarette packet.

"Hello, what's this?" he mumbled as he opened the box. Inside were two vials, one labeled *Indigo One* and the other *Indigo Two*. He closed the box and put it in his shirt pocket along with the letter and the bill. Then he pulled his key ring out of his trousers pocket. Attached to it was a small penlight, and he turned it on and shone it into the drawer cavity. He could see another small object at the very back of the cavity.

He stuck his hand in again and attempted to grasp it between his fingers, but it was too small and too far back. He went over to a kitchen drawer and returned with a pair of tongs. He reached into the cavity with the tongs and this time managed to grip the object and pull it out. He saw that it was another plastic box about half the size of the first one. When he opened this box, he saw a glass vial that contained a reddish fluid, but this vial had no label.

He retrieved the other box from his pocket and opened it again. He held up the vial labeled *Indigo One* and saw that it contained a milky white liquid. Then he held up the one labeled *Indigo Two* and saw that it contained a blackish red fluid.

He closed the boxes and placed them on the kitchen table. Then he sat down and tried to sort things out. These were obviously the samples referred to on the veterinarian's bill, he thought. He wondered if they were samples of blood and saliva from Black Angus, but why was there a third vial that had no label? Why did his father have them, and why would he get Black Angus samples from Barbados anyway? Even more puzzling, why did his father's passport not have a stamp for this latest trip to Barbados?

He was just wondering if he should tell Peggy about all these discoveries when the kitchen door opened and she walked in.

"It's time for a cup of tea," she pronounced as she shrugged out of her jacket. "Good news, George. I think we're getting closer to finding out where the Foot and Mouth originated. I have Bonderbrook's horse log that shows lots of comings and goings and inseminations."

"Congratulations, Peg," said George, sharing her excitement at this news. "I'll put the kettle on. Do you have any more samples to analyze?"

"Just a couple, this time from the deer," said Peggy as she held up two familiar vacuum-sealed vials. "I'll get on with that while you make the tea. What are these, George?" asked Peggy, having discovered the two boxes on the table.

"I don't know. I found them hidden away with Dad's passport. They appear to contain fluid samples," said George as he put the teakettle on to boil.

Peggy put the first deer saliva sample into the analyzer, and the graph appeared on the monitor screen.

"Bingo! This sample does not contain any virus," she said excitedly. "Now for the second sample." When the new graph came up, Peggy smiled. "Thank goodness, this sample doesn't contain a virus either. That means the deer are free from infection and cannot spread the disease."

"Isn't that strange?" asked George, wrinkling his brow. "The horses share the same pasture with the deer and one would think the deer would also have it, as it spreads so easily."

"I don't know the reason for that, but it's a blessing."

"But not for the deer, Peggy. Won't they still have to be slaughtered?"

"Yes, I'm afraid so. It's government policy, and nothing can be done to change it. Now, let's see what your vials contain," said Peggy. She opened the larger of the two boxes.

George carried two cups of tea over to the table and placed one near Peggy. "Here you are," he said as he sat down in the chair near Peggy.

"Thanks, George," said Peggy taking a sip of tea. "Let's do *Indigo One* first." She sat her cup of tea on the table, plucked the vial out of the box and placed it in the analyzer.

"What do we have here? It's certainly not a Black Angus sample," said Peggy as she examined the graph that had appeared on the computer screen. "I will try to find out what it is."

She tapped a key on the keyboard and the graph changed to display a different waveform.

"It's horse semen," said Peggy excitedly. "Why on earth would your father have that?"

"Maybe it's got something to do with Lord Bonderbrook," George guessed.

"Brilliant," said Peggy touching the keyboard.

George watched her change screens until Lord Bonderbrook's thoroughbreds came up again. Peggy scrolled down through the list, and then selected the foal named Sally May. "Well, what do you know! The DNA from the sample shows that it comes from the stallion that sired Sally May."

"Does the stallion have Foot and Mouth?"

"No, clean as a whistle. No sign of any diseases."

"Can you tell what the horse's name is and who owns him?"

"I certainly can. The name of the horse is Thundercloud, and his owners are Lord and Lady Kimberly in Barbados."

"I wonder what my dad is doing with a sample of Thundercloud's semen," said George. "He must have been on an errand for Lord Bonderbrook. Perhaps *Indigo Two* will give us an explanation."

Peggy exchanged vials and the green light flashed as the laser scanned the sample. The graph came up, and Peggy sucked in her breath. "Well, fancy that. It's human blood. What was your father doing with that?"

"I have no idea," said George in surprise. "I assumed it was a sample from his herd. Can you find out who the sample is from?"

Peggy went to the DNA data bank, tapped a couple of keys, and waited for the result. "Mmmmm. It's a male specimen but it doesn't give a name. I can summarize his ancestry though," she said peering at the screen.

"You can tell that?" asked George incredulously. "What sort of ancestry?"

"One half African, one quarter Carib Indian, and one quarter Scot," said Peggy, scrolling down through the information on the screen.

"Can't you find the name?" asked George. "Perhaps that would tell us why Dad has his blood sample."

"I'll give it another try, George. There's another data field that might have the answer," said Peggy as she typed in a command on the keyboard. Another set of data came up on the screen, and Peggy shook her head. "Sorry, I can't identify the person, because there is a block on his name. That probably means the person is not a subject of Great Britain, and according to international law, I cannot access that information."

"Is there anything you can deduce from what you know so far?" asked George, disappointment registering in his voice.

"I'll go back to the other data and see what else I can learn," said Peggy. After a while she said, "It looks to me as if this is a male who comes from a Caribbean Island and has a great deal of British influence."

"Barbados?" interjected George.

"Possibly, or even Jamaica," said Peggy. "Both those islands have populations with similar DNA."

"Can you check this other sample?" asked George handing her the unmarked vial.

Peggy exchanged the vial with the one in the analyzer and waited for the result.

"This is blood also, George. Just a moment - I have to calibrate the analyzer again." Peggy inserted a blue filter in front of the laser beam and pushed a button. "There you are, George, another DNA curve, but this one belongs to a female."

"Is there any match with *Indigo Two*?" asked George excitedly.

"All we have to do is overlay the DNA curves, like so," said Peggy. "Amazing! The two blood samples are from the same family, and the female is between twenty-eight and thirty-five years of age."

"Can you tell the relationship?"

"The male's blood sample comes from her father, that's for sure," said Peggy.

"Can you find out her name?" asked George eagerly.

"Yes, I'm giving it a try," said Peggy as she concentrated on the screen. "I can't find it yet, George, but I'll try something else."

Peggy brought up various data screens, examined each closely, and finally shook her head. "I'm sorry, George. The name is not here."

"I think the samples came from Barbados, Peg," said George. He pulled the letter and the bill out of his pocket." I found this bill amongst Dad's things. It gives him authorization to leave the country with two specimens - *Indigo One* and *Indigo Two*."

Peggy scrutinized the veterinarian's bill. "Well, that confirms what the analyzer told us - that the specimens come from the Caribbean. Veterinarian Association of Barbados," Peggy read aloud. "What in earth's name does a veterinarian have to do with a human blood sample? I can understand *Indigo One* - the horse semen," she said with a puzzled look.

"I wondered about that, too. It's a mystery," said George.

"Hmmm ... perhaps the bill was a ploy in order to get the samples out of Barbados without causing curiosity. It would be easy to assume both samples were from the horse," Peggy speculated.

"And then, what about the unlabeled sample? The one for the female? That's not mentioned on the veterinarian's bill," said George. "I just wish there was a way to find out her name."

Peggy sat back in her chair and thought for a moment. Then she went back to the computer keyboard and quickly typed in some numbers. "I'm trying for medical records now. I just made a general inquiry for records for an unknown patient with the DNA that matches the female's," she explained.

They both watched the screen for a response. It took several seconds for the computer to search the data banks. Then the screen displayed a ninety-nine percent match.

"Her name is Denise Downing," said Peggy, clapping her hands. "She has both Barbados and British citizenship. That explains why we were not able to find her name in the DNA data bank."

"Why is that?" asked George.

"Dual citizenship means she is in between jurisdictions, and each jurisdiction is governed by different laws," explained Peggy.

"What about her father?" asked George peering at the screen. "Do the medical records name her parents?"

"No. The father's name is blocked, which means he is foreign, and the same thing with the mother."

"Both from Barbados?" asked George.

"I think it's safe to assume that, considering this Denise has citizenship both in Britain and Barbados. Let's see what else we can find out from the medical records." Peggy began to scroll through the information.

"Look at this, George," said Peggy pointing at the screen. "She has been in the UK for two years. Her doctor is located in East Croydon and her address is Chesterfield House in East Croydon. Good Heavens, George! It looks as if she has something similar to Mad Cow disease ... Let me look further. I can't be sure, but ..." Peggy clicked on a button several times to enlarge the data. "By jingle, it is symptoms of Mad Cow and ..." She hesitated for an instant. "It's possible it's the same genetically engineered variety your dad has."

"What!" exclaimed George.

Peggy concentrated on the display. "Look here, George. Her doctor is prescribing *KG9004.* I've never heard of that before."

"*KG9004* ..." repeated George.

Peggy went to a medication search engine, and entered the name of the drug. "Look here, George," she said. "There is no such drug named *KG9004.* It isn't listed."

"Do you think it's something that could help Dad?"

"I don't know. We'd have to find out what it is and where it comes from and if is being used for treating Mad Cow, or something else."

"I'm getting confused with it all, Peg," said George, shaking his head.

"It is baffling, George. Your dad and Denise Downing both have the same genetically engineered Mad Cow Disease. Denise's father is unknown, and she is being treated with an unknown drug."

"And Denise and her father come from Barbados," added George.

"And this drug could very well help your dad," said Peggy.

"Do you think it could be a breakthrough?" asked George hopefully.

"It certainly could be, George, if in fact this drug is being used to treat Mad Cow."

"How can we find out? Is there a way to get our hands on some of this *KG9004,* do you think?" asked George. Peggy shrugged her shoulders. "I know!" cried George, snapping his fingers. "Do the medical records show if Denise has any brothers or sisters?"

Peggy went back to the medical data display and clicked the mouse several times. Then she shook her head. "No brothers or sisters, but she has an uncle. His name is Roger Clemens, address 16 Sarre Road, West Hamstead, London."

"Does he have Mad Cow too?"

"Fortunately not. Suffers from rheumatoid arthritis and is being treated for that."

"Bugger! Dad is involved in all this somehow. I wish he could tell us what he knows."

"Well, he can't tell you, George, at least not until he comes out of his coma. I wish he could. It would save a lot of time."

"All I am interested in is getting him cured."

Peggy looked at her watch and turned the computer off.

"Well, George, I think that's all we can do for today. First thing tomorrow, I must get back to the work at hand. I don't want the Army to shoot everything in sight. If you don't mind, I'd like to take you up on your offer to stay here tonight. It will save me time in the morning."

"Of course, Peggy. I'd be delighted for you to stay. While I was looking for my dad's passport, I happened to find a bottle of Johnny Walker Black. Are you up for a few drinks?"

Peggy gave him a mischievous smile. "That sounds just right. We can have a couple of drinks before dinner. Remember, we have the roast chicken dinner for tonight. All I have to do is put it in the oven. I also have more wine that we can have with dinner."

"Right! I'll make a couple of drinks right now," said George, jumping up and tipping over his chair. It fell to the floor with a loud crash and they both jumped at the noise. Then they burst out laughing.

"My, my, such enthusiasm, George. I do believe you're up for a drink!"

"Yes, indeed. It's been a long day and it's time to unwind," said George. He set the chair back to an upright position, and went to the kitchen counter to make the drinks while Peggy shut down her equipment for the night.

After he returned to the table with their drinks and they had saluted each other and taken a couple of sips, George grew serious for a moment. "What's next, Peggy? Is there anything I can do? I want to make myself useful."

"Well, we need to find out more about Denise Downing and verify that she has the same disease as your dad. You can be my virus detective and investigate for me, if you want."

"I'm willing to do anything to help my dad," said George.

"Right you are. So, the first thing you could do is to go up to East Croydon tomorrow and pay Ms. Downing a visit. See if you can find out what is really wrong with her and perhaps get a sample of that drug."

"That sounds like a good idea," said George. Then he looked down at his feet. "Will you ah ... be able to give me a lift to the train station? I can't drive."

"Can't drive?" asked Peggy with an amused grin. "You certainly look old enough to me."

"Lost my license. Got caught drinking and driving. It was my third DUI, and now I'm banned for ten years," mumbled George, refusing to look at Peggy.

"Think nothing of it, George. Those things happen. I was charged with a DUI a couple of years ago - was stopped for going around a roundabout five times." Peggy laughed and held up her glass. "Drink up, George. Here's a toast to you. You certainly seem to enjoy yourself - venereal diseases and DUIs - what a combination!"

"I can explain that ..." said George, raising his glass.

*   *   *

Chapter 8

W ADHURST TRAIN STATION was busy the next morning. Commuters crowded the platform waiting for the fast train to London. The regulars knew just where to stand so that when the train stopped they would be in front of their favorite carriage and could walk right on to their usual seats.

George, dressed in a black trench coat over an out-of-date gray suit, was holding a black briefcase in one hand and the early morning newspaper in the other. When the train pulled in and stopped, he climbed aboard and found a seat opposite an off-duty train guard who was reading the horse racing news. After stowing his briefcase on the luggage rack above the seat, he gratefully flopped down in the seat and blankly stared out the window.

A thunderstorm was pounding in his head and his stomach was gurgling. He thought about last night but couldn't remember anything after dinner. This morning he'd had a shock when he awoke to find Peggy in his bed, and they were both quite naked. He had been red with embarrassment, but Peggy was not in the least inhibited. She had smiled, given him a peck on the cheek, bounced out of bed and headed for the bathroom with no concern whatsoever for her nudity.

When she came out of the bathroom, she scooped up her clothes from the floor, and stood in the doorway joking about fish and oysters, which he didn't understand at all, and then she told him to hurry up and dress while she fixed breakfast. George felt a little twitch as he remembered how she had looked without clothes, which was not bad at all, he thought. He wished he could remember what had happened after dinner.

When the train pulled out of the station and began to pick up speed, the guard in the seat opposite him put down his paper and smiled. "The train will be delayed when it reaches Bridgefield," he remarked. "All trains will be disinfected there again."

"It needs to be done, I'm afraid," said George, looking sadly at his stained wet shoes. "I'm willing to do my part to stop the outbreaks. It's a sorry state of affairs for all those animals to be slaughtered. My father has lost his entire herd of prize Black Angus."

"I know. It's a good thing they made provisions at Wadhurst station, even though it doesn't do much for your shoes," said the guard, looking down at his own stained boots. He shook his head sadly. "So many of our local farmers have been devastated."

"I hope the Government will make adequate compensation," said George. "Otherwise many farmers will go bankrupt, and you know where that will lead."

"Yes. The Europeans will be able to charge what they like for meat," said the guard. "We should never have joined that Common Market. Should have stayed with the Commonwealth. Damned Europeans have not done us any good, and I never did like the French. France has been a thorn in England's side ever since I can remember. At least Canada and Australia did their best to help us when we needed it. The Europeans just stood back and watched and waited for the opportunity to take care of their own self interests."

"That's not necessarily true," said George. "I worked for the Foreign Office for many years, and I am in a position to know that the Europeans have backed Britain on many occasions," said George. "I do agree with you about the French, however."

The guard leaned forward and looked closely at George. "I say, aren't you George Goater?" he asked. "Did you go to school in Wadhurst?"

"Yes," said George, looking at the guard in surprise. "I went to Best Beach and my father owns Ivy Farm. He has lived there for nearly fifty years."

"I thought as much. My name is Harry Higgins. Don't you remember me? I went to school with you."

George looked more closely at the guard and then smiled. "Of course, Harry, now I do. I'm so glad you said something. Otherwise, I wouldn't have recognized you. I haven't seen you in donkey's years. I'm so pleased to see you again."

"Heard you were back," said Harry. "How is your dad doing? I heard he had a heart attack when he found out his cattle had Foot and Mouth."

"Dad is going to be all right. He is getting good care at Bridgefield Hospital," answered George carefully.

"Are they sure it was a heart attack?" asked Harry. "Sometimes the doctors don't know for sure."

"I'm quite sure it was a heart attack. I have faith in his doctor," said George rather abruptly.

"There's a rumor going around the village that your dad has some sort of tropical disease that he picked up on one of his foreign travels."

"The last time he left the country was eighteen months ago, Harry. If he had picked up something it would have shown up long before now."

"It wasn't eighteen months ago, George. It was last month. I know that for sure because my cousin Jack drives a taxi and he took your father directly to Heathrow Airport. Your father told Jack it was an emergency and he couldn't wait for a train, as he had to be in Bridgetown, Barbados that same day."

"Bridgetown, Barbados. He never told me he was going there," said George with a frown.

"He was only gone a couple of days. My cousin met him at the airport and brought him back to his farm."

"I'm surprised. Dad normally tells me about his trips ..." said George, as the squealing of the train wheels indicated they were coming to a stop.

"It's Bridgefield. We have to get off," said Harry. "They are going to wash the floors with disinfectant and it will take half an hour. We might as well get a cup of tea and I'll look for my cousin. If he is around he can tell you more about your dad's trip to Barbados."

George followed Harry to a small tea stand on the station platform. Many other passengers had the same idea, however, and all the seats were taken.

"We can use the guard's office," said Harry, speaking in a low voice into George's ear. "Follow me."

George followed Harry to the end of the platform where Harry opened a small door and held it open for George to enter.

"We're in luck, George. There's still tea in the teapot," said Harry, lifting the lid on an electric tea urn. He looked around and found two enameled mugs, which he placed on a small table. He poured strong tea into each cup and motioned for George to sit down. "Make yourself at home, George. I'll see if Jack is at the taxi stand."

Harry left, and George sat at the small table sipping the strong tea. A few minutes later Harry returned with a tall younger man following him.

"This is my cousin Jack Gibson," said Harry. "Jack, this is George Goater, my old school chum."

"Pleased to meet you, Mr. Goater," said Jack, stepping over to the table and shaking George's hand. He pulled up a chair and straddled it backwards. "Harry says you have some questions about your dad's trip to Barbados."

"That's right. To be truthful, I'm quite puzzled. Did Dad give you a reason for going to Barbados on such short notice? He never told me he was going."

Jack shook his head. "Your dad didn't say very much about it. He said that he had to go quickly because it was an emergency. He was in such a hurry that he forgot his passport. I offered to go back and get it for him, but he said there wasn't time. He ended up contacting a friend who was able to make arrangements for him to make the Barbados trip without his passport. He was adamant that nothing should delay him. He must have gotten short notice because he had only a small leather briefcase with him. I guess he didn't have time to pack a suitcase."

"That is odd," said George. "Did he happen to say who the friend was?"

"No name, but I remember him telling me it was a friend at the Commonwealth Office."

"You met him at the airport when he returned?" asked George.

"That's right. He made arrangements with me before he left," said Jack.

"How did he appear to you when he returned? Did he seem ill?"

"No. He looked haggard, but that's to be expected from such a
long flight. He did say he was very tired and had a bad headache, as he'd
had little sleep. I tried to joke with him, saying he was probably tired with
eyestrain from watching all those topless ladies on the beach, but he was in
a somber mood. I couldn't get him to smile the whole way back, and he
said very little."

"Is there anything else you remember, Jack?"

Jack took a sip of tea that Harry had poured for him as he thought for a
moment. "There is something that seemed rather strange at the time. When
I picked him up at Heathrow, he was carrying his briefcase and a small
parcel. I remember the parcel for sure, because I tried to make a joke about
it. I said something like, 'Oh, Mr. Goater, you shouldn't have!' as if I thought
he had brought me a gift. He didn't laugh - just looked at me as if he hadn't
heard me."

"Did he take the parcel back to the farm with him?"

"That's another odd thing. He posted it at Heathrow before we left. I
made a joke about that too. I said it was a long way to come just to post a
parcel. He just glared at me and said it was quicker to post it here than in
Barbados and to mind my own business. He seemed to be very concerned
about it. He was not his normal self. He seemed to have a lot weighing on
his mind."

"Did you notice the address on the parcel, Jack?" asked George.

At that instant the announcement that the train for London was
departing and all passengers should be aboard came blaring over the
loudspeakers.

"Come on, Jack, did you see the address?" asked Harry excitedly as he
and George jumped to their feet.

"I can't remember," said Jack as he followed George and Harry
out onto the platform.

The train's whistle sounded and George quickly opened a carriage door
and stepped in just as the train began to move forward.

"I hope your father recovers quickly," called out Harry through
cupped hands as he and Jack walked alongside the train. "Sorry to hear about
his cattle."

"West Hamstead, the address was in West Hamstead," cried out

Jack, waving both arms over his head. "Yes, yes, I remember now - it was West Hamstead."

The strong acrid odor of disinfectant in the carriage made the passengers cough and sneeze and tears ran down their cheeks. One passenger reached to open a window to let some fresh air in, but another passenger yelled at him to leave the window closed until they reached Sevenoaks. "What's the point of sanitizing if you let the virus in from outside?" shouted the passenger.

When the train stopped at Seven Oaks more passengers boarded and gasped and wheezed at the invasive odor. This time no one said anything when the same passenger reached to open a window. A small cheer went up from the commuters when a strong breeze of fresh air blew into the carriage.

Throughout all this, George did not take much notice. He was deep in thought about his father's trip and the parcel with the West Hamstead address. He remembered that Denise Downing's uncle lived in West Hamstead. Was this just a coincidence, or was his father tied up in something involving Denise Downing and her uncle? After all, Peggy had said that Denise Downing had the same genetically engineered strain of Mad Cow Disease that his father had. He was still deep in thought when the train pulled in to Charring Cross Station.

George got off the train and found himself in a madhouse of commuters rushing to get to their places of work on time. The delay at Bridgefield had made his train late, and most of his fellow passengers were sprinting through the station either to try to get a taxi or to catch the next underground train.

George walked slowly as commuters dodged around him. He found the platform where he would catch the next East Croydon train and went to buy a ticket. The cashier said that there would be an hour's wait before the train reached Charring Cross, so George found a seat and unfolded his newspaper.

He was reading the latest news about the Foot and Mouth outbreaks when he heard a familiar voice.

"Hello, George. Fancy seeing you here."

He looked up from the newspaper and saw Stan Straw smiling down at him.

"Well, hello, Stan. What are you doing here? Do you have the day off?"

"Nah, I have to go down to Gatwick Airport to bring back lost luggage for some high mucky muck. I do other things besides checking people in and out at the Foreign Office, you know," said Stan. He wrinkled his nose. "Good God, George! You smell like my toilet. Where in dickens have you been?"

"Oh, I've been sanitized. I'm pure now - no fear of me carrying Foot and Mouth. If you don't believe me, just look at my shoes."

"By the look of it, you have foot rot," said Stan with a chuckle as he observed George's white-stained shoes. "So where are you off to?"

"Going to visit an old friend in East Croydon. I haven't seen her for years."

"I imagine now that you're retired, you have plenty of time to look up old friends."

"By the way," said George, changing the subject. "That was quite a mess last Saturday morning. It looked as if bombs had gone off. I've never seen anything like it - burning cars and police everywhere."

"It wasn't the farmers that did that, George," said Stan with a scowl. "Bloody hooligans just out to cause trouble. Wish they would lock the buggers up ... Oh, here's our train now. We'd better get on or we might not find a seat. It's a long way to have to stand."

George picked up his briefcase, and he and Stan hurried to the train where they managed to find seats opposite each other. After only a few minutes the train pulled out of the station leaving behind a number of out-of-breath passengers who had not made it on time.

After he was settled in his seat, George opened his briefcase and looked at the computer paper Peggy had given him. He squinted at it and wrinkled his brow.

"Is that your bank statement?" asked Stan curiously. "If it were mine, it would all be printed in red instead of black."

George laughed. "No, it's just a hard copy of some computer data and I can't understand it. It's just a lot of mumbo jumbo to me."

"I'm no good at that type of thing either," said Stan, shaking his head. "I just leave it to the kids to figure out. When I went to school there were no computers, and life was much easier."

"I know what you mean," said George as he gave up and folded the computer paper and put it back in his briefcase. "Kids today play with computers the way we used to play with tiddly winks."

"I heard about your father's farm in the news," said Stan with a sympathetic look. "They said it was a prized herd of Black Angus. Damned Foot and Mouth. The whole thing is out of control. According to the news this morning, over sixty percent of all our sheep and cattle will have to be slaughtered. It will destroy our livestock industry, and on top of that, it's causing heart attacks, just like what happened to your dad. I hope he is recovering?"

"He seems to be doing nicely, but it may take quite a while before he is back to normal," said George.

"I see Lord Bonderbrook's estate is quarantined too," said Stan. "What a pity his horses have to be destroyed. I've made a lot of money betting on Bonderbrook's horses."

"I didn't know you were a gambler, Stan."

"Just now and again," said Stan. "I did very well when Sunset won the Grand National."

"It is a bloody shame for all those horses to be destroyed," said George, looking down at his hands folded in his lap.

"The papers said the Lord's horses had to be destroyed because they were inside the quarantined area. Said they've traced this outbreak to a flock of sheep a Sussex farmer imported from Belgium."

"What? A flock of sheep from Belgium," said George, sitting up in his seat.

"That's right," said Stan. He pointed at the paper in his lap.

George tried to compose himself. "I'm surprised they could track it down so quickly. Perhaps they'll soon discover the source of Mad Cow as well."

"They think they have, George. The paper says that it came from imported meat."

"Imported from where, Stan?"

Stan picked up the paper and looked for the article.

"Here it is, George. It says that several years ago a Chinese restaurant in Nottingham served beef illegally imported from China, and it turns out it was from cattle infected with Mad Cow."

"Bugger, Stan! Do you believe it?

"I don't know what to think."

"Well, whatever the cause of it all, the fact remains that Dad has lost his herd. Such a bloody shame."

"I just hope the government compensates him well," said Stan. "Your dad had a valuable herd, and it will be hard to replace."

"I wonder where Lord Bonderbrook is," said George suddenly shifting to another topic.

Stan frowned. "Now that's a curious thing. No one seems to be sure. The news just keeps on saying he can't be reached. The general consensus is that he is in Brussels involved in some European matter. I just hope it has something to do with putting pressure on the French and getting the European Union to lift its ban on importing meat from outside, at least until this crisis is over. As it is now, we can't import meat from Australia or America because of the ban, even though they've offered to help."

"It would be interesting to know what Lord Bonderbrook is doing," said George. "If I were still at the Foreign Office, I might hear something about it, but now ..."

"I can take a hint," said Stan with a chuckle. "I'll keep my ear to the ground, and if I hear anything, I'll ask Sherry to email you."

Stan paused and looked at George with a grin. "By the way, speaking of Sherry, is there anything between the two of you?"

"Afraid not, Stan. It's against civil service policy to become romantically involved with someone in the same office, you know."

"Well, you don't have to worry about that now that you are retired, do you, George?" Stan winked at him. "You should give her a call and ask her out. She just might take you up on it. No harm in trying. Opportunity is for those who try."

"Well, she has told me two or three times now to call her for a lunch date when I'm in London ..." said George blushing slightly.

"There you go," said Stan. "I happen to know she fancies you, you lucky sod."

"How do you know that?" asked George, hope springing in his chest.

"On Friday night at your retirement party, she was looking for you and when she saw you with those two girls, she seemed quite annoyed. I tried to explain to her that they were old friends, but I think she knew what was going on. She probably overheard someone joking about it. Most of us had contributed to your 'retirement gift,' you know.

"Speaking of that, how was it, George? I want to be sure my contribution was well used."

"Not to worry, Stan. They certainly did their part to provide more than just entertainment, even though I can't remember much of it," said George with a smile. "Whoever came up with that idea? It was certainly a memorable retirement gift."

"East Croydon. Remember to take your personal belongings with you when you disembark," said a pleasant female voice over the intercom.

George stood up, collected his briefcase and looked down at Stan. "Well, Stan, it was nice seeing you again. Have a good trip to Gatwick and good luck in finding the lost luggage. Don't forget to let me know if you hear anything about Lord Bonderbook," said George as the train pulled into East Croyden.

"That I will, George, and I'll also put in a good word with Sherry," said Stan winking. "I wouldn't be surprised if you soon have a date with her."

"I will definitely call her when I'm in London," said George with a light heart as he walked to the carriage door to disembark.

When he was outside the station, George stopped and retrieved a sheet of directions from his pocket. Peggy had printed out the directions to Chesterfield House from her computer the night before. He looked at the sheet of paper, and then turned left past the flower shop. He continued walking briskly, stopping occasionally to consult the directions.

After about ten minutes he found himself standing outside the large wrought iron gates at the entrance to Chesterfield House. He looked about and noticed a polished brass name plate on the London brick column. Leaning closer, he read the embossed words: *Chesterfield House, Private Hospital. To gain admittance, please push button below.* George pushed the button. No response. Finally, on his tenth push of the button, a woman's voice answered over the intercom at the gate.

"Can I help you?"

"Yes. I'm here to see Denise Downing," said George in an official voice.

"Are you a relation of Ms. Downing's?"

"Yes, I'm her step uncle," he blurted out without thinking.

"Visitors have to give twenty-four hours' notice, and she has no scheduled visitors today."

"I'm Mr. Downing, and I am her uncle," said George in a firm voice.

"An uncle, you say? I thought you said step uncle."

"Yes, that's right, and I've traveled a great distance to see my niece. I insist on seeing her today."

"You will have to come back tomorrow, Sir. No visitors allowed today. You can visit her at three tomorrow afternoon."

"Look here. If I can't see her today, I will report this to the Board of Governors. It seems you are not aware that family members have to have access to patients. It's the law," George blustered, making it up as he went.

"You're wrong, Sir. Hospitals only have to allow visitors during posted visiting times."

"I just want to see her for a minute or two. I have to leave tonight and it may be a year or two before I can get back," said George in a wheedling tone.

He waited for a reply, but none came, and he was about to give up when he heard the woman's voice again.

"Mr. Downing, I've just checked on Ms. Downing and she is under sedation. If I let you see her you must be very quiet."

"Yes, yes. I promise not to disturb her. I just want to see her," said George gleefully.

A loud buzzing sound made George jump, and then he saw the gate begin to slowly open. He quickly walked through as soon as the gate had opened wide enough, and he followed a circular driveway to the main entrance. After climbing the flagstone steps to the entrance he heard another buzzing sound and then the noise of sliding bolts and the turning of a key in a lock. George patiently waited as the large barred door began to open.

"Come in, Sir," said the same voice he had heard over the intercom. As he walked through the open door, George saw that the voice belonged to a rather gaunt looking nurse. "It's not the normal visiting time, but under the circumstances we have decided to make an exception and allow you to make a short visit. Please remember, Ms. Downing is under medication and you are not to disturb her."

George nodded and followed the nurse to a small waiting area. She locked the door and disappeared into an adjacent room. Finding a comfortable seat, George sat down and surveyed the surroundings. The entrance door had four old-fashioned bolts with padlocks. The main key lock had a pick shield and there was a keypad with a small red light glowing at the right-hand side of the door. The sun shone through the iron bars on the windows, casting shadows on the floor. George wondered if all this was to keep people from getting in or to keep them from getting out.

"I will take you to see Ms. Downing now, Sir," said the nurse, suddenly appearing at the door to the adjacent room. "Follow me. Her room is this way," she said as she held the door open.

George stood up clutching his briefcase and followed the nurse down a green carpeted corridor until they reached a white door that was bolted on the outside.

"Just a moment, Sir," said the nurse as she peered through a small window in the door.

George looked over her shoulder into the room. He saw it was like any other private hospital room, with brightly-colored furniture and matching drapes that were drawn. An elegant light fixture illuminated the room, and George saw a young black woman lying in an oversized hospital bed with railings. He saw that she was strapped down in the bed.

"Remember, Ms. Downing is under sedation so please do not disturb her," the nurse reminded him as she slid back the bolt on the door. "I'll give you five minutes, Mr. Downing, and that's all."

"Thank you, Nurse," whispered George as the nurse quietly opened the door. "Are the restraining straps necessary?"

"I'm afraid so," whispered the nurse. "They keep Ms. Downing from harming herself or others. Normally she is under heavy sedation but when she is not she can be very restless."

"Will she recognize me or know that I am here?"

"Very unlikely, Mr. Downing. The medication affects her optic nerve and she cannot see clearly."

"What sort of medication?" asked George, forgetting to whisper.

The nurse held a finger up to her lips. "A nerve relaxant to calm her down. She can get excited very easily," she whispered.

"Does she have emotional problems?"

"No, but she loses muscle control and has violent convulsions," said the nurse turning away from the door and looking at George. "You seem very inquisitive, Mr. Downing. If you weren't a family member, I could not be telling you all this."

"Thank you for answering my questions. It helps me to understand her condition," said George humbly.

The nurse smiled at George and pushed the door open wider. "That's quite all right, Mr. Downing. I'll be back in five minutes and remember what I said. By the way, in case Ms. Downing does become excited push the emergency button next to her bed."

George walked into the room as silently as he could. The nurse pulled the door closed and he heard the lock engage. As quietly as possible, he picked up a chair and placed it close to the head of the bed and sat down. He looked at the young woman lying there. She appeared to be in her early thirties and her skin was the color of polished ebony. Her hair had recently been washed and done up in dreadlocks. To George's surprise, her large brown eyes were wide open and she appeared to be looking directly at him.

"Hello, Denise," said George in a soft voice. "I'm a friend."

She did not answer. Her unblinking eyes continued to stare at him.

"I've come a long way to see you."

Still no answer.

"You come from Barbados, Denise?"

George watched as her lips curled into a faint smile. Then her mouth opened as if she were trying to speak. "Yoooo noooo. Yoooo noooo," she said.

"Know what, Denise?" asked George, leaning closer to hear better.

"Yoooo noooo?" she cried, nearly breaking his eardrum.

George quickly drew back and saw that her tongue was now protruding from her mouth.

"The weather in Barbados is wonderful," said George soothingly, attempting to calm her down. "Bridgetown is a city."

"Ees, ees! Bigetoon!" she shrieked. Her body tensed and heaved against the restraints.

George quickly pushed the emergency button and within seconds the door opened and the nurse hurried into the room.

"I was being very quiet, but she was awake and became excited," said George apologetically.

"You must leave now, Sir," demanded the nurse. "Ms. Downing is getting too overwrought and I'll have to give her a higher dose of sedative."

"I will come back later today when she has settled down," said George as he watched Denise's body heaving against the restraints.

The nurse shook her head as she attempted to hold Denise's flailing arm in order to take her pulse. "That will not be possible, Mr. Downing. Denise has to rest."

"But I have plans to leave tonight and I don't know when I'll be back this way," George said, reverting to his wheedling tone.

The nurse shook her head again. "No, Mr. Downing. You shouldn't even be here now. If the doctor found out that I let you in, I would be in trouble. I only allowed you to come in because Denise doesn't have many visitors. As soon as I have her calmed down again, you will have to leave."

George watched the nurse stroke Denise's forehead and speak soothingly to her. Despite these efforts to calm her, Denise continued to shake and heave uncontrollably. After a few more moments, the nurse walked over to a medicine cabinet. She unlocked it with a key on her key ring and retrieved a syringe and a vial of clear fluid.

"Do you need any help?" asked George, watching as the nurse punctured the vial with the needle and began to draw the fluid into the syringe.

"If you could hold her arm out straight, it would make it easier for me to give her the injection," said the nurse. She placed the empty medication vial on top of the cabinet and walked back to Denise's bedside.

As George walked past the cabinet on his way to Denise, he glanced at the empty vial and saw the label. As he went by, he glimpsed *KG9004* printed on the label.

George held Denise's arm out straight as gently as he could, while the nurse injected the fluid. Almost instantaneously Denise's body relaxed and she went to sleep.

"What is the medication you are using?" asked George.

"I'"s a new experimental drug, but I don't know its composition, Mr. Downing. I just administer it according to the doctor's instructions."

"Where does the doctor get it?"

"I don't know that either. As I said, I just administer it according to the doctor's instructions."

"Aren't you curious, Nurse?"

The nurse shook her head and shrugged. "All I know is that it calms Denise and I'm happy for that."

"What is wrong with her?"

"The doctor believes she has Genetic Encephalitis."

"Never heard of that before," said George. "Do you get it from mosquito bites?"

"I don't know, and I really can't answer any more of your questions, Mr. Downing." The nurse looked at her watch. "It's past the time for you to leave."

"Is the medication helping her to get better?" George persisted.

"No more questions, Mr. Downing," said the nurse in an agitated tone as she walked to the door. "You have been here too long as it is, and now you must leave."

As George passed the medicine cabinet on his way to the door, he reached over and grabbed the empty vial and quickly stuffed it in his coat pocket. He glanced at the nurse. She had been opening the door and appeared not to have noticed his thievery.

"Is Denise's illness similar to Cj Disease?" George asked as he stepped through the door.

The nurse hesitated, then quickly closed and locked the door and looked at George suspiciously. "Why would you say that, Mr. Downing? What makes you think it's Cj?"

"The newspapers are reporting there is an outbreak of it, and I wondered if Denise may have it, that's all," he said in what he hoped was an innocent tone of voice.

"I told you no more questions," said the nurse in a stern voice.

"From what I've read about Mad Cow, it appears that Denise has the symptoms, and I am really worried about her because there is no cure for it," said George in as concerned a voice as he could muster.

The nurse looked at him and her face softened. She looked up and down the corridor and seeing no one, turned back to George. "I'm not supposed to discuss the details of the doctor's diagnoses," she said in a very low voice, "but I will tell you in confidence that whatever Denise has, it has attacked her brain cells in a similar way to Creutzfelt-Jacob. The doctor says Denise's disease may have come from a gene passed on from one of her parents."

"Which parent?" asked George in a low tone. He and the nurse were standing so close together that their foreheads were nearly touching.

"It didn't come from Denise's mother," whispered the nurse, glancing over her shoulder again. "We have checked her mother's medical records, you see, but unfortunately there is no information about who her father is. It was one of those instances in which the mother refused to disclose the name of the father when Denise was born."

"Why not ask her mother who the father is? Surely, she would be willing to tell now if she knows that it could help save Denise's life."

The nurse shook her head sadly. "It's not possible, I'm afraid. You see, Denise's mother was killed in a car accident in Barbados about three years ago."

"I see," said George. "That's too bad."

The nurse suddenly looked at him suspiciously. "Well, you being an uncle, you should have known that."

George caught his breath and hoped she hadn't noticed. "Oh, my mother was Denise's mother's mother by a second marriage and I've lived in South Africa for the last thirty years," he said waving his hand. "I didn't communicate with my stepsister for many years because my mother thought that she had brought disgrace to the family."

"That's a shame," said the nurse indignantly. "In this day and age it shouldn't matter. A child is still a child, regardless of its parentage. I thought that attitude against unmarried mothers had disappeared twenty-five years ago."

"Does Denise ever have any visitors?" asked George, quickly changing the subject. "If there are any family members, I would certainly like to make contact and unite the family again. The animosity has gone on too long."

"Yes," said the nurse. "Her uncle visits sometimes. He has trouble getting here, what with his handicap and being in a wheelchair and all." She looked at George suspiciously again. "You must know him."

"Oh, that's right," said George quickly. "I haven't seen him for years, but I know he lives in West Hamstead. It's a pity he has rheumatoid arthritis."

"That doesn't make sense. If you haven't seen him for years, how would you know that?"

"He is her uncle and his mother writes to my mother," George blurted.

"What a mixed up family, Mr. Downing."

"Does he have the same disease as Denise?" asked George quickly.

"No. We tested him," said the nurse. She looked around the corridor again and then said to George in a low voice, "I've said enough already. You must not repeat what I have told you. A patient's medical information is supposed to be strictly confidential."

"I understand. I won't say anything," said George in a conspiratorial tone.

The nurse looked at him suspiciously. "Say, as a relative of Denise's, why aren't you talking to her doctor anyway instead of asking me all these questions?"

"You must understand, Nurse. I'm very concerned about Denise and I want to be sure she is getting the best medical care. I don't have time to talk with her doctor because I have to leave tonight."

The nurse continued to appraise George suspiciously. "You don't have the dark skin and features of someone from Barbados. I think you are an impostor and are not related to Denise at all."

"It's like this, Nurse ..."

Before he could say anything further, the nurse blew a whistle that was on a chain around her neck. "That's enough Mr. Downing, or whoever you are. You will leave this hospital immediately and don't come back. I'm going to report this to the authorities and if you try to come back again you will be arrested."

With that, two burly men in orderlies" uniforms burst out of a door at the end of the corridor and ran up to them.

"I can explain, Nurse ..."

"Escort this man off the premises!" shouted the nurse.

The orderlies grabbed George's arms and rushed him out of the building, down the driveway, and out of the wrought iron gates.

As the gates clanged shut, George found himself sitting in a mud puddle, weakly shouting, "I can explain ... !"

*   *   *

Chapter 9

T HE FOUR O"CLOCK train from London pulled into Wadhurst Station. Six passengers alighted from the train carriages and George was one of them. The blue haze and the odor of burning animal carcasses still filled the air.

As George walked hurriedly from the platform to the station entrance, it began to rain. He stood under a canopy looking for Peggy's car. After a few minutes he spotted her pulling into the station.

"Jump in George before you get wet," called Peggy through an open car window as she pulled up next to him. "I'm in a hurry."

George opened the car door and quickly jumped in. Peggy put her foot on the accelerator and the wheels spun and squealed on the wet road as the car gathered speed.

"Well, George. What did you find out?" asked Peggy gripping the steering wheel and concentrating on the road. "I've made some progress myself."

"I got in to see Denise Downing," replied George. "It's all very peculiar. She is in hospital all right, but she seems to be the only patient. Didn't see or hear any others. It's not like a regular hospital - more like a hotel, but with bars on the windows and many locks on the doors. I don't know if it is to keep Denise in or to keep other people out."

"What condition was Denise in? Did you talk to her?" asked Peggy still tightly gripping the steering wheel with both hands.

"That was weird too. She was heavily sedated and was strapped to a bed. I couldn't really have a conversation with her. All she said was 'eees, eees, Brigeton,' when I mentioned Bridgetown, Barbados."

"Did you ask any questions about her illness?"

"I spoke to the nurse about that, and she said Denise had a hereditary disease which must have been passed down by her father. I also asked the nurse if Denise had Mad Cow Disease, and she became suspicious. In the end I was thrown out of the hospital right into a mud puddle."

"I wondered how you got mud all over the back of your coat," said Peggy with a laugh. "I thought you had been carousing again. Did you find out about Roger Clemens?"

"A little. I found out he's in a wheelchair."

"And what about Denise's mother and father?"

"Her mother was killed two years ago in a car accident in Barbados, and the father is unknown. Apparently, Denise's mother was not married at the time of Denise's birth, and she refused to name the father."

"The drug, George. Did you find out anything about that?"

"Yes, and I may have a sample, because I managed to nick an empty vial after the nurse gave Denise an injection," George said proudly. He took the vial out of his coat pocket and held it up for Peggy to see.

"Well done, George!" exclaimed Peggy. "That's great news. My analyzer should be able to tell us what's in it."

"What about you, Peg? Any new developments?" asked George.

"Yes, we had a visitor. A friend of your father's stopped by. He said he was in the area and thought he would drop in to see what the conditions were at the farm. He was very concerned about your dad's health and wanted to know if there was anything he could do to help."

"Did he say who he was?"

Peggy grinned. "Yes, he did, but I already knew who he was from the tabloids. It was Julian Fleet. He said he knew your father from when he worked for the Government."

"Julian Fleet?" exclaimed George. "You mean that playboy that's always in the papers? The one all the women are ga-ga over?"

"The very one," said Peggy with a broad smile that sent a jealous twinge through George's gut. "He was very well dressed and polite and looks even better in person than in the papers or on the telly. And I had to meet him dressed in my charming florescent field jacket!"

George frowned. "That's strange, Peg. I don't remember Dad ever mentioning that he knew him. He's really not the type my dad would have as a friend. Did he say anything else?"

"Not really, but he did seem curious about my investigation."

"Did you tell him anything, Peg?" asked George with concern.

"No, George. I couldn't do that because it was none of his business. In fact, I haven't told anybody. I just told Mr. Fleet that government policy forbade me from speaking with anyone outside the Ministry of Health about my findings."

"Great, Peg. Did he say anything else?"

"He was curious and kept probing about the edges, but I didn't tell him anything. He was only there for about half an hour, and then he left."

Peggy gripped the steering wheel harder as she drove through a large puddle that sent a wave of water up both sides of the car.

"Did he say anything about me?" asked George frowning.

"He asked if you were enjoying your retirement. I told him you hadn't had the chance to retire because you were dealing with your dad's heart attack and the Foot and Mouth outbreak, and that you were eager to help me. That's all," said Peggy as she steered the car around a sharp bend in the road. "Are you sure you don't know him, George? He seemed to know all about you."

"No," said George shaking his head. "I've never met him. I only know of him through what I read in the newspapers."

"There is something else, George, now that I come to think about it. He wanted to know if you enjoyed your retirement party, and if you had returned the tuxedo you rented."

"What?" exclaimed George. "How on earth would he know about the retirement party, and especially about the rented tuxedo?"

Peggy shrugged. "Perhaps he knew someone who went to your party."

"I shouldn't think so, Peg. Can't imagine anyone involved with the Foreign Office knowing someone as flamboyant as Julian Fleet."

"Maybe he knows one of the women who work there," she said. "God knows, he doesn't have any problem getting acquainted with women. I couldn't believe it when he showed up at the farmhouse. I almost forgot my 'professional demeanor'." Peggy giggled and pressed down on the accelerator causing the car to jump forward through another puddle.

"Hey!" yelled George, gripping the door handle as the car skewed to one side. "Watch what you're doing! You women are all alike - falling for Fleet's good looks."

"It's more than looks, George," Peggy said with a knowing grin.

George pouted for a moment. "Well, I don't understand why he would be nosing around my dad's farm," he said.

Peggy took her eyes off the road briefly and gave him a little smile. "Oh, don't be suspicious, George. I'm sure there is nothing to be worried about."

Peggy put her foot down on the accelerator and George sat in silence as the car sped along in the pouring rain.

*　　*　　*

The lights in the parking lot at Bridgefield Hospital reflected off the driving rain as nurses hurried along under their brightly-colored umbrellas. An ambulance had just pulled up at the emergency entrance when the black Jaguar pulled in and parked close to the visitors" entrance. Julian Fleet got out of the car and pulled up the lapels of his raincoat as he walked hurriedly into the hospital. He paused at the information desk, took off his driving gloves and smoothed down his jet-black hair. The receptionist looked up at him and smiled invitingly.

"Can I help you, Sir?" she asked in her sexiest voice.

"Is it possible to see Bill Goater, young lady?" inquired Fleet. "I'm a close friend of his - Julian Fleet."

"Oh, yes, Sir. I know who you are," gushed the receptionist, blushing.

"Yes, love. I've come down from London to see Bill, and I know it is past visiting hours, but I'm sure you can let me in to see him for a few minutes?" Fleet dazzled her with one of his smiles.

The receptionist gulped. "Oh dear. I'm really quite sorry, Mr. Fleet, but we cannot allow visitors at this time of night."

"I am a close friend, and I've driven all the way from London.

Surely you can make allowances for that," said Fleet, leaning on the reception desk and looking directly into her eyes.

"I'm truly sorry, Mr. Fleet, but it is hospital policy, and I could lose my job if I let you in to see him," she said, nearly in tears because of her inability to accommodate him.

Fleet leaned back and slapped his hand on the desk. "Well, I must see him. I haven't come all this way to be turned down." He noticed the receptionist was about to burst into tears. He smiled kindly at her. "It's all right, love," he said in a gentler tone. "It's not your fault, and I understand you must abide by the rules. Could you please ask whoever is in charge tonight to step out here? I really must see Mr. Goater tonight."

The receptionist smiled. "Oh, yes, Sir. That would be Mr. Jenkins. I'll page him right away."

She was rewarded with another of Fleet's smiles as she dialed a number and then her voice came over the intercom. "Paging Mr. Jenkins. Mr. Jenkins, please come to reception."

Within seconds, a short pudgy man wearing wire-rimmed glasses came into the room through a swinging door. "What is it, Brenda?" he asked as he glanced at Fleet who was leaning on one elbow on the reception desk.

"This gentleman wants to see Mr. Goater, but it is after visiting hours, and he is not a family member," she said, looking adoringly at Fleet.

Jenkins turned toward Fleet, but before he could say anything, Fleet straightened up and put out his hand. "Pleased to meet you, Mr. Jenkins. My name is Julian Fleet. May I have a word with you in private?"

"No harm in that," replied Jenkins shaking Fleet's hand. "We can talk over here."

Fleet followed Jenkins to a grouping of chairs in a far corner of the reception area and sat down. He and Jenkins spoke for a few moments, and the receptionist strained to hear what they were saying, but they were speaking in such low voices that she couldn't make anything out.

She quickly looked down at her desk as she saw the two men stand and shake hands again. Then they both walked back over to her desk, and Jenkins leaned over it. "It will be all right for Mr. Fleet to see

Mr. Goater, Brenda. Call the ward sister and tell her to give Mr. Fleet her full cooperation."

"Yes, Sir," said Brenda. She picked up the phone as Jenkins walked off with a wave of his hand and a smile at Fleet.

Fleet looked back at Brenda and winked at her as she spoke to the ward sister.

"The sister will meet you at the end of the corridor through those doors," she said with a smile as she put down the phone.

"Thank you so very much, Brenda. You've been quite charming," said Fleet as he walked toward the door, and Brenda's heart raced so fast that she felt quite giddy.

*   *   *

Peggy and George were back at the farmhouse. They had barely taken the time to remove their coats in their haste to analyze the drug sample George had brought from Chesterfield House. Peggy quickly turned on the computer and the analyzer. George handed her the vial, and Peggy carefully ran a cotton swab around the inside of it. Then, she carefully wiped the swab on a small glass slide and inserted it into a slot in the analyzer.

"I just hope there is enough residue to make a sufficient sample for the analyzer," she said as she made some adjustments on the analyzer and then turned her attention to the computer screen.

George was peering anxiously over her shoulder at the screen expecting the usual graph and waveform to appear, but nothing happened. The screen remained blank.

Peggy shook her head. "I'll change filters. Perhaps I'm using the wrong light wavelength," she said as she turned a dial on the front of the analyzer.

"Now there is something," said George as a straight line appeared on the screen.

"I can't make heads or tails out of that, George," said Peggy as she looked closely at the screen. "The sample doesn't seem to reflect or absorb light like normal compounds do. I'll try changing the laser frequency and see if that helps."

George watched her turn a switch on the analyzer and then he looked back at the screen. It was blank.

Peggy increased the laser pulse rate. Nothing happened. She shook her head. "We're not getting a waveform at all," said Peggy. "The analyzer indicates there is enough to sample, but it can't analyze it. I'm at a loss for what to do now."

"What a shame," said George in a disappointed tone. He thought for a moment and snapped his fingers. "I know. Let's take a look at the vial itself. Perhaps there's a clue there."

"Of course, George. Why didn't I think of that?" said Peggy.

George picked up the vial between his thumb and index finger and they both looked at it closely.

"That's odd," said Peggy frowning. "The label just says *KG9004* and nothing else. Not the dosage, or the name of the company that made it, or anything else."

"The nurse said it was an experimental drug," said George.

"Even so, if it were an experimental drug, it should be identified as such on the label," said Peggy shaking her head.

George rolled the vial between his fingers and then turned it upside down. "Aha, there's something here, Peg," he said excitedly. "Do you see the lettering embossed on the glass?"

Peggy took the vial from George and examined the lettering on the bottom of the vial closely. "It's not English, George, and it's not French or German, either," she said slowly.

"Try looking down from the inside, Peg. That may be the way to read it," suggested George.

Peggy turned the vial over and squinted down through the neck at the bottom. "No, I still can't read it," she said.

"Let me try," said George, and Peggy handed him the vial. He looked down through the neck for a moment, and then sat up in surprise. "Bloody hell, It's Russian!" he exclaimed. "I had to read Russian when I worked at the Foreign Office. That's why I know. It's apparently the name of the company that manufactured the vial - it says *Alexia-Moscow*."

"Never heard of that," said Peggy, "but then I'm not familiar with Russian drug companies. How odd, George. Why would an English doctor be treating Denise with a drug manufactured in Russia?"

"And we can't find out what it is made of," said George with a sigh. He and Peggy looked at each other in disappointment, and then George's face lit up. "Maybe there's a way I can find out more about the company. I'll call up one of my old office pals at the Foreign Office and ask him to run the name through the F.O. computers. The Foreign Office keeps lists of most foreign companies."

"That's a great idea, George," said Peggy enthusiastically.

George looked around the table. "Where are those vials my dad brought from Barbados?" he asked uneasily.

"I sent them to my supervisor for further analysis," said Peggy.

George looked at her in surprise.

"It's possible he can get clearance to analyze the father's blood sample and find out who he is, plus I wanted him to take a closer look at this genetically engineered variety of Mad Cow that is showing up in Denise's blood," she explained.

"Will we get them back?" asked George in alarm. "I don't know why my dad hid them up, and I wouldn't want to put him in any kind of jeopardy."

"Not to worry, George. We'll get them back, and besides, my supervisor has high-level security clearance, and I have complete trust in him. While he's doing his analysis, we can concentrate on trying to find out what this *KG9004* is. Just think what a breakthrough it would be if it turns out it's a cure for Mad Cow!"

"Well, all right - just so long as I get those vials back. I'll call my friend at the F.O. first thing in the morning. It shouldn't take long to find out," said George. He stood up and walked over to the kitchen counter. "Now, how about a drink?" he asked as he held up the half-full bottle of Johnny Walker.

"Yes," said Peggy with a grin. "Then we'll have the rest of the roast chicken and a bottle of Merlot and go to bed," she said.

"In that order?" asked George.

Peggy just smiled, walked over and took the drink from him. "We'll see," she said.

*   *   *

At nine o'clock the next morning George used his mobile phone to call his old department at the Foreign Office. After speaking briefly with the receptionist he asked to be put through to Adam Freeman's office. The phone rang several times and then George heard Adam's familiar voice. "Good morning. This is Adam Freeman."

"What are you doing there so early? I thought civil servants worked bankers" hours," said George.

"Hello, George," said Adam with a laugh. "Pleased to hear from you. How is retirement going?"

"What with Dad in the hospital and Foot and Mouth on the farm, I've hardly had an opportunity to enjoy my days of leisure," said George.

"Oh, yes, George, I heard about that. Hope your father is getting over his heart attack?"

"He seems to be responding well to the medication."

"That's good news, George."

"I need a favor, Adam, if you don't mind."

"Of course, George. What is it?"

"I need some information about a Russian company. Could you look it up in the data banks?"

"Now you know it would be against policy for me to look it up for a private citizen," teased Adam. "What is the name of the company?"

"*Alexia* located in Moscow."

"Hold on while I check the data bank." George heard Adam put the phone down. He walked about in the kitchen and looked out the window while he waited. In a few minutes, Adam was back on the line.

"Sorry, George. There's no company by that name. I checked Moscow first and then all of Russia and it's not there. Are you sure you have the right spelling?"

"Pretty much, Adam," said George sounding disappointed. "Is there any other name that comes close?"

Adam put down the phone again.

"*Alexiam, Alexus, Almex* and *Alcomax*," he said when he came back. "Those are the only company names I can find that come close, George."

George frowned. "How about taking a look at *Alexiam*, Adam? Maybe I forgot the *m*."

"That's my George, always forgetting something," said Adam jokingly as he put the phone down again.

He was soon back on the line. "*Alexiam* is located in Moscow. Has three thousand employees and branch offices in Kursk, St. Petersburg, Uralisk and Vladivostok."

"What do they do?" asked George.

"The computer doesn't say. All it says is what I've told you. Why do you want to know, George? Are you looking for a job to supplement your pension?" asked Adam with a chuckle.

George laughed. "No, Adam, as paltry as it is. I'm helping a doctor with some research and she thought *Alexiam* was a drug company."

"A lady doctor, eh? You're certainly not letting the grass grow under your feet are you? This lady doctor wouldn't be treating your father, would she, George?"

"No, she is in a different medical field," said George somewhat impatiently, tiring of Adam's jibes.

Adam's voice grew serious. "Just a minute, George. I just thought of another place to look."

George held the mobile to his ear as he paced around the kitchen. He grew tired and switched it to the other ear. He began to think the connection had been broken and was about to call back, when Adam suddenly picked up the phone.

"Sorry for the delay, George, but it took some doing. Now, you won't believe what I found. I went to the classified data bank, and guess what! *Alexiam* is a top secret Russian military research group that specializes in biochemical weapons. MI6 just recently discovered it."

"What? Biochemical weapons!" George was shocked. "Now that's one for the book."

"It certainly is, George. Even more puzzling is how would your lady doctor know the name of a top secret group?"

"She discovered the name on a glass medicine vial," said George.

"That's a serious matter, George," said Adam with concern in his voice. "How would a Russian medicine vial finish up in the UK?"

"I have no idea, Adam."

"Well, I would keep quiet about it, George, or your doctor friend might come to the attention of MI5, and you know what they are like."

"You mean she might be hustled away in the night and never be heard of again?" said George with a laugh.

"It's no joking matter, George," said Adam, lowering his voice. "And keep me out of it. If MI5 found out I gave you the information, I would be in serious trouble."

"And I could lose my pension," said George. "Don't worry, Adam. I won't say a word."

There was no response. After a moment, George said, "Adam, are you there?"

"Just a minute, George," said Adam. "I have someone here who wants to talk to you. I'll get off now."

"Thanks for the help, Adam," said George.

"Just don't forget what I said," said Adam.

George waited for a second, and then a whispery, sexy voice came over the line that made him beam from ear to ear. "Hello, George. Are you in London? You promised to call me for lunch, you know."

George glanced outside the kitchen window and saw that Peggy was nowhere in sight. "No, I'm not in London today, Sherry," he said, "but I'll be there tomorrow. Would you like to meet me at noon outside the Embankment underground on the Charring Cross side, and we'll have a nice long lunch?"

"Yes, George, that would be fine. It's a date then," said Sherry. "I'll see you tomorrow."

George had just turned off his mobile phone and was still grinning from ear to ear when Peggy walked in.

"You look like the cat that swallowed the canary, George. What's up?"

"Oh, I have some news," he said. "Some very interesting news indeed."

*   *   *

Chapter 10

G EORGE WALKED BRISKLY out of the Kilburn underground station in London. As he turned left, he did not notice the man in the light tan raincoat who began to follow him. George paused briefly when he came to Mill Lane and consulted a map he was carrying. Then he turned onto Mill Lane and walked hurriedly until he reached Sarre Road. Number 16 was an attached house with a small garden in front. An untrimmed boxwood hedge hung over the steps leading to the front door. He climbed the tiled steps and rang the doorbell.

"What is your business here, Sir?" boomed a policeman who suddenly appeared at the foot of the steps.

"Uh, ... I'm looking for Roger Clemens," answered George startled at the sound of the officer's sharp voice.

"Do you some identification, Sir?" The policeman walked up the steps to where George was standing.

George winced and fumbled for his wallet. "I'm afraid all I have with me is my old business card," he said.

The policeman looked at the card and then gave it back to George. "What do you want to see Roger Clemens about Mr. Goater?"

George thought quickly. "I, uh ... I just wanted to see if he wants an electric wheelchair," he said.

"Did you now, Sir? And why would Mr. Clemens be wanting an electric wheelchair?" asked the policeman looking curiously at George.

"So he can get around easier," said George lamely.

"Did you make arrangements to see him this morning, Sir?"

George frowned. "No, Constable. I was in the area and just dropped by hoping to find him at home."

"Well, Mr. Clemens is not available, Mr. Goater," said the constable with a grim expression.

"Not available?" asked George.

"No. Mr. Clemens has been missing for twenty-four hours."

"I didn't know that, Constable," said George in a startled voice. "I hope he is all right."

"Stay where you are, Sir," ordered the policeman. Then he whispered into his lapel microphone.

Almost immediately a police car pulled up and the officer took George by the arm and escorted him to the car. George opened his mouth to protest, but the officer frowned at him and shook his head. George got in the car, and the officer driving it put on the siren and sped to Kilburn Police Station where another officer opened the car door and led George into the station, down a corridor and into an interview room.

A balding man dressed in a well-worn but pressed suit got up from his seat at a metal table that took up most of the room. "Have a seat, Sir," he said, indicating a chair on the other side of the table.

"Why am I here?" demanded George after he sat down. "I've done nothing wrong."

"My name is Chief Inspector Donaldson of Scotland Yard, and you are here to assist us in our inquiries into the disappearance of Mr. Roger Clemens."

"I don't know anything about Mr. Clemens's disappearance," said George in a sincere voice.

"You told the constable you wanted to see Mr. Clemens about a wheelchair?" asked the inspector as he looked down at a notepad on the table in front of him.

"Yes," said George. "I thought he would like to have an electric one to make it easier for him to get around."

The inspector looked at him curiously. "And what is wrong with Mr. Clemens that makes you think he needs a wheelchair?"

"He has rheumatoid arthritis," said George confidently.

"How do you know that?" asked the inspector still looking at George curiously.

George hesitated. "A friend of mine told me," he said as he felt a nervous twitch in his right eyelid.

"And the name of this friend, Mr. Goater?"

George felt droplets of cold sweat forming on his forehead and the twitch in his eye grew more intense. He clammed up.

"Answer the question, please, Mr. Goater," said the inspector staring at him intensely across the table.

George took out a handkerchief and mopped his face.

"Are you nervous, Mr. Goater?"

"No," replied George quickly. "It's just that it's hot in here, and I think I'm coming down with the flu."

"Well, that shouldn't prevent you from answering my question, Mr. Goater. Now, what is the name of your friend?" said the inspector in a harsh voice.

"A doctor told me. He told me that Roger needed an electric wheelchair," George blustered.

The inspector waved his hand impatiently. "Come on, Mr. Goater. You are trying my patience. What is this doctor's name?"

"All I can say is that it was a doctor who told me. If I told you more, I would be violating doctor-patient privilege and that would be against the law," said George somewhat smugly.

The inspector banged his fist on the table making George jump. "Utter rubbish, Mr. Goater!" he shouted. "Stop trying to be clever and give me the name of the person who told you!"

George felt his heart beat increase, and his shirt collar suddenly felt very tight. All he could do was sit there. He could not look the inspector in the eye.

"Very well, then, Mr. Goater. I have no alternative but to hold you for further questioning," said the inspector, his patience having run out. "The disappearance of Mr. Roger Clemens is a very serious matter and your cooperation is needed. Perhaps some time in a cell will help you come up with some answers."

"I need a solicitor," said George feebly, as the inspector walked to the door. "You can't question me without my solicitor being present."

The inspector turned back and glared at him. "I see how it is, Mr. Goater. You know more about this case than what you are letting on, and you are keeping important information from the police. Now that is a serious matter - impeding an investigation of a possible crime!" shouted the inspector, narrowing his eyes.

"I'm entitled to legal counsel. You have no right to treat me this way," said George meekly, the twitch in his eye turning into a pounding throb.

The chief inspector appeared not to have heard him. He opened the door and called out a name. He held the door open until a tall, skinny redheaded man entered the room.

"Detective Nickerson, we are holding Mr. George Goater here in our inquiries into the disappearance of Mr. Roger Clemens."

George"s eyes grew large. "You can't do that. I've done nothing wrong," he said feeling a twitch start up in his other eye.

"Don't tell me what I can and cannot do, Mr. Goater!" exploded the inspector. He turned to Nickerson and jerked his head in George's direction. "Detective Nickerson, take Mr. Goater away." He stormed out of the room.

"Come this way, Mr. Goater," said Nickerson as he reached out to take George's arm.

George stood up and the detective led him down a flight of steps and into a small holding cell. Nickerson left and a constable locked the cell door and stood at attention with his back towards George.

George sat down on a metal chair and held his head in his hands. "This is not cricket," he muttered. Half an hour went by and then he heard footsteps coming down the stairs. It was Detective Nickerson.

"We can let Mr. Goater go," he said to the constable. "There is no need to keep him any longer."

George rubbed his eyes in disbelief as he stood up and waited for the constable to open the cell door.

"Sorry for any inconvenience, Sir," said Nickerson in an apologetic voice. "It was an error on our part."

"I can't understand it," said George indignantly. "You put me through a grilling and then just let me go?"

"Just routine, Sir."

"Have you found Roger Clemens?" asked George as he brushed lint off his coat with his hand.

"We are still continuing our inquiries," said Nickerson noncommittally as he followed George up the stairs.

*   *   *

George left the police station in a daze. As he walked slowly back toward Kilburn underground station, he noticed a well-preserved suit of armor in an antique shop window and stopped to look at it.

"Nice suit of armor, isn't it?" said a man in a tan raincoat who walked up and looked into the window as well. "I'll bet they want an arm and a leg for it."

"Yes, I expect so," said George absent-mindedly. "It looks like it was made in the fifteen hundreds."

"Between fifteen-twenty and fifteen-fifty, I'd say," said the man who stood gazing into the window with his arms behind his back.

"Are you a collector of armor?" asked George, looking at the man curiously.

The man shook his head. "No, just interested, that's all, but when I was a kid I use to collect swords."

"They would be worth a pretty penny today," remarked George.

"I lost them playing marbles," said the man. "Utterly stupid. Wagering old Norman swords in a game of knocking little glass balls around."

"I did a stupid thing, too," said George, smiling at the memory. "When I was fifteen, I traded my collection of Roman coins for a kiss from Daphne Blodget."

"Well, at least you got something in exchange," said the man, and he and George shared a good laugh. Then the man put out his hand. "Peter Jones," he said, introducing himself.

"George Goater," said George shaking his hand. Then he turned to walk away. "Where are you headed?" asked Jones.

"Kilburn underground," said George, pausing.

"Me too," said Jones. "I'll walk along with you."

"Pleased to have you," said George with a smile as the two of them walked on together.

"It"s been terrible weather. Haven't seen so much rain in years," remarked Jones as he kept pace with George.

"Yes, it has been unusually wet."

"I hope you don't mind me asking, but didn't I see you in a police car earlier?" asked Jones casually.

George stopped walking and looked at him in surprise. "Yes, that's right," he said suspiciously. "I was assisting the police in some inquiries."

"Something to do with the disappearance of Roger Clemens?" asked Jones in a pleasant tone as he stood looking at George.

George frowned at him and narrowed his eyes. "How would you know that?" he asked cautiously.

Jones shrugged his shoulders nonchalantly. "It was in this morning's newspaper. Said the police are conducting an investigation into the disappearance of a Mr. Roger Clemens and that they are seeking the public's help."

"I haven't seen the papers today. I didn't know he was missing," said George.

"It was on the telly, too."

"I didn't watch that either. Had better things to do this morning."

"Were you able to give the police any leads?"

"No, I couldn't help them," said George abruptly. He began walking again at a faster pace.

"I say, slow down there, George," said Jones with a grin as he tried to keep pace. "We're not in a marathon, you know."

George ignored him and walked even faster. Jones reached out and grabbed his arm. "It's quite all right, George," he said. "I'm a private investigator."

George stopped abruptly and looked at Jones again. "What a coincidence," he said. "Are you looking for Roger Clemens as well?"

"Not particularly. I'm just curious as to how somebody in a wheelchair could suddenly disappear without anyone noticing anything."

"That crossed my mind, too," said George as he began walking again, this time at a more leisurely pace.

"Do you have time for a cup of tea?" asked Jones, pointing at a small teashop up ahead of them.

George looked at his watch. "Yes, but I mustn't be long. I have to meet someone across town at noon."

"Right," said Jones. He opened the door of the teashop and allowed George to walk in ahead of him.

They found a table with a view of the street and sat down.

"Two teas please," called out Jones to a waitress who was standing nearby.

She smiled broadly and went behind the counter. She soon emerged with two full cups of tea and brought them to their table. "Anything else?" she asked as she put the cups down in front of them.

Both Jones and George shook their heads, and the waitress went back to her position in front of the counter awaiting the next customer.

George lifted the teacup in both hands and looked questioningly at Jones. "You said you were an investigator?"

Jones smiled and nodded his head. "How important is it for you to find Roger Clemens?"

George started and spilled a bit of his tea. "Not very," he replied warily. "All I wanted to do was to give him an electric wheelchair."

"That doesn't sound like a plausible reason for wanting to see him," said Jones with a smile as he casually sipped his tea.

"Why not? I just wanted to help him and thought an electric wheelchair would help him get around easier," said George defensively.

"The reason it doesn't sound plausible, George, is because Roger Clemens already has an electric wheelchair," said Jones as he put his cup down.

George sank back in his chair and stared at Jones in disbelief.

Jones smiled at him. "Surely, you didn't tell the police that story, George?"

George shook his head in dismay. "I'm afraid I did."

Jones picked up the sugar dispenser and watched as the sugar poured into his cup. Then he put the dispenser down and stirred his tea with a plastic spoon.

"I feel like a fool," said George quietly.

"No need to feel that way," said Jones in a calm voice. "How would you know that he had an electric wheelchair anyway?"

George's face brightened a bit. "You're right. I didn't know. How would I?"

"That settles it, George. No need to worry. If the police had doubts about it you would be still at the station. Do you want me to find out what happened to Roger so you can give him another electric wheelchair?"

"No need for that, Mr. Jones. The police are looking for him anyway."

"I just thought you might be interested. That's all," said Jones with a knowing look.

George looked at him cautiously. "Well, as it happens, I am very concerned about Mr. Clemens, but I'm sure you would be expensive to hire."

"Two hundred pounds a day plus expenses," said Jones nodding his head.

"I can't afford that," said George. "I'm trying to live on a civil servant's pension, and my ex-wife takes half of that."

"Well, I can certainly sympathize," said Jones. "I worked for a private security firm that decided I was 'redundant' three years ago. The redundancy payoff was enough for me to live on for six months, but my wife ran through that before I knew it. I started my own investigation business to make ends meet. The business has grown and I am doing all right now, I'm happy to say."

"Congratulations on your success, Mr. Jones. You are still too costly for me, however," said George shaking his head.

Jones looked at George and held up his hand. "I'll tell you what I will do, George. I won't charge you a fee. If I do find Roger Clemens before the police do, I would benefit from the publicity. It would be very good for my business, you see."

"I see," said George with a grin. "You're envisioning headlines that would read something like *Police Stumped; Private Investigator Finds Missing Man in Wheelchair.*"

"Something like that would suit me fine," said Jones. "All those wealthy people who want certain matters to be handled discreetly would flock to my door." He chuckled. Then his face grew serious as he looked at George over his teacup. "There was more to you wanting to see Roger Clemens than the wheelchair, wasn't there, George?"

George fidgeted and fumbled nervously with the teaspoon, which flew out of his hand and landed on the floor under the table. "Well, you see," he said slowly, "Roger has a niece who is seriously ill, and I wanted him to know about it."

"What is her name?" asked Jones, as he withdrew a small notebook and a pencil from a pocket in his raincoat.

"Denise Downing," said George hesitantly.

"Where is she?" asked Jones as he wrote down the name.

"Chesterfield Hospital in East Croydon," said George relaxing a bit.

"That's a good start for me, George. Is there anything else?"

George shook his head. "Nothing else." He looked at his watch. "I must get going or I will be late for my appointment."

"Right," said Jones with a smile as he put his notebook away. "Better take one of these," he said as he pulled a business card out of another pocket and handed it to George.

George took out his wallet and placed Jones's card in it. Then he pulled out one of his own cards and a pen from his shirt pocket. He crossed out the Foreign Office information and wrote down his mobile phone number. "You can call me anytime," he said as he handed it to Jones. He stood up to leave. "I really must get going, or I will miss the train."

Jones nodded. "It was a pleasure meeting you, George. I'll take care of the bill," he added, holding up his hand as he saw George fumbling in his pocket for change.

"Thanks for the tea then," said George with a smile, and he walked hurriedly out of the teashop.

Jones put his hand into his trousers pocket and pulled out five pounds as he watched George walk out the door. He placed the five pounds on the table and walked out of the teashop. He then followed George at a discreet distance until he saw him walk into the underground station and head toward the Jubilee Line. When George had disappeared from view, Jones went to a pay phone on the corner and dialed a number.

*   *   *

George walked up the moving stairs from the platform and emerged at the entrance of the Embankment underground station fifteen minutes before noon. There were hordes of people milling about and it had started to drizzle, so he walked up the road a bit towards Charring Cross Station and found a shop awning to stand under while he waited for Sherry Davenport to appear.

"Hi ya' George," said a male voice with an American accent.

George spun around and saw Sylvester Monroe and Chester Abrams standing quite close to him, one on either side.

"What are you doing here?" gasped George.

"We told you we'd be in touch," said Monroe, inching closer to George so that he was nearly in his face.

"That's right," said Abrams, also moving in closer. "You've surely had time to think about our little proposition by now?"

"I thought you had forgotten about me - maybe found someone else to do your dirty work," said George, swallowing hard. He tried to back away, but he was up against the shop window.

"Oh, no George, how could we forget our video star and that great performance at the Savoy?" said Monroe with an evil grin.

George reddened and looked to see if anyone was standing near enough to hear. "Please don't let Sherry Davenport show up right now," he prayed silently. "No need to talk about that in public," he said aloud. "You know it is embarrassing me."

"Oh, Gee! We wouldn't want to embarrass you, George," said Monroe with a sly wink at Abrams. "It was just a reminder in case you forgot," he added.

"What do you want?" said George angrily. "If it's blackmail, you can forget about it. I will not do any of your dirty work, do you hear?"

"We haven't asked you to do anything yet," said Abrams, moving even closer to George. "How do you know it's dirty work?"

"The last time I saw you, you wanted me to find something, but you didn't know what it was. Do you know now?" asked George.

Abrams and Monroe huddled even closer to George with their hands in their coat pockets. They looked up and down the road.

"Yes, George, we know what we want, and you're going to get it for us," Abrams said softly.

"And if you don't, we still have your gala performance to show around on the Internet, and the Foreign Office will have no option but to withdraw your pension in order to avoid a scandal," Monroe reminded him.

"You know I can't afford to lose my pension," said George miserably. "Oh, why me? Why can't you pick on someone else?"

"You're acting as if we want you to do something wrong, Georgy Porgy," said Abrams. "Now, surely you don't think we'd want you to commit a crime or anything like that? What we want you to do is for the good of your country, after all."

"You haven't said what it is."

"A copy of a document, that's all, George. Just a copy," said Monroe.

"Document. What document?"

"A copy of the agreement between Great Britain and Russia, that's all, George. Just a copy."

"You're out of your mind," said George with a snort. "There isn't any agreement. It's just an unsubstantiated rumor."

"*The London Times* would not print an unsubstantiated rumor, would they, George?" asked Abrams glancing at Monroe.

"Well, they have!" said George heatedly, not realizing his voice was becoming louder. "It was probably all a pack of lies just to increase their circulation. It's all balderdash, or bullshit, as you Americans would call it!"

"How do you know it was, George? How do you know there isn't a treaty between Russia and the UK?" asked Abrams in a whisper. He had taken hold of George's right coat lapel and pulled him up on his tiptoes right into his face. "We must be absolutely sure about this."

"You know where I worked. You know I was in the European Section. I am telling you with absolute certainty that there is no treaty. If there were, I would certainly have heard about it. It would be impossible to keep that quiet in the Foreign Office!" said George, his voice rising in desperation.

Monroe stepped in and grabbed George's other lapel. "Are you absolutely sure that there's nothing to it, George?" he asked, yanking George up even higher on his tiptoes. "We would not take it kindly if you are lying to us, you know."

"How many times do I have to say it? Yes, I am absolutely sure! Yes! Yes! Yes! Yes!" he shouted, not realizing his voice had reached such a level that it carried up and down the street.

"Here, here now! What are you two doing to that poor man?" exclaimed a gray-haired little old lady who had sought shelter from the rain under the same awning. She whacked Monroe on the arm with her walking stick. "You're not trying to proposition him, are you? That's utterly disgusting!"

Monroe and Abrams let go of George's lapels, and the three men stepped back from each other.

"We were just having a private conversation, Ma'am," said Abrams in an innocent tone.

"That's right," said Monroe. "It wasn't what you think."

"Aha! Americans! I should have known. You Americans think you can go to other countries and get away with all kinds of obscenities!" She whacked Monroe on the arm with her walking stick again. "There are gay clubs for that sort of thing, which is disgusting enough, but to put on a display in a public thoroughfare is utterly despicable! I've a good mind to call the police!"

She raised her walking stick again, and both Monroe and Abrams put up an arm to shield themselves.

"Really, Ma'am, you have it wrong. We're not gay at all. We like women," said Abrams.

"What did you say?" yelled the old woman, becoming even more inflamed. "So that's what you're up to! The three of you with a woman, indeed! That's even more disgusting!" She jabbed at both Monroe and Abrams with her walking stick as they dodged and parried.

By now a crowd had formed, and the old lady sensed she had an audience. She lunged at Monroe and Abrams with her walking stick as if she was in a fencing match. "How dare you come to this country and perform your lewd, perverted acts in public! Get back to where you came from!" she yelled.

"Here! Here!" called out several members of the crowd.

Abrams and Monroe stood there dumbstruck. Their training had not included dealing with a furious little old lady wielding a walking stick, especially one that had a crowd backing her.

During all this confusion, George had turned toward the shop window as if he had been standing there looking in. Then he quietly sidled away until he was a short distance down the road. He looked back at the scene, and saw that the lady had raised her walking stick in the air and was waving it around.

"You're worse than farm animals, and you should be whipped in public!" she roared.

"That's right! You tell them, Lady!" yelled a male voice from the crowd.

"Take that!" shouted the lady as she whacked Monroe on the arm again.

"That's it! Give it to them, the dirty bastards!" yelled another male voice from the crowd.

A cheer went up and the sound of sirens didn't phase the crowd. Monroe and Abrams froze where they were standing.

George walked a little further up the street. He turned to look, and the last thing he saw was the riot police forcing the crowd to disperse. The lady was talking to a constable waving her stick in the air as Monroe and Abrams were bundled into a police car.

George couldn't help but grin at the scene. He was standing there chuckling to himself when Sherry Davenport walked up.

"Hello, George. I'm sorry I'm late," she said kissing him on the cheek.

George smiled at her. "No problem, Sherry. I've been watching some sort of commotion down the street."

Sherry looked down the road at the dispersing crowd and the police car driving away. "What was that all about?" she asked.

"Apparently, two American tough guys were making sexual advances to an Englishman and an old lady came to the rescue."

"How disgusting, George. What is this world coming to?" said Sherry shaking her head.

"My, you look smashing," said George noticing Sherry's silk plum-colored suit. He was pleased that she had dressed up for their date rather than wearing her usual drab office attire. "Where would you like to have lunch?" he asked.

Sherry gave him a sparkling smile that set his heart racing. "Let's go to the Savoy, shall we, George?"

George hesitated, turning slightly red as he remembered the last time he had been at the Savoy.

Sherry must have read his mind, because she smiled and tucked her arm under his. "Come on, George. There is nothing to be embarrassed about. People get tipsy at their retirement parties all the time."

George relaxed and smiled at her. "Well, all right, then," he said, patting her hand, as they began walking towards Charring Cross Road. George did not notice Peter Jones trailing along a half block behind them.

When they reached the Savoy, they saw the luncheon crowd mingling at the entryway. Uniformed doormen were busy greeting well-dressed ladies and gentlemen arriving in expensive automobiles or in taxis.

George shook his head as he surveyed this scene. "I'm sure we would need reservations for this, Sherry. Perhaps we should go somewhere else."

Sherry smiled and tugged on his arm. "Don't worry, George. I took care of that," she said. "We have one of the best tables in the restaurant - it was going to be a surprise."

George looked startled and then he gave her a flirtatious smile. "That was thoughtful of you, Sherry. I hope you are not planning to take advantage of me."

Sherry laughed. "It's hardly a candlelight dinner, George, but if lunch works out, perhaps there will be candlelight dinners."

"Mmmmm, I think I would like that," murmured George as he squeezed her hand. As they walked up to the hotel entryway, a doorman tipped his hat and held the door open for them. George nodded and smiled at the doorman as they walked through into the lobby of the Savoy.

"I feel out of place, Sherry," said George self-consciously as he observed the crowd around them. "If you had told me, I would have worn better clothes and brought along a pair of dress shoes," he said, looking down at his disinfectant-stained shoes.

"Not to worry, George. Clothes do not make the man, at least in my opinion," she said with a smile. She tugged on his arm, and they walked through the huge lobby to the restaurant located at the back of the hotel.

A tall prominent-looking man with a David Niven mustache and dressed in a black pinstriped suit walked past them, and then turned around abruptly. "I say, George. Fancy seeing you here," he said.

"It's Sir Alfred Rid, the Foreign Minister," whispered George to Sherry as he turned to acknowledge him.

"How are you my dear fellow?" asked Sir Alfred as he extended his hand to George and glanced at Sherry.

"Sir Alfred," said George as he shook his hand. He noticed Sir Alfred's eyes straying past him toward Sherry. "May I introduce Ms. Sherry Davenport?" he said.

"You certainly may, old chap!" replied Sir Alfred as he took Sherry's hand and bent over it. "Sir Alfred Rid at your service," he said.

"It's a pleasure to meet you, Sir Alfred," said Sherry politely.

"I like your hair, Ms. Davenport. It suits you well," said Sir Alfred, standing back slightly and admiring her.

"I noticed that too," interjected George.

Sir Alfred turned his attention back to George. "How is your father, George? Going to be all right, I hope?"

"I can't be sure yet, but he is in stable condition."

"That's good to hear. Well, I must be on my way. A pleasure meeting you ..." He paused and looked at Sherry again. "I say, do you work for the Foreign Office, Ms. Davenport?"

Sherry glanced at George. "Yes, Sir Alfred. I worked with George in the European Section."

"Well now, perhaps I will be seeing you again. In fact, I will make a point of it," he said, smiling directly at her. "Must be off now," he added, looking at George. "I do hope William gets better soon. Give him my regards."

"Dirty old man," said George under his breath as they watched Sir Alfred walk away.

"I thought he was rather charming, George," said Sherry in a teasing tone.

George looked at her and saw that she was grinning at him. He laughed, and they turned and walked on to the restaurant. The maitre d" showed them to a quiet table with a view of the terrace at the back of the restaurant. After they were seated, an immaculately dressed waiter handed each of them a luncheon menu and a wine list.

"Do you fancy wine or champagne?" asked Sherry as she opened the wine list.

"The last time I had champagne here I finished up in ..." George stopped, embarrassed.

"Finished up where, George?" asked Sherry innocently.

"In bed early," said George and quickly looked down at his luncheon menu.

The wine steward walked over to their table and stood stiffly at attention. "Have you decided on a wine, Madame?" he asked, noticing that Sherry had the wine list.

"Yes," said Sherry grinning at George across the table. "We'll have a bottle of the Dom Perignon champagne."

The wine steward bowed, took the wine list and went off to get their champagne.

"What's new on the grapevine at the office, Sherry?" asked George.

"Oh, there's a big flap on, George. *The Times* article about that so-called treaty has everyone in a tizzy. Everyone's been interviewed by MI5. They want to find out if anyone in the department had anything to do with it."

"Did you?" asked George with a grin.

"Did you, George?" countered Sherry with a smile.

"No, I knew nothing about it. I swear. I just read the article like everyone else," said George in a guilty voice.

"Just kidding, George," said Sherry waving her hand at him. "I didn't mean to imply that you did."

The wine steward returned with a large silver bucket and a stand. He placed the bucket on the stand beside the table, and placed a champagne glass in front of each of them. Then he pulled the bottle of champagne from the ice in the bucket and held it up for Sherry's inspection. She looked at the label and nodded at him. He opened the bottle with a loud pop of the cork, and poured a bit of champagne into Sherry's glass. Again he stood back waiting. Sherry picked up the glass, looked at the frothy bubbles, and then took a sip. She rolled her eyes in appreciation. "It"s lovely," she said with a smile and a nod at the wine steward who then filled both their glasses, put the bottle back in the ice bucket and went away.

After they had toasted and taken sips of the champagne, George returned to the conversation they had been having. "It doesn"t make sense, Sherry," he said shaking his head. "*The Times* is well respected for printing only accurate information, and yet the Prime Minister denies there is a treaty, and the department hasn't a clue."

"It could be that the opposition party is behind it," speculated Sherry. "They are always looking for ways to discredit the Prime Minister."

"If so, they've achieved their purpose. The Government has lost its majority and now there will be a general election."

"Only when the Prime Minister says so, George. It appears he is stalling off an election until the Foot and Mouth is under control, and that could take months."

"Well, that makes sense to me, Sherry. I wouldn't like to see the disease spread, and, unfortunately, I'm in a position to know all about that because of my dad's herd having to be destroyed," said George with a frown. He took another sip of champagne.

"I know, George. It is terrible," commiserated Sherry. "I also read about Lord Bonderbrook's horses. It is such a pity."

George was surprised to see tears glistening in Sherry's eyes. "I wonder if he knows yet. His stable lad said he was out of the country and couldn't be reached. Tied up in some EU business," he said.

Sherry took another sip of champagne, put the glass down and looked out of the window at the terrace for a moment. Then she looked back at George, and he saw that she still had tears in her eyes. "I shouldn't be telling you this, George," she said in a low voice. "Lord Bonderbrook was flown back from Brussels late last night and is now in hospital."

Sherry looked out the window again. "Officially he had a heart attack, but rumor has it he has had a nervous breakdown."

"It probably happened when he found out about his horses having to be destroyed," said George not quite understanding why Sherry appeared to be so upset about Lord Bonderbrook. "My father had a heart attack, too, and they think it was brought on by the shock of learning about his herd of prized Black Angus."

"Have you seen your dad?" asked Sherry, looking at him again.

"Yes," said George. He looked at her curiously.

"Lord Bonderbrook cannot have any visitors," she said.

"That's understandable, Sherry. If he is in intensive care, they are probably not allowing visitors other than immediate family. After he is better in a day or so, I'm sure visitors will be allowed."

Sherry shook her head sadly. "That's not it, George. The hospital they took him to is at Stonehurst, a secure Air Force Base that is being patrolled by armed guards. Only people who have high level clearance are allowed in."

George picked up his champagne glass and looked at her with concern. "I don't understand why you are concerned about it, Sherry. After all, Lord Bonderbrook is a high level diplomat and he will get the best possible treatment."

"There is something else, George," said Sherry, now dabbing at her eyes with the linen napkin.

"What is it, Sherry?" George asked in alarm as he took a sip of champagne.

"Lord Bonderbrook is my uncle."

"Your uncle!" exclaimed George, choking on the champagne. "I never knew that, Sherry."

"Not many people do," said Sherry with a slight smile. "I didn't want my connection to influence anyone, especially at work. I didn't want people thinking I was getting special treatment, you see. I even changed my name. My real name is Bonderbrook, not Davenport."

George's eyes widened. "That is a surprise, Sherry. I would never have guessed," he said looking at her in awe. She smiled at him, and he relaxed and smiled back. "But surely the authorities are keeping Lord Bonderbrook's family informed of his condition?" he asked.

Sherry glanced at her empty champagne glass and then leaned across the table and said in a low voice, "Not a word, George. It seems they are keeping everything hush-hush. They seem to be keeping his illness under wraps for some reason."

"How did you find out about it, Sherry?" asked George, leaning forward and speaking in a low voice.

Sherry looked around the restaurant as if to see if anyone would hear her. Then she looked back at George. "I overheard a telephone conversation between ..." she looked around the restaurant again and leaned further over the table. "Between Coby, the head of EU liaison, and someone else. I heard Coby mention my uncle's name, so I stood outside his office and eavesdropped."

"You said no visitors are allowed to see the Lord?"

"That's right, George. According to what I overheard, Coby was being told not to tell anyone where my uncle was because visitors were prohibited."

"Who was he talking to?"

"I don't know," said Sherry with a frown. "Coby didn't call him by name, but he did call him 'Sir'."

"Must be his boss," surmised George.

"But my uncle is his boss," said Sherry.

"I think you are being overly concerned, Sherry. High officials who become ill are usually brought back to the country without public announcement. In a day or so, there will be a press release," he said comfortingly as he reached across the table and patted her hand.

Sherry smiled at him. "You're probably right. Thanks for making me feel better."

George beckoned to the wine steward who was watching their table from a distance. "Bring us another bottle," said George as the wine steward emptied the first bottle into their glasses.

When he had gone, Sherry said, "Perhaps we'd better order. Have you decided what you want yet?"

"I'm in between the Dover sole and the pheasant under glass," he said, opening his menu again.

"I'm having the Dover sole," said Sherry. "They fix it especially well here."

"Then that's what I'll have, too," said George smiling. He picked up his champagne glass and was about to propose another toast, when his mobile phone began bleeping.

He frowned and plucked it out of his pocket. "Now, who could that be?" he mumbled. "Sorry," he apologized to Sherry. He pressed the „Yes" button to take the call, and Doctor Stevenson's face appeared on the video screen.

"Yes, Doctor Stevenson?" George said anxiously, trying to keep his voice down.

"Mr. Goater, I do not want to unduly alarm you, but there has been an incident in your father's hospital room, and we are required by law to inform you."

"What!" exclaimed George in a louder voice and Sherry looked at him in alarm.

"Yes," said the Doctor. "Someone posing as an orderly was discovered in your father's room tampering with one of the IV drip bottles. When the nurse walked in, the person ran out of the room and escaped from the hospital. We have checked your father's medication and everything is fine. We now have a policeman posted around the clock outside your father's door."

"Does Dad know about it?" asked George.

"No, he is still under heavy sedation, but it might be good if you could stop by the hospital as soon as possible."

"Of course," said George. "I'll be there late this afternoon. I'm in London right now."

George clicked off the connection and put his cell phone back in his pocket. Sherry was looking at him with concern. "What is it, George? Not bad news, I hope," she said.

George shook his head and looked at her with a frown. "An odd thing has happened. Someone dressed as an orderly was caught in Dad's room trying to tamper with his medication."

"Oh, how horrid," said Sherry. "Why on earth would someone want to do that?"

"I don't know, but I intend to find out," said George slowly. He picked up his champagne glass and drained it. Then he reached for the bottle and refilled both their glasses.

*   *   *

Chapter 11

I T WAS DARK outside when George came out of the hospital and looked around. He stood at the curb for only a short time before Peggy drove up. She had been waiting in the car park for him to appear. George had called her from the train station in London.

"How is your father?" she asked the second he opened the door to climb in.

"Dad was not harmed by the intruder, thank God," said George as he buckled his seat belt. "The nurse walked into the room at just the right time to scare him off before he could do anything."

"That's good news, George. You say the police are guarding his room now?" asked Peggy as she turned onto the main road.

"That's right. They have an officer stationed outside his door around the clock now."

"Any leads as to who the intruder was? Did the nurse see his face?"

"Afraid not. The nurse couldn't really describe him as he was wearing a surgical mask. She was sure it was a man, though, and said he was tall."

"Well, that's something anyway," said Peggy as they came to the outskirts of Bridgefield.

"The doctor did have some good news," said George, his face brightening. "It seems he has been trying a new vaccine on Dad that seems to be working. He can't talk yet, but he did open his eyes for a bit."

"Did you find out what this new vaccine is? Maybe it's the same thing they are using on Denise Downing," asked Peggy, glancing over at him with an eager expression.

"I asked the doctor, and he said it doesn't really have a name yet. He got it from a research institute in Edinburgh. I even asked him if it was called *KG9004*, but he had never heard of that," said George. "The doctor says he still doesn't know for sure if Dad has Cj."

"Perhaps that's because your father has a genetically engineered variety," speculated Peggy.

George shrugged his shoulders. "As long as the vaccine works, that's all I care about."

Peggy glanced over at George again. "Don't get your hopes up too high, George. Even if the vaccine makes him better, chances are he will never return to normal because Mad Cow destroys part of the brain. He may not be able to remember anything or talk again. The symptoms are similar to having a major stroke."

George nodded and tears sprang to his eyes. "Such a bloody shame. I hope Dad doesn't finish up as a vegetable. I just wish they had had this vaccine at the outset, not only for Dad, but for all the thousands who have it as well."

"I know," said Peggy sadly. "Perhaps the vaccine will at least prevent others from getting it." She slowed down as they drove through Wadhurst. After she had turned onto the road that led to the Goater farm, she said, "By the way, I did an analysis on Cj today, and it isn't as I had originally thought. My assumption was that the people who have the disease are widely dispersed throughout the country, and it turns out that's not the case at all."

"What do you mean, Peg?" asked George with a frown. "I thought Mad Cow showed up in clusters around the country because of the distribution of contaminated meat to local areas."

"That is what happened in the earlier outbreaks, but this one is quite different. I'll show you what I mean when we get back to the farm."

Peggy put her foot down on the accelerator, and they were soon at the farm. Peggy drove up to the gate leading to the kitchen door and turned off the engine. Without speaking, they both climbed out quickly and hurried into the kitchen.

As soon as they had turned the lights on, Peggy immediately went to her computer without stopping to take her coat off. "Here, George. Take a look at this geographical analysis. The black dots indicate where the people with Mad Cow live."

George looked at the sheet of paper Peggy handed him. It was a computer printout of a map that showed all the towns from Nottinghamshire in the north to Leicestershire in the south. George's attention was immediately drawn to Fordham, a town close to Nottingham.

"Do you see what I mean?" asked Peggy watching George's face for a reaction.

George frowned as he examined the map and then looked up at Peggy in surprise. "Yes, the black spots indicating the Mad Cow outbreak form a definite pattern," he said with a puzzled expression. "It's a sort of funnel pattern that begins in Fordham and grows wider as it goes south." He looked down at the map again. "I see there are a few other black marks in other parts of the country, but the large majority of them are concentrated in this funnel." He looked back up at Peggy with question marks in his eyes.

Peggy nodded her head. "That's right, George. It seems this version of Cj originated close to Fordham."

George put the map down on the table and, deep in thought, slowly removed his coat and hung it up on the coat tree.

"There is something else, George. Look at this," said Peggy. She handed him another sheet of paper as she came over to remove her jacket and hang it up.

George looked at the paper and shook his head. "I don't know what it means. It's just sets of numbers to me, Peg."

"It means there is no one under the age of twenty-seven who is infected. Not one single person!" exclaimed Peggy.

George looked at her in surprise. "That's strange. What does age have to do with it?"

"I can't be sure," said Peggy shaking her head, "but now look at this. All the cases of Mad Cow are of the same variety that Denise and your Dad have."

"Do you think the authorities are aware of this funnel pattern?" asked George.

"Oh, I'm sure they must be," said Peggy.

"It is strange   ... seems there's something funny going on," said George.

Both of them were silent for a moment mulling over this latest development. Then Peggy turned off the computer and stood up. "I'll make us some tea and some sandwiches, and while I'm doing that, you can tell me about your trip to London," she said.

George recapped his day, telling her about Roger Clemens's disappearance, his encounter with the police, and Peter Jones the private investigator arriving on the scene. He omitted his encounter with Abrams and Monroe as well as his lunch with Sherry.

As they sat down at the kitchen table to eat, he said, "I'm still bothered by this Jones character offering to find Roger Clemens without charging me anything. I wonder if I made a mistake in agreeing to let him in on the investigation."

Peggy smiled at him across the table. "Oh, I shouldn't worry about it, George. If he does find Roger Clemens, so much the better. Besides, you don't have to tell him everything anyway."

"I suppose you're right ..."

"As to our investigation, I think Denise Downing is the key. We need to find out more about her and why Barbados is in the picture."

George nodded and was about to take a bite of his sandwich when his mobile phone rang. He took it out of his pocket and flipped open the cover. "George Goater," he said.

"George, this is Peter Jones."

"Mr. Jones, I didn't expect to hear from you so soon," said George looking at Peggy and raising his eyebrow. He put the phone in speaker mode so she could hear what he was saying.

"I work fast," said Jones. "Here's what I found out. Roger Clemens's housekeeper reported him missing early yesterday, and his niece Denise Downing has also disappeared. It seems someone who looks a lot like you visited her just before she went missing."

"How could she disappear? She was in a private hospital."

"I don't know all the details yet, but I do know she was taken away in a car bearing diplomatic plates. I'm checking to see what embassy the car is registered to, and I'll let you know when I find out."

"What about Roger?"

"I don't know any more yet, George. I'll let you know when I do."

"Thanks for the information, but tell me again the reason you are so interested in investigating for free," said George for Peggy's benefit.

"I told you I'm doing it for the publicity."

"That's it? Just publicity?"

"Yes, George. Why not? It makes perfect sense to me. It's a good opportunity to get my name out there to potential clients."

"It was just a coincidence that we met?"

"Yes, George. If I hadn't seen you being hauled off by the police at Roger Clemens's house, I wouldn't be talking to you now."

"Well, that makes sense, I suppose," said George.

"Hold on, George. I have another call."

George heard a click as Jones put him on hold and picked up another line.

"What do you think?" said George in a low voice to Peggy.

"I think he's on the up and up," she whispered. "I told you not to worry."

"Are you there, George?" Jones was back on the line.

"I'm here," said George.

"I just got word that the car that took Denise away was registered to the United States Embassy. Why the Americans would be involved beats me."

"That is odd," said George raising an eyebrow in surprise. "Do you know where they took her?"

"No, but I will find out. That may take a bit, so I'll ring off now and talk to you later."

George put the cell phone back into his pocket and looked at Peggy questioningly.

"The plot thickens," she said. "Why in heaven's name would the Americans be involved?"

"I'm sure Jones will find out," said George with a grin. Then he frowned. "This Jones chap seems to come up with information very quickly. I still wonder if there's more to this than what he says."

"Now, now George. You're worrying again. Whatever his motive, he seems to be making good progress, and so far it's all to our benefit. See what he has to say tomorrow."

"Yes, Peg. I suppose you're right," said George slowly. Then he waved his hand and smiled. "Say, Peg, I'm curious. Can you get access to anyone's file in that medical records data base?"

Peggy grinned. "Why, George? Do want to look up old girlfriends to see how that venereal disease got on your record?"

George ignored her teasing. "I'm just wondering about Lord Bonderbrook," he said with a serious face.

Peggy's smile faded and she turned serious also. "I wouldn't be able to get access to Lord Bonderbrook's records, George. His file would be blocked for security reasons just like any other high government official. If I tried to gain access, my supervisor would call me on the carpet. The computer would ID me, and that is a no-no. But why do you ask?"

"I just wondered, Peg. Curiosity, that's all."

Peggy stretched her arms and yawned. "Let's have an early night, George. We both need to relax."

"Well, it's difficult for me to relax with you in my bed," said George.

"I don't know about that," said Peggy. "I think I'm able to make

you relax pretty well."

*   *   *

The next morning George had an inspiration while he was shaving. He quickly dressed and went into the kitchen where Peggy was fixing breakfast.

"We need to go to Barbados, Peg. I feel certain that's where we'll find the answers to Dad's and Denise's illness. Perhaps we can locate Denise's family and find out who her father is, and discover what Dad was doing there."

"Barbados! You must be crazy. We just can't take off like that," exclaimed Peggy.

"Why not, Peg? The samples my dad had all point to Barbados, and so does Denise's heritage. Besides, the weather here is lousy, and we could continue our investigation under the Caribbean sun - combine business with pleasure. What do you say?"

"Well, I don't know ..." said Peggy as she turned the bacon over in the frying pan.

"Well, I am going, with or without you. It would be better to have you along, but if you can't go, you can't go."

Peggy glanced over at the computer and analyzer and then at the clock on the wall. "I have to see if I can get the time off. I'll try George. That's all I can do. I'll call my supervisor and see what he says. He'll be in at nine."

"Good," said George. He sat down at the table and started to take a sip of his tea when his cell phone rang. He pulled it from his pocket and flipped the cover down.

"Good morning, George. This is Peter Jones."

"Hello, Mr. Jones. Any news this morning?"

"Yes. Denise Downing was flown to America on an unscheduled flight. My contacts at Heathrow said people who are not associated with the American Embassy accompanied her."

"Did they know who these people were?"

"Afraid not, but never fear, I'll find out more today," said Jones. "I'll call you later."

He hung up, and George switched off the connection and put his phone back in his pocket.

"That was Peter Jones. Says Denise was flown to America, and he doesn't know who is behind it."

"Flown to America?" repeated Peggy as she brought two plates of eggs and bacon to the table. "Perhaps Denise has relations there?"

George shrugged his shoulders, and they both attacked their eggs and bacon.

When George had finished, he leaned back in his chair to sip his tea. He looked at his watch. "It's nine o'clock, Peg." he said.

*　　*　　*

Chapter 12

I T WAS SLEETING in Washington, D.C. President Forbes and his cabinet had embarked on formulating the new administration's policies. So far, the foreign policy had been entirely centered on the British-Russian military treaty. Despite the President's orders, neither the State Department nor the CIA had been able to obtain the actual text of the agreement. President Forbes stepped into the Oval Office after adjourning the morning's cabinet meeting. General Kingsman was waiting for him.

"What news today, Hank?" asked Forbes as he went over to shake hands with his old friend.

"We are making progress," said Kingsman as he shook Forbes's hand. After he and the President sat down, he said, "We've just brought back the last one we know about from England, and she is now in our special medical facility in Maryland."

"Where in Maryland?" asked Forbes.

"Green Gate, Glenn," said Kingsman in a low voice.

"Why did you choose Green Gate? I thought the CIA abandoned that air base years ago."

"I chose it because it's isolated, but it's also close to D.C. and it still has an operational runway. We didn't want to cause attention when the plane landed."

"How many do you have now, Hank?"

"One from Great Britain and the twins from here that I told you about a couple of days ago. We think that's all there is."

"Is there any treatment?"

Kingsman shook his head sadly. "Not at the moment, but the one from England came with an experimental drug, and we are monitoring the effects of it."

"Did you encounter any problems in recovering the one from England?" asked Forbes.

"Nothing of any significance."

Forbes sat forward in his chair. "What does that mean, Hank? I know you well enough to know that „nothing of any significance" means there was something."

Kingsman grinned. "It's really nothing. It's just that a retired British Foreign Office official has been bouncing around the edges, but he's not a problem. He doesn't know anything, and now that the woman has been moved here, he won't be able to go any further."

"Well, he must know something, or else why would he be snooping around?"

"You know how the Brits are, Mr. President," said Kingsman.

"No. How are they, Hank?"

"They're always suspicious and sticking their noses into everything," said Kingsman with another grin.

"I think you've hit the nail on the head," said Forbes with a small chuckle. "By the looks of things, they are suspicious of us, and that's why they've decided to cuddle up to Russia." The President grew serious as he looked at his old friend. "Any ideas about why the Brits are so suspicious of us?" he asked.

Kingsman shook his head. "Better ask the CIA."

"Give me a break!" said Forbes with a smirk. "Those jokers can't even get their hands on the treaty, let alone figure out why. Not only that, but also two of their operatives were arrested two days ago for harassing an Englishman. Now the Prime Minister is upset with us because the CIA was poking around in the UK." He pointed at Kingsman. "And that's off the record, Hank."

Kingsman grinned. "Of course, Glenn. I didn't hear a thing."

"Good," said Forbes. "Now, back to your mission. Where are you at now?"

"Tracking the cause of exposure."

"Any clues?"

"Not yet," said Kingsman. "It's not easy. No documentation and it's been buried deep."

Forbes nodded. "I know what you mean, Hank. Nobody wanted it to surface - too much at stake. Not only here, but over there too."

"Yes, Glenn, you're right. I understand why, and I'll make sure this is resolved without causing any embarrassment. You can count on me. I've handpicked all my people and I would trust any one of them with my life. There will be no leaks, and that's a fact."

"Sure, Hank. I trust you. Are you going to have any problems with using Green Gate?"

"There shouldn't be. The cover story I'm using, in case the media notices something's going on there, is that it is being prepared for Presidential purposes," said Kingsman.

Forbes smiled. "Care to share with me what 'Presidential purposes,' just in case some reporter asks me a question?"

"How about we're restoring a couple of hangars and the runway so you can escape the rigors of the Presidency to fly your own plane for recreational purposes?" asked Kingsman.

Forbes laughed. "That'll fly," he said.

"So to speak," added Kingsman with a chuckle.

"So, what's your next move?" asked Forbes, turning serious again.

"We're going to do a complete medical workup on each of them to see if there are any similarities," said Kingsman, leaning forward in his chair.

"What about this Brit that's snooping around?"

"We've got him under surveillance to see what he discovers. It's a possibility he might find out more than what we know," said Kingsman.

"Be careful, Hank. There may be more to this guy than you think. A retired government official - especially from the Foreign Office - digging around seems a little too coincidental to me. Maybe he's a plant," said Forbes.

Kingsman burst out laughing. "Oh, God! If you could only see this guy! He's no James Bond, and that's a fact. Anyway, he's not intelligent enough to be working for British intelligence and he drinks too much. Besides, we've checked him out thoroughly and know he was just a low-level bureaucrat working in the European Section of the Foreign Office."

Forbes smiled and stood up. "Ok, Hank, I believe you. I'll let you get on with it." There was a knock on the door. Forbes nodded his head at the door. "The country awaits," he said.

Kingsman picked up his titanium attaché case, saluted the President silently, and left by a side door.

*   *   *

Within an hour, General Howard Kingsman, dressed in civilian clothes, arrived at Green Gate air base. He was flying a Cessna 680 and was the sole occupant of the light plane. As he landed, the Cessna's wheels skidded and bounced on the cracked and pot holed runway. When he taxied up to an abandoned air terminal building, a black Lincoln Continental appeared from a nearby derelict aircraft hangar and pulled up beside the Cessna.

Kingsman cut the engine and quickly got out of the plane and climbed into the rear of the Lincoln. As soon as he closed his door, the car began moving and sped towards a one-story brick building situated in a grove of trees at the end of a badly worn asphalt road.

A security guard wearing a black uniform and a black baseball cap bearing the emblem of a private security company stepped out of the shadow of the building holding a cell phone to his right ear. As the Lincoln approached, he closed the phone and slid it into his breast pocket. The Lincoln stopped in front of the entrance of the red brick building and the guard opened the door and stepped back.

The entrance door to the building swung open and a short balding man wearing spectacles and a white doctor's jacket walked out.

Kingsman got out of the car and walked quickly towards the door. "Good morning, Doctor Hinkle," he said. "The weather is pleasant for this time of year."

"There are some new developments, General," the doctor blurted out. "The results are confusing. Their toxins are the same."

Kingsman glanced over his shoulder at the guard, and grabbed the doctor's arm. He hurriedly led him into the building and then into a small room. He closed the door and turned on the doctor angrily. "Hinkle, how many times do I have to remind you not to say anything in front of people outside this building, and don't ever call me *General* in front of them. This matter must be kept one hundred percent confidential!"

"I'm sorry, General," said the doctor meekly. He took off his glasses and rubbed his eyes. "I wasn't thinking. I had my mind on the results of our tests, and I was eager to tell you."

Hank relaxed and smiled. "Apology accepted. Just don't forget in the future." He pointed to a couple of metal chairs at a small table. "Let's sit down, and you can tell me your news. I'm all ears."

As soon as they sat down, the doctor began speaking excitedly. "As I said, there is only one toxin, General - not two as we had assumed." The doctor put his glasses back on and watched Kingsman for his reaction.

Hank frowned. "Are you sure, Doctor? We've assumed all along that they were different because they come from different places."

"Yes, General, I'm sure. At first I wasn't sure, but we've tested them time and time again and the result is always the same. There is only one toxin." Doctor Hinkle opened a thick file folder that was lying on the table and extracted a folded paper.

"Look at these results from our analytical toxin spectrometer," he continued as he unfolded the long sheet of graph paper and spread it out on the table. "If the toxins were different, the peaks and valleys would not match precisely when we overlay them, but look," he said pointing.

Hank had risen to his feet and leaned on both his hands on the table to see better. He looked where the doctor was pointing. "Yes, I see it," he said slowly. "They are the same."

"The red line belongs to the one from England, and the blue and green lines belong to the twins from our side of the water. As you can see, the blue and green lines match perfectly with the red," said the doctor.

Hank sat back down in his chair and gazed at the plotted lines for a while as Hinkle sat watching him for a reaction.

"This is not good, Doctor," said Hank frowning. "We must be absolutely sure beyond the shadow of a doubt." He pointed a finger at Hinkle. "If there is an error in your test results, there would be the devil to pay - far beyond your wildest imagination."

Hinkle paled. "There is no mistake, General," he said defensively. "All the tests were monitored closely, and I can assure you they were done according to procedure."

Hank shook his head. "That's not it, Doctor. You had only three samples to work with. What we need are more samples. We must have samples from a much larger group than three individuals." He noticed the defensive look on Hinkle's face. "Don't get me wrong – I'm not criticizing your testing with what you had to work with. All I'm saying is that having only three samples limits the diagnosis. Don't you agree?"

The doctor sat looking at Hank for a moment and then retrieved an ink pen from his breast pocket. He turned the graph paper over and started to write. Hank watched curiously as Hinkle scribbled down what appeared to be a formula and then a bunch of numbers. After a few minutes, the doctor murmured a number that Hank couldn't hear and then he double-checked his computation. Once he was satisfied, he looked up at Hank reluctantly. "To have absolute confidence in the result, we would have to test a minimum of sixty-five samples, General."

Hank looked at him in disbelief. "Sixty-five!" he exclaimed. "You'd better give me an idea of where to look for them, then. The three we have now took a lot of finding and then a lot of trouble in getting them here, and we don't have that kind of time, Doctor!"

"I may have an answer," said Hinkle. He opened the file again and pulled out several sheets of paper that had been stapled together. He examined each of the sheets closely and then looked up at Hank with the hint of a smile. "These are the DNAs of our three, and I believe they will provide clues as to where to look for more candidates."

"I'm listening," said Hank impatiently.

"According to her genetic fingerprint, the one from England comes from the Caribbean originally. The reason I say that is because she is one-half West African, one-quarter native Caribbean Indian - both Carib and Arawak - and one-quarter Scot."

"That narrows it down a little, but the Caribbean is still a large area, Doctor," said Hank.

The doctor smiled. "I can narrow it down even further. I'd suggest looking in Barbados."

"Why Barbados?"

Hinkle had anticipated the question and was ready with an answer. "Because Barbados is one of the islands that was settled by Britain, and according to the woman's DNA, the number of generations of her British ancestry dates back to when the British first colonized the island."

"I guess that answers it for the one from England," said Hank, "but what about the twins?"

The doctor flipped the sheet of paper over and looked at the next one. "Well, of course, the DNA tells us they are twins, and they are a quarter Polynesian, a quarter Chinese and half Caucasian. Based on that, I would search in the Hawaiian Islands." He looked at the paper again. "To narrow it down further, I'd say you should start on the Big Island - Hawaii."

"Can you provide me with any other information that would be of help so I can get on with the search as quickly as possible?"

"I have quite a bit on the twins, but hardly any on the one from England," said the doctor as he pulled three folders from the file on the table. "These are up to date, General," he said handing the folders to Hank.

Hank opened his titanium briefcase and put the folders inside. Then, he locked it and stood up. "Now, Doctor, let's go see your subjects."

The doctor nodded and led the way out of the room and along a wide corridor where security guards in black uniforms stood at attention where other corridors crossed their path. Finally, the doctor stopped outside an airlock door and instructed a guard to let them in. The guard swiped a card key through the electronic door lock and the door slid open. After they entered, the door automatically closed.

They were in a small chamber where several suits of white protective clothing hung on hooks along one wall. They pulled the protective suits on over their other clothes, and then donned white surgical masks and caps. When they were ready, Hinkle pushed a button and another door slid open. They entered a second chamber, and the door closed behind them. There was a swishing of filtered air and the humming of vacuum pumps. When the chamber pressurized another door opened automatically, and they entered a medium-sized isolation room.

Hank saw that there was only one subject in a hospital bed in the comfortably furnished room. When he and the doctor walked up to the bed a nurse wearing protective clothing like their own, but blue in color, stood up from where she was sitting on the other side of the bed. Hank looked at the bed and saw a young black woman with her hair braided in cornrows curled up in a fetal position.

"This is the one from England. She is under medication," the doctor said in a low voice. He motioned towards the intravenous tube in the woman's arm, and then at the various monitoring devices placed around the bed.

Hank was about to say something when the young woman opened her huge brown eyes and looked directly at him. Her eyes rolled with fear as she tried to focus on him. Noticing her anxiety the doctor leaned over her and gently stroked her forehead. "It's all right, Denise. You have a visitor."

Denise's eyes continued to roll and her body began to heave with sufficient force to throw off the blanket and sheet that covered her, exposing the padded body restraints.

"Moo maa, moo maa!" she cried in an agonized voice as her body continued to thrash about against the padded straps.

The doctor hastily adjusted the drip flow on the intravenous tube and the nurse pulled up the sheet and blanket. In a few seconds Denise's eyes closed and the moaning and twitching stopped.

"The toxin has attacked her nervous system and she can't control her muscles, which causes spasms and convulsions," said the doctor quietly as he leaned over her. "Can you hear me?" he asked in a soft voice. "Denise, can you hear me?"

The doctor looked at Hank and shook his head. Hank stepped closer to the bed. "My name is Hank," he said softly. "I just came by to say hello."

As Hank and the doctor continued to look down at her, without warning her eyes opened and her eyelashes fluttered as she looked from one to the other. The white protective suits seemed to frighten her, and her body began to twitch again.

"It's all right, Denise," said the doctor soothingly. "We are dressed in special doctor's uniforms, and there is nothing to be frightened of."

Denise's head rolled toward the nurse, and then back again. "On't no yuu. Geet way of meee."

"It's ok, Denise, we are trying to help you," said the doctor again.

"Airre um I?" she asked fearfully rolling her eyes around the room.

"You're in a private nursing facility, Denise. There is no need to be frightened."

Denise's eyes rolled around the room again and then back to them. Fear was written on her face, and her body started to twitch again.

"Denise, I will come and visit you later today," said the doctor softly as he again adjusted a valve on the drip tube. Within seconds Denise's eyes closed and she fell into a deep sleep.

Hank followed the doctor silently back to the door and then through another airlock chamber into another isolation room. This room was furnished much the same as the first, but had two beds instead of one. The beds were placed against walls opposite of each other. As they entered the room, a woman wearing a white protective suit like theirs rose from a desk where a number of papers were strewn.

She walked over to them. "Good morning, Doctor Hinkle," she said in a low throaty voice. She looked up at Hank curiously. He noticed that she had eyes the color of deep green pools with small golden flecks of sunshine playing on them. Thick dark lashes surrounded them. Her eyes made him wonder what the rest of her looked like under that mask and protective gear.

"This is Hank. He is here to visit the patients," said Hinkle. "Hank, this is Doctor Elliot. She is a specialist in toxicology and neuropsychology."

Doctor Elliot's green eyes crinkled at the corners as she smiled up at Hank behind her mask. She extended her hand. "Pleased to meet you, Hank."

Hank shook her hand, which he happened to notice was small and warm through the protective glove. "You too, Doctor Elliot. Believe me, the pleasure is all mine."

"How are the twins today, Doctor Elliot?" asked Hinkle

"Both are in stable condition, Doctor Hinkle," she said, turning abruptly away from Hank. "The latest medication has kept them in a deep sleep and there has been no more restlessness."

The doctor and Hank walked over to one bed while Doctor Elliot followed. Doctor Hinkle unclipped the medical chart from the end of the bed and looked at it closely while Hank pretended to be interested in the electronic displays on the monitors that were stacked one on top of another against the wall.

"I see there is still a level of toxin in the blood," commented Hinkle as he replaced the chart. "The blood filtering doesn't seem to be working?"

"No, it's not," said Doctor Elliot, "and it's not working for the other twin either."

"Why isn't it working? Do you know?" Hank asked speaking directly to Doctor Elliot.

She nodded. "I think I might," she said. She thought for a moment and then went over to look at an electronic screen on one of the monitors that displayed wavy lines. "It appears that the molecular structure of the toxin is such that it adheres to the red blood cells and they cannot be filtered out. It's my theory that the first toxin has mutated to allow itself to break through the red blood cell wall and the filter cannot distinguish between healthy and contaminated cells. I don't believe filtration will work, but Doctor Hinkle does not agree with me on that issue."

"We shouldn't be airing our professional differences in front of Hank, Doctor Elliot," said Hinkle glaring at her over his mask.

Hank put up a hand. "It's all right, Doctor Hinkle." He turned his attention back to Doctor Elliot. "Now, Doctor, I'm interested in knowing what you think will work, professional disagreements be damned. After all, the objective is to find a cure ASAP."

"I do have another theory, Hank. May I call you Hank?" she asked.

Hank nodded. "Of course."

"Well, Hank, my theory is that If we had samples of the toxin before it mutated we could learn how the mutation works and develop an antitoxin that would force it to detach itself from the cells."

"The trouble with that theory is that it's never been tested," said Doctor Hinkle, looking at Hank. "Doctor Elliot's theory is purely speculation. There is no evidence to prove it will work or that it can even be done."

"But Doctor, that is old-school thinking. All I need are a few samples of the original toxin to begin the work. I am ninety-nine percent sure that it will work," said Doctor Elliot.

"No, I don't agree, Doctor! It would be a waste of time, and time is of the essence here!" said Doctor Hinkle heatedly, his voice rising.

Doctor Elliot's eyes were angry over her mask, and she started to rebut Hinkle's statement, but Hank, who was standing between the two doctors, held up his hands.

"Whoa! There's no sense arguing. Doctor Elliot's theory makes sense to me. Why not try it? After all, nothing that you are using now is working," said Hank, feeling like a referee.

"No, I still don't agree, General! It won't work, and we'll be wasting our time, and besides, I am the one in charge here and I say no. Our best bet would be to find ways to improve the blood filtering," said Hinkle, his voice now at a feverish pitch.

Hank's temper flared. He grabbed Hinkle's arm and began to steer him towards the door. "Excuse us for a moment, Doctor Elliot," he said. "I need to talk to Doctor Hinkle in private."

He dragged Hinkle to the airlock door and pushed the button with his free hand. The door slid open, and Hank pulled him into the airlock chamber and the door slid shut. As soon as the door was closed, Hank turned to Hinkle angrily. "You're fired, Hinkle!" he yelled. "It's clear to me that your piddling around is impeding progress and taking up precious time! And not only that, but you called me 'General' again!"

Hinkle had turned white. "But, General ..." he stammered.

"No buts about it, Doctor. You're fired, and you will have to be sequestered until we're finished here because I don't trust you not to open your big mouth outside." He pushed another button and the door on the other side of the chamber slid open. He shoved Hinkle through the door. "After all, *I'm* the one in charge here, not you!" he yelled as the door slid shut behind Hinkle.

Hank pushed the button on the other side of the chamber, the door opened, and he walked back into the twins" isolation room brushing his hands together.

Doctor Elliot's eyes were wide over her mask. "Are you really a general?" she asked.

"That's right, and as of now, I am placing you in charge," said Hank gruffly. He smiled slightly as her eyes grew even wider. "My name is General Howard Kingsman. I am in command of this operation and from now on you will be reporting directly to me."

"In charge?" she asked when she found her voice. "Are you sure? I've never been in charge of a project of this magnitude before."

"Yes, I'm sure, Doctor. Just think of this as a battlefield, and you've just been promoted because your commanding officer has been demoted. If I didn't think you were up to it, I wouldn't have put you in control. I'm used to making quick judgements and decisions because that's my job," said Hank, amused at the look in her eyes.

Her eyes dropped. "Yes, Sir. Should I call you General or ..."

"No! Never call me General unless you see me in uniform. Always call me Hank. It's very important that you remember that because my involvement in this operation is strictly confidential and it must continue to be that way. Now that you know that, tell me what you need to test your theory."

"I'll need to have more patients with the same toxin in order to find a sample of the one that has not mutated. That's the hard part. The rest will go fast, because once I can analyze the mutation, I will be able to develop an antitoxin quickly."

"And where do you propose I begin looking for these 'samples'?" asked Hank.

"In the case of the twins, we know from their DNA that their heritage is Hawaiian and we know they were from the island of Hawaii, the Big Island."

Hank nodded. "That matches what Hinkle told me. And what about the one from England?"

"You'd have to go to Barbados to search for more like her," said Doctor Elliot without hesitation.

Hank smiled. "Right on again, Doctor. We don't have to worry about her for the time being. We'll start with the Hawaiians. What else do we know about these twins?"

The doctor walked over to her desk and typed in a command on her computer keyboard that brought up a profile of the twins.

"There is no information about their parents other than what their DNA tells us - that the mother's heritage is Polynesian and Chinese, and that the father is Caucasian. The twins were in an orphanage on the Big Island until they were three months old. Then they were brought to the mainland and an American couple adopted them."

Hank frowned as he looked at the computer screen. "I knew that," he said. "About them being brought over here, but I don't know why." He paused and scratched his head. Then he shrugged. "Hinkle must have mentioned it," he said. "What happened next?"

Doctor Elliot turned back to the screen. "When they were five years old they exhibited learning difficulties, at that time believed to be the result of alcohol consumed by their biological mother while she was pregnant. Despite the learning problems, both of them graduated from high school, enlisted in the Army and served in Iraq. After serving five years there, they were brought back to Camp Pendleton where they were trained in counter terrorist operations. After al Quada blew up the oil tanker *World Enterprise* they both went to Yemen as part of a Special Forces team. During a raid on a suspected al Quada training camp they both came down with a nervous disorder, diagnosed as toxin poisoning by a military doctor two years ago."

"Yes, I'm familiar with their military history," said Hank. "That's why we were able to find them and bring them here."

The doctor looked at him with a raised brow. "I don't understand how twins with the same toxin poisoning came to be here in the first place, and now a young woman from Barbados with the same toxin."

Hank shook his head. "All I can tell you is they were discovered by some very bright doctors. I can't tell you any more, because there are certain things about this operation that only I can know. Do you understand?"

Doctor Elliot looked at him curiously and nodded her head. "I see," she said. "I shouldn't be asking too many questions, right?"

"That's right," said Hank. "Now, Doctor, what's the first thing we need to do?"

"Find the twins" biological parents if they are still alive."

"All right, Doctor. That means we go to the island of Hawaii first thing tomorrow morning," said Hank looking at his watch.

"We?" asked Doctor Elliot in surprise.

Hank smiled at her. "That's right, Doctor. I think it would be a good idea for you to go with me. It will speed things up." He jerked a thumb over his shoulder in the direction of the twins. "There isn't much you can do for them right now anyway, is there?"

"Well ..." she said frowning slightly. "I need more samples to develop the antitoxin ... and I know what to look for. There are trained assistants who can look after the patients here ..."

Hank waved his hand. "Then it makes sense for you to come with me. Be at the terminal building tomorrow at o-seven hundred, and I'll pick you up. Bring along the necessary gear, but try to pack light." He turned and walked over to the door to the airlock chamber and pushed the button.

The doctor's eyes were wide with surprise again. "Which terminal?" she managed to ask as the door slid open.

"The one at the end of the gravel road. I'll be the one in the white Gulf Stream Jet," he said pausing at the door with a smile that reached his eyes. "You see, I'm very good at flying very fast planes."

"As long as you don't do acrobatics, it will be fine by me," said Doctor Elliot as Hank stepped through the door into the airlock chamber.

*   *   *

Chapter 13

G EORGE SPENT MOST of the day Friday making travel arrangements for Barbados. Being short of money, he decided to book through an online travel service since it was the least expensive way. Peggy had approval from her supervisor to take ten days off beginning Monday.

Throughout the day George expected to hear from Peter Jones, but the investigator didn't call. Then, just as he and Peggy were about to go to bed George's mobile phone rang.

"Any more news?" asked George excitedly, seeing that it was Jones calling from the caller identification message on the mobile's display screen.

"Yes, George," said Jones. "I spoke to a friend at Heathrow Airport and he confirmed that the car that took Denise to the airport is registered to the American Embassy. Also, he says they didn't take her through passport control, which seems very strange."

"Sounds like a kidnapping," said George. "Maybe we should notify the authorities."

"We have no proof, George," said Jones quickly. "It's just hearsay. Who would believe us?"

"I see what you mean," said George glancing over at Peggy who was watching him with raised eyebrows. "What about Denise? Have you found out any more about her background?"

"Yes, I did. It seems Denise has been in a nursing home since she was ten years old. Originally, she was in a private facility in Barbados, but when her medical condition deteriorated an English nurse brought her to East Croydon."

"What sort of medical condition?"

"She has a nervous disorder that causes episodes of uncontrollable muscle spasms, similar to epilepsy. There's a name for it. Just a minute, I have it written down," said Jones. George could hear paper rustling, and Jones came back on the line. "It's called Genetic Encephalitis. It's a genetic mutation passed on by one of her parents."

"Have you found out anything about her parents?" asked George eagerly.

"No, I haven't had chance to look into that yet."

"Can you look into it? It would be very useful to know."

"Sure. I'll see if I can get hold of her medical records, and maybe that will tell us who her parents are."

"It would also be good to know who was in the car with her when she was taken to the airport. Surely it couldn't have been the Ambassador," said George with a laugh.

Jones laughed also. "I'll find out what I can about that, but it may be difficult. The Americans are very tight-lipped."

"Give it a try, won't you Peter," said George and clicked off the connection. He looked at Peggy. "According to Jones, Denise has a genetic disorder," he said.

Peggy smiled. "Well, that's understandable. Mad Cow could be confused with other neurological disorders. I hope you still have confidence in my abilities."

"Let's go to bed, and I'll show you how much confidence I have," said George, grinning at her.

"Confidence in what?" asked Peggy with a flirtatious smile.

"That's for me to know and for you to find out," said George with a laugh.

"Touché," said Peggy. "By the way, are you going to tell Jones that you're going to Barbados?" she asked turning serious.

"No, there's no reason for him to know," said George. "It might be interesting to see how long it takes him to find out."

"But he'll know when he calls you, won't he?"

"No, I'm on WorldNet. He won't know where I am," said George.

"Why don't you want him to know?"

"Because I'm still wondering why he's doing all this for free. I don't quite trust him," said George with a frown.

"But you trust me, don't you, Love?" said Peggy with a sly grin, and George walked over and took her hand and pulled her up from the sofa.

"You know I do," he said as he led her to his bedroom.

*　　*　　*

After they had parked Peggy's car in the Gatwick Airport long-term parking, George and Peggy made their way into the terminal building and looked for the Low Fare Holiday counter. People were rushing in every possible direction pushing carts piled high with luggage as they sought out the check-in counter for their airline. Several lines had formed at the Low Fare Holiday counter, and George and Peggy joined the queue at the end of the economy line.

At last it was their turn to check in, and they walked up to the counter where a representative greeted them with a pleasant smile. George handed both of their passports and electronic tickets to her. The representative checked their passport photos and names and handed them back. Then she looked at the electronic tickets and entered some information on the computer. She looked at the screen and frowned and then entered more information on the computer.

"Is there a problem?" asked George anxiously. "I made the reservations online."

The representative did not respond as she continued to concentrate on the computer screen. Then she looked back at George and said in a pleasant voice, "I'm sorry, Sir. It will just take a moment to sort this out. There seems to be an ambiguity."

"What do you think it is, George?" whispered Peggy. "Did you pay for the tickets online too? Maybe that is the problem."

Before George had time to respond, a distinguished-looking man dressed in a navy blue blazer and gray trousers walked up to the representative from a door behind the counter. He whispered something to the representative, and she nodded her head and smiled at George. "I must apologize for the delay, Sir, but your electronic ticket doesn't match the reservations on our computer ..."

"That's right," interrupted the man in the blue blazer. "Mr. Goater, both you and your companion are flying in the first class cabin, and you'll be staying in the Britannia Suite at the Palm Shores resort in Barbados."

"What? Oh, no, that's wrong! I can't afford first class or the Palm Shores," George blurted out. "I made reservations for economy seats and the Skeleton Beach Hotel."

"Not to worry, Mr. Goater," said the man with a smile. "The whole lot has already been paid for."

"Oh, George. You old dear. Trying to surprise me, is that it? Well, it's a wonderful surprise," gushed Peggy, leaning her head on his arm.

"No, no," said George still looking at the representatives. "I'm absolutely sure I paid for the economy rate, and ..."

"I shouldn't complain, Sir, if I were you. It's a long flight to Barbados and much more comfortable in first class, as well as all the free champagne you can drink."

George's mouth snapped shut and his face brightened. "Yes, I see what you mean," he said. "And you say it's all paid for?"

"That's correct," said the female representative with a huge smile as she tapped on the keyboard. A printer spit out two boarding passes and she handed them to George. "There will be a representative to greet you when you arrive in Barbados and take you to the hotel, Mr. Goater. Meanwhile, you can wait in the VIP Lounge just behind that red door over there until your flight is called. Just show the receptionist your boarding passes for admittance."

George thanked her and he and Peggy carried their small travel bags and walked over to the red door. When they entered the door, they found themselves in lavish surroundings that seemed more like the lobby of the Ritz than an airport lounge.

After they had shown their boarding passes to the receptionist, they walked in and found two overstuffed velvet chairs with a cocktail table in a secluded corner.

The moment they sat down, a waiter dressed in tails appeared. "Cocktails, Sir?" he asked. George looked at Peggy. She smiled and without hesitation said, "I believe I'll have a *Cosmopolitan*."

"And for you Sir?" asked the waiter.

"I'll have the same," he said having no idea what a *Cosmopolitan* was.

"What's the matter, George?" asked Peggy when the waiter had gone to get their drinks. George appeared to be in a daze.

"I still don't get it," he said, pulling his ticket confirmation out of his pocket. "I know I bought economy tickets. Look at this," he said, thrusting the confirmation into her hands.

Peggy held the confirmation up so she could read it in the dim light cast by a floor lamp behind their chairs. "You're absolutely right. It does show that you booked economy tickets and a room at the Skeleton Beach Hotel. It is a mystery." She handed the confirmation back to George and thought for a moment. "I know! I'll bet it's one of those computer errors. I've heard of it happening to other people where they were accidentally upgraded. I'm sure that must be what's happened, and all we have to do is relax and enjoy it at the agency's expense. This is exciting, George. I've never been on a first class holiday, have you?"

"No, I haven't. Could never afford it," said George still looking worried. "Remember, this is supposed to be a working holiday ..." He stopped as the waiter walked up with two huge martini glasses on a tray. He placed napkins in front of them and set the drinks down with a flourish.

George started to reach into his pocket, but the waiter put up a hand to stop him. "No need for that, Sir. Everything is complimentary," he said as he twirled the tray and walked away.

George picked up the martini glass and looked at the pinkish liquid in it. "So what's in a *Cosmopolitan*?" he asked.

"Straight Russian vodka with a tiny splash of cranberry juice and a hint of lemon, shaken, not stirred," said Peggy, picking up her glass.

"Vodka, you say?" George grinned and touched his glass to hers. "Well, here's to a first-class working vacation then."

*   *   *

After two rounds of *Cosmopolitans*, an airline steward walked up to them. "Mr. Goater?" he asked.

"That's right," said George. "See, I still remember my name," he added as an aside to Peggy who giggled at him.

"We are boarding first-class passengers now. Please follow me," said the steward trying not to grin at the interchange between George and Peggy.

They followed the steward through a private security screening station and were soon seated in sumptuous dove-gray leather reclining seats. The first-class stewardess appeared with two crystal flutes of champagne, which they sipped while the other passengers were boarding.

After it appeared that the last stragglers had boarded, a stewardess walked up and down the cabins checking passengers against a list she was holding. When she passed George and Peggy who so far were the only two passengers in first class, George leaned over to Peggy and whispered, "So far so good. We didn't get booted out of first class."

"Will you stop worrying, George? Everything is going to be all right," said Peggy with a hint of exasperation in her voice.

The captain's voice came over the intercom. "Ladies and Gentlemen, there will be a slight delay before we can take off. There is nothing to worry about. Because of the delay, we are offering a complimentary glass of champagne. Sit back, relax and enjoy, and we will take off before long."

While the cabin stewardesses handed out champagne in plastic glasses to the other passengers, the first-class stewardess returned with a bottle of Dom Perignon and filled George and Peggy's glasses.

"What's the cause of the delay?" asked George as the stewardess was filling his glass.

The stewardess smiled at him. "Nothing to worry about, Sir. We have a missing passenger who has checked in but has not yet boarded. He should be here any minute now."

The stewardess walked back up to the front of the plane and stood waiting at the door. In a few moments, George and Peggy heard the sound of rapid footsteps on the ramp outside the door. The stewardess walked forward to the door with a smile, and they heard the muffled sound of a man's voice apologizing for being late. George and Peggy were looking expectantly at the front of the plane when the man stepped around the corner.

"Bugger me, if it isn't Stan!" said George breaking out in a huge grin. "What a surprise!"

Stan looked at George in surprise and grinned. "George! We meet again!" he said. "Seems I've seen more of you since you retired than I did when you were working," he said as he walked to the first-class seat across the aisle from George. As Stan was stowing his luggage and getting settled in his seat, George leaned over to Peggy who was looking at Stan curiously. "It's Stan Straw. He's a security guard at the Foreign Office," he explained.

"So you're the cause of our delay, Stan," said George when Stan had buckled his seat belt. "What happened?"

"Oh, I got lost and went to the wrong gate," said Stan with a grimace, "but I'm here now."

"Are you going to Barbados on Foreign Office business?" asked George curiously. He was wondering how Stan could afford to be in first class on a security guard's pay.

Stan shook his head. "Oh, no, George. I was lucky on the horses so I'm treating myself to a holiday in the sun."

"We've been lucky too," said Peggy, leaning forward slightly so that Stan could see her on the other side of George.

"Oh, sorry, Peggy," said George. "Peggy this is Stan Straw. Stan, meet my companion Peggy Valentine."

"Pleased to meet you Peggy. Lucky, you say? What? On the lottery?" asked Stan leaning forward and looking at Peggy.

"No, not that," said Peggy. "We got upgraded to first class. We think it was a computer error," she said with a laugh.

"Shush," said George poking her in the ribs with his elbow, and pointing to the front where the stewardess was just coming out of the galley.

She collected their empty champagne glasses and smiled. "This is just for takeoff," she assured them, noticing the disappointed look on George's face. "I'll be back with more champagne and fresh glasses as soon as we're airborne and the captain has turned off the seatbelt sign."

As the plane was roaring down the runway at full speed about to lift off, the harsh, acrid smell of jet fuel filled the plane and passengers began to sneeze and cough.

The captain's voice soon came over the intercom. "Ladies and gentlemen, there is no cause for alarm. The cabin air will improve in a minute or two. Wind conditions during takeoff caused fuel vapors to get into the ventilation system. Please accept my apologies."

"Well, fancy that," said Stan with a gravelly voice. "I've never been on a plane where that's happened." He began to cough and wheeze.

George looked at Stan with alarm as he saw that he was red-faced and gagging as he coughed. George was about to get out of his seat and see if he needed to perform the Heimlich maneuver on Stan, when the stewardess came running down the aisle with a plastic cup of water and some tissues.

"Here, Sir. Try to drink some water," she said handing Stan the cup of water.

Stan took it and managed to sip some water in between coughs. The stewardess handed him the tissues, and he blew his nose several times. Finally, the coughing subsided, and he leaned back in his seat, relieved. "Sorry about that, but I have asthma, and it can be touched off by anything in the air," he said in a nasal tone. "I'm all right now."

"I never knew that, Stan," said George still looking at Stan with concern.

"Yes. It was brought on by tear gas when I worked in the British Embassy in Jakarta. Riot police broke up demonstrations outside the Embassy gates," said Stan as he put his head back on the headrest.

George raised his eyebrows in surprise. "I never knew you worked directly for the Diplomatic Corps."

"Ho, yes," he said with a slight smile and a far-off look. "Before I began working for the Foreign Office I worked in many countries, including Barbados."

"Well, I never!" exclaimed George. "I've never been to Barbados before."

"Nor have I," said Peggy. "What is it like?"

"Great!" said Stan with an enthusiastic smile. "Lovely beaches and beautiful people. Best island in the Caribbean in my opinion."

"Where are you staying?" asked Peggy. "We are staying at the Palm Shores Resort."

"Oh, I'm up the road from that posh place," said Stan with a chuckle.

"One of my friends from my diplomatic days has a small cottage right on the beach. It's nothing fancy, just the bare essentials, and that suits me fine. The place where you are staying is a haven for the rich and famous. That's not my style - I like to go native."

"You're lucky to have a place like that where you can do as you please," said George wistfully. "I suppose where we're staying, we'll have to be on our best behavior at all times. And I bet the food is expensive and the drinks will cost an arm and a leg," he groused.

"Did I hear you say drinks?" asked the stewardess as she walked up to them. "I'm taking orders now. We have a full bar in first class. What would you like?"

Stan opted for a gin and tonic while George and Peggy decided they wanted more *Cosmopolitans*. The stewardess soon returned with three glasses on a silver tray. "I will be serving breakfast in half an hour," she said, handing them small engraved menus.

"Well, Cheers! Here's to a great holiday," said Stan raising his glass and clinking it against George's across the aisle.

*   *   *

Nine hours, six glasses of champagne and four *Cosmopolitans* later, George wobbled down the steps of the plane at Grantley Adams International Airport in Barbados. Stan went ahead of him and Peggy brought up the rear, just in case. The humidity hit them like a hot wet towel. At the bottom of the steps George stood swaying to and fro and Stan grabbed his arm to steady him. When Peggy stepped down to the tarmac, she took his other arm, and Stan led them toward the immigration terminal.

Outside the door, a reggae band played a Bob Marley song to welcome the passengers to Barbados. George looked from Stan to Peggy with a foolish grin. "Are we there?" he asked in a drunken voice.

"Yes, George," said Peggy. "Now we have to go through passport control, so try to straighten up so they won't know how tipsy you are."

"It's all right," said Stan. "Just follow me and I'll get you through."

Stan led the way, and Peggy, still holding on to George, followed him into the terminal. Long lines of passengers had already formed at each immigration official's station.

"Stand here," said Stan to Peggy, indicating a spot just inside the door. Peggy nodded, and stood holding on to the swaying George, as Stan walked over to a black man dressed in an immigration officer's uniform. Stan and the officer grinned at each other and shook hands. Then Stan pointed in the direction of George and Peggy, and the officer looked at them with a huge grin. He beckoned to them to come over.

"Welcome to paradise, Mr. and Mrs. Goater," said the officer when they walked up. "I understand you are good friends of Mr. Stan." He held out a hand to George.

"That's right," said George shaking his hand. "Pleased to be here," he said in a fairly normal voice. Stan and Peggy looked at each other in relief. George had apparently sobered up somewhat.

"To save you any delay, follow me and I will take you through immigration," said the officer.

George reached into his pocket and brought out his passport as Peggy began to open her carry-on bag. The officer held up his hand. "No need for those," he said still grinning. "Being friends of Mr. Stan is good enough. Just follow me."

Stan smiled at George and Peggy, and motioned for them to follow the officer, who led them to the front of one of the lines and straight through the immigration station. The officer at the station simply smiled and nodded at them as they passed through. When they were well inside the terminal, the official stopped. Stan smiled and shook hands with him, slipping him a twenty-pound note in the process. The officer grinned and turned to walk back to his station. As he passed George and Peggy, he said, "Have a fine holiday in beautiful Barbados."

Stan beckoned to them, and George and Peggy followed him towards the baggage carousel. When they came up to the outskirts of the crowd standing around the carousel, Stan stopped and looked around. A porter waved at him from the other side of the carousel, and Stan waved back. The porter grinned and walked over carrying a large suitcase.

"Good to see you, Mr. Stan," said the porter. He put the suitcase down and gave Stan a hug.

"Good to see you, too, Louis," said Stan patting the porter on the back.

Louis released Stan from his hug and looked at George and Peggy who were standing nearby. "Are you friends of Mr. Stan?" he asked.

"They are," said Stan before George or Peggy could respond. "Louis, this is Mr. George and Ms. Peggy."

Louis beamed and shook hands with both George and Peggy. "Do you have luggage? I will get it for you."

"No, thank you, Louis," said Peggy. "We just have what we are carrying."

"Do you need a taxi?"

"No, someone from the hotel is supposed to meet us."

Louis grinned and without a word took George and Peggy's carryon bags, picked up Stan's suitcase, and led them outside.

Again, the humidity hit them, and the sun was hot even though it was low in the western sky. Lines of taxis and mini-buses queued at the curbside. Crowds of people were mingling around trying to determine what sort of transportation they should take.

"It's bloody hot here," said Stan, mopping his forehead with a handkerchief.

"Phew, that's for sure. I'm already sweating," said George, shrugging out of his dark jacket and opening his shirt collar.

"It's probably all that alcohol coming out," said Peggy, grinning at him.

"That's why you can drink a lot here - you sweat it out the minute it goes down, isn't that right Louis?" said Stan laughing.

"Yeah, Mon. It takes a lot of rum to get us Bajans drunk," said Louis, grinning as he put the luggage down on the concrete pavement.

"Mr. George Goater! Calling Mr. George Goater!" boomed out a voice.

George looked toward where the voice was coming and saw a young black man dressed in a red blazer and white trousers. He was standing by a white stretch limousine holding up a sign with George's name printed on it in big block letters.

"Over here!" called out George raising his hand and waving it in the air.

The young man looked toward them and leaned the sign against the car.

"That's your ride?" asked Stan looking at the young man as he hurried towards them.

"Mr. Goater?" asked the man politely as he walked up to them.

"Yes," answered George returning his smile. "I suppose you're the Palm Shores driver."

"And Philip, the son of Nick and Anna," added Stan with a chuckle.

The young man looked at Stan in surprise. After a few moments his face broke out in a huge grin. "Mr. Stan!" he said. "It's so good to see you again." He saw Louis standing nearby with the luggage and grinned at him, and Louis nodded and grinned in recognition.

"Good to see you again, Philip," said Stan putting his arm around Philip and hugging him.

"Are you friends of Mr. Stan?" asked Philip turning back to George and Peggy after he had greeted Stan.

"Yes, they are. It's Mr. George and Ms. Peggy," said Stan before George could respond.

"I will give you all a ride then. Do you mind, Mr. George?" said Philip after he had shaken hands with George and Peggy.

"Not at all," said George. "I was just about to suggest it myself, as Stan is staying up the road from the Palm Shores."

Philip happily nodded his head. "Oh, yes, I know. Mr. Stan always stays at Jonkanoo Cottage."

"No, I'll take the luggage to the car," said Louis as Philip started to pick up the bags. He carried Stan's suitcase and George and Peggy's carry-on bags to the car and Philip opened the trunk. After he had stowed the baggage in the trunk, Louis turned and gave Stan a departing hug. Stan gave him a five-pound note, but Louis looked at it and shook his head. "I cannot take money from a friend," he said handing the note back to Stan. "If Mr. Stan gave money to all his friends he couldn't afford to come to Barbados to see us."

"Good for you, Louis," said Stan as he put the money back into his pocket. "Give my best wishes to Martha and the rest of the family." He climbed into the back of the limousine where George and Peggy had already settled themselves.

Philip opened the window behind him so he could communicate with the passengers. He started the limo and cautiously pulled into a traffic lane. At a roundabout, he headed north toward Speightstown. The passengers sat in silence as they looked out at the passing cane fields and scenery cast in the glow of the late afternoon sun.

After a while, Peggy broke the silence. "You seem to know everyone, Stan, and they certainly remember you."

"I know a few," said Stan. "As I said, I've spent some time here and you can't help making friends. Bajans are very easy-going, friendly people, isn't that right, Philip?"

Philip glanced at them in the rearview mirror as he slowed the car to take a sharp curve in the road. "Yes, and Mr. Stan is very popular with us because he is very friendly to everyone. He is not like the rich and famous staying at the Palm Shores, who act like all Bajans are their servants."

"It wasn't my idea to stay there," said George quickly. "I'm not rich and famous - just a poor retired civil servant."

"How long are you staying, George?" asked Stan, frowning slightly and shaking his head at George to indicate he should not discuss his monetary status.

"Seven days," said Peggy, helping Stan to change the subject. "I'm looking forward to the sunshine and those white sandy beaches I have heard so much about."

Philip smiled and glanced at her in the rearview mirror. "It's all true, Ms. Peggy. We have the best sunshine and beaches in the Caribbean," he said proudly. "You won't want to leave. No one ever does. I've driven people to the airport in tears."

"It's because of the hotel bill," said Stan with a chuckle. "The Palm Shores is very dear."

"Mr. George doesn't have to worry," commented Philip. "His bill is prepaid."

"Prepaid? I haven't prepaid anything," said George.

"Keep quiet, George," whispered Peggy nudging him with her elbow. Then she said louder for Stan"s benefit. "It's that computer error again."

"That's right, George," said Stan. "Don't look a gift horse in the mouth. As they say here, „Don't worry. Be happy"."

Forty-five minutes later, Philip turned the car onto a hard-packed dirt space and parked under a breadfruit tree next to a small cottage. The cottage was painted a bright marine blue with hot pink trim. Palm trees and a variety of other tropical plants surrounded and overhung the cottage. A small flight of three concrete steps led up to a crude wooden front door. The steps were painted hot pink, and directly above them painted in hot pink on the side of the cottage was the single word *Jonkanoo*.

"Here we are," said Stan enthusiastically. "Jonkanoo Cottage. It hasn't changed at all."

"It's charming," said Peggy as she noticed a black cat ducking into the undergrowth. "Wake up, George," she said.

George stirred but didn't awaken. He had dozed off about midway during the trip. Peggy reached over and gently squeezed his hand. "George, wake up. We have arrived at Stan's cottage."

George slowly opened his eyes and blinked several times to adjust to the light.

"Looks like one of those postcards we saw at the airport," he murmured as he looked at the cottage.

Philip climbed out of the car and went to open the trunk.

"Why don't you come in for a while," said Stan as he opened the car door. "Then you can see the inside and watch the sunset from the deck."

"Come on, George," said Peggy. "I would like to see it."

George opened the door on his side and they both got out. Philip lifted Stan's suitcase out of the trunk and led the way up the concrete steps to the front door. Stan followed directly behind him with Peggy and George bringing up the rear.

"Now where's the key?" murmured Stan as he looked around the tiny entryway. "Ho, yes, here it is," he said as he spied the key hanging on a rusty nail close to the door.

"That's not very safe. It's in plain sight," said George.

Philip grinned at him. "A key is just a formality here, Mr. George. The door is locked to keep it from blowing open in the wind more than anything else. Everyone trusts everyone here. For Bajans, there is no such thing as taking something that doesn't belong to you."

"That's right," said Stan as he opened the door. He flipped a crude light switch just inside the door, and the others followed him into a long narrow sitting room.

George and Peggy looked around. The room was furnished with well-used mismatched furniture that included a large black vinyl sofa, and two sagging overstuffed chairs upholstered in brown corduroy. A low scarred wooden table sat in front of the sofa. On it were stacks of out-of-date magazines with torn covers, and on another side table was an old-fashioned black telephone that had a dial. The walls and floor were constructed of unfinished rough wooden planks and light from the outside came in through cracks in the walls. A floor fan stood in one corner of the room. When Stan turned it on, it turned from side to side with a rattling whine.

"It's very basic," said Stan. "Come see the rest of it," he said as he led them through a door into another hallway. "Here's my bedroom," he said as he led them into a tiny whitewashed room. There was a single bed in the center of the room with a bare light bulb dangling over it.

Stan showed them the rest of the cottage, which consisted of a bathroom and a small kitchen with a fully stocked refrigerator. He grabbed a six-pack of Banks beer and led them through a door in the kitchen onto a huge two-level deck. The deck had a spectacular view of the Caribbean Sea through a frame of tropical foliage.

George, Peggy and Philip followed Stan to the lower deck level that had a latticework fence along the end. Stan walked to the end of the deck and put the beer down on a plastic table.

"What a wonderful view, Stan," said Peggy looking over the fence at the end of the deck. Gentle waves washed up on the white sandy beach directly below. As she stared at the beach she noticed movement out of the corner of her eye. She looked closer and saw a sand crab sitting atop a mound of sand where it had been digging a hole.

"It's paradise," said Stan using a bottle opener to pry off the beer caps. "I spend most of my time out here, either on the deck or down below on the beach."

"I can see why," said George. "There's no need to be inside the cottage except to sleep."

"That's right. Sometimes I even sleep out here on the deck," said Stan.

They all took Stan's lead in helping themselves to the opened bottles of beer and sitting down in white plastic lawn chairs facing the ocean where the sun was nearly touching the western horizon.

"A toast," announced Philip holding out his beer bottle in an outstretched hand. "Welcome to my island. Here's to happy times in Barbados."

The other three tapped their bottles against his and sipped the cool beer as they sat in silence listening to the waves lapping on the sand and the palms rustling in the warm breeze. They watched the sun as it slowly disappeared below the horizon leaving in its wake a brilliant sunset of red and pink streaks across the sky.

"Do you know someone named Denise Downing? She grew up here in Barbados," said Peggy suddenly when the sunset began to give way to the dark indigo of the night sky.

"Denise who?" asked Stan, startled out of his reverie.

"Downing. She was born here thirty-four years ago."

"Can't say that I do. I don't remember that name," said Stan taking another sip of beer. He looked at Philip with a frown. "What about you, Philip? She would be around your age."

Philip looked down into his beer bottle and thought for a moment. Then he looked up at Peggy. "The name doesn't seem familiar, Ms. Peggy. Is she a friend of yours?"

"Not really a friend," said George looking at Peggy. "Peggy is interested in genealogy, and Denise Downing comes from Barbados, and Peggy is trying to trace her heritage."

"It's a small island. It should be easy to find out about her," commented Stan lazily.

"Well, I don't know her, and I've lived here all my life," said Philip somewhat testily, looking at Stan.

"If she was from here, Philip would certainly know her," said Stan. "Perhaps you have the wrong island. Maybe she's from Bimini or Bermuda instead of Barbados."

"No," said Peggy. "I'm sure she's from Barbados."

Stan shrugged. "Well, I can ask around. Maybe somebody knew her. How about another beer? I have plenty," he said, noticing George's empty beer bottle.

George started to accept but noticed Peggy glowering at him. "I

Don't think so, Stan," he said. "It's been a long day, and we need to check in and all of that yet."

"Yes, Stan," said Peggy. "We'd best be going now. Thank you for showing us the cottage. It's truly charming. You must come visit us and let us buy you a drink."

"Ho! I don't think I'd fit in with all those la-de-da types," said Stan as he got up to walk them to the door.

Philip had driven only a short distance south when he turned into a brightly illuminated driveway and stopped at a security gate. A security guard walked up and looked in at Philip. He grinned and then signaled to another guard to open the gate.

The gate swung open and Philip drove through and continued down a cobblestone avenue lined on both sides with royal palms. Garlands of white lights wrapped around the palm trunks lit up the avenue. A sound like hundreds of small bells chiming came through the open windows of the limousine.

Peggy sucked in her breath. "How beautiful! It looks like fairyland," she exclaimed. "What is that sound?"

"Tree frogs," explained Philip. "They sit in the trees and other plants and sing at night. They love the Palm Shores because of the many gardens full of every kind of tropical plant imaginable."

"Isn't it wonderful, George!" exclaimed Peggy.

George offered no comment, and Peggy saw that he had dozed off again, his head resting on the plush leather seat. His mouth was wide open.

When Philip drove around a slight curve, a large Georgian style building came into view. It was lit by hundreds of floodlights.

"Here's the main hotel," said Philip as he stopped under a massive portico. "Welcome to Palm Shores."

As soon as the car stopped two Bajan men attired in azure blue blazers and matching pith helmets stepped forward and opened the two rear doors of the limousine.

"Wake up, George. We're at the hotel," said Peggy shaking his shoulder.

George mumbled something and groggily climbed out of the car. Peggy climbed out on her side and smiled at the doorman.

Philip had opened the trunk, and a bellhop reached in and pulled out their two carry-ons. "Is this all?" he asked in surprise. Philip nodded and the bellhop took the bags into the lobby of the hotel.

"Thank you so much, Philip," said Peggy as George reached into his pocket for a tip.

Philip held up his hand. "No, Mr. George. It is not necessary to tip me because the limousine service is part of the package. Save your tip for the bellhop."

"That's very decent of you," said George as he shook hands with Philip. "Thank you for everything."

"I will see you tomorrow," said Philip as he climbed into the driver's seat.

George and Peggy watched as Philip drove away down the circular drive, and then they walked into the hotel.

As they walked through the lobby, Peggy commented on the architecture and the furnishings from the sparkling crystal chandelier overhead to the pink marble floor below.

A beautifully dressed young Bajan woman greeted them at the reception desk. "Mr. George and Ms. Peggy, welcome to paradise and the Palm Shores," she said in a soft musical voice.

George had pulled out his wallet and was fumbling through it looking for his identification and a credit card. The receptionist shook her head smiling at him. "That won't be necessary, Mr. George. Everything has been taken care of. All you need to do is sign for the keys."

George put his wallet back into his pocket and stepped up to the counter to sign the paper the receptionist placed in front of him. Then she gave him two card keys and a black envelope with the Palm Shores insignia engraved on it in gold. "The envelope contains two gold identity cards. Use these cards for meals, drinks or any resort activities," she said.

"How am I going to pay for it all? Don't you want a credit card?" asked George.

"No, Mr. George. It is not necessary as everything that you charge has been paid in advance."

"Who paid?" asked George. "I certainly haven't." Peggy rolled her eyes at him as the receptionist looked at the computer terminal.

The receptionist smiled at him. "It doesn't say, Mr. George. All it says is that your stay here has been prepaid. No other details are given."

"If the computer says that, it must be true," said Peggy through gritted teeth. "Come, George. You're tired, so let's go to the room and get settled."

The receptionist smiled understandingly. "Yes, you've had a long journey, and the jet lag can take its toll."

"And I"'s way past our bedtime," said Peggy, "It's after three in the morning at home."

"The elevator is to the right. Robert will show you and take you to your suite," said the receptionist as she motioned to the bellhop who had their bags.

When they got off the elevator on the seventh floor, the bellhop led the way to Number 711 with *Britannia Suite* engraved on a brass nameplate on the door. He took one of the card keys and opened the door. He stepped aside for George and Peggy to enter, and then he followed with their bags.

*　　*　　*

Chapter 14

D OCTOR JANE ELLIOT arrived at the terminal early. She wanted to be there to see Hank fly in. It was still dark, but there was the hint of a rising sun. A black-clad security guard stood in the background. Just as the sun had surfaced on the horizon, she heard the faint droning of a plane in the distance. She smiled as she looked at her watch. "Right on time," she thought.

Soon the droning turned into a roar and the jet's landing lights came into view. The deafening roar of the plane as it landed on the uneven runway surface set up a vibration that rattled the sheet iron on the terminal building. Doctor Elliot looked up in alarm and quickly walked out and away from the building.

She watched as the plane taxied to the terminal, its landing lights revealing the large cloud of dust and debris stirred up by the two jet engines. The plane came to a stop outside the terminal. A few minutes later the engines shut down and the exit door opened.

"Good morning, Doctor Elliot," said Hank with a smile as he bounded down the ramp. He was dressed in full uniform.

"Good Morning, ... General Kingsman," said Doctor Elliot staring at Hank's uniform. "I see you are in uniform today." She also noticed the strongly etched features of his tanned face and was surprised to see that under his hat his hair was a streaked blonde color.

"I had to wear the damned thing," said Hank. "We'll be flying in and out of Air Force bases, and it will save us at lot of trouble." He looked her over from head to foot, taking in her casual safari style pants and jacket, her long dark hair caught back in a loose French braid, and her beautifully curved lips the color of ripe watermelon. He caught his breath. "You certainly aren't dressed very doctorly today, Doctor," he said with a grin.

She smiled up at him, noticing again as she had when he wore the surgical mask how the grin set his marine blue eyes dancing. "I'm looking forward to warm weather and some sunshine," she said. "I don't generally wear doctor's garb when I'm doing field work."

"I'll carry your bags on and stow them. We'd better get going. It's a long way to Hawaii from here," said Hank. He picked up two large bags from the tarmac and started to reach for the two smaller bags, but Doctor Elliot beat him to it.

"I'm not helpless," she said.

"I'm sure of that," said Hank with a grin. "Come on. Let's go." He led the way up the ramp and into the plane. He stowed her two large bags in a compartment at the back of the plane.

"What's all that?" asked Doctor Elliot seeing a large number of boxes, cases and bags already stowed in the compartment.

"Supplies for Hawaii," said Hank as he motioned for her to place her two small bags on top of the large ones.

She looked at him questioningly and he just smiled. "You'll see. Come on, follow me."

She followed him through a luxuriously appointed cabin that looked like a combination living room and office. She noticed a fax machine and a computer, and there was a bar near the front with bottles and glasses in custom-made slots to keep them from flying around while the plane was in the air. At the front of the cabin there was a small kitchenette. "My, my," she said. "All the comforts of home."

"That's right," said Hank. "It's like a flying RV. There's even a king-sized bed in the other compartment at the rear of this cabin. That might come in handy."

She looked at him with a frown. What did he mean by that remark, she wondered? She tried to find a clue in his eyes, but he had turned away and was walking on up to the front of the aircraft.

He opened the door that separated the pilot's compartment from the main cabin. "I'll be the pilot and you can be the co-pilot," he said motioning for her to sit in the co-pilot's chair.

He saw the look on her face and laughed. "Don't worry, Doc. You don't have to do any flying. All you have to do is enjoy the scenery and my company."

"Buckle up, Doc," he reminded her as he climbed into the pilot's seat and buckled his own seat belt.

"Roger, Gen."

"Gen?" he asked looking at her curiously.

"Sure. If you're going to call me Doc, I might as well call you Gen," she said.

Hank laughed. "I see. I take it you don't like to be called Doc."

"It always reminds me of Doc on 'Gunsmoke' or Doc Holiday, and they weren't exactly how I picture myself," she said smiling.

"Well, since we're alone, why don't you just call me Hank?" he said as he flipped some switches on the instrument panel.

"Roger, Hank," she said with a grin. "And you can call me Jane."

He looked over at her and grinned. "All right, Jane, are you ready for takeoff?"

"As ready as I'll ever be," she said. "Let's go!"

Hank started the engines and taxied the short distance to the runway. He turned the plane so it was pointed at the length of the runway, revved the engines, and they were soon airborne.

When the plane reached cruising altitude, Hank entered a command on a touch screen on the left side of the instrument panel. Then he turned to Jane. "I've put her on automatic pilot now. In five hours we'll land at the Air Force base in Medford, Oregon to refuel. We can go back and sit in the cabin now if you like."

Jane shook her head. "No, I like sitting up here where I can see out, and even more important, watch the instrument panel. Besides, this is a comfortable seat," she said patting the arm of the leather seat.

Hank laughed. "You don't trust Rollo?"

"Who's Rollo?"

"The automatic pilot," said Hank with a laugh. "It's ok. Up front suits me fine," he said with that smile that reached his eyes, and Jane relaxed and smiled too.

Hank pushed a lever and swiveled his seat so he was facing Jane's seat and showed her how to do the same. "Now, Jane, tell me how you know about 'Gunsmoke'? You"re not old enough to remember that. You're only forty-four."

"My dad had all the 'Gunsmoke' episodes on VCR, and I used to watch them over and over with him," she said with a far away look in her eyes. Then she suddenly frowned. "How do you know I'm forty-four?" she asked suspiciously.

"Oh, I know all about you," he said waving a hand. "I've read your file several times."

"My file? What file?" asked Jane startled.

"I have a file on everyone involved in this project," said Hank seriously. "Let's just say I have access to certain intelligence sources that gathered the information for me."

"I see," said Jane in a miffed tone of voice. "The FBI are pretty thorough, or so I'm told."

Hank shook his head. "It wasn't the FBI or the CIA - just a source that I can command for top secret work, and they are very thorough, even more so than the FBI. And that's all I can say about it."

"Well, just exactly what do you know about me?" asked Jane still miffed.

"Well, for starters I know you were born in Halstead, Kansas, the only child of Doctor Winston Elliot and Janine Cole Elliot. You grew up in the small town of Pawnee, Kansas where you were valedictorian of your graduating class. You received a scholarship to Kansas University where you earned your bachelor's in English and Journalism in three years.

"After graduation, you taught high school English in Prairie, Kansas for two years, and you were married for one year. In 1996 both your parents were killed in a car accident, and you used your small inheritance to enroll in pre-med at Harvard. You soon discovered a duel interest - medical research in toxicology and in neuropsychology - so you specialized in both. After your internship and residency at Boston Hospital, you distinguished yourself at Mayo Clinic, and in 2010 Johns Hopkins lured you away where you remain today. End of story. Have I missed anything?"

Jane looked at him in disbelief. "No, you seem to know it all, except for the color of my underwear."

"Well, believe me, I'd want to conduct my own research on that," said Hank with a twinkle in his eye and a sly grin.

"Are you coming on to me, General?" asked Jane without the hint of a smile.

"What do you think?" asked Hank still grinning. "You're a good looking woman, and you're smart and single to boot." He reached over and squeezed her knee.

Jane grabbed his hand and smartly thrust it off her knee. "Really, General! I don't know where you would get the idea that I'm that kind of woman!"

"And what kind of woman is that?" asked Hank with a cocked eyebrow.

"You know very well what I mean!" Jane shouted. "I did not come along on this trip to be your plaything. I'm here to do a job, and that's what I intend to do, so you can keep your hands to yourself!"

Hank was both surprised and embarrassed to see that tears of humiliation had sprung into her eyes. He felt like a little kid who had his hands slapped for reaching into the cookie jar. "You're absolutely right, Jane ... Doctor. I had no business doing that. I don't know what got into me and I apologize," he said humbly.

Jane sniffed self-righteously and then could not help smiling at Hank's chastised look. She couldn't believe she had just chewed out a general. "Well, no harm done. At least you apologized and that's something." They were both silent for a moment, and then Jane cleared her throat. "Now I would like to know about you, Hank. It's only fair since you know my whole life story."

Hank stroked his chin and smiled. "What would you like to know about me, Jane?"

"What is the real reason you are taking me to Hawaii?"

Hank looked at her in surprise. "You already know the reason. We are trying to find the biological parents of the Hawaiian twins and anyone else who may have the same toxin in their systems - particularly in its original state before it mutated."

"What is the reason for all the secrecy?"

Hank waved a hand. "There's no more secrecy than what is usual in the case of identifying unknown diseases. We don't want to cause any unnecessary alarm among the public."

"Well, I find it all very strange, Hank," said Jane with a puzzled expression. "When I looked at my paycheck, I saw that it didn't come from a regular source. It was issued by a commercial bank, not from any government agency or the military."

Hank's smile faded. "That is because you are not a government employee. You are on lease from Johns Hopkins to a subcontractor to a contractor. All you should be concerned about is getting paid, not where it's coming from," he said gruffly.

"And does this contractor perchance have a contract with the Defense Department? It must be the Defense Department; otherwise, why would a General be in charge of the project?" said Jane ignoring his evasiveness.

"You are out of line, Doctor," said Hank, his anger flaring. "You know everything you need to know. No more questions about the project. I've told you all I can. Soldiers do not question their commanding officers. If they did we'd never win a war."

"Yes, Sir, General, Sir! I wasn't aware I was a soldier and that we are at war!" said Jane sarcastically, giving him a mock salute.

"It was just an analogy," said Hank huffily. "No more questions about the project."

"All right. What about yourself then? Are you married?" she asked abruptly.

The abrupt shift in the line of questioning startled Hank, but at the same time, he was relieved that she had gotten off the topic of the project. He looked at her and slowly shook his head. "No," he said.

"Ever been?" she asked.

"No."

"Why not?"

"I didn't think I could handle being married to the Air Force and a woman at the same time. Didn't think it would be fair to her," he said. He looked down for a moment and then back up at her with a wistful smile. "Now that I'm nearing retirement, though, I wonder if I made the right decision - no one to share retirement with, no kids, no grandkids to take fishing."

Jane's face softened. "I feel the same. You know from reading my file that I've only been married that one year right out of college. I had several opportunities along the way, but my career seemed much more interesting than the men. Now I sometimes feel as if there's a void in my life that the work can't fill, and I want it all. Now I know I could handle it all - that I wouldn't have to make a choice between one or the other. That is, of course, if I met the right person."

They both sat contemplating this for a second and then Jane brightened. "Hank, can I ask you another question? It's related to the project, but not really about the project itself I don't think."

Hank smiled. "Sure, Jane. I'll tell you if it's something I can't answer."

"Well, I can understand why we are interested in the twins from America, but why would we be interested in this woman from Barbados?"

"Because she has the same symptoms as the twins, and now we know it's the same toxin. I can't tell you how we found her, so don't ask," said Hank holding up his hand as he anticipated her next question.

"You know, I'm not a hundred percent sure it is a toxin," said Jane wrinkling her forehead. "The symptoms are similar to another disease."

"And what is that?" asked Hank.

"What the British call Mad Cow Disease," said Jane. "The medical name is Creutzfeld-Jacobs Disease, or Cj for short."

Hank sat up straight in his chair. "Mad Cow? Isn't that caused by a virus?"

"No it's not. I believe the British have figured it out. Here, let me show you what I mean." Jane unbuckled her seat belt and went back into the cabin. Soon she returned with her laptop computer. She opened the case and put it on her lap. After she had booted it up, she typed a command on the keyboard and a document appeared on the screen. She turned the laptop sideways so Hank could see.

"This document is from the British Ministry of Health," she said.

Hank looked at her in alarm. "The British? Have you been in touch with any of your counterparts in England?"

"No," said Jane looking at him curiously and wondering why he was upset about the possibility she had been talking to anyone in England. "I downloaded it from the Internet," she explained.

"Oh, I see," said Hank obviously relieved. "Ok, tell me, but please tell me in layman's terms. Remember, "'m just a military man."

Jane grinned at him. "Ha! Just a military man, indeed. You understand more than you let on, I'm sure of that."

"Maybe ..." said Hank pleasantly agreeing with her.

"All right, then. Pay attention, please," said Jane in a teasing tone. Then she grew serious. "From what I've learned, all three of them could be exhibiting symptoms of a variant of Mad Cow."

"Variant? What does that mean?" asked Hank.

"The Mad Cow Disease that affects cattle is different from the one that attacks humans and that is why they call it a variant."

"I see," said Hank. "You said it is not a virus? What is it then, and how do humans get it?"

"As you can see here," said Jane scrolling down to the second page of the document on the laptop, "Research has led the British to conclude that the disease is caused in cattle by an abnormal protein and humans get it by eating the infected meat."

"Because of an abnormal protein in the meat? How does that work?" asked Hank peering at the laptop screen.

"This abnormal protein is unlike regular proteins that multiply generically. Rather, the abnormal protein multiplies by converting good protein to its own type," she explained, pointing to a diagram on the screen.

"You mean something like cloning?" asked Hank.

"Exactly," said Jane with a smile. "You see, you know more than you let on."

Hank ignored that remark and sat back in his chair. "Well, how do these proteins kill people?"

"Just so you know, these cloned proteins are called prions," said Jane, "and these prions attack and kill brain cells which ultimately kills the person."

"What symptoms do the victims have?" asked Hank.

"Unsteadiness, insomnia and dementia are the most prominent symptoms. On the average, most people live six months after being diagnosed."

"Do you think the British theory is correct?" asked Hank.

Jane nodded. "Yes, it makes sense and I have no reason to doubt it. Besides the British have more experience with the disease and have conducted more research into its causes than we have."

"So the virus in humans comes from eating red meat that has these abnormal proteins ..." mused Hank.

"Yes, that's what the research shows. But remember, it is not a virus ... or bacteria for that matter," Jane reminded him. "That is because it does not multiply on its own; it mutates healthy protein."

"Not a virus ... yes, you said that before," said Hank. "You see I'm not so smart when it comes to medical terminology."

Jane smiled at him and shook her head. "You're not alone. Most people do think it's a virus. And really only someone with medical training would know the difference."

"Well that makes me feel a little better," said Hank with a grin. He put his hands on his knees and stood up. "Turn that thing off. It's time for a cup of coffee and a break from all the techno-medical stuff."

"That sounds great. I haven't had my shot of caffeine for the day," said Jane as she shut down the laptop.

While Hank went back to the galley, she put the laptop back in its case and then sat looking out to see if she could determine what part of the country they were flying over. She could not see the ground. All she could see was a blanket of clouds below them that looked like a giant puffy goose down quilt.

Hank returned balancing a tray with two large coffee mugs and a plate of two donuts. "Help yourself," he said holding the tray out to her. She took the cup with the black coffee and a jelly donut.

He looked down at the tray and frowned. "I was sure that you would want coffee with sugar and cream and a plain donut," he said. "Boy, was I wrong."

Jane laughed. "You've been around men too long, all sitting around perpetuating these myths about women."

Hank shook his head and went back to the galley. He threw out the coffee with cream, poured himself a cup of black coffee and exchanged the plain donut for a jelly one.

*   *   *

When the jet touched down at the Air Force base in Medford, Oregon, an officer in a staff car was waiting on the tarmac to meet them. As the Gulf Stream rolled to a stop the sun broke through an opening in the snow clouds that covered the sky. There had been a heavy snow shower just before the plane landed, and the tarmac was covered with a thin coat of melting snow.

When the door of the Gulf Stream opened the staff officer got out of the car and stood at attention. He saluted when he saw Hank emerge from the plane, and Hank returned the salute as he came down the ramp. Jane followed him, smiling at the staff officer.

"Good morning, General," said the officer as Hank walked up to the car. He stepped to the rear and opened the back door.

"Had some snow I see," said Hank as he climbed into the back seat, leaving Jane to climb in after him. The officer nodded slightly at her as she entered and then closed the door and got into the driver's seat.

"Have the plane ready in an hour," said Hank in a brisk voice. "And inform flight control my destination will be Kahlula Air Force Base on the island of Hawaii."

"Will there be any passengers, Sir?" asked the officer glancing at Jane in the rearview mirror. "I need to know what provisions to lay in, Sir," he explained when he saw Hank frowning at him in the mirror.

"Just one," said Hank tersely.

"Very well, Sir," said the officer. He released the footbrake and drove towards a large white building.

Hank did not speak during the drive, and Jane, taking his lead, remained silent also. When they arrived at the building, the driver held open the door, and Hank got out. He returned the officer's salute and strode rapidly toward the building. Jane scrambled to get out of the car and ran to catch up to him. She followed him into a large comfortable reception room.

Hank turned and motioned for her to take a seat in a comfortable armchair near a large stone fireplace where massive oak logs were burning.

"Would you like a late breakfast, Doctor?" asked Hank as he pushed a button on the wall across the room. It set off a buzzing noise.

"Sure, that would be nice. I would like ham and scrambled eggs and black coffee."

The buzzing stopped and a panel slid back revealing a smiling Hispanic man wearing a chef"s hat.

"Two large ham and eggs and two large black coffees. Make one order of eggs scrambled and the other sunny side up," said Hank.

"Yes, Sir," said the chef and the panel slid shut.

"I have a question, General," said Jane. He turned and nodded at her to continue. "Don't you have to file a passenger list with the flight plan?"

"No, Doctor," said Hank in a sharp tone. "I'm a general, and if you can't trust a general, who can you trust?"

Another Hispanic man dressed in a waiter's uniform entered the room through a door next to the sliding panel. Hank paced around the room, hands behind his back, and Jane sat staring into the fireplace while the waiter set a dining table in a corner of the room.

When the waiter left, Hank went over to the table and pulled out a chair. He motioned to Jane. "Time for chow, Doctor," he said.

Jane walked over to the table and was surprised to discover that the great high and mighty general was holding the chair out for her. Hank sat down opposite her, and the waiter immediately appeared with their food.

When the waiter disappeared again, Hank and Jane began to eat, remaining silent and avoiding eye contact throughout the meal. Hank seemed preoccupied, and Jane was at a loss for words, finding it difficult to talk to him when he was in his military mode.

When they finished, Hank led the way back to the fireplace holding his freshly filled coffee cup. Jane did the same and they sat in facing armchairs in front of the fire. While the waiter cleared the table, they sat sipping their coffee silently staring at the crackling logs in the fireplace. When he had gone, Jane looked at Hank. "Did I do something wrong, General?" she asked softly.

Hank looked at her in surprise and then glanced at the door across the room. He looked at her again and gave her one of his smiles. "No, Jane," he said in a very low voice. "I just have to keep up appearances and make sure no one overhears anything about our project. It is vital to the welfare of the country."

Jane surprised him by reaching over and squeezing his hand. "I understand why you are acting this way," she said in a near whisper, "even though I don't know the reason. I hope you will come to trust me enough to share the burden of this secrecy. It must be difficult carrying the whole load by yourself."

He looked directly into her eyes for a long moment. She did not flinch or look away. Finally, he smiled slightly and looked down at her hand in his. He squeezed it gently. "Yes, Jane. I will tell you when the time is right," he said.

*   *   *

Chapter 15

GEORGE AND PEGGY woke up to the sound of a knock on the door. "Message for Mr. Goater," called out a man in a singsong voice.

"Slide it under the door," yelled George in a grumpy voice.

"Message for Mr. Goater. It isn't written down," the voice persisted.

"Sod it!" said George. He got out of bed, looked down at himself and saw that he had not a stitch on. He hastily grabbed a pair of corduroy trousers lying on the floor and pulled them on as he hopped to the door.

He was still pulling up the zipper on the trousers when he opened the door. A very dark Bajan man dressed in a messenger's uniform stood grinning in at him. "Good afternoon, Mr. Goater," he said with a slight bow and an even broader grin. "I have a message for you from the hotel manager."

"Is it afternoon already?" asked George running a hand through his rumpled hair.

"Yes, Mr. Goater. It is two o'clock on the island of Barbados," said the man in his singsong voice.

"Must be jet lag," said George fuzzily.

"The Manager of the Royal Palms cordially invites you and your guest to a dinner party tonight at eight in the Queen Elizabeth Ballroom on the top floor," sang the messenger.

"Oh, that's the message from the manager? Thanks very much," said George in a relieved tone. He expected that any minute the management would discover the computer error and he would have to pay for his stay in this expensive hotel.

"I'"s black tie. No formal wear? Don't worry. Be happy. I can get formal wear for you," sang the Bajan again as he looked at George's crumpled trousers and bare chest.

"No, we didn't bring any formal wear. Thought we were staying at a cheaper place," said George.

"George!" shouted Peggy from the bed in an indignant voice. "Just tell the messenger we will call down later for the formal wear."

"Yes, Madam. Just call the valet's desk, and he will bring beautiful clothes," the messenger sang. He paused and looked at George.

"Is that all?" asked George.

"Yes, Mr. Goater, that is all the message," he sang. Then he stood there grinning at George.

George finally got the hint and reached into his pocket and pulled out a ten-penny piece. He gave it to the messenger. The man stood looking at the coin in his hand and then at George. "Ah, Mon, what is this? I don't recognize it," he said in a regular voice.

"It's a tenth of an English pound," said George.

"Not true, Mon. The English do not deal in pounds; they deal in kilos. I think you are playing a joke on me," said the messenger still beaming at him with his hand open.

"George, don't be stupid. Give the man fifty pee," shouted Peggy from the bed.

George reached in his pocket again and felt the coins inside. He felt a fifty pence coin and placed it in the messenger's hand. The man looked at the coin in his hand, grinned and walked off down the hall. As George was closing the door, he heard him singing, "Ten pee, fifty pee. It beats me. A dollar, yes - a pee, no. A dollar for a beer, not a pee for a beer, but beer will make you pee, pee, pee."

George took off his trousers and got back into bed.

"What is that, George?" asked Peggy, pointing at a small envelope on the bedside table on George's side of the bed.

"It must be a written invitation to the manager's party," said George picking up the envelope and handing it to Peggy. He frowned. "If we already had a written invitation, why did that messenger have to sing it to us?" He thought for a moment. "Probably to get a tip," he said, talking to himself.

Peggy opened the envelope and pulled out a small piece of paper. "George, you are wrong. It's not an invitation. It's some other kind of message scribbled down on a piece of notepaper. I don't see a signature," she said, turning the paper over and looking inside the envelope. "It doesn't say who it's from."

"Well, what does it say?" asked George in frustration.

"It says, 'I will meet you in the Coconut Lounge at seven tonight. Don''t worry about who I am. I will know you'."

"That's strange," said George. "Why don't they want to say who they are? And how did this message get into our room in the first place?"

Peggy shrugged as she examined the paper and the envelope again. "I haven't a clue," she said.

"Well, it looks as if we are going to stop off for drinks in the Coconut Lounge before we go to the manager's dinner. It will be interesting to see who turns up," said George. "Maybe it's the person who is paying our bill," he added as he lay down and put his head on the pillow. "Didn't realize this jet lag would affect me this way. I need more sleep, or I will be a dead fish tonight," he said closing his eyes.

Suddenly he felt something and his eyes snapped open. "Bloody hell, what are you doing?" he said.

Peggy came up from under the covers grinning. "I was just checking to see if you are a dead fish right now," she said.

"Oh, is that so?" said George with a grin. "Well, let's just see what the oyster is up to." He ducked under the covers. "It appears that when your oyster came out of its shell it never found its way back," he said when he came up for air.

"You are a dirty old man, George," said Peggy giggling as she threw the covers off the two of them. "I think it's time I went fishing."

Soon George was panting heavily. "That's enough! That's enough! Fishy wants to swim upstream and spawn now!"

"Hold on fish! Oyster wants to play some more," said Peggy as she straddled him. She introduced the fish to the oyster.

George lay transfixed, watching as Peggy rocked back and forth on top of him. "Fish is ready to spawn now!" he yelled. He rolled over on top of her.

After a bit he felt the oyster tighten around him and then relax. Peggy looked up at him. "What's going on? Are you done?" she asked as he continued to thrust.

"I'm still working on it, Peg," he said breathlessly, clinching his eyes shut and trying to concentrate.

"Hurry up then," she said looking bored. "I' m getting tired of this."

*   *   *

A little before seven George and Peggy took the elevator down to the lobby. Peggy was dressed in a beaded black evening gown and three-inch black satin stiletto heels. George was wearing a white linen dinner jacket with black trousers, cummerbund and bow tie. They had chosen these from a selection of formal wear that the valet had brought to their room.

"This place is like a palace," said Peggy, looking at the molded ceiling, the ornate light fixtures and the marble beneath their feet. "We'll be mixing with the rich and famous tonight."

"Well, I won't be seeing anyone that I know," said George. "If anyone does recognize me they will wonder how I can afford to stay here."

"Oh, for heaven's sake, George! Just say you have won the lottery," said Peggy in an exasperated tone.

They walked through the lobby and down some half-circular steps onto a stone terrace where they could see the moon's reflection in the ocean. Surrounding the terrace were dozens of palm trees with garlands of tiny lights wrapped around their trunks.

"Just look at this, George. Isn't it marvelous?" sighed Peggy.

"Yes, it is," said George. "There is nothing like this at Hastings."

"There's the Coconut Lounge," said Peggy pointing at a large open-air pavilion with a thatched roof. They could hear the lively music of a steel band playing nearby. "Let's find a seat."

They entered the Coconut Lounge and saw that it was filled with people wearing formal attire. "They must all have the same idea," mumbled George. "A drink before going to the manager's party."

They looked around for a table and found one that had recently been vacated near the bar.

A Bajan cocktail waitress dressed in a white and gold outfit walked up to their table. "Good evening, Sir and Madam, would you like a cocktail?" she asked as a young man dressed in white shorts and an azure blue shirt came over and began cleaning their table.

"How much are they?" asked George.

Peggy kicked him under the table. "Don't take notice of my friend, here. He's just joking," she said with a smile at the waitress.

"That's all right. I'm used to it. All our English guests ask that not realizing this resort is all-inclusive," said the waitress with a smile.

"All-inclusive?" asked George, rubbing his shin under the table.

"Yes, Sir. Food and beverages and resort activities are all included in your daily rate. There is no additional cost."

"You knew that, George," said Peggy kicking him on the shin again. George winced.

"He's all right. He suffers from indigestion, that's all," said Peggy with a wicked grin at George. "He likes oysters and sometimes he overindulges." She looked back at the waitress. "What drinks do you recommend?"

"The rum punch is excellent here, especially the *Caribbean Crackup* that has five kinds of rum plus curacao, triple sec, pernod, and a splash of chartreuse."

"The *Caribbean Crackup* sounds wonderful. We'll both have one," said Peggy without bothering to consult George.

The waitress went to the bar and soon returned with their order. She placed a glass the size of a fishbowl in front of each of them. They contained a blue liquid and a skewer of pineapple slices, lime peel and maraschino cherries plus a large clear plastic straw and a tiny paper umbrella. "This should get you off to a good start," said the waitress with a smile.

"It's not champagne, but it packs a punch," said Peggy noticing George looking skeptically at the drink.

George looked at Peggy suspiciously as she bent over her glass to take a sip of the drink through the straw. Why would she say that about champagne, he wondered? Did she know about his antics at the

Savoy? George took a sip of the punch through his straw still wondering about Peggy's remark. His thoughts were soon broken when a man dressed in a black tuxedo passed their table and then turned back to them.

"Is that Peggy Valentine?" he said, smiling down at Peggy.

Peggy looked up from her drink in surprise and then broke out in a smile. "Well, I never! If it isn't David Richmond," she said. "It's a pleasure seeing you again."

"You do look lovely this evening, Peggy," he said smiling at her. Then he looked across the table at George.

"David, this George Goater. George, this is David Richmond," said Peggy.

George stood up and shook David's hand and sat down again without saying a word.

"What brings you back to Barbados, Peggy?" asked David. "Is it business again?"

Peggy cocked an eyebrow at him. "Oh, David, you're mistaken. I've never been to Barbados before. You must be thinking of Jamaica. Remember? I saw you there when I was on holiday, not on business, three years ago."

David started to shake his head when he noticed Peggy's expression. She was looking intensely at him nodding her head slightly toward George. "Oh, yes," he said quickly. "It was in Jamaica and you were on holiday, not on business. Sorry, my error."

He turned quickly to George. "So what brings you to Barbados, Mr. Goater. Are you on holiday?"

"Not quite ...," said George and then he felt Peggy kicking him under the table again. "Oh, uh, yes ... on holiday," he finished.

"And what line of business are you in, Mr. Goater?" continued David.

"Oh, I'm a retired civil servant," said George matter-of-factly.

"I say, pensions must have improved for you to afford to stay here," said David with a snide grin.

"I won the lottery - ten million pounds," shouted George to be heard over the steel band, but at that moment, the band stopped playing and his voice carried throughout the lounge. The entire bar went silent, and people looked over at George's table. In a few minutes, they turned back to their own tables and the lounge buzzed with conversation again. George was red with embarrassment.

"Ten million. You are a lucky man, Mr. Goater," said David winking at Peggy.

"David, David," called out a feminine voice from two tables away.

David looked over and waved. "Coming, Love," he said in a voice loud enough for her to hear. "I must be off," he said in a lower voice turning back to George and Peggy. "I can't keep a beautiful lady waiting."

Just as he was about to leave, he looked at Peggy with a wicked grin. "By the way, are you still raising fish, Peggy?" he asked.

"Yes, and she is in the oyster business, too!" blurted out George before Peggy had a chance to say anything. He felt her foot stabbing his shin again.

"Aha!" said David, shaking his finger at Peggy. "I knew you were here on business," and with that he left.

After David was out of earshot, George glared at Peggy across the table. "So, does your friend like oysters, too?" he asked sarcastically.

"No. David is a surgeon, and he specializes in sex change operations. He is really a woman, you see. He's here to meet potential clients."

George's mouth fell open and he stared at Peggy, shocked. Peggy laughed at his reaction. "You see David and I both have oysters," she said laughing even harder.

"Were you ever a man?" asked George when he had recovered his composure.

This brought on another gale of laughter from Peggy that brought tears to her eyes. "Hell no! I've always had an oyster," she said, wiping her eyes.

"Well, something certainly seems to be humorous. What's the joke about oysters?" Another man dressed in a tuxedo with a blonde on his arm had stopped at their table and was smiling down at them.

It was Peggy's turn to be embarrassed. "Oh, nothing really. Just a private joke," she said. "Fancy seeing you again, Mr. Fleet, and in Barbados of all places."

"What's with this Mr. Fleet business? Call me Julian." He looked over at George. "I don't believe I've had the pleasure," he said extending his hand. "Julian Fleet here, and this is Lady Dimshire," he said indicating the young blonde thing on his arm.

"George Goater," said George, getting up and shaking Fleet's hand. "Your Ladyship," he said with a slight bow in the blonde's direction.

"Charmed, I'm sure," said Lady Dimshire in a shockingly high-pitched voice that grated on George's nerves.

"George Goater, the son of Bill Goater, of course," said Fleet, drawing George's attention away from the blonde. "I missed meeting you when I stopped in at your father's farm last week. I suppose Ms. Valentine told you?"

"Peggy," interjected Peggy looking up at Fleet adoringly.

He smiled down at her. "Peggy," he said. He looked back at George.

"Yes," said George. "Peggy told me. Said you are a friend of Dad's. I didn't know that. How did you meet?"

"Oh, it was when he was with the Commonwealth Office," said Fleet vaguely. "I do hope he is recovering from his heart attack?"

"He seems to be getting better, but he's not out of the woods yet," said George. He wrinkled his brow. "By the way, Mr. Fleet, I've been meaning to ask you how you knew about my retirement party at the Savoy and my rented tuxedo."

Fleet waved a hand elegantly, showing off a diamond and onyx cufflink. "Oh, I have a suite at the Savoy. I'm there nearly every night, you know, and I always know what goes on."

George opened his mouth to ask more questions, but Peggy jumped in. "Why don't you join us, Julian?" she asked still looking up adoringly at Fleet.

"It would be an honor, Peggy. All right by you, my dear?" he asked patting Lady Dimshire's arm.

"Charmed, I'm sure," she said in the same high-pitched tone that set George's teeth on edge, but it didn't seem to bother Fleet.

George got up and moved to the seat next to Peggy so that Fleet would be facing her and he would be facing Her Ladyship.

"Are you here on holiday or business, Mr. Fleet?" asked George when they were settled at the table. He was irritated to see that both of the women were looking at Fleet with stars in their eyes.

"Please call me Julian. I'm here for a bit of both, George - a little of this and a little of that," he said with a twinkle in his eye that caused the blonde to giggle and Peggy to blush.

"I see, ... a mixture of business and pleasure," said George trying to keep the conversation going.

"More pleasure than business," said the blonde with another giggle.

"And what sort of business are you in, Your Ladyship, or are you on holiday also?" asked George grinning at her and getting in the spirit of things. He took another long sip of his *Caribbean Crackup*.

"Don't be so out of it, George," said Peggy frowning at George who was still grinning at the blonde. "Everyone knows Her Ladyship is a fashion model. In fact, I saw on the notice board by the lift that she is modeling swim wear at the Grecian Pool tomorrow."

"She certainly is," said Fleet enthusiastically.

"Yes, and Julian has already seen the collection," said Her Ladyship with another giggle. "I gave him a special viewing this morning."

"From what I've read about Mr. Fleet, I didn't think he was interested in seeing ladies with clothes on," said George, laughing at his own attempt at a joke. He felt a tremendous kick just below his knee.

"Take no notice of George. He has had too much to drink," said Peggy in an apologetic tone.

Fleet smiled. "No harm done. In fact I found it rather humorous," he said, which set off another bout of giggling from Her Ladyship.

Her Ladyship looked across the table at George and batted her eyelashes. "I heard you say you won ten million on the lottery. Therefore, you can call me Zoë," she said.

George was getting set to explain about the lottery when Fleet glanced at his watch. "Well, I'm afraid we must be off now. We are invited to the manager's party, and it starts at eight."

"We are invited, too," said Peggy as Fleet stood up. "Perhaps you can show us the way?"

"It would be a pleasure," said Fleet as he held out his arm to Peggy.

Fleet had Peggy on one side and Zoë on the other, and they walked out of the bar. George quickly sucked down the rest of his drink, jumped up and followed. They seemed to have forgotten all about him. Fleet was talking and each of the women were looking up at him, hanging on his every word. "Totally disgusting," muttered George as he brought up the rear.

When they stepped off the lift on the top floor, they heard the beat of reggae music. As they walked toward the double doors of the Queen Elizabeth Ballroom, George realized the music was coming from within. A huge Bajan dressed in the white and gold uniform of the resort stood at the door and smiled broadly as they approached.

"Good evening, Mr. Fleet," he said cordially as Julian passed through the door with Peggy and Zoë on his arms.

George attempted to follow, but the Bajan stepped in front of him, blocking the entrance. He held out his white-gloved hand. "May I see your invitation, Sir?" he said.

"Peggy - one of the ladies with Mr. Fleet - has it," said George pointing into the ballroom.

"Which one?" asked the doorman. "The older blonde or the younger one?"

"The older one," said George embarrassed that people were now queuing up behind him.

The doorman motioned to a young woman dressed in a black suit with a gold nametag. When she came over, the doorman whispered something to her, and she looked at George and nodded. Then she disappeared into the ballroom.

"Would you mind stepping aside for a moment, Sir, while we verify your invitation," said the doorman.

George stood out of the way near the door and waited for the young woman to return, and then it dawned on him that they did not have a written invitation. The messenger had simply told them they were invited, but had left nothing with them to present at the door.

He went to the doorman again to try to explain, but before he could say anything, the doorman shook his head. "Sorry, Sir. No admittance without a written invitation."

"That's what I just came to tell you," said George. "It's true there was no printed invitation, but a messenger came to our door this afternoon and invited us with a singing telegram of sorts."

The doorman started chuckling. "Oh, I am truly sorry, Sir, but that was Silly Billy. He's not quite right in the head, and he likes to dress up and play these practical jokes on our guests," said the doorman twirling a finger at his ear. "We try to keep him out of the hotel, but somehow he manages to get in from time to time. I'm sorry, but I can't admit you without a written invitation."

"But my friend is already inside," said George raising his voice. "If she can get in why can't I?"

"The hostess asked both ladies if they knew you and they said they didn't," said the doorman impatiently. "I'm afraid you'll have to leave now."

"But Mr. Fleet knows me. Ask him," said George in desperation. The doorman looked at him, rolled his eyes and motioned to the young woman in black again. She came over and he whispered to her. She looked at George with a raised eyebrow, and then turned and went into the ballroom.

"Stand here, Sir," said the doorman, pointing to a spot just outside the door so that the other guests could get by.

George stood there impatiently shifting his weight from one leg to the other. "Bloody balls up," he muttered. After what seemed an eternity, George saw the young woman walking towards the ballroom door, and just behind her was Julian Fleet.

Fleet walked up to him. "Having difficulties?" he asked.

"Some crazy person played a joke on us," said George angrily. "He told us we were invited but did not leave a printed invitation."

"A practical joke," said Fleet shaking his head. "A shame you had to wait all this time. Come with me," he said. As they passed the doorman, Fleet said, "This gentleman is with me." The doorman grinned at George as they walked into the ballroom.

George followed Fleet as he wound his way through a crowd of people to a table where Peggy and Lady Dimshire were seated.

"Where have you been George?" asked Peggy when George sat down.

He glared at her. "Thanks for nothing," he said. "At least you could have said you knew me."

Peggy looked at him in surprise. "What do you mean? That's a funny thing for you to say."

"Why didn't you tell the hostess that you knew me?"

"What hostess? I wasn't asked anything by any hostess," she said.

George started to say more about the incident, but Lady Dimshire leaned across to him giving him a bird's eye view of her cleavage and patting him on the arm. "You have some catching up to do," she said with a giggle. "We've had two glasses of champagne already." She smiled and George felt a silken toe rubbing up and down his right leg under his trousers.

George was mesmerized at the sight of her ample breasts that seemed about to pop out of the top of her gown at any moment. He decided her voice wasn't so grating after all.

*   *   *

At nine the next morning George awoke to find himself alone in the king-sized bed. He lifted his pounding head off the pillow long enough to see if Peggy's side of the bed was rumpled. It was not. He carefully laid his throbbing head back down on the pillow, pulled the sheet up over his head and in a few seconds was sound asleep again.

At ten o'clock a loud pounding on the door woke him again. He did not come out from under the sheet, hoping whoever was out there would go away. The pounding continued even louder, and then he heard Peggy shouting.

"George, are you in there?" she yelled. "Open this door immediately!"

George rubbed his blurry eyes and stumbled out of bed naked. Keeping his balance by holding onto the furniture, he slowly inched his way to the door.

"George!" Peggy yelled, sending a bolt of pain through his head.

"Sod off!" he called out weakly. "Go back to where you have come from and leave me in peace."

"George, I am telling you to open this door, or I will get hotel security up here to do it!"

"Bugger!" muttered George as he leaned against the wall and clutched his head with one hand and opened the door slowly with the other.

Peggy burst into the room still in her evening gown. "What a fine chap you are!" she yelled, pointing at his bare body. "You embarrassed the hell out of me, you twerp!"

George did not answer. Still clutching his head with one hand, he felt his way along the furniture back to the bed where he stumbled in and pulled the sheet up over his head.

"Never until my dying day will I ever forget you and your despicable performance! You are the crudest person I've ever known. You embarrassed everyone!" Peggy marched over to the bed and snatched the sheet away from George. "What do you have to say for yourself, you miserable sod!"

George put his hands over his face, opened one eye and peered through his fingers. "What did I do?" he asked weakly.

"You got up on the stage and talked through the microphone about me and oysters and fish swimming upstream to spawn, that's what!" Peggy's face had turned red with anger and embarrassment. "It was utterly despicable! Even Julian and Zoë laughed at me. I was made a fool of, the laughing stock of the party. I shall never be able to show my face again. You rat!"

"I don't remember anything about it," mumbled George still looking at her through his fingers.

"You would say that! Don't try and make excuses. Surely you remember falling off the stage right onto someone's table and having to be carried out of the room by two security guards! And you were still shouting about oysters all the way out of the ballroom. Oh, I will never ever forgive you for that!"

"It must have been the champagne," said George in a meek voice. "It goes straight to my head."

"Not to your head, stupid! To your mouth! Oysters indeed!" Peggy had worked herself up into a frenzy. Her face was a livid red.

George slowly removed his hands from his face and looked at her with a miserable expression. "I don't know what to say, Peg, except that I am sorry and I didn't know what I was doing. I didn't mean to embarrass you. Where did you stay last night?"

"I spent most of the night watching Lady Dumb Shit cozy up to Julian. What a bimbo! I can't see what Julian sees in her."

"Perhaps he likes her oyster," said George without thinking.

"You little turd!" yelled Peggy, taking her spiked heel off and thrashing him with it. "Take that!"

"Stop, Peg! That hurts!" said George, covering up as much of his exposed body as he could with his arms.

Peggy abruptly turned away and walked to the other side of the bed. "Anyway, I'm packing my things and moving in with a lady friend. I don't want any more to do with you. From now on you can keep yourself company, you little pipsqueak," she said in a slightly calmer voice.

George took the opportunity to cover himself with the sheet again. "What about the research? Are you going to dump that too?"

"I have a good mind to, but it wouldn't be ethical - too many lives at stake. I will continue, and I expect you to do your share."

"Yes, I will help as much as I can," said George, relieved that she seemed to be calming down.

Peggy whirled around and pointed a finger at him from the other side of the bed. "I want to make it clear there will be no more sex! From now on our relationship will be strictly professional. Do you understand?"

George nodded and cowered under the sheet as Peggy hastily packed her things. When she finished, she picked up her bag and strode to the door where she turned on him again. "I'll leave the laptop and the analyzer here. This suite is going to be our office, so you'd better be up early.

From now on, we keep normal office hours, and another thing – get your arse out of bed! You''ve been in Barbados nearly two days, and not one ounce of sunshine has fallen on you!"

George sat up in bed. "This new arrangement suits me just fine," he said becoming peeved at her attitude. "What is your friend's name and room number, in case I need to get hold of you - strictly for business reasons, of course," he asked sarcastically.

"David in Room 107," said Peggy smugly.

"David, the sex change surgeon?" gasped George.

"Yes, that's right. As you recall, he has an oyster, too."

George gasped again. "What? You mean you have hooked up with another oyster?"

"That's right, George. I'm in the mood for oysters now. Much better than your miserable old smelly minnow," she said as she walked out the door slamming it behind her.

George sank back on the pillow and sulked. He was revolted at the revelation that Peggy was a switch hitter and he had slept with her. Then he remembered Yin and Yang and shrank down in the bed closing his eyes. After a few moments, he suddenly sat up chuckling out loud. What in the world was going on? In the past week or so he'd had more kinky sexual experiences than he'd had in his entire life. Even though he couldn't remember the kinkiest one, he reminded himself.

He was reminiscing about waking up in bed at the Savoy with Yin and Yang, when his mobile phone rang. George picked it up from the bedside table and hesitantly pushed the receive button.

"Hello, George." Peter Jones's face appeared on the tiny video screen.

George took a deep breath and turned off the video function. "Hello, Mr. Jones. I was just about to go down for breakfast," said George forgetting about the time difference.

"Breakfast? At this time of evening?" queried Jones.

"That's right," said George quickly. "I like breakfast for supper, if you know what I mean."

There was an awkward pause, and then Jones laughed. "Yes, yes, I get your meaning. Quite funny, that. But on to business - I have some important news."

"Yes?" asked George eagerly.

"First, Denise Downing was taken to America."

George frowned. "That's not news. You told me that already."

"That's right, George, but I didn't tell you where in America."

"Where then?" asked George rubbing his right temple in an effort to stop the throbbing.

"She was flown to Green Gate, an abandoned Air Force base close to Washington, D.C."

"Who took her there?" asked George in surprise.

"I don't know yet, but I am working on it," said Jones.

George held the mobile phone up and looked at it. It seemed to have gone dead. "Are you still there, Mr. Jones?" he asked, putting the phone back to his ear.

"Yes. The other news is that Denise Downing's uncle Roger was taken to Stonehurst Air Base in an unmarked car in the middle of the night."

George sat up straight. "What? Stonehurst Air Base, you say?" He frowned and tried to remember. Wasn't that the name of the air base where Lord Bonderbrook had been taken after his heart attack?

"That's right, Stonehurst. It's a secure base. Armed patrols, no one in except higher ups, that type of thing."

"What is Roger Clemens doing there?"

"I don't know that yet either, but I will find out," said Jones. "By the way, I'm pleased your Dad is recovering from his heart attack. Not able to speak yet, but much better just the same, what?"

"My father! How did you find out about that?" asked George suspiciously.

"That was easy, George. William Goater, formerly of the Commonwealth Office, is your father, is he not? There was an article about his condition in *The Times*."

"Thank you for the news about Dad," said George relieved.

"But that shouldn't be news to you, George, what with you being right there at the farm and close to Bridgefield."

George's right temple began to throb again. "That's right, I did know. I read the same article in *The Times.*" George grimaced as he realized he'd made another blunder. "That is, the article just confirmed what the doctor had told me," he added lamely. "Is there anything else, Mr. Jones? I'm in a bit of a hurry as I can hear the kettle boiling in the kitchen."

"Nothing more right now, George, but I will call you again the moment I find out any more."

"Right, then. Thanks for calling and I'll look forward to hearing from you," said George.

"Cheerio, then. Enjoy the sunshine," said Jones and switched off the connection.

George looked at his mobile phone with a frown. What did that crack about the sunshine mean? Did Jones know he was in Barbados?

George didn't dwell on it. It was probably the hangover making him overly sensitive, he thought. He struggled out of bed and into the shower. After a long hot shower, he had a careful shave and dressed in dark Bermuda shorts, a multi-striped Rugby shirt and sandals.

He found his way out of the lobby and looked for directions to a restaurant that was serving breakfast. He looked around and noticed a bar on the other side of a huge swimming pool with a waterfall. He made his way down the half-circular steps from the lobby, around the pool and towards the bar. Along the way, he noticed people glancing at him and turning to whisper to their companions. He overheard a man in a blue bathing suit saying the word *oyster* to another man in a Panama hat and olive green shorts. By the time he arrived at the bar he was red from embarrassment.

He found a secluded table in a corner overlooking the white sandy beach. He looked straight ahead at the sand and ocean, not daring to look around.

A few minutes later a Bajan cocktail waitress dressed in the familiar white and gold outfit beamed down at him. "Good morning, Mr. George. Would you like a beverage?"

"Just breakfast please," answered George politely.

"Sorry, Mr. George. Breakfast is not served in the bar. It is being served up there on the terrace," she said pointing to the other side of the pool.

"My mistake," murmured George getting up from the table. Now he had to endure walking the gauntlet again all along the other side of the pool. He looked straight ahead, trying to ignore the grins, whispers and snickers as he walked by dozens of sunbathers on his way to the terrace.

The terrace was crowded, and George looked about for another secluded table, but the only vacant table he saw was right in the center of the terrace. As he was considering what to do, an obese boy who was sitting with two adults at a nearby table pointed at him. "Look, Dad, it's the oyster man!" he shouted.

George quickly turned around and stepped behind a palm tree as heads all around the terrace swiveled in his direction. He was staring down into the pot that held the palm when he felt a tap on his shoulder.

"Good morning, George," said the unmistakable voice of Julian Fleet. "Why don't you come and join us?"

George cautiously turned around to face Fleet who was resplendent in white linen trousers, black and white silk shirt, and Armani sunglasses.

"I don't want to cause you any embarrassment," he said looking down at his feet.

"Not at all, old chap," said Fleet clapping him on the shoulder. "Here, walk with me. Our table is just over there."

George looked where he pointed and saw Zoë sitting at a table under an umbrella in the far corner of the terrace. He swallowed hard and nodded at Fleet. "All right, then," he said, bracing himself for the walk.

Fleet led the way as if parting the waters. He smiled and nodded at the other diners as he walked by, and they were so thrilled to be noticed by Fleet that they paid no attention at all to George.

"Hello, George," said Zoë, giggling and motioning for him to sit next to her. "You are quite famous today."

"Notorious is the more appropriate word, eh George?" said Fleet with a chuckle as he sat down on the other side of Zoë.

"But tell me, George, what your oyster joke meant. I didn't understand it," said Zoë looking at him with her big blue eyes. "Especially the part about the fish swimming upstream. What do fish have to do with oysters anyway?"

Fleet looked at George with a grin. "Zoë, love, I think George is tired of talking about oysters. I'll explain it to you later."

Zoë looked at Fleet adoringly. "All right, Julikins. I love the way you explain things."

George looked down at the menu and decided he was in dire need of a Bloody Mary, maybe two or three. The waitress came and Fleet ordered mimosas for Zoë and himself and a Bloody Mary for George. When the waitress brought their drinks, they ordered the standard English breakfast with tea.

"What are your plans for today, George?" asked Fleet after they'd all taken sips of their drinks.

"I think I will lie on the beach and get some sun."

"Be careful not to get a sunburn," said Zoë. "There's nothing worse than being in bed with a sunburn. You need a cover-up. I always wear mine," she said, pointing down at the see-through gold mesh that she was wearing over a gold lame bikini.

George stared at her breasts barely contained by the skimpy bra underneath the cover-up that covered nothing up.

"Do you like it?" she asked noticing George staring.

"Like what?" asked George guiltily as he quickly looked up.

"The cover-up of course, you silly boy," she said swatting him playfully on the arm.

"That? Oh, yes," said George. "I don't have a cover-up. Perhaps you'd loan me yours," he teased, starting to feel better after several swigs of the Bloody Mary.

"But then what would I wear?" she asked with a coquettish smile.

"Your other suit, of course," said Julian, winking at George.

Zoë looked up at Julian. "What other suit?" she asked innocently.

"You know," said Julian looking at her seriously. "Your birthday suit."

Zoë sat staring at him with a puzzled look for several seconds as Julian looked at her with a deadpan expression. Suddenly, she smiled and swatted him on the arm. "Oh, I get it, Julian. You're so naughty!"

After breakfast, George headed toward the beach, while Julian and Zoë headed for the lobby. They had told George they were going on a tour of the island and would be back in the late afternoon.

As he walked down onto the crowded white sandy beach, George found a beach chair under a large sun umbrella. He took off his Rugby shirt and sandals and lay down on his back on the chair. He watched bikini clad women playing in the surf for a while and then watched the couples lying together in the sand. He yawned, his eyelids drooped and soon he was fast asleep.

About an hour later he awoke to find Philip, the limo driver, standing over him.

"Hello, Mr. George. How are you today?"

George blinked in the bright sunlight and shaded his eyes with his hand. "Well, hello, Philip. What are you doing here? Are you a beach boy as well as a limo driver?"

"No," said Philip looking around. He looked back at George. "Sorry I missed you last night, Mr. George," he said in a low voice. "At the last minute I had to pick up someone at the airport and I didn't get back to the hotel until seven-thirty. When I came into the lounge, you were busy talking to another couple at your table so I didn't interrupt."

"But you are here now, Philip," said George, not understanding what Philip was talking about. "Why don't you take a seat?" he added, pointing to a nearby empty sun chair.

"Where is Ms. Peggy?" Philip asked, looking around again as he drew up the empty chair.

"Peggy has found a new friend," answered George sarcastically. "She makes friends easily."

"I see," said Philip, looking around again. "I'd better be going then."

"Come and sit down and I'll buy you a beer, Philip," said George waving at the empty chair.

"It's kind of you, Mr. George, but I don't have much time." Philip sat down and looked uneasily around the crowded beach. "I checked around with some boys I used to go to school with and I have some information about Denise Downing," he said out of the corner of his mouth as he continued to look around the beach. "I wanted to pass it along to Ms. Peggy."

"You can tell me, Philip," said George sitting up on the side of his chair. "I will tell Peggy when I see her later today."

Philip did not look at George. He said in a low voice that George strained to hear, "Denise's grandparents are still alive, and they live in Speightstown."

"Her mother's parents or her fathe'"'s?" asked George.

"Her mother's," said Philip still looking straight ahead.

"How can we find them, Philip?"

"Very easy, Mr. George. They live in a house directly on the beach. It is a very old house and needs repairs and the purple paint is peeling off. You can't miss it, Mr. George. It is just before you get to Speightstown on the beach between two new hotels - the Virgin Nights and the Happy Caribbean Days."

"What are their names?"

"Malcolm and Beth Downing. They are very old, Mr. George, and may be forgetful."

"How do we get to Speightstown?"

"That's easy, Mr. George. Just walk north on the beach for about ten minutes." Philip got up and dusted the sand off his trousers. "I must get back to the car now, Mr. George," he said. "I'm not allowed to be on the beach or to talk to the guests."

Philip turned to walk away and then looked back at George with a worried expression. "Please don't tell anyone except Ms. Peggy what I told you," he said in a low voice. Then he smiled and said in a normal voice, "Be sure to keep out of the full sun, Mr. George."

George nodded and watched as Philip walked away.

"Bugger! Why all the mystery?" wondered George.

George lay back in the sun chair contemplating what to say to Peggy. As he thought of Peggy, he grew peeved again at her dumping him for the sex change surgeon who was really a woman. Then he began to feel sorry for himself. After all it was his idea to come to Barbados and now he was alone and had no female companionship. He looked around the beach again. Everywhere he looked there were couples, and he was alone. Perhaps he would feel better after another nap. He closed his eyes.

By mid-day the shadow of the umbrella had shifted exposing George to the full strength of the Barbados sun, but he slept on.

"Wake up, Sir. You are getting sunburned. I have something to put on it," said a masculine voice interrupting George's dream about a dead fish that had washed up on the beach and was frying in the sun.

George tried to open his eyes, but his eyelids protested painfully. He tried again and found himself squinting up into the bright sun. He tried to sit up, but the tight burning sensation of his broiled skin caused him to gasp and lay down again.

"Don't move, Sir," said the voice. As George squinted up painfully, he saw that it belonged to a Bajan man who was wearing a white tee shirt bearing the hotel's insignia in gold. The Bajan adjusted the umbrella so that it shaded George's chair again. Then he knelt down in the sand beside the chair. "I have ointment to relieve the pain."

George caught his breath as the Bajan gently smeared a clear thick ointment on his shoulders, arms, chest, stomach, legs and feet. It felt icy cold on his burning skin, and then the burning sensation lessened considerably as the ointment penetrated. "And now your face, Sir."

George closed his eyes as he felt the cooling ointment on his neck, face and eyelids. That is why he neither saw nor felt the Bajan slip a packet into the pocket of his shorts.

"Does that feel better, Sir?"

George opened his eyes and saw the man standing over him. He sat up cautiously and flexed his shoulders as he looked down at his red skin. "Absolutely. Whatever that is, it certainly did the trick. I don't feel the sunburn at all now."

"We like to take of our guests, Sir," said the Bajan, holding out a large plastic bottle about half full of the clear white gel. "This is aloe, the best thing for burns. Take this and put it on every two hours, and your burn will be gone by morning."

"Thanks very much," said George gratefully as he took the ointment.

"Are you English, Sir?" asked the Bajan with a grin.

"That's right," said George.

"That accounts for it then. Only mad cows and Englishmen lay out in the mid-day sun." He bent over and slapped his thigh, laughing at his joke.

George laughed at the Bajan. "That's right, but you've got it slightly wrong: I'"s 'Only mad *dogs* - not cows - and Englishmen go out in the noonday sun'."

"Oh, right, Sir!" said the Bajan laughing even harder. George joined him. They were laughing so hard that nearby sunbathers looked over wondering what the joke was.

"Now, don't forget to put that aloe on again in a couple of hours," said the Bajan, as he turned to walk back up the beach.

"Thanks very much!" called George after him, and the Bajan waved a hand behind his back as he walked away.

George watched him go. Then he slowly sat up and swung his legs over to the side of the chair. In doing so, he didn't notice the packet that fell out of his shorts pocket and down through the slats in the beach chair into a depression in the sand. After he had put on his sandals, George slowly got up from the chair. In doing so, the chair moved in the sand and buried the packet lying beneath it.

George put his Rugby shirt back on and walked back up to the bar by the swimming pool. This time he found a seat at the bar and ordered a Banks beer. He sat drinking the beer straight out of the bottle and gazing into the mirror over the bar in front of him. He gritted his teeth. In the mirror he saw Peggy walking towards him.

"Hello, George. I see you have had too much sun. Does it hurt?" she asked as she climbed up on the white leather barstool next to him.

"Why aren't you with David, your lady friend?" asked George still looking at her in the mirror with a snide grin.

"Stop it, George. I just came over to see if you are all right. I'm concerned about you. You looked terrible this morning and now you are badly sunburnt."

"The hangover is gone and the sunburn looks worse than it is. One of the beach lads rubbed this ointment on me - aloe, I think it's called." He showed her the plastic bottle. "Great stuff. It really took the sting out of the burn."

"Well, I'm pleased to hear that, George, because you are red as a beet," said Peggy.

"It's your fault," said George. "You're the one who told me to get my arse out of bed and get some sun, as I recall."

"Will you stop, George? Let bygones be bygones. We have work to do together, after all," said Peggy. "Which reminds me. Who do you think sent us the note about meeting us in the Coconut Lounge at seven last night? Do you think it was David or Julian?"

"No ...," George started and then stopped short. He snapped his fingers and turned to her with a smile. "No. It wasn't either of them, but I know who it was!"

"Well, out with it!" said Peggy as George sat there grinning and taking a swig of his beer.

"It was Philip," he said with a mysterious smile.

"Philip?"

"Yes, Philip the driver, remember?"

"Oh, him," said Peggy. "How do you know it was Philip?"

"He came over to me while I was on the beach. Said he had to pick up some people at the airport and didn't get back until seven-thirty. Said he looked in at the lounge, but we were talking to another couple at our table, so he didn't interrupt. He's the one who sent us the note as it turns out."

George took another long sip of beer as Peggy looked at him impatiently. "Well, what did he want?" she asked.

"He said he asked around and found out Denise Downing's grandparents are still alive and they live just along the beach. They are her mother's parents, and their names are Malcolm and Beth Downing."

Peggy frowned. "Downing? So, Downing is her mother's maiden name after all."

"That's what we suspected, isn't it? That Denise's mother was not married when she was born and that's why the father's name is not known?" asked George.

"Yes, that's right," said Peggy still looking puzzled, and then she shrugged her shoulders. "That's the only explanation. Well, we must go and visit these grandparents. Perhaps they can shed some light on who her father is."

"Tomorrow morning suits me fine, but what about you?" asked George. "Do you have plans?"

"No plans for tomorrow, George. David has patients all day, and I will be free to go with you."

"Free?" asked George with a snort. "What does she do? Keep you handcuffed to the bed?"

"Don't be crude, George," sniffed Peggy as the barman walked up.

"Banks beer for the lady?" asked the barman smiling.

George nodded. "And another for me, too," he said.

"May we join you?" asked a voice behind them that made Peggy's face light up.

George glanced in the mirror and saw that Julian and Zoë were walking toward them. He turned around on his bar seat just as the barman walked back with the two Banks beers. "Ho, back from your island tour I see," said George with a smile.

"Welcome, Mr. Fleet," said the barman. "Will it be the usual?"

"Yes, Timothy. Two Black Jamaicans over ice, and be sure it's over, not under."

Zoë giggled as she looked at George. "Oh, George! You certainly have a sunburn. Does it hurt?"

"Only when someone mentions it," said George grinning at her.

"I have something that will make you feel better," said Zoë reaching in her large gold beach bag and pulling out a plastic bottle of baby oil.

"I already have some wonderful stuff," said George, smiling and showing her his bottle of aloe. "It's called aloe, and it really cools the skin."

"Oh, really?" said Zoë, looking at the baby oil. "What I have normally heats things up." She looked at George and giggled and George and

Julian both laughed while Peggy looked away pretending she hadn't heard.

The barman brought the Black Jamaicans. "Over not under, just the way you like," he said handing them to Fleet.

"Thank you, my good man," said Fleet handing one of the drinks to Zoë. He raised his glass. "Here's to fun in the Barbados sun," he said, and they all raised their drinks and took a sip.

"What plans does everyone have for tonight?" asked Peggy casually as she placed her beer bottle on the bar.

"Unfortunately, I have a business engagement that may last until midnight," said Fleet looking down into his drink.

"What?" exclaimed Zoë, looking at him with wide eyes. "I thought you were taking me to that Italian restaurant in Holetown for dinner."

"I'm sorry, Zoë," said Fleet smiling at her sympathetically. "I only found out a short while ago. I promise to take you to the Italian place tomorrow night."

Zoë's eyes turned cloudy with disappointment and her bottom lip protruded in a pout.

"A bit of a letdown, I should say," observed George.

Fleet looked at George and then at Peggy and smiled. "What about you, old man," he said, turning back to George. "Any plans for tonight?"

"I was thinking of having an early night. All that sun made me tired."

"Sun, my foot," said Peggy. "You're still suffering from a hangover from last night's drinking."

All of them laughed as George looked down with a sheepish grin. Zoë leaned close to him and stroked his arm. "Would you take me to the Italian restaurant tonight, George?" she asked in a little girl voice.

George looked up at Fleet.

Fleet grinned. "Splendid idea," he said enthusiastically. "Be my guest, George. You and Zoë have a splendid time. I don't like to disappoint Her Ladyship."

The sun immediately broke through the clouds in Zoë's eyes and she beamed at Fleet and then at George. "Oh, brilliant! Thank you ever so much, Julian. Oh, we'll have such a good time, George," she babbled.

"And what about you, Peggy? Do you and David have plans?" asked Fleet.

"No, David is having dinner with potential clients, and I have no plans to speak of," said Peggy with a downcast look.

"Well, now, Peggy, I shouldn't despair," said Fleet, his eyes sparkling. "It's early yet. You're in Barbados, and anything can happen." He smiled and Peggy looked up at him and returned the smile.

"That is for sure," said George. "I never thought I'd get a sun tan so quickly or be escorting a Lady to dinner either."

*   *   *

Chapter 16

W HEN THE GULF Stream touched down at Kahlula Air
Force Base on the Big Island of Hawaii, the sun was high in the sky.
During the second leg of the flight from Medford, Jane had elaborated
on her theories about how the Mad Cow variant affected humans and
what potential cures might be developed. Hank listened intently to
what she had to say. He found her theories fascinating, and as he listened,
he began to realize that he was becoming more and more fascinated
with the doctor herself. He found it more and more difficult to tear his
gaze away from the gold-flecked green pools of her eyes, and he caught
himself wondering what lay beneath that safari outfit.

After the plane landed and began to taxi, Jane looked out the window at the
air base bathed in the bright glow of the mid-day sun. As Hank turned the
plane at the end of the runway and headed for a dark green building that
resembled a plantation house, Jane looked over at him in surprise. "This base
looks as if it is deserted," she said.

Hank looked over at her. "In this case, looks are not deceiving.
Kahlula is an abandoned base. I was stationed here when it was
operational thirty-five years ago. Haven't been back since, but when
we decided we had to come to the Big Island, I thought it would be the
perfect place to stay for security reasons. No one will know we're here,
and we can conduct our search without fear of discovery."

"You mean there's no one here?" asked Jane somewhat
apprehensively.

Hank grinned. "That's right. We have the place all to ourselves.
The only personnel in the area is a small detachment of Army Military

Police who guard the perimeter to make sure no one gets in just in case there's any unexploded ordnance or other hazardous materials."

"But don't they patrol the base itself?"

Hank shook his head. "No, they just patrol the perimeter, which is enclosed by an electric twelve-foot chain link fence topped off with four more feet of barbed wire. They do not have clearance to enter the base itself, but in case they did, I would just pull rank on them anyway."

"But if it's abandoned, how will we ..."

"Eat, sleep and so forth?" asked Hank anticipating her question. Jane nodded.

"Don't worry. I've taken care of everything," he said. "That's what all those boxes are in the cargo bay - food and supplies for a month's stay if necessary. All I need to do is turn on the electricity and the water, and voila, all the comforts of home."

"Sounds as if you've thought of everything," said Jane still looking skeptical as Hank pulled the plane up close to the plantation-style building.

"Welcome to the Hotel Kahlula," he said as he cut the engines.

"What is this building?" asked Jane.

"The commanding officer's headquarters," said Hank with a grin. "Since we have the place to ourselves, might as well stay in the most comfortable place."

Hank unbuckled his seat belt and got up. "Come on, Doctor. I'll have you set up for business in no time, and then we can have dinner. Steak tonight," he added.

"What about the plane?" asked Jane as she started to unbuckle her seat belt. "Aren't you afraid someone might spot it from the air or even from the perimeter?"

"Not much chance of that," said Hank. "But just in case, I'll park it in that empty hangar over there after we're finished unloading."

Jane looked out the window in the direction Hank had indicated and saw a corrugated steel hangar about one hundred yards from the commanding officer's quarters. She nodded and began to relax slightly. Hank seemed to have everything under control.

She followed him back to the cargo bay and picked up her two small bags. He picked up the two larger ones and led the way to the exit door. Hank opened the door and lowered the ramp. He stepped out.

"It's been a long day. I'm really looking forward to a bath ..." remarked Jane as she followed him out onto the ramp. She never finished her comment as she ran into Hank who had stopped abruptly in front of her.

"What's wrong?" she asked, as he stood frozen in front of her halfway down the exit ramp. She looked around his shoulder to see what he was looking at. At the bottom of the ramp stood two ancient Chinese men dressed identically in black pajama-style pants and long-sleeved jackets with mandarin collars. They both wore sandals on their feet and straw coolie hats over long wispy gray-streaked hair on their heads. They stood with arms crossed in front of them, their hands tucked inside the sleeves of their jackets.

"What the hell," muttered Hank. He slowly continued walking down the ramp with Jane hesitantly bringing up the rear.

As he neared the bottom, one of the men stepped forward and kowtowed. "Welcome to Kahlula," he said in a very pronounced Chinese accent.

"Thank you," said Hank, stepping onto the pavement and putting down the bags. "And who may I ask are you?"

"I am Chih Chong Woo, and this my brother Yong Cha Woo," he said bowing his head. The other man also bowed when he was introduced.

"And what are you doing here? This is an abandoned base, and no one is supposed to be inside," said Hank authoritatively.

Chih looked at him in surprise. "Always live here," he said. "Me, Yong Cha and our parents before us always live at Kahlula. Others too, but now we only ones left. We caretakers. You need house boy?"

"I see," said Hank. "Well, I am General Hank and this is Doctor Jane. We are here on vacation for a week or so. We are going to stay in the CO's headquarters. Do you know what kind of shape it's in?"

"Vely good shape. We take care many years," said Chih proudly. "We take care you while you stay?"

"Can you cook?" asked Hank.

"Vely good cook," said Chih pointing to himself. "Yong Cha raise many vegetables in garden. Yong Cha take care outside. I take care inside," he said pointing to Yong Cha who bowed again.

"All right then," said Hank nodding at them. "We can use the help. You can be houseboys starting now. We have many boxes of supplies. You can start by carrying them in and unpacking. We have food for dinner tonight, and both of us would like to shower, change clothes and relax before dinner. Can you handle all that?"

"You bet, General Hank," said Chih, motioning to Yong Cha. Yong Cha hurried forward and picked up the two bags sitting on the tarmac and then turned to Jane, holding out an arm. She smiled at him and handed him her two small bags. Chih scurried ahead and opened the door to the plantation house and stood to one side while Hank and Jane walked in. Yong Cha followed with the bags.

"Oh, how wonderful!" exclaimed Jane looking around at the comfortable island-style architecture and furnishings. Teakwood, rattan and bamboo abounded with palm leaf ceiling fans in every room. "Oh, Chih, you have done a marvelous job of keeping this up," she said as she walked from the large sitting room into the open-air lanai.

Chih grinned with pleasure. "Thank you, Doctor Jane. It is beautiful, no?"

"Absolutely gorgeous," agreed Jane as she admired the potted palms, ti plants and orchids grouped around the lanai. "Look, Hank!" she exclaimed pointing at a pool full of brightly-colored koi. "Isn't it wonderful?"

Hank grinned at her enthusiasm. "It will do," he said. "Not too bad for camping out on an abandoned air base."

Chih showed Jane to a large bedroom with an adjoining bathroom and a door that opened out onto the lanai. Hank had an identical room on the other side of the sitting room that also opened onto the lanai.

While Yong Cha carried in the rest of the supplies from the plane and Chih took charge of the kitchen, Jane stripped off her safari garb and took a long cool shower. Then she dressed in a long sarong-style skirt and matching halter in a teal and violet Hawaiian floral print. She brushed her shoulder-length dark brunette hair and let it fall in waves around her face. Then she slipped on a pair of gold thongs and, totally refreshed, wandered out onto the lanai.

Hank was already there, ensconced in a comfortable rattan armchair with a file on his lap and a drink at his elbow on a bamboo side table.

She saw that he had changed into well-worn Levi's, sandals and a marine-blue tee shirt that matched the color of his eyes. He glanced up and saw her and let out a low whistle. "Wow! You definitely don't look very doctorly now, Doctor," he said with an admiring smile.

Jane felt her face grow warm. Was she actually blushing, she wondered? She covered up with a mischievous smile. "Well, you don't look very generally either, General," she said, noticing how the Levi's and tee shirt revealed his lean muscular frame. She quickly looked away at the pool, pretending to have great interest in the koi that were splashing and milling about.

Hank put down his file and got up. He pulled another rattan armchair over near his. "Come sit down and have a drink. Chih says dinner will be ready in an hour," he said, sitting down and picking up the file again.

"All right," said Jane smiling and walking over to the chair. "What's that you're drinking?"

"A *Mai Tai*," said Hank. "Want one? Chih makes a mean one."

"That sounds great," said Jane settling into the chair.

Chih suddenly appeared as if by magic with a *Mai Tai* on a tray. He placed it on the bamboo table next to Jane. "*Mai Tai*, Doctor Jane," he said.

"Thank you, Chih," said Jane smiling at him. "My, we were certainly lucky to meet you and Yong Cha."

Chih beamed with pleasure and returned to the kitchen.

"What are you studying?" asked Jane after she had taken a sip of the *Mai Tai*.

Hank looked up from the file. "It's the twin'" file. I've been reading through it again. The orphanage they were at is called Kalimahi and it is about twenty-five miles north of here. I thought we should start by going there first thing tomorrow. What say you?"

Jane nodded. "Yes, that makes sense. Perhaps we'll be able to find out who their parents were, but how are we going to get there?"

"No problemo," said Hank with a grin as he picked up his drink. "There's a jeep in the hangar where I stashed the plane. Like other things around here, our Chinese friends kept it up, and there's still gas in the pumps at the old PX, according to Yong Cha."

"Chih and Yong Cha are quite the pair, aren't they?" said Jane lowering her voice. "What's their story do you suppose? I didn't think there was supposed to be anyone here."

"I'm not sure what the deal is, but I'm going to find out. I'll have a long talk with them tomorrow," said Hank. He started to say more, but stopped when Chih magically appeared again and announced dinner.

*   *   *

At seven-thirty the next morning, Hank pulled the jeep up in front of the house, and Jane came out clad in khaki shorts, teal blue tee shirt, and sunglasses perched on top of her head. She had a backpack that she slung in the back seat before climbing into the Passenger's seat.

"Ready?" asked Hank, smiling at her from behind his aviator sunglasses.

"Roger!" said Jane. She pulled her sunglasses down over her eyes and looked at him. "Let's roll!" she said with a grin.

"Yes, Ma'am!" said Hank with a mock salute. He put the jeep in gear and they were soon barreling along over a pitted asphalt road that led north toward a chain of high green mountains. After about twenty miles, the paved road gave way to a red dirt road that snaked its way through thick tropical vegetation.

In another twenty minutes, they rounded a curve and came out into a large clearing. In the distance they could see a large building with a rusty steel roof. Several small dilapidated buildings surrounded it.

As the jeep bounced along over the rough road toward the buildings, Jane noticed no signs of life - no one working in the surrounding fields, no barking dogs, no children at play.

As they drew closer, Jane saw a wooden sign hanging askew on the larger building. It said simply *Kalimahi*.

Hank came to a screeching stop in front of the main building kicking up a cloud of red dust. After it settled, Hank and Jane slowly got out of the jeep and stood looking up at the building. They looked at each other, and Hank shook his head. "Appears to be abandoned," he said.

"Just like the air base," said Jane.

Hank nodded. "Well, let's look around. Maybe we'll find something that will give us some clues. Maybe we can find out where the people who ran the orphanage have gone."

They began their search in the main building. Hank led the way, testing the shaky, rotting boards of the veranda, and Jane followed in his footsteps. The door opened with a loud creaking protest from its rusted hinges.

They walked into a large room littered with rotting furniture and shredded paper. Rats scattered in all directions, diving for cover under furniture and in holes in the walls and floorboards. Jane wrinkled her nose at the musty odor of rot and the smell of animal and bird droppings.

They carefully crossed the room, and Hank kicked a termite-infested door that fell with a loud crash on the rotting floor. This set up a flurry of squawking and a beating of wings as nesting birds flew out of the door in a panic, causing Hank and Jane to duck and cover their heads with their arms.

"Yuck!" exclaimed Jane in disgust as she felt something skim over the top of her head.

After a bit the noise and dust settled, and Hank rose cautiously from where he was crouching. "It's ok now, Jane. I think they have all gone," he said.

Jane followed him through the door into what used to be a large kitchen. Shelves above the kerosene cooking stoves still contained crockery, and corroded pots and pans hung uselessly on rusty nails. A long plain wooden dining table balanced on rotting legs. Cups, plates, knives and forks remained where they had been laid for a meal, and a chair had been drawn up at each place setting. Jane counted twenty settings.

Over everything, spiders had woven a vast network of webs in which hundreds of insects had become ensnared.

Hank kicked down another door at the far end of the kitchen, and hot musty air billowed out to greet them. "Must have been the dormitory," commented Hank as he peered into the room.

Jane followed him through the doorway and saw a shaft of sunlight coming in through open doors at the far side of the room. The doors swung and creaked in the breeze. Small iron beds lined the walls, and rats scurried from their nests in the mildewed mattresses. At the foot of each bed stood a large steel trunk. Jane stopped at the first trunk and tried to lift its hinged lid. It budged slightly. Hank saw what she was trying to do and came over and lifted the lid for her.

Neatly stacked inside and preserved by the metal trunk were children's books, wooden toys, and ironed and folded clothes. Jane and Hank looked at each other in surprise. Then Jane reached down and pulled out a Bible that was lying on top of another book.

She carefully opened the cover and looked up at Hank. "Here's some writing," she said. Hank looked at her inquisitively and she looked back down at the page. "It says, *May God be with you in work and play. May your life be filled with joy, and may God's love be with you always, sweet Abigail.* It's signed *Sister Mary Rose.*"

Jane looked up at Hank again. He was staring at her with a strange expression. "I wonder what happened here, Hank? Why would everyone have left without taking their belongings, and why would the table still be set and all the kitchenware still here if they had moved somewhere else?"

"Something happened here ..." said Hank, looking over her head as if he were in a room by himself.

"What? What happened here, Hank?" asked Jane putting her hand on his arm.

He slowly looked down at her as if he was waking from a dream. "What did you say?"

Jane looked at him with concern as his eyes slowly focused on her. "You said something happened here. I asked you what," she reminded him.

He shook his head. "I don't know," he said, "but I feel as if I should know ..." He frowned at Jane for a moment and then shrugged. "Nope. I don't know anything about this. Something here must have reminded me of something similar - a sort of déjà vu thing, I guess. Well, let's look around outside and see if we can find anything else."

He turned to walk out the open doors at the far end of the room, and Jane stood looking at him curiously for a moment before she followed.

Holding on to a rusty iron rail, Jane followed Hank down rotting wooden steps into an area that was once a garden. Hank glanced around the overgrown garden and then continued along a faint dirt path with Jane right behind him. When he reached an opening in the sagging chicken wire fence that surrounded the garden, he stopped and looked beyond the opening and then turned to face Jane who had stopped behind him. Jane was surprised to see that his eyes were sad and watery. He quickly put his sunglasses back on.

"I'm sorry," he said in a low tone, his voice cracking.

Before Jane could respond, Hank reached out and took her by the arm. "I'm really sorry, Jane," he said in a tortured voice. "I am so sorry."

He gently led her through the opening in the fence as Jane continued to stare at him dumbstruck. She was trying to think of something to say, when he stopped and dropped her arm. And then she saw them.

Gravestones. Rows of them.

She ran forward to the first row, and read four of the inscriptions: *Abigail Evans, 1978-1985; Timothy Evans, 1976-1985; Sister Mary Rose, 1918-1985; Father James O'Shaunessy, 1928-1985."*

She went quickly to the second row, then the third and fourth and finally to the tenth and last row, scanning a few of the inscriptions as she went. Then she went back to where Hank remained frozen near the opening. "They all appear to have died in 1985," she said. "There are ten rows with about ten graves in each row, so that makes a total of ..."

"One hundred and nine," said Hank in an uninflected tone like an automaton. "Eighty-four children and twenty-five adults."

"How do you know that?" asked Jane in surprise. "I thought you had never been here?"

"I just know," said Hank in the same dead voice. "I don't know why."

"What happened here?" asked Jane. "Why did they all die at the same time?"

"Something happened here ..." said Hank. Suddenly, he turned and walked back through the garden and into the dormitory, leaving Jane standing there looking after him with a puzzled, concerned expression.

She turned and looked at the graves again. After a while, she retraced her footsteps through the garden, the dormitory, the kitchen, the front room and back out the front door. Hank was sitting in the jeep looking straight ahead. When she climbed into the jeep, he did not look at her. He simply started the engine, put the jeep in gear and drove back the way they had come.

On the drive back, Jane looked at Hank several times, but he did not look at her or speak. When he pulled up in front of their headquarters, he switched off the engine, and Jane asked, "What's wrong, Hank?" He did not look at her. He climbed out of the jeep as if he hadn't heard her and walked into the house without saying a word to Chih who stood smiling in the doorway to greet them.

Jane slowly got out of the jeep and collected her backpack from the back seat. She walked up to the door and smiled at Chih who had a worried expression on his face. "Hello, Chih," she said.

"Hello, Doctor Jane," he said with a slight bow. "Is something wrong with General Hank? Is he unhappy with Chih?" he asked anxiously.

"No, he is not unhappy with you, Chih," said Jane comforting him with a pat on the arm. "Something seems to have upset him, but I don't know what exactly." She walked on into the large sitting room and Chih followed. She saw that Hank was not in the room or on the lanai. He had apparently gone directly into his bedroom. She turned back to Chih. "You said you have always lived here, Chih - you and your brother and your parents?"

"Yes, Doctor Jane," said Chih with another bow.

"Perhaps you can tell me what happened at that orphanage, Kalimahi," she said.

"Ah, Kalimahi," said Chih. "Is that where you have been?"

Jane nodded. "We found a graveyard there. Everyone seems to have died at the same time, in 1985."

"My brother and I were born in a house very near Kalimahi. Our father was the gardener there, and our mother cleaned and did laundry. They are also buried at Kalimahi - Sung Chin and Mae Lai Woo."

"Oh, then you must know what happened there," said Jane.

Chih shook his head. "No, Doctor Jane. I do not know what caused them to die because my brother and I were here and not there. We were working here at the base."

"The base was operational at that time?" asked Jane.

"Oh, yes, Doctor Jane. Many aircraft, many fry boys."

"Fry boys?" asked Jane with a frown.

"Yes, you know the ones who fry the planes," Chih explained, moving his hand in the air to illustrate a plane in motion.

"Oh, I understand!" said Jane with a laugh. "Fly boys. What did you and Yong Cha do on the base?"

"I Number One Houseboy for C.O.," said Chih proudly. "Yong Cha vely good with making things work. He work in hangar, make planes run."

"So the base was operational in 1985 ..." said Jane. Then she snapped her fingers. "I just realized something!" she exclaimed. "This base is cordoned off by a high fence all the way around isn't it, Chih?"

Chih nodded. "Yes, Doctor Jane."

"Well, I just realized we didn't go through a security fence on our way to the orphanage. Does that mean the orphanage is on the base?" she asked.

Chih nodded. "Yes, Doctor Jane. Kalimahi is on base. So is honorable parenst' house where I born."

"Really! So you were born on the base?"

Chih shook his head. "Oh, no, Doctor Jane. House not on base when I born. Kalimahi not always on base either."

"That's interesting," remarked Jane. "Do you know when the base was expanded to include them?"

"No, Doctor Jane. Memory has faded. It has been so for many years."

"What about Yong Cha? Would he remember?"

"Not know, Doctor Jane. We don't speak of old days. Yong Cha still goes to honorable parents' house. Maybe he remember more than me." Jane's eyes lit up with excitement. "Do you think Yong Cha would take me to the house?" Then she frowned. "How does he get there? It's too far to walk."

Chih laughed and waved his hand. "Oh, Yong Cha drive jeep. I tol' you he make things work. He go to house two, three times a week. Has vegetable garden there. Vely proud of garden. Maybe vely proud to show you. I ask when he come for dinner."

"Oh, that would be splendid, Chih," said Jane enthusiastically. "I would love to see the house and the garden." She wandered out onto the lanai and Chih followed. She looked at the koi lazing about in the pond for a moment and then turned to Chih. "Right now, I think I would like one of your *Mai Tais*, and then I am going to take a nap. Yesterday was a long day, and I think I've got a bit of jet lag."

"Vely good, Doctor Jane," said Chih with a bow. "I serve dinner on lanai tonight at eight," he said as he went to fetch her *Mai Tai*.

*   *   *

Hank did not appear for dinner that evening. Chih brought a *Mai Tai* to Jane when she emerged from her room at seven-thirty. At eight he reappeared on the lanai to tell Jane dinner was ready. "What about General Hank?" asked Chih.

"I don't know," said Jane. "Perhaps you should knock on his door and tell him dinner is ready."

Chih bowed and went to the door of Hank's bedroom and knocked. No response. He knocked louder and said in a loud voice, "Dinner is ready, General Hank!"

"Go away!" called a gruff voice from within, and Chih shrugged his shoulders and turned back to Jane.

Jane smiled at him. "General Hank is probably tired from jet lag, too. Go ahead and bring the dinner, and if he comes out, I'll let you know."

Chih nodded and went off to the kitchen. Before long he returned with a plate of barbecued pork, grilled pineapple and baked yams. As he sat it down on the table in front of Jane's chair, he said, "Yong Cha say he take you to house tomalla, Doctor Jane. He will be outside at nine if ok with you."

"Yes," said Jane with a smile. "Tell him I'll be ready, and thank you."

Jane ate her dinner in silence, enjoying the peacefulness of the lanai. Chih came and took her plate, brought her rice pudding and coffee for dessert. When she had finished that, Chih removed the dishes and retired for the night to his room off the kitchen. Throughout it all there was no sign of Hank.

Jane sat for a while listening to the quiet night sounds and watching the moon playing hide and seek among the palms. At last she decided to go to her room. She had just opened the door from the lanai when a loud crash from Hank's room broke the silence causing her to jump. "No! No! No! Oh, God, No!" he yelled, his voice carrying throughout the house.

Jane raced to the door of his room that opened onto the lanai. "Hank!" she cried, pounding on the door. "Hank! Are you all right?"

"Oh God, oh God, oh God!" he yelled. "I'm sorry! I'm sorry! I'm sorry!"

"Hank!" yelled Jane again as she pounded on the door.

Another crash emanated from the room. Then silence.

"Hank?"

No response.

"Hank, are you all right?" Jane yelled again as Chih hurried up to her.

"What is wrong, Doctor Jane?" he asked out of breath.

"I don't know ... it's General Hank. Something is wrong. I'm going in to see," said Jane, her heart pounding. She turned the doorknob and found the door unlocked. She threw the door open and ran into the room with Chih on her heels.

It was pitch black in the room and she stopped short trying to remember where the light switch was. Chih quickly flipped on a switch just inside the door, and the soft light from a wall sconce illuminated the room. Jane found herself staring at a bed full of rumpled twisted sheets, but there was no one in it. Then they heard a low moan coming from the far side of the bed.

Jane and Chih quickly went to the side of the bed and looked down. There was Hank sprawled on the floor, face down, dressed only in his skivvies. Jane knelt down and saw blood oozing from a gash over Hank's right eyebrow. "Help me get him back into bed, Chih," she said. "He must have hit his head on the corner of the nightstand."

With Chih's help Jane managed to wrestle Hank back into the bed on his back. She straightened out the sheets and drew one up over him to chest level. Hank did not wake up, and Jane thought he had knocked himself out when his head struck the night table until she noticed the half-empty bottle of Jack Daniels on the other nightstand.

Jane sent Chih to her room to fetch her doctor's bag and then to the kitchen for a basin of hot water while she sat on the bed next to Hank and stroked his forehead and smoothed back his sweat-drenched hair. Suddenly, he began to thrash about, flailing his head from side to side on the pillow. "No! Oh God, no!" he blurted out again as Chih came into the room. "No! No! Oh God, I'm sorry!"

"Quick, Chih, hand me that bag, and come here and hold him so he doesn't hurt himself," she said. Chih did as she instructed, and Jane quickly dug in her doctor's bag and brought out a vial and a syringe. She broke the seal on the vial, inserted the needle and drew the fluid into the syringe.

When she returned to the bed she was surprised to see that Hank was completely calm. Chih sat next to him holding Hank's right hand palm up in his left hand. With the index finger of his right hand, Chih was gently probing various places on Hank's palm.

"What are you doing, Chih?" asked Jane, holding the syringe upright to keep it from leaking.

"Ancient Chinese cure to draw out demons," he said without looking up. He continued to apply pressure with his finger to various spots on Hank's palm.

Jane smiled. "Is that what they call acupressure?"

Chih nodded. "That's what it called in West."

"Well it certainly seems to be working," she observed. "I was going to give him this sedative, but it doesn't appear to be necessary. I'm going to put a couple of stitches in that gash over his eyebrow. Will the acupressure keep him calm, or should I inject some lidocaine?"

"No need, Doctor Jane. This keep him from feeling pain."

Jane cleaned the wound with antiseptic and then sewed up the gash with four small neat stitches while Chih continued to apply acupressure to Hank's palm. She stepped back and surveyed her work as she put her things away. Hank was sleeping peacefully, the anxiety gone from his face.

"Looks as if he is all right now, Chih," she said. "I believe I'll stay here tonight just in case he starts thrashing around again. I don't want him to hurt himself again."

"Yes, Doctor Jane. He should be peaceful now," said Chih, gently placing Hank's hand down on the sheet where it covered his chest. "If you need help, call out and I come again."

"Thank you, Chih. Your healing touch seems to have done the trick."

Chih bowed and left the room closing the door behind him.

Jane quietly went into the bathroom and turned on a dim nightlight. Then she switched off the light in the bedroom, took off her sarong skirt and matching short-sleeved jacket, and still wearing her tank top and bikini panties very carefully climbed into the other side of the king-sized bed. She lay rigidly still listening to Hank's quiet breathing. After about half an hour, she turned onto her side with her back to Hank and dozed off satisfied that he was sleeping peacefully.

Several hours later, a warm tickling sensation on her neck half-awoke her. "I'm sorry," Hank was whispering in her ear. "I'm so sorry." He had turned on his side and had an arm over her. She felt the hard muscular warmth of his chest against her back. "I'm sorry," he murmured again, stroking her arm, his fingers brushing across the side of her breast as he did so.

Jane sighed and turned towards him. "It's all right, darling," she said, laying her head on his chest and putting her arm around him. "It's all right," she repeated as she went back to sleep.

The early morning light filtering into the room brought Jane gradually back to consciousness. She slowly opened her eyes and wondered where she was. She saw tanned skin covered with golden springy hair and then she remembered. She felt the gentle rise and fall of Hank's chest below her head and felt her face grow hot. "Oh, my God. What am I doing?" she thought. She gently and ever so slowly raised her head off his chest hoping not to awaken him. She looked up from beneath her lashes directly into blue eyes gazing back at her with an amused expression.

"Where did you come from?" he asked in a low voice, the hint of a smile curling his lips.

"Oh, dear," she said. "I must have fallen asleep ... that is, you were having a nightmare or something and you banged your head and I had to stitch you up and I didn't want you to bang your head again and I decided to stay in here with you. I didn't mean to ... that is ... I'm sorry."

"It's all right, Jane," he said with a tender smile as he cupped her face in his hands. He closed his eyes and drew her to him, pressing his lips on hers.

*   *   *

Chapter 17

A FTER GETTING LOST three times, George finally stumbled his way to his room after his night out at the Italian restaurant with Zoë. As usual, he'd had numerous drinks including five Banks beers before they left, two *Mai Tais* in the bar while they were waiting to be called in for dinner, two bottles of Chianti Classico with dinner and four *Sambucas* after dinner. When they returned to the resort, they had gone into the Coconut Lounge where Fleet was waiting at a table with Peggy and David to collect Zoë, and he had two *Caribbean Crackups* to top it all off.

Perhaps that is why, when he finally found his room, he did not notice the two Bajan men dressed in island shirts and linen trousers who were standing by his door. As he fumbled drunkenly for his key, one of the men stepped forward and showed him a badge identifying himself and his partner as police. "Mr. Goater?" inquired the man politely.

George nodded as he finally pulled his card key out of his wallet and promptly dropped it on the floor. He started to reach down to pick it up, but the Bajan said, "Allow me," and picked it up for him. "We must search your room, Mr. Goater," he said. "May I?" he asked, holding the card key to the slot on the door.

"Why not?" said George, waving his hand and weaving about. "Got nothing to hide, 'cept maybe some oysters." He laughed raucously punctuated by a loud hiccup at the end.

The Bajans looked at him questioningly, and the one with the key shook his head as he inserted the key into the slot. He opened the door and led the way into the room. The other Bajan followed George, holding out his arms on either side of George as he lurched from side to side.

Inside the suite, George lurched his way to the bed and fell on it face down. "Got to sleep now," he said in a muffled voice, his nose smashed into the pillow. Nearly immediately, loud snores filled the room.

The two Bajans looked at each other and shook their heads. Then they went about the task of searching George's room. They paid particular attention to the shorts he had worn on the beach that afternoon, and then they looked in all the drawers, the cupboards, under the furniture and under the bed. They ran their hands under the mattress as George snored away on top and searched the clothes he was wearing. They looked in the bathroom through all his toiletries and even in the toilet tank.

At last, coming up empty-handed they met at the door to the suite. "Must have been a false lead," muttered one of the men in a low voice. The other nodded and they looked back at the bed. George was still sound asleep snoring away. They quietly left the room, placing the "Do Not Disturb" sign on the door as they left.

*　　*　　*

When Peggy telephoned and woke George at ten the next morning, he did not remember the two men who had searched his room. All he was aware of was the pain of another hangover and the pain of his sunburn. While Peggy waited for him on the terrace, he took a shower and gingerly smeared aloe over his lobster-red skin, and then he shaved very carefully and as gently as possible. When he went to put on the shorts and Rugby shirt he had worn the day before, he found the shirt in a wad on the floor of the bathroom, but the shorts were not there. He looked around the suite and finally found them lying under his carry-on bag in the closet. All the pockets were turned out. He shook his head as he straightened them out and put them on. How did the shorts get in here, he wondered. He had no recollection of putting them there when he had changed clothes before going to dinner the night before.

When he met Peggy on the terrace, she had already had breakfast and was drinking tea. As George slowly sat down, she grinned. "Looks as if you had red wine and lobster at the Italian restaurant last night, George. At least your eyes and skin certainly look like it."

George grimaced at her from behind his sunglasses. "Not in the mood for any of your jokes this morning, Peg," he said. "All I want is a Bloody Mary and then we can go on up the beach to see Denise's grandparents."

"Suit yourself," said Peggy, shrugging her shoulders. "All I want is to get our business over with so I can go to the horse races with David."

After George had his Bloody Mary and a piece of toast, he and Peggy walked down to the beach and headed north on the white sand. He walked closest to the water at arm's length from Peggy along the white sandy beach. The sea was calm with gentle surf, and the waves lapped close to where George was walking. Peggy stopped for a moment to take off her beach sandals and place them in a plastic bag she was carrying. George paid no attention and continued to walk aimlessly along the edge of the lapping waves in his socks and black leather shoes.

A fallen palm tree blocked the beach and Peggy paused and timed the surf to walk around it. When she reached the dry sand on the other side, George followed without paying attention to the surf. Suddenly a high wave broke on the shoreline and engulfed him, sucking him out to deeper water as it receded.

"George!" called Peggy seeing only his head bobbing in the water. "George, are you all right?"

When the wave receded further, George managed to half-swim half-crawl to shore where he flopped down on the dry soft sand. "Bugger! Now I'm soaked," he muttered feebly.

"Do you need any help?" called out a familiar voice.

Peggy looked around and saw Stan rushing towards them.

"I saw what happened, Peggy," said Stan. "The cottage is just there." He pointed a short distance up the beach. "Is George all right?" he asked looking at George who was lying on his stomach in the sand. "And why in bloody hell is he wearing shoes and socks?"

"Oh, he thinks he is on Brighton Beach," said Peggy with a scornful wave of her hand. "He's afraid he'll get tar on his feet."

"Are you all right, George?" asked Stan leaning over him.

George slowly and painfully got up on his hands and knees and then to his feet. "I'm all right now," he mumbled, looking down and trying to brush the caked wet sand off his soaked clothes.

"Come on, George. Come on over to the cottage. I have some dry clothes you can wear," said Stan with an amused smile.

"Splendid, Stan," said Peggy. "Perhaps you could lend him some beach shoes too?"

"Sure, I've got plenty of extra pairs of thongs lying about," said Stan as he turned to lead the way to the cottage.

At the steps that led up to the deck of the cottage, Stan pointed to a crude outdoor shower that had a flimsy bamboo screen around it. "Strip off your wet clothes and shower off in there, George, and I'll be right back with some dry clothes."

George did as he was told, and Peggy followed Stan up the steps to the deck and sat down on a deck chair. Stan disappeared into the cottage and soon returned with a shirt, shorts, thongs and a large brightly colored towel that had the words *Bajan Pride* printed on it.

Stan looked down over the deck railing into the shower where George stood shivering under the cold water. "Blimey, George, you look like a lobster!" he said observing George's sunburned skin.

George did not answer. He just looked up at him with a miserable frown.

Stan took pity on him. "Dry off with this towel - gently, mind you - and I'll get some aloe for you to put on your skin before you put these clothes on."

George nodded obediently as Stan handed him the towel.

After George had dried himself off, smeared aloe all over his sunburnt areas, and dressed, he joined Stan and Peggy on the deck.

"Taking a morning walk, George?" asked Stan handing him a Banks beer. "It's such a beautiful day, but then every day is a beautiful day in Paradise."

"We are walking to Speightstown," said Peggy before George could answer. "It's only a short distance from here."

"Oh it is, is it? Who told you that?" said Stan with a laugh.

"Philip," said George. "He said it was about a ten minute walk from Palm Shores."

Stan was about to take a sip of his beer. His hand with the beer bottle paused in mid-air. "When did you see Philip?" he asked with a frown.

"On the beach at the resort yesterday afternoon," said George, looking out at the passersby on the sand below. "I hope he doesn't get into trouble because he talked to me. He said he's not allowed onto the beach or to talk with the guests."

"What did he tell you?" asked Stan in a gruff voice.

George looked at Stan in surprise at the tone of his voice. Stan quickly wiped the frown off his face and smiled reassuringly at George. "He told me where to find Denise Downing's grandparents, that's all. You remember Peggy was asking him if he knew her the other night when we were over here."

"Oh, sure, I remember. He said he didn't know her. He must have remembered something about her later."

"That's right," said George. "Said he had talked to some of the chaps he'd gone to school with and they had told him about her grandparents still being alive."

"I see," said Stan casually raising the bottle to his lips. "You know, I'd like to take a walk along the beach myself. Mind if I come along with you?"

"We'd love to have you, wouldn't we, George?" said Peggy. "You can help us find the place, and besides, if George gets swept away again, you can help rescue him."

"That I can," said Stan laughing. "I can also give you a guided tour along the way. All right by you, George?"

"Sure. Suit yourself, but I don't think I'll be falling in the water again. That salt water doesn't exactly help the sunburn. From now on, I'm walking high up on the beach away from the surf," said George with a small grin.

"All right then, let's go," said Stan draining his beer bottle and plunking it down on a plastic table.

Stan led the way up the beach walking on sand and then around points on rocky outcroppings and then back on sand again. As George and Peggy followed close in his wake, he gave a running commentary on the owners of the expensive beachfront estates that they passed.

After half an hour, Peggy looked at her watch and stopped to rub a spot on her right foot where a blister seemed to be forming. "This is definitely more than a ten-minute walk," she commented.

Stan looked back over his shoulder and laughed. "Oh, it's ten minutes all right - in Bajan time, which has no known relationship to real time. But don't despair. It won't be long now. Speightstown is just beyond that cove up ahead."

As they came upon the cove, they had to walk inland slightly through the perimeter of a small public park where some Bajans were roasting chicken over an open fire. There was a bright magenta colored rowboat pulled up in the sand near them.

As George walked passed, a young Bajan man with a blue bandana tied on his head rose from his perch on a log near the fire and fell into stride alongside him. "Hey, Mon, you want to buy cure for that sunburn?" he asked, holding up a plastic tube of aloe gel.

George shook his head and kept walking. "No. Already have some," he said.

"In that case, how about boat ride?" persisted the Bajan, pointing at the rowboat. "Hundred dollars for one hour."

Again George shook his head and plowed on through the sand, but the Bajan kept walking beside him. "Here is present for you," he said holding out a small branch with shiny leaves on it.

"No, no, no!" said George raising his voice in exasperation.

Stan heard him and looked back. "Hey, there, Jo-Jo. You go on. We're not interested, you understand?"

The Bajan stopped short in his tracks and grinned. "Ok, Mr. Stan. I go back to boat. You come buy fish on way back, yeah?"

"Maybe," said Stan, waving good-naturedly at him. "I'll stop by and see what you have."

The Bajan returned to his seat by the fire as Stan led George and Peggy around the point into the cove. "We must be close now," said George. "There are the two new hotels, I take it."

"Yes, that one just ahead is the Virgin Nights," said Stan. "The Happy Caribbean Days is at the other end of the cove."

"So that means Denise's grandparents live somewhere in the middle of the cove, in between the two hotels," commented Peggy. "Didn't you say It's a house with peeling purple paint, George?"

"That's right. That's what Philip said."

Stan stopped and looked at them. "Peeling purple paint? I know exactly the house you mean, and I know who lives there as well - Malcolm and Beth. What a coincidence. Didn't know they had a granddaughter. What did you want to tell them about this granddaughter?"

"Oh, it's nothing really," said Peggy quickly before George could respond. "It's just a bit of genealogical research I've been doing for a lark. We're not even sure these are the ones who are related to our Denise Downing."

"I see. Just a lark ... Well, there's the house you're looking for. You know your way back, so I'll go on back to the cottage now. Stop in on your way back and we'll have a beer," said Stan.

"Thanks, Stan. We'll do that," said George. He looked in the direction Stan had pointed. They were right in front of the house that sat back just a few feet from the high tide line in the sand in a small grove of palms and breadfruit trees. Between them and the house was a lone palm and in the shade of it sat two elderly Bajans cleaning fish. A long rope tied to the palm lay in the sand. As George followed it with his eyes, he saw that the rope disappeared in the surf and that it was apparently connected to a bright blue rowboat that bobbed in the surf about fifty yards off shore.

As he and Peggy started to pass the elderly couple on their way to the purple house, George nodded at them and they grinned up at him. George smiled and said, "Hello. We are looking for Malcolm and Beth. Do they live in that house there?"

One of the Bajans looked at the house George was pointing at and grinned and nodded.

"Thanks very much," said George with another smile, and he and Peggy continued walking toward the house.

"Is Malcolm or Beth here?" called out George through the open door of the shack. The interior was dimly lit. There were no windows, and the only light came through the open door.

Hearing no response, George poked his head in the door and looked about but saw no one. At last, satisfied that no one was at home, he and Peggy turned to leave and again passed the elderly couple who was cleaning fish.

"Would you know when Malcolm and Beth will be back home?" asked George.

The Bajan man looked out at the ocean and then back at George with a smile. "They will be back in house when the sun is hottest."

"Is that between Noon and two o'clock?" asked Peggy politely.

Both the Bajans smiled and nodded their heads in agreement. Then as Peggy and George started to walk away, the Bajan man said, "Is it necessary to talk to Malcolm and Beth in their house?"

George looked back in surprise and saw that the two Bajans were grinning and chuckling as they continued to concentrate on scaling the fish. "No, I guess it is not necessary to talk to them in their house," he said slowly.

"Then you can talk to us here!" said the man looking up and waving the scaling knife in the air. Both Bajans broke out in guffaws of laughter.

George and Peggy looked at each other and grinned. "Does that mean that you are ... ?" asked George.

"That's right," said the elderly Bajan woman. "I am Beth and this is my husband Malcolm. We are not in our house right now. We are in our office. If you want to talk to us, you can talk here."

Peggy and George sat down on a fallen palm trunk in the white sand and introduced themselves.

"Are you here to buy flying fish? Someone must have told you we have the best on the island," said Malcolm, wiping the fish scales from his knife on a piece of palm bark.

"No, thank you. We're here to talk to you about your granddaughter Denise Downing," said Peggy.

Both Malcolm and Beth stopped what they were doing and looked at Peggy with serious faces. "Is Denise ... Is our granddaughter all right?" asked Malcolm in a soft voice.

"She isn't very well, I'm afraid to say. She has a very bad illness," continued Peggy in a sympathetic tone, "and we are here to see if anyone else has the same type of illness."

Malcolm gave Beth a strange look and then started cleaning fish again.

"What about her uncle?" asked Beth as she too resumed cleaning fish. "Roger is just fine," said George watching her closely, "but he still uses a wheelchair."

"What sort of illness do you say Denise has?" asked Beth not looking up.

"It is a sort of nervous disorder. She has trouble speaking and is unable to control her muscular spasms," said George.

"No different than when she left here," said Malcolm shaking his head as he cleaned the fish scales from his knife. "She would have been better off staying here than in England. Beth and I told them to let her stay, but they wouldn't listen. They just took her away."

"Who took her away?" asked George.

"Those people who work for ..." said Beth.

"Now, now, Beth," said Malcolm looking at her sharply. "We don't know that for sure." He looked around to see if there was anyone in earshot, and then turned back to George and Peggy. "You'd better buy some fish now before we run out," he said in a loud voice.

"What people?" asked George.

Both Malcolm and Beth concentrated on the fish they were cleaning. They did not look up or answer.

"Do you know of anyone else who is ill like Denise?" asked Peggy, trying another tack.

No response.

"I'd like to buy five pounds worth of fish," said George suddenly.

Without looking up Malcolm reached into a white plastic bucket and brought out a large handful of small silvery fish. With the other hand he held open a clear large plastic bag and continued to scoop fish out of the bucket and place them in the bag until it was full. Finally, he looked at George and held out the bag to him. "That will be twenty Bajan dollars," he said.

"Twenty dollars!" exclaimed George, eyeing the huge bag of fish. "I didn't want that many fish."

"You said five pounds," said Malcolm with a shrug.

"I meant five pounds worth, not five pounds of fish," said George frowning.

Malcolm looked confused. Peggy jumped in. "It's all right. I"'s our mistake. Give Malcolm the money, George," she said, glaring at George as she saw him opening his mouth to object to the price.

George grimaced at her and reached into his pocket for his wallet. After he had paid Malcolm, he looked closer at the fish in the bag. "Lovely fish," he said. "What sort are they?"

"Reef perch. Malcolm catches them at night using a lantern," said Beth with pride. "He has been a fisherman all his life. That is his fishing boat," she said pointing to the blue rowboat they had noticed earlier.

"It must be difficult to fish out in the sea without an engine," commented George as he looked at the boat.

"I'm nearly eighty-nine years old and I have never had a boat with an engine. The best fishing is done the old way - an engine scares the fish away," said Malcolm.

"Have you lived here all your life?" asked Peggy.

Malcolm nodded. "All my life, except when I went to fight for the King in the Second World War. After I enlisted, I was on my way to Singapore to fight the Japanese when the British surrendered, so I finished up in Egypt."

"Amazing," exclaimed George. "I didn't know Bajans fought in the British Army."

"Oh, yes, many island people fought for King and Country," said Beth proudly, patting Malcolm's shoulder.

"But the British would never admit that we did," said Malcolm scowling. "Just shipped us back when the war was over. Not even a thank you."

"Now, now, Malcolm. That was a long time ago and these English people had nothing to do with that," said Beth looking apologetically at George and Peggy.

"George quickly jumped in. "Don't worry. I understand how you feel, Malcolm. I worked for the Foreign Office, and I know my history. It was many years before the British government acknowledged the contributions of the common soldier."

"And that's not all the British did either," said Malcolm, warming up to the topic that was obviously a bone of contention with him. "They caused bad things to happen here."

George and Peggy glanced at each other. "What do you mean?" asked Peggy.

"For five years there wasn't any fish, and Malcolm blames the British for that," said Beth picking up the scaling knife again. "He blames the British for nearly everything."

"Including Denise's condition," added Malcolm in a bitter tone of voice.

"Malcolm, you don't know that for sure. You are only guessing," said Beth quickly, glancing again at George and Peggy apologetically.

George and Peggy glanced at each other again. "By the way," said Peggy, trying to sound casual. "We were wondering if you can tell us who Denise's father is? Is he from Barbados also?"

Malcolm and Beth looked at each other with something akin to fear in their eyes. "We don't know. Never did," said Malcolm abruptly.

"Cecily never would tell, and now she's dead," added Beth with a faraway sad look in her eyes.

"Cecily was your daughter? Denise's mother?" asked Peggy gently. Beth nodded.

Malcolm threw down his scaling knife in the sand. "That's enough. We don't want to talk about it anymore. Too many sad memories and nothing can be done to change anything." He stood up as if to indicate the conversation was over.

George and Peggy quickly stood up. "Well, we will be off now. Thank you for talking with us," said Peggy.

"Yes," said George, clutching the bag of fish. "We want to get back to our friend's cottage to cook these fish for lunch while they're still fresh."

"Your friend wouldn't happen to be named Stan who is staying at Jonkanoo Cottage, would he?" asked Malcolm.

"Yes, that's right, but how did you ... ?" asked Peggy in surprise.

"I thought I saw him with you when you walked up," he said looking at Beth with a frown. "How do you know him?" he asked turning his attention back to George and Peggy.

"I used to work with Stan at the Foreign Office in London," said George. "He is a security guard there. Just happened to be taking a holiday here at the same time we were."

"Foreign Office?" queried Malcolm. "I thought he worked for the Commonwealth Office. In fact, I know he did, because he was here during the time of the Grenada crisis." Malcolm paused and looked closely at George. "Did you say your last name is Goater?"

George nodded. "That's right. George Goater."

"Any relation to Bill Goater?"

George looked at him in surprise. "Yes. Bill Goater is my father, and he worked at the Commonwealth Office."

"Yes, I know him. He and Stan were both here."

"Are you sure?"

"As sure as anything," said Malcolm. "They were both with the Commonwealth Office."

"That's right," added Beth. "As a matter of fact, your father came to see us not that long ago - about three weeks, wasn't it, Malcolm?"

Malcolm gave her an intense look. "That's enough, Beth," he said. "George and Peggy need to get back to Stan's before the fish go bad, and we have many more to clean before it gets too hot."

Beth looked down quickly and nodded, and Malcolm sat down again and picked up his scaling knife. "Hope you like the fish," he said.

George and Peggy took the hint. "I'm sure we will," said George. "It was nice to meet you. I will tell my father I saw you. He is recovering from a heart attack."

Malcolm dropped the knife. "Bill had a heart attack? When?" he asked with great concern etched on his features.

"A little over a week ago. His prize Black Angus herd came down with Foot and Mouth and had to be destroyed. They think that's what brought on the heart attack," said George.

"That would have been just after he was here ..." said Beth looking at Malcolm.

Malcolm shook his head at her and she sat down and picked up her scaling knife without looking at George and Peggy.

"Well, give your father our best. Hope he recovers from his heart attack soon," said Malcolm. He picked up his scaling knife again and plucked a fish out of a nearby tub of water.

It was clear the conversation was over, so George and Peggy began walking back along the beach. When they had rounded the point and were out of sight of Malcolm and Beth, they paused and sat down on a fallen palm tree and sat looking out at the sea.

"This is all very strange, Peg," said George. "Malcolm and Beth saw my dad when he was here the last time, and my dad brings back samples of Denise's blood and her father's blood, but they say they don't know who the father is. Do you believe that?"

Peggy shook her head. "No. They are very obviously not telling everything they know for some reason or other. And that remark about those people taking Denise to England ..."

"Another thing - why would Malcolm think the British were responsible for Denise's illness, and why would my dad have connections with them?"

"Not only that, but did you notice their reaction when they found out you are a friend of Stan? Most of the Bajans we've met all seem to know Stan and think he's wonderful, but that didn't seem to be their opinion. In fact, they seemed sort of wary about him didn't you think?"

George nodded. "Also, from what they said, it sounds as if my dad and Stan were both working for the Commonwealth Office and were both here at the same time. It almost sounded as if they were working together, and Stan has never mentioned that he knows my dad personally."

"Methinks Mr. Stan knows a lot more than what he's telling," said Peggy. "Maybe we can get some information out of him. Let's go back to the cottage and make a present of the fish, and while we're having a nice sociable lunch and a couple of friendly drinks, I'll try to draw him out a bit."

"That's a good idea, Peg, but I am wary of telling him too much of what we know. There was a rumor going round the Foreign Office that Stan worked for British Intelligence at one time, and if he did, I don't know how that connects to my dad. I wouldn't like to unwittingly do something that will jeopardize my dad. Now that I think of it, Stan seems to have been popping up a bit too much recently. He just happened to be on the same train when I was going to East Croyden to see

Denise, and now here he just happens to be on the same flight to Barbados."

"That sounds odd, George. If Stan was with British Intelligence, why is he just a guard now at the Foreign Office?"

George shrugged his shoulders and then grinned. "Maybe the same thing that happened to me. Perhaps he was forced to take early retirement and took the guard position at the F.O. in order to make ends meet."

"Perhaps ..." said Peggy, "or maybe he's still in with them and the guard job is just a cover."

"Well, whatever the case, I don't trust him," said George. "We just need to be careful what we tell him."

"I agree," said Peggy. "Leave it to me. I can play the innocent in this situation much better than you can."

"Ho!" snorted George derisively. "It seems to be the only situation in which you can play the innocent and get away with it!"

Peggy slapped him on the arm. "Cut it out, George. Let bygones be bygones. We're on the same side, after all."

George looked at the anger in her eyes and relented. "Yes, I suppose you're right. Sorry, Peg."

"All right then. Let's go see what we can weasel out of Mr. Stan," said Peggy, getting up and brushing sand from her shorts.

When they arrived at Jonkanoo Cottage, Stan was sitting on the deck drinking a bottle of beer. As George and Peggy climbed the steps from the beach to the deck, Stan said, "I hung your clothes out to dry, George. Had several offers to buy your Rugby shirt." He laughed as he motioned to them to take seats on the deck.

"That's quite a bag of fish you've got there," he commented as he saw the huge plastic bag George was holding.

"That's right," said George grinning. "I bought them from Malcolm and Beth. I asked for five pounds worth, but got five pounds of fish instead. Peggy and I thought we'd bring them here and share with you. Should make a good lunch. The only catch is that you have to cook them."

"Oh, there's no catch to it as they've already been caught," said Stan grinning. "I'll cook them, no problem. Reef perch are very tasty.

I'll just put them in the refrigerator and we can have some beer before lunch. They don't take long to cook," he added over his shoulder as he carried the bag of fish into the open door that led to the kitchen. He soon returned with a six-pack of frosty bottles of Banks beer.

"There's enough fish in there to feed an army," he remarked as he handed a bottle of beer to Peggy and then one to George.

"Were you ever in the Army, Stan?" asked Peggy with a smile as she lifted her bottle of beer in a salute to him.

"No, I was in the Navy - the Royal Navy." Stan's eyes twinkled as he sat back down and picked up his beer bottle. "I sailed the Seven Seas."

"Lucky you, Stan. I was always stuck in the Foreign Office. Never went anywhere - not even a minor overseas posting," said George forlornly.

"What did you do in the Navy, Stan?" asked Peggy.

"Initially I was a signalman, but I finished up as a radio operator."

"What did you do after you left the Navy?" asked George.

Stan contemplated his beer bottle for a moment, took a large swig and grinned. "Like you, George, I worked for the government."

"Have you been a security guard all those years?" asked George.

"Oh, you might say that. I've done many types of guarding over the years," he replied with a mysterious grin.

"That must be exciting, Stan," said Peggy smiling admiringly at him. "What kinds of things did you guard?"

Stan gave her another mysterious smile. "George knows what I mean."

He looked at George for confirmation, and George said, "Sure, I know what you do. You search bags and check people who enter and leave the ministry buildings to make sure they're all on the up and up."

"That's true," said Stan with a laugh, "but my work hasn't always been that mundane."

"Didn't you tell us that you worked for the Commonwealth Office when you were in Barbados?" asked Peggy, casually taking a sip of her beer.

"That's right," said Stan.

"Well, you know my dad worked for the Commonwealth Office,

and I recall that he spent some time here. Did you know him?" asked George.

Stan looked at his beer bottle and then out at the ocean. "You know, I think I did know your dad many years ago here in Barbados." He paused and then a slow smile came over his face. "Yes, Bill Goater. As a matter of fact, Bill and I worked together on several overseas assignments."

"What?" cried George. "You never told me you knew my dad!"

Stan looked directly at George with the hint of a smile and shook his head. "I couldn't really let on, George, because our work together was strictly confidential."

"What does that mean, Stan? That you were a secret agent?" asked Peggy with wide innocent eyes and a giggle.

"Oh, nothing like that," said Stan."I worked for British Imports and Exports, that's all," he said with a chuckle. "Can't really talk about it."

"When were you stationed in Barbados?" asked George.

"Quite a while back. I was here in 1983. So was your dad, George," said Stan.

"Were you working for British Imports and Exports then?" asked Peggy.

Stan looked at her and chuckled. "Not going to give up, are you, Ms. Peggy? Yes, I was. My job was to help the government in Barbados do some exporting, especially to Cuba. You know, back then Castro was a major threat in the Caribbean, and we thought he was trying to help the Russians build an airbase on Grenada. Of course, communism was against everything British Imports and Exports stood for."

"Hmmm, how exciting," said Peggy, giving Stan another of her wide-eyed innocent looks. "Do you mean that you were in the business of quote, unquote, exporting Cubans?"

"Can't say," said Stan with his mysterious smile.

"I see what you mean. How exciting. Are you still working for British Imports and Exports?" asked Peggy.

Stan put down his empty beer bottle and rose from his chair. "I think it's time we had lunch. How would you like your fish cooked? The Bajan way or the Cuban way?"

"Definitely the Bajan way," said Peggy with a laugh. "I wouldn't want to be exported!"

Stan laughed and strode off to the kitchen leaving George and Peggy to relax on the deck with the rest of the beer. As they stared out at the sparkling blue sea and the people walking along the beach, Peggy said in a low voice, "Well, now we know. He as much as admitted that he worked for intelligence. Do you think he is telling the truth or just bragging?"

"It's difficult to say," said George with a frown. "He does seem to know a lot about the Caribbean, and the Bajans all seem to know him ..."

"And Malcolm and Beth seemed very leery of him ..." said Peggy. "I wonder if he knows anything about the fish disappearing for five years. I think I'll ask him."

"This is all bloody strange," said George. "I can't begin to think how my dad is all mixed up in this ..."

"Oh, look! Can you see that sand crab that just popped out of its hole?" said Peggy in a loud voice as she saw Stan emerging from the kitchen out of the corner of her eye.

"Here we are," said Stan. He set down a huge platter of fish that had been dipped in a light coating of flour and cornmeal and fried in olive oil. He handed out paper plates and napkins. "Dig in. I'll be back with some bread and butter to go with it, and I can see we need more beer," he said noticing the empty beer bottles.

By the time Stan had returned, George and Peggy had already wolfed down two fish apiece. "This is absolutely delicious," marveled Peggy. "It's better even than plaice or Dover sole, and it takes a lot to beat that."

"Yes, Bajan fish is the best in the world," said Stan as he filled his own paper plate with fish and several slices of buttered bread.

"Speaking of Bajan fish, Malcolm told us that all the fish died some time ago. Were you here when it happened, Stan?" asked Peggy as she took another bite of fish.

"Yes. I remember it well. It wreaked havoc on their economy. No fish for a number of years - about five, as I recall," said Stan as he placed one of the fish between two slices of buttered bread. "It was a bloody disaster. Cost them a pretty penny to bring in fish from Jamaica and Trinidad."

"Why did the fish die, Stan?" asked George, wiping his fingers on a paper napkin.

"I don't really know," said Stan frowning. "Rumor had it that the Cubans had something to do with it. A sort of retaliation for ..." He hesitated and then took a bite of his fish sandwich.

"Retaliation for what, Stan?" prompted George.

"Remember what I said about exporting to Cuba, George? Well, the Bajan Prime Minister rounded up and booted out a bunch of Cubans who were suspected of plotting to overthrow the government. That upset Castro, and the rumor was he got his own back by killing the fish."

"That sounds a bit far-fetched doesn't it?" commented Peggy.

"No, something like that really did happen," said George, his eyes lighting up. "I remember now. The Americans accused Castro of contaminating the fishing grounds in the Caribbean for political purposes. It's all coming back to me now. It was after America invaded Granada. That's right. President Reagan, at the time, got the Caribbean nations to back him in the invasion. So I think there may very well have been some basis to that rumor."

"Regardless of that, I still find it difficult to believe the Cubans would have contaminated the fishing grounds because they would have been cutting off their own nose to spite their face. It would have been almost impossible to contaminate someone else's fishing grounds without affecting their own," said Peggy. "The ocean currents could take it anywhere."

"That's right, Peggy. It all sounds rather fishy to me," said Stan with a grin.

All three laughed at Stan's little pun and clinked their beer bottles together.

"Now it's my turn to ask some questions," said Stan. "It's only fair, what?"

"Sure," said Peggy. "Turnabout's fair play. What do you want to know?"

"All right, then," said Stan raising his beer bottle. "What is the real reason you have an interest in this Denise Downing and her grandparents?"

"We already told you ..." began George, but Stan held up a hand.

"No, don't tell me it's a genealogy project for a lark. That doesn't make sense. I'm sure it's much more than that, or you wouldn't be going to all this trouble especially when you're here for a holiday."

George looked at Peggy, and she nodded. "The truth is, Stan, I am a doctor and am involved in treating Denise Downing. She has a life-threatening disease that we believe is hereditary. Our research indicates that it may have come down from the father's side, and if we can find the father, we may be able to come up with a cure."

"What sort of disease is it?"

George looked intensely at Peggy.

"It appears to be a rare form of Multiple Sclerosis," said Peggy looking back at George with the hint of a smile. George took a gulp of his beer and looked out at the surf.

"Well, if Denise's last name is Downing, her father would have to be Malcolm and Beth's son," speculated Stan.

Peggy shook her head. "No, Denise's mother is their daughter Cecily. Denise was apparently born out of wedlock, and that's why her last name is Downing."

"I see," said Stan frowning and gazing out at the beach. "Did you ask Malcolm and Beth who Denise's father is?"

"Oh, of course, but they say they don't know - that Cecily would never say," said Peggy with a shrug.

"Well, why don't you ask Cecily herself?"

"Can't do that either. Cecily was killed in a car accident two years ago in Bridgetown and apparently took it with her to her grave. We're at a dead end I'm afraid. It's a pity because I feel confident that if I knew who her father is I could find a cure for her. As it is, she is likely to die within the year," said Peggy shaking her head sadly.

Stan picked up the last piece of fish and the last two slices of bread and made a sandwich. George and Peggy glanced at each other.

"It's a bit of a puzzle," said Stan taking a bite of the sandwich and chewing slowly. "The only thing I can suggest is to ask Philip if any of his old school mates know anything. Surely someone who knew Cecily would know who she was going about with."

"Philip seemed a little reluctant to give us the names of her grandparents," said George. "He kept looking around and acting as if it was very hush-hush, but maybe that was because he wasn't supposed to be talking to me on the beach and was afraid his manager would spot him."

Stan waved his beer bottle and shook his head. "More likely it's because he doesn't know you. Bajans are very leery of confiding in tourists. I'll ask him if you like. He's known me for years and certainly trusts me."

Peggy reached over and put her hand on Stan's arm. "Oh, would you, Stan? That would be most helpful - you might be able to help save a life. Thank you so much." Tears sprang up in her eyes.

Stan smiled at her and patted her hand. "That's quite all right. Willing to help in any way I can. I'll let you know what I find out."

Peggy smiled and withdrew her hand and looked at her watch. "Thanks ever so much for everything, Stan. I'm afraid I must be going. I have plans to go to the races with some friends later this afternoon."

"Oh? I'm going also," said Stan. "It's the big race of the year - the Gold Cup. Thundercloud is expected to win it hands down."

George looked at Peggy and then at Stan. "Thundercloud? I've heard of that horse ..."

"Oh, everyone that's up on racing has heard of Thundercloud. He's Lord and Lady Kimberly"s champ - he sired many a winner both here and in England. Costs a pretty penny to hire him for stud I can assure you!" said Stan enthusiastically.

"Yes, I can imagine. I believe I know someone who owns a filly by him. By Jove, I'd like to see him run. What time do the races start?" asked George, his eyes shining.

"Four o'clock," said Stan. "Say, George, if you don't have plans to go with someone, why not come along with me? I can get seats in the owners' box, and you can meet everyone who's anyone in Barbados. What do you say?"

"Sounds great," said George excitedly. He jumped up and looked down at himself. "I'll have to go back to the hotel and change clothes, though."

"Plenty of time for that," said Stan with a grin. "Walk on back with Peggy and I'll come by in a taxi to pick you up at three-thirty. Be out at the main entrance."

"Done!" said George. He scooped up his clothes from the deck rail as Peggy said good-bye to Stan.

After they were a short distance down the beach out of eyesight of the cottage, Peggy looked over at George with a grin. "Didn't know you had an interest in horse racing, George."

"I do now," said George grinning back at her.

*   *   *

Chapter 18

A T NINE THAT morning, Doctor Jane Elliot met Yong Cha who had pulled up in the jeep outside their headquarters. "Hello, Yong Cha. Thank you for offering to take me on a tour of the orphanage and your parents" house. I hope you don't mind. Hank and Chih have decided to come along also. They'll be here in a moment."

"No problem, Doctor Jane," said Yong Cha with a good-natured grin.

Jane grinned and slung her backpack into the back seat of the jeep and climbed in. She was grateful Yong Cha had not been looking directly at her when she had mentioned Hank's name because she had been unable to keep the hot blush off her face as she remembered his touch earlier that morning. She felt like a fourteen-year-old who'd just had her first kiss.

Her heart did another somersault when the door to the house opened and Hank strode out with Chih right behind him. His tight Levi's and black tee shirt set off his lean muscular frame. He took off his aviator sunglasses as he walked up to the jeep, and although he nodded at Yong Cha, he was looking only at her. "Good morning," he said with a smile. "Did you have a good night's sleep?"

"I certainly did!" said Jane smiling into his eyes, and then she stopped short and burst out laughing. "Where in the world did you get that?" she asked pointing at his tee shirt. It had a large portrait of Mickey Mouse dressed in a general's uniform.

Hank laughed. "Like it? My ten-year-old nephew gave it to me as a Christmas present, and I always wear it when I'm in good spirits."

"And are you in good spirits?" asked Jane with a teasing smile.

"The absolute best," said Hank as he climbed into the back seat with her. "I certainly woke up on the right side of the bed this morning." He winked at her and then turned to Chih. "Come on Chih, chop! chop! Get in and let's go," he said putting his aviator glasses back on.

"All right, General Hank," said Chih, grinning at Hank and Jane. He climbed in the front seat next to Yong Cha. Yong Cha started the jeep with a roar, put it into gear, and they were off in the same direction Hank and Jane had taken the day before.

"So, tell me about yourselves," said Jane. "Chih said you were born in your parents" house near the orphanage and that you were working on the base when it was active. How long ago was that?"

"We were living here with many others working on a sugar cane plantation. When the Air Force took it over as a base, we continued working here. That was just after Ronald Reagan became President of U.S. - about thirty-five years ago," said Yong Cha.

"Thirty-five years ago? How old were you then?" asked Jane.

"In early fifties, right Chih?" Yong Cha looked at Chih, and Chih nodded in agreement.

"What? How old are you now?" asked Jane incredulously.

"Chih is eldest - eighty-seven now, and I eighty-five."

"You're kidding!" exclaimed Jane. "You certainly look and act much younger than that. I would have thought you were in your sixties!"

Yong Cha and Chih glanced at each other and chuckled. "Thank you, Doctor Jane, for compliment," said Chih.

By this time they had reached the dirt road and Yong Cha was steering the jeep through the tropical growth on the way to the ruins of the orphanage.

"Didn't you say you were stationed here about thirty-five years ago, Hank?" asked Jane.

Hank had been gazing out at the scenery silently listening to the interchange between Jane and the Chinese brothers. Now he looked over at Jane. "Yes, that's right," he said slowly. "I was here for about two years. I was a captain then."

"Then you were here at the same time. Do you remember General Hank?" she asked Chih.

"No," said Chih, "but my memory has faded. Do you, Yong Cha?"

Yong Cha shook his head as he concentrated on the road. "No. I knew many of the fry boys because of working on planes, but there was another group stationed at another part of the base that did not mix with the regulars. We heard they were involved in top secret testing of some kind. Maybe General Hank was with them?"

"What about it, Hank? Were you part of that group?" Jane looked back at Hank, but he was looking out at the scenery again and refused to look at her.

"I don't really know," he said in a low voice.

Jane looked at him for a second, took the hint and decided not to continue this line of questioning.

The jeep came out into the clearing and now they could see the dilapidated buildings of the orphanage. As Yong Cha pulled up outside the orphanage and turned off the engine, Jane leaned forward and put her hand on the back of the front seat. "Chih said your parents worked here at the orphanage and that they died here along with all the others who are buried here," she said gently to Yong Cha. "Do you know what happened here?"

"That's right," said Yong Cha, gazing at the dilapidated buildings with a sad expression. "Honorable parents worked here at orphanage. Sing Chin Woo was gardener and Mae Lai Woo worked inside." They all fell silent for a moment, and then Yong Cha said, "Not sure what caused everyone to die. No one ever said. All I remember about that time is strange looking plane."

"Plane?" asked Jane.

Yong Cha nodded, still gazing at the buildings. "Yes, it was different from other planes - looked like black kite. I remember seeing it in sky same day people at orphanage found dead."

"Do you know anything about that, Hank?" asked Jane looking over at him.

Hank startled everyone by slamming his hand on the side of the jeep. "No!" he yelled. "No! I don't know anything about that!" He abruptly climbed out of the jeep and strode off a few paces. Then he stood with his back to them looking at the blue-green chain of mountains that rose beyond the orphanage, his hands stuck into the hip pockets of his Levi's.

Yong Cha, Chih and Jane all looked at each other in surprise. Finally Yong Cha started to get out of the jeep. "Come," he said. "I show you house of my parents where Chih and I were born."

Jane nodded, grabbed her backpack and scrambled out of the back seat of the jeep. Chih got out of the front and he and Yong Cha began walking along a path that led past Hank and around the perimeter of the orphanage. Jane followed and stopped just in front of Hank where she began struggling to get her arms through the backpack. She looked over her shoulder up at Hank. "Do you mind?" she asked with a smile.

Hank started out of his reverie and helped her put the backpack on. "What do you have in there? The kitchen sink?" he asked in his normal tone of voice, grinning down at her.

"That's right," she said returning his grin. "You never know when it might come in handy."

Hank motioned for her to go ahead of him, and they walked on up the path where Yong Cha and Chih were waiting for them to catch up.

After about a ten-minute hike along the trail that wound through a lush tropical forest, they came upon a small immaculate house with a red roof curved up at the eaves in the Chinese style. They went through a red arch with Chinese characters painted in gold into a small courtyard. Yong Cha and Chih paused and turned to look at their guests with welcoming smiles.

"My word! This is fabulous," said Jane looking about at the simple elegance of the courtyard where a few stones, plants and sand had been arranged to create a sense of harmonious balance.

"What does the writing mean?" asked Hank curiously looking at the gold characters on the arch.

"Name of house," said Chih. "Honorable parents name it House of Joy and Harmony."

"I can certainly see why," said Jane admiring the richly carved and lacquered wood that adorned the entrance of the house.

"Come. We show you rest," said Yong Cha. He went up one step onto the tiny veranda and opened the sliding panels that served as a door.

Jane and Hank followed the brothers" example by taking off their shoes just inside the door and slipping into house sandals. Jane shrugged out of her backpack and left it beside her Nikes. As they followed the brothers through the house they marveled at the exquisite lacquered Chinese furniture and the many watercolor paintings.

Yong Cha opened another set of sliding panels at the back of the house, and they came out onto a lanai overlooking an immaculate garden. Carefully swept paths bordered the various vegetable beds and bamboo screens surrounded the perimeter. Lush flowering plants were placed strategically, and water trickled pleasantly down rock shelves into a small pool near the lanai. At the rear of the garden, water fell down rocks into a bamboo funnel that was balanced on a fulcrum. When the funnel filled, it tipped and made a thumping noise as it struck a rock and emptied the water into the pool below. "Scares off rodents and other garden pests," explained Yong Cha.

After they had taken a tour of the garden, Chih said, "Now we show you special place."

Hank and Jane followed the brothers back to the front door where they put on their shoes and Jane collected her backpack once more. They followed Chih out to the entry gate and waited for Yong Cha to close the sliding panels. Then they walked up a steep path at the side of the house that wound its way up and up through a tangled tropical forest. Finally they came into a clearing and discovered they were at the top of a mountain. A kiosk-like structure with a roof and walled in on three sides faced a red octagonal pagoda.

Yong Cha and Chih stood on either side of the open structure beckoning to Hank and Jane who were standing at the head of the trail gaping in surprise at these buildings in so remote a location.

"Welcome to Tea House of Sing Chin and Mae Lai," said Chih as they walked up onto the slate stones that paved the floor of the teahouse

"Please to sit," said Yong Cha, motioning at cushions on the floor.

Hank and Jane did as they were told and sat down cross-legged on the cushions. They found that they were facing the pagoda and beyond that, they could see the blue Pacific sparkling in the distance and the white foam of the surf breaking on a black sand beach far below.

Chih and Yong Cha bowed reverently toward the pagoda before they also sat down on cushions. They both sat in silence facing the pagoda, and Jane and Hank did the same, sensing that this was some sort of holy place for the two Chinese men.

After a time, Yong Cha broke the silence. "This is where we come to meditate and honor parents," he said. "Honorable parents are buried in pagoda."

"But I thought they were buried at the orphanage ..." said Jane, turning to him in surprise.

"They were buried there at first, but many years later, after everyone gone, Chih and I move them here and build pagoda and tea house," explained Yong Cha with a proud look.

"What do you mean, after everyone was gone?" asked Jane.

"Everyone who was confined to the base," said Yong Cha. "They all gone now except me and Chih."

Jane looked at him with a puzzled expression. "I don't understand."

"When Air Force leave, they fenced in whole area including orphanage and where we are now, and all of us who living here had to stay," said Chih.

"What? That's strange," said Jane. "Why would they do that?"

Chih shrugged his shoulders. "We never knew why. They not tell us."

"How many people ended up being confined here?"

"Eighty-five beside us."

Jane looked at Hank in alarm, but he was looking out at the pagoda and the ocean beyond and seemed not to be aware of the conversation.

"Eighty-five? How could they keep that many people inside this area all those years?"

"Oh, not hard," said Chih. "We all live here anyway. They just put fence around whole area and patrol outside to make sure no one come in or go out."

"And now you and Yong Cha are the only ones left who are living here?" asked Jane with an incredulous look. "What happened to the others?"

"They all die over the years."

"I still don't understand. Surely, you must have some idea of why the Air Force did this? What happened right before?"

Yong Cha thought for a moment, creasing his brow. "There were strange people who came to the base dressed like what they wear in outer space. I remember that. After they were here for a day or so, they told us they were enlarging the base and none of us could leave and nobody could come in. I think it had something to do with that plane."

"Plane?" asked Jane with a frown.

"Yes, you remember. The one I told you about that looked like a kite," Yong Cha explained.

Jane looked at Hank. "Do you remember anything about when they closed down the base, Hank? Were you still here when they did that?"

Hank frowned and concentrated. "Somehow it seems familiar, but I just don't remember ... must have heard something about it after I left."

Jane studied Hank with a curious expression for a moment. Then she turned back to Chih and Yong Cha. "We happen to know of two young men who were at the orphanage and are still living," she said. "We were wondering if you might remember them."

Chih looked at Yong Cha and Yong Cha frowned. "Oh, no, Doctor Jane. You must be mistaken. Nobody living who was at orphanage. Nobody living who was on base except the two of us."

"Our records show that they were at Kalimahi Orphanage until they were three months old, and their ages put them here right at the time all those people at the orphanage died," said Jane. She paused and noticed that Hank was looking out at the ocean again. He seemed to have no interest in the conversation. "By the way, these two young men are identical twins, and although their mother was Hawaiian, they have blue eyes and blonde hair," she added.

Yong Cha frowned as he searched his memory. "Hawaiian twins with blonde hair, blue eyes ..."

"I remember!" said Chih suddenly. "You remember, too, Yong Cha. Honorable mother deliver them - name Cory and Cody, born to Alicia Kalima."

Yong Cha's eyes lit up. "Ah, yes! Now I remember. Alicia Kalima ..." He paused and frowned again. "Reason I not remember at first is because you say twins were at orphanage. Cory and Cody were not at orphanage because of Father James."

"What do you mean?" asked Jane.

"Alicia, she try get orphanage to take them, but Father James refuse. He say Catholic orphanage cannot take children born out of wedlock if parent is living. Alicia, she get desperate. Can't support children; not know for sure who father is," said Yong Cha.

"That right," added Chih noticing Jane's look of confusion. "Alicia good looking girl. She earn money going out with fry boys. Obvious twins" father is American, but Alicia go with so many, she not know which one is father."

"I see," said Jane, looking at Hank with a small grin.

Hank looked at her but did not smile. "Alicia ... Alicia Kalima ..." he said softly almost as if he was talking to himself.

"Do you remember her, Hank?" asked Jane, watching his expression closely.

"No ... no, I'm almost certain that I don't remember her," he said. He was looking out toward the ocean again.

Jane watched Hank for a second and then she turned back to Chih. "So what happened to the twins then?"

"Alicia commit suicide to force Father James to take twins into orphanage," he said with a sad expression.

"Oh, my God!" exclaimed Jane, shocked. "What a horrible thing to do! Surely she could have found the father or found a way to raise them without resorting to that!"

"Alicia, she not able to face humiliation. She outcast when she have children without being married. She not know of any other way out. That's the way things were in island society in those days - maybe even now, for all we know," said Yong Cha.

"Did you hear that, Hank? That's terrible! The twins" mother committed suicide," she said.

"Yes, I heard," said Hank still looking out at the ocean. "I heard about it all right, but I don't remember."

Jane looked at him with an odd expression again. What in the world was wrong with him, she wondered.

"What happened then? Did Father James take the twins into the orphanage?" asked Jane.

Chih shook his head. "No, Father James say Alicia cannot be buried in Catholic cemetery because she commit suicide, and he say twins would be too big a disruption at the orphanage because they looked so much different from other children. So he get elderly people to take care of them until someone took them to mainland."

"Do you know who took care of them?" asked Jane.

"Old Chinese couple who live near mountains on other side of orphanage. You remember, Yong Cha?" asked Chih.

Yong Cha thought for a moment and then nodded. "Wang and Ling-Ling Chan. They die many years ago - not long after Air Force abandon base."

"That's right. That was their name," Chih agreed.

"From our records, we know who adopted the twins when they were brought to the mainland, but we don't know who brought them to the mainland. Did you ever hear about that?"

Both brothers shook their heads. "No. We never know about that. Wang and Ling-Ling refuse to talk about it. Seem like it was secret for some reason," said Yong Cha.

"Well, that puts a new wrinkle in things, don't you think, Hank? We thought the twins were at the orphanage, but it turns out they were not. Our records on that score are incorrect," said Jane, looking at Hank again.

Hank looked at her and nodded slowly. He had just opened his mouth to say something when the sound of an approaching helicopter caused them all to look toward the ocean side of the mountain. The thwacking of the blades grew so loud it was impossible to speak and be heard. Suddenly, the helicopter popped above the rim of the mountain. "Put your hands up and do not move!" yelled a voice over a megaphone. They saw soldiers dressed in camouflage fatigues training rifles on them through the open doors of the helicopter as it started to set down in the clearing.

Even before the helicopter had set down four soldiers boiled out of the sides of it and ran crouching under the blades toward them with their weapons held in front of it at the ready.

Jane, Chih and Yong Cha looked to Hank for direction. "Do as they say," he said, rising to his feet and putting his hands up. "I'll have this sorted out in no time."

They followed his example and rose to their feet, standing in the teahouse with their arms up in the air.

Hank recognized the insignia of a lieutenant in the lead. He was apparently in charge. "Who is your commanding officer, Lieutenant?" he asked in an authoritative voice.

"Sit down and hands on top of your heads!" shouted the Lieutenant. "This area is off limits to anyone. What are you doing here?"

"I am on official business, and I am a General," said Hank as Jane, Chih and Yong Cha sat down and placed their hands on their heads.

"I am in charge here!" shouted the Lieutenant. He prodded Hank in the chest with the barrel of his rifle. "Get down and put your hands on your head."

"You are making a mistake, Lieutenant. I far outrank you and you will not hear the end of this," Hank cautioned him.

"We'll see about that," said the Lieutenant.   "Produce your identification."

"I don't have it with me. It's back at headquarters, but I assure you I am a general, and I have a reason for being here that you are not privy to. Who is your C.O.?" Hank's face was beginning to flush with anger at the impertinence of this subordinate.

"Sure, sure. Like I really believe you. If you're who you say you are, you would have identification on you." The lieutenant's face was harsh and sweaty from the humidity of the hot sun and tropical forest. "Now, are you going to get down, or do I have to help you with the butt of my rifle?"

Hank glared at him. "Why you little ..." he began.

The lieutenant raised his rifle threateningly, which infuriated Hank even further. "Why you little S.O.B., I'll have you demoted!" he said, provoking the lieutenant to point the rifle at his midsection.

"Get down, I said, or face the consequences!" he roared.

Hank grudgingly sat down and put his hands on his head. "You'll be sorry about this," he said.

"Sure, sure. Tell it to the Marines," said the lieutenant, motioning to his men who trained their weapons on the prisoners. "Now, I'm going to ask again," he said looking at Jane. "Who are you and what are you doing inside this restricted area?"

"I'm a doctor and I'm conducting research on a rare tropical disease," said Jane.

The lieutenant snorted. "Right, and I come from the moon. What about you two?" he asked turning to Chih and Yong Cha.

"We live here," said Chih, answering for both of them.

"Sure you do!" exploded the lieutenant. "No one has lived here for thirty years. Well, we'll just have to take you to headquarters and put you in the brig and then maybe your memory will come back to you and you'll tell us the real reason you're here. As of now, you are all under military arrest."

"God damn it, Lieutenant! I told you I'm an Air Force General, and these people are with me," yelled Hank.

The lieutenant looked at him sternly and then he grinned snidely. "Oh, pardon me, Sir. I don't know why I didn't notice sooner. Of course you're a general, Sir." He looked at his men and pointed at Hank's tee shirt. "Stand at attention, men. It's General Mickey Mouse!"

*   *   *

After a half-hour ride in the helicopter, their armed escort led Hank, Jane, Chih and Yong Cha into a large single-story building that served as the commanding officer's headquarters on the Army base. Inside, they were led into separate rooms where they waited in solitude to be interrogated.

After about an hour, the interrogator, dressed in a crisply pressed captain's uniform, walked smartly into Hank's room holding a clipboard. He walked over to where Hank had been pacing up and down behind a metal folding table, placed the clipboard on the table, and stuck out his hand to Hank. "Captain Robert Benson," he said. "I'm here to ask you a few questions."

Hank shook the captain's hand. "Well, Captain. My name is General Howard Kingsman of the Air Force, and I am a special aid to the President of the United States."

"So you say, but I am told you have no identification to prove your claim," said Captain Benson. "I need to know what you were doing inside the restricted area."

"Who is your commanding officer, Captain? I will only speak to him. The sooner the better, and this whole matter can be cleared up." Hank had drawn himself up to his full height and was looking down on Captain Benson who was a head shorter.

"General Armstrong Sutton is in charge here, but you cannot speak to him ..."

"And why the hell not?" shouted Hank, his temper flaring.

Captain Benson bridled at the tone of Hank's voice. "Because he is away from the base at the moment, and I am in charge of this matter."

"Well, you'd better be contacting him, then, and he can verify my identity through the Pentagon. I'm not saying anything more to you or anyone else lower in rank than a general," said Hank.

"Then you will have to be detained for several days. General Sutton will not be back until Friday."

"Oh, for God's sake! You can certainly get hold of him, and tell him he'd better get his butt back here and get this straightened out right away, or you'll all be sorry. I'm operating on orders from the President and it can't wait. If Sutton will check it out, he'll understand, so you'd better get hold of him pronto unless you want to spend the rest of your military career on Rat Island!"

Benson's temper flared at Hank's combative tone, but his demeanor suddenly changed to surprise at the mention of Rat Island. "Rat Island? You mean that old deserted outpost in the Aleutians? It hasn't been used since World War II and it's restricted. How do you know about that?" he asked suspiciously.

"Because I just know, that"s all," said Hank. "That should convince you that I'm who I say I am, anyway' Anyone who's not in the military would not likely know about Rat Island, now would they?"

Benson was still frowning at him. "Well, maybe ..."

"No ifs ands or buts about it! That's all I'm saying to you. Your mission is to get hold of Sutton and get him back here right now. Otherwise, believe me, you will all be sorry," said Hank with an air of finality. Then he turned his back on Benson, crossed his arms and stood rigidly looking at a map that hung on the wall.

Benson shrugged his shoulders, picked up his clipboard and quietly walked out of the room. He walked a few paces down the hallway and nodded at two guards outside another doorway. They saluted and opened the door for him to enter.

Jane looked up quickly as she heard the door open. Then she rose to her feet from the metal chair as she saw the captain enter the room.

He walked up to her, placed his clipboard down on the table and extended his hand. "Captain Robert Benson," he said.

Jane smiled slightly and took his hand. "Doctor Jane Elliot."

"Doctor Elliot, please have a seat," said the captain politely, waiting for her to sit back down in the metal chair before he sat in another one across the table from her. He pulled his clipboard over and looked at it for a second before raising his head and looking at her. "Now then, I'm told you're a doctor and doing research on a rare tropical disease?"

"That's correct," nodded Jane. "I am consultant for a subcontractor to a contractor who is working for General Kingsman."

"A consultant for a subcontractor to a contractor who works for General Kingsman?" repeated Captain Benson with a puzzled look, his pen poised above the clipboard.

"That's correct, Captain. You have it right."

"Does General Kingsman pay your salary?"

"No," said Jane shaking her head.

Captain Benson raised an eyebrow and made a note on the clipboard. "What were you doing in the restricted area, Doctor?" he asked without looking up.

"I was with the General, and that's all I can say about it, Captain. You will have to ask the General that question."

"Are you sure he's who he says he is? Is he really an Air Force general - General Howard Kingsman?" asked Benson raising his eyes to her again.

Jane nodded and smiled. "Oh, yes, I'm quite sure of that. By the way, why is that area restricted?"

"It's dangerous for anyone to be in there," said Benson without thinking. He was taken off guard by her sudden question.

"Why is it dangerous?"

"Unexploded ordnance left over from the base's operational days," said Benson quickly.

"What sort of ordnance?"

"Oh, ammunition mostly, but I'm the one who's asking questions here. What were you doing in there?"

"I told you, you'll have to ask the General."

"Very well," said Benson, rising to his feet. "I have no choice but to detain you here until we get this sorted out. The guards will show you to some quarters."

"But I'm a civilian and I know my rights. The Army cannot detain me," said Jane as Benson strode toward the door. He did not reply and she was left sitting alone until the two guards came to take her away.

Captain Benson questioned Chih and Yong Cha and, like the lieutenant, was surprised to learn that they had been living inside the base all those years. Other than that, he learned nothing new about Hank and Jane.

The four detainees were put into separate guarded quarters for the night.

At nine o'clock the next morning there was a knock at Hank's door and when he opened it, Captain Benson saluted him. "Good morning, General Kingsman, Sir," he said. "General Sutton checked out your identity as you asked, and he has returned to the base and is ready to meet with you."

Hank grinned as he returned the captain's salute. "That's more like it, Captain Benson. Lead the way."

"Yes, Sir!" said Benson saluting again and turning on his heel. A passing lieutenant looked back over his shoulder and shook his head in surprise at seeing the captain saluting a man dressed in Levi's and a Mickey Mouse tee shirt.

"Good morning, General Kingsman," said a beefy-faced man in an Army general's uniform as Hank passed through the door into his office. "I am General Armstrong Sutton. I am sorry we had to detain you, and I hope your quarters were satisfactory."

"I've been in worse places," said Hank as he exchanged salutes with Sutton. He sat down in a chair in front of Sutton's desk, and Sutton resumed his seat behind his desk.

"Now then, General. The Pentagon confirms that you are, in fact, General Howard Kingsman, and that you are still active in the Air Force and that you are a special aid to the President," said

Sutton rocking back in his chair and steepling his fingers together in front of his chin.

"That's right," said Hank. "So now you know who I am, you can have your boys take me back where they found me so I can get on with my mission."

Sutton sat forward and leaned across the desk. "I'm afraid it's not that simple, General. No one - and I mean no one, general or not - is allowed inside that area. That's why I'm here - for the sole purpose of making sure no one goes in or out of that base."

Hank leaned forward on the desk also and looked directly into Sutton's eyes. "Believe me, General Sutton, I have every right to be inside that base, and I outrank you on this because I am acting on orders from the very top," he said in a low voice.

"The very top ... you mean ... ?" asked Sutton in a hushed voice.

Hank nodded gravely. "That's right. The Commander in Chief."

Sutton's eyes grew wide and then he frowned. "How am I to know that for sure? I can't let you back into that base unless I'm absolutely certain that you're acting on orders from a source higher than my own."

Hank paused for a moment and leaned back in his chair. "Do you have a secure line there?" he asked, pointing to a bank of telephones that sat on the General's desk.

Sutton nodded and shoved a red phone over towards Hank's side of the desk.

Hank leaned forward again and picked up the receiver and began tapping in numbers on the keypad. As he waited for an answer, he held up a finger to Sutton and then he smiled. "Are you alone?" he asked into the receiver.

There was a pause as Hank held the receiver to his ear and looked at Sutton with a smile. Then he said into the receiver, "Making progress here, but ran into a small snag. I have someone here who needs to hear from you that I have full authority to be where I'm at and doing what I'm doing."

There was another pause and then Hank chuckled. "That's the problem. I can't pull rank. He's a general, too. Name's General Armstrong Sutton - Army."

Hank listened for another second and nodded. He put his hand over the receiver and looked at Sutton. "He wants to talk to you," he said.

Sutton drew himself up in his chair, smoothed back his hair and nodded. Hank switched on the video display and President Glenn Forbes's face filled the screen.

"General Sutton?" he asked.

"Yes, Sir, President Forbes," said Sutton, holding himself rigidly at attention.

"General Sutton, as your Commander in Chief, I order you to cooperate with General Kingsman in anything he demands. He is acting on my behalf in a matter of critical national security. If you get any flak from any of your higher-ups, have 'em call me and I'll confirm it to them, understood?"

"Yes, Sir!" said General Sutton. "It's a pleasure to act on your behalf, Sir."

"Good," said Forbes. Then he grinned at Sutton. "What's that accent? You from Oklahoma by any chance?"

Sutton relaxed slightly and grinned back. "Sure am - Tulsa-bred, born and raised."

"Glad to hear it. Oklahomans and Kansans have been good neighbors for a long time. I know I can count on you to help General Kingsman out. Remember, if you need anything verified from me, just have 'em call here at the White House."

"Yes, Sir, President Forbes," said Sutton.

"Good. Okay now, Hank?" asked Forbes.

Hank got back on the receiver and grinned at Forbes. "Thanks, Mr. President. Everything's ok now. You should be hearing from me soon."

"Looking forward to it," said Forbes and the two of them hung up.

Within an hour, Hank, Jane, Chih and Yong Cha were preparing to board a helicopter that would take them back to the base.

"With the compliments of General Sutton, Sir," said Captain Benson who was supervising the loading of a case of champagne, a case of Jack Daniels and a sealed box of fifty pounds of mahi mahi packed in dry ice.

"Thank General Sutton for me. We'll make good use of it," said Hank.

"Yes, Sir," said Captain Benson, standing back from the helicopter as the blades began to whirl. He saluted.

Hank returned the salute and boarded the helicopter. Jane, Chih and Yong Cha were already strapped into seats behind the pilot, and Hank took the seat up front next to the pilot.

"Ready, Sir?" asked the pilot, looking over at Hank.

Hank put on his aviator sunglasses and grinned. "Sure am, Lieutenant. Let „er rip."

The helicopter lifted off and they soon had a bird's eye view of the extent of the security fence that surrounded the base.

"Just look at that fence! It goes on forever!" exclaimed Jane.

"Yes, Doctor Jane. It goes on for many miles. That is why we live there for so many years not really feeling fenced in, because it surrounds such a large area," said Yong Cha.

"Why was the fence put up and the base sealed off?" asked Jane. "Captain Benson said it had something to do with unexploded ordnance."

"I heard it was because of contamination, and that was about thirty-five years ago," said the pilot.

"Contaminated with what?" asked Jane.

The pilot shook his head as he looked out the window. "I don't know. Don't even know if the contamination story is true - just a rumor."

"I still think it had something to do with that plane," said Yong Cha. "It was some kind of special plane."

"Special plane?" asked the pilot.

Suddenly Hank turned to him with a stern look. "Lieutenant, you are out of line," he said in a raised voice. "This is all classified information and you should not be talking about it."

The pilot glanced over at Hank in surprise. "I'm sorry, Sir. I didn't know," he said apologetically.

"Well, now you do, so be careful what you say," said Hank gruffly. He turned his face away and looked out the window on his right side.

Feeling chastised, the pilot completed the rest of the trip in silence. After a while, Jane struck up a mundane conversation with Chih and Yong Cha about the flora and fauna of the island.

In about half an hour, the rusted red roofs of the dilapidated orphanage buildings came into view. "Here's the orphanage coming up," said the pilot, looking over at Hank. "This is where I'm supposed to drop you, isn't it?"

Hank looked down at the orphanage below. "Oh, God! It's the orphanage!" he cried in a strangled voice. "Oh, no, no, no! It's the orphanage!"

The pilot kept looking at Hank, but Hank didn't look at him. He just kept looking down at the scene below. Finally the pilot glanced back at Jane who was intently watching Hank with concern. She glanced over at the pilot and saw that he was looking at her. "Yes, Lieutenant. We left our jeep in front of the gate to the orphanage. That's where we want you to drop us," she said.

"Oh, God! Oh, no! It's the orphanage!" cried Hank again as the helicopter touched down near the jeep.

*　　*　　*

Chapter 19

W HEN STAN AND George entered the glass enclosed Owner's Box at the top of the tiers of seats at the race track, it was already packed. Up here, people were dressed up - the men in blazers and linen trousers, the women in frilly chiffon dresses and wide-brimmed straw hats. They were standing about in clusters sipping champagne and eating delicate canapés being passed around by Bajan waiters dressed in tuxedos. This crowd appeared to be mostly white, with a small scattering of well-dressed Bajans.

Fortunately, taking Peggy's advice, George had dressed in his navy blue blazer and light gray trousers. "Bloody hell, Stan. This looks just like Ascot - the type of thing my ex-wife is into. I'd be more comfortable with the regular types down below."

Stan laughed. "I know what you mean. I usually prefer mixing with the regulars also, but this is a once-a-year event - The Gold Cup. There's only one race, and afterward, there is a big gala for the owners at the Palm Shores. Let's go over and place our bets. Then we can enjoy the food and drink before the race starts."

George followed Stan who wound his way through the crowd toward the back of the enclosure. As they joined the queue in front of one of the windows, a huge muscular Bajan man dressed in a butter-colored linen suit, silk tropical-print shirt and a straw Fedora-style hat the color of cream was just turning away from the window next to them after placing his bet. He placed a wad of tickets inside his wallet and returned it to his inside jacket pocket. He looked up just as he was passing Stan and George and stopped abruptly. "Hello, Stan," he said. "Haven't seen you for a while."

Stan grinned and held out his hand. "Ambrose. Good to see you. One of your horses running today?"

The man shook his head and did not return Stan's smile. "No. My filly Caracas Queen will be ready next year. Then, we'll give Thundercloud and Lord Kimberly a run for the money. Next year, I'm betting we can say good-bye to Lord Kimberly, but for now I'm betting on Thundercloud," he said glancing at George.

"Ambrose, this is an English friend of mine - George Goater. George, this is Ambrose Reynaud," said Stan.

"Mr. Reynaud," said George. He shook hands with the big man and felt positively engulfed. The man must be over six foot five, he estimated.

"Mr. Goater," said Reynaud. George noticed that, unlike the other Bajans he had met, this one did not smile and he didn't call him "Mr. George."

The Bajan stepped back and looked at George appraisingly. "Any relation to Bill Goater?" he asked.

George was so surprised at this question that he could only nod.

"Bill Goater is his father," said Stan quickly.

"I hear he is not well," said Reynaud.

"That's right," said George, recovering his speech. "He had a heart attack, but he is getting better."

"Is that right? A heart attack, and he's getting better?" said Reynaud looking at Stan.

Stan simply nodded with a grim expression.

"I see," said Reynaud. He looked at his watch, which George noticed was a Rolex. "Well, I am meeting some people so I've got to get over to my seat now. Hope your luck is better today, Stan."

"It was a pleasure meeting you, Mr. Reynaud," said George as he watched the big man stroll away.

George turned back to Stan and saw that he was frowning as he watched Reynaud walk away.

"Who is this Reynaud chap?" asked George. "Seems very influential."

"What?" asked Stan, jolted out of his inner thoughts. "Oh, yes.

Ambrose Reynaud is very influential indeed. He is the leader of the opposition party and after the next election will very likely be the next Prime Minister of Barbados."

"What does he do for a living? Seems quite wealthy to own racehorses and to be dressed as he is. Did you notice the size of the diamond in that ring and the Rolex watch?"

Stan smiled slightly and nodded. "Yes, he is quite wealthy. Possibly the wealthiest man in Barbados. He has business interests in Venezuela."

"Oil?" asked George.

Stan's smile broadened. "Yes, I believe it is oil."

"Who is the current Prime Minister of Barbados?" asked George after they had placed their bets. He had bet five Barbados dollars on Thundercloud to win, place or show.

"A chap named Owen Haynes, the leader of the National Democratic Party," said Stan. "In fact, he and his wife are right over there." Stan pointed to a tall slender Bajan dressed in a black blazer and white linen trousers. Standing next to him was a lithe elegantly dressed woman whose skin was the color of café a lait. A cluster of English people surrounded them. As George and Stan approached, a woman wearing a large floppy hat turned her head in their direction. It was Peggy. She smiled and beckoned to them to come over.

"Hello, George. Hello, Stan," she said as they joined the fringe of the group. "Placed your bets on Thundercloud, I hope?"

"That's right," said George winking at her. "They say Thundercloud is the favorite." He glanced around the group and saw Julian Fleet, Zoë and David. Fleet was saying something to the Prime Minister who inclined his head toward him with an amused look. Zoë was engaged in conversation with a rather pudgy blonde woman and a tall fair-haired gentleman dressed from head to foot in dove gray, while David had the attention of the Prime Minister's wife.

"Well, I see the gang's all here," remarked George. "Who is that talking to Zoë?"

"Why, that's Lord and Lady Kimberly, owners of Thundercloud," said Peggy.

At that instant Fleet noticed George. "George, old man," he said.

"There's some people here you should meet." He looked at Stan curiously. "I don't believe I've had the pleasure," he said extending his hand.

"Stan Straw, Mr. Fleet," said Stan shaking his hand. "I'd know you anywhere from all the newspaper coverage."

Fleet laughed. "Shouldn't believe half of what you read," he said. "Just call me Julian. I take it you're a friend of George's?"

"That's right," said Stan. "I work at the Foreign Office where George worked before he retired."

"And what brings you to Barbados, Stan?"

"Won a bit of money at the races and decided to treat myself to a holiday."

"Yes, it was a real coincidence," said George with a laugh. "We ended up being on the same flight together."

"Come," said Fleet. "Allow me to introduce you to the Right Honorable Owen Haynes, Prime Minister of Barbados. And this is his lovely lady Genevieve. George Goater and Stan Straw, Prime Minister."

The Prime Minister inclined his head toward Stan. "Hello, Stan. I haven't seen you for a while," he said. Then he turned to George. "Mr. Goater, a pleasure. Mr. Fleet tells me you are Bill Goater's son."

"That is correct," said George. "It's a pleasure to meet you, Sir."

"Did I hear you say you're the son of Bill Goater?" asked the fair-haired man who had been talking to Zoë.

"Allow me," said Fleet. "George, Lord and Lady Kimberly."

"My lord, milady," said George, bowing his head slightly toward each of them.

Lord Kimberly reached over and gave him a hearty clap on the shoulder. "Nonsense, dear fellow! No need for such formalities. Bill Goater and I have been close friends for donkey's years. How is Bill?"

"Not well, I'm afraid. Had a heart attack two weeks ago, but is recovering," said George. "Oh, pardon me. This is my friend Stan Straw."

"Of course it is," said Lord Kimberly, glancing at Stan. "I know Stan. How are you?"

"Quite well, my lord. Had to come to wager on Thundercloud. He's such a sure winner," said Stan with a grin.

Lord Kimberly waved his champagne glass. "Well, let us hope he keeps up his reputation today. Certainly helps with his stud fees, which keeps us in bread and butter, what?" They all laughed. "Well, best drink up. The race begins in fifteen minutes." He beckoned and a couple of waiters appeared with trays of champagne and canapés. As George took a flute of champagne from one of the waiter's trays and turned to select a canapé, he didn't notice when a passing waiter slipped a small packet into the pocket of his blazer.

George and Stan sat with Fleet, Zoë, Peggy and David to watch the race. The Prime Minister and his wife, along with the owners of the horses, had gone down to sit on a grandstand that had been especially erected for this event in the inner oval of the track. The Prime Minister officially announced the race. As the horses were being led into the starting gate, George started to perspire from the champagne and the excitement. He took off his blazer and absent-mindedly draped it upside down on the back of his chair. The gates flew open with a loud buzzing noise, and the race was on. Everyone jumped to his feet to watch the race and consequently, no one noticed the small packet that slid out of George's blazer pocket and onto the floor under the chair.

As predicted, Thundercloud won, and everyone sat down to watch as the sleek black stallion was led into the winner's circle, where Lord and Lady Kimberly joined him to receive the Gold Cup. While the ceremonies were taking place the jockey stood beside Thundercloud and held his bridle. Suddenly, the horse began frantically tossing his head and skittering, and the observers became gradually aware that there was another person in the winner's circle. A young Bajan man dressed in baggy pants, running shoes and a baseball cap was hanging onto Thundercloud's bridle on the other side of the jockey. The jockey was attempting to swat the newcomer with his riding crop as the horse continued to pitch and toss.

Just as the rest of the people in the winner's circle were becoming aware that something was awry, four policemen rushed into the circle and grabbed the young man. They quickly cuffed his hands behind his back and dragged him away down the length of the track.

"Bloody hell! What was that all about?" asked George.

"Oh, probably some bloke who is on drugs and just wanted to touch the winner," said Stan. "Happens all the time."

"I don't know," said Peggy looking at Stan with a frown. "Looked as if he was trying to do something to the horse. Almost like he had a needle in his hand."

"Oh, no," said Stan waving a hand in dismissal. "I'm sure it was nothing like that. Just someone who got a little overly exuberant, that's all. Anyway, I'm sure the police will sort it all out."

After the ceremonies were over, people collected their winnings and exited the owner's box. Most of them were on their way to the Palm Shores for the Gold Cup Winner's Gala. As George and Stan made their way down to the lower level, two policemen walked up to them.

"Hello, Lloyd," said Stan to the older officer.

"Hello, Mr. Stan," said the officer. "Is this your friend?"

Stan nodded. "Yes. He's a friend from England. Mr. George Goater."

"I'm sorry, Mr. Stan. We need him to come with us for a moment
- in there," he said pointing toward the men's toilet.

"What? Why?" exclaimed George.

"I'm sorry, Mr. Goater, but we need to search you. Please come with us."

"Search me for what?" exclaimed George. "I've done nothing wrong. Tell them, Stan."

Stan looked at George and patted his arm. "It's ok, George. I'm sure there's nothing wrong. Best to go with them and get it over. I'll wait right here. It won't take long, I'm sure."

"Well, ok, but be sure to wait here for me ..." said George as the policemen took him by the arms and led him toward the toilet.

A short while later, Lloyd, the older of the two policemen, emerged from the door to the toilet and walked over to Stan. "No problem," he said. "We didn't find anything on your friend. Had a tip, but it must have been a false one. He'll be out in a moment as soon as he gets his clothes back on."

"Well that's good to hear, Lloyd," said Stan. "Can you tell me what you were searching for?"

"Drugs - cocaine, but he is clean."

"I see. I know George drinks a bit, but had no idea he'd be into cocaine," remarked Stan as he saw a red-faced George staggering out of the door to the toilet with the other policeman right behind him.

After the policemen left, Stan turned to George. "Are you all right, George?" he asked.

George was looking down at the ground and refused to look up at him. "Bloody hell! You can't believe where they searched me. Nobody in their right mind would hide anything there - I won't be able to sit down for a week."

*   *   *

Every Friday and Saturday night is festival night in Oistins, a town just south of the area known as The Gap where most of the middle-class tourists stay. Locals come by the thousands to eat, drink and dance at this outdoor fish market where hundreds of Bajans operate rum, beer and food stands. Eyes and mouths water from the smoke of dozens of barbecue grills where fish, chicken and pork are being prepared Bajan style. Noses are overwhelmed with a hodgepodge of aromas ranging from raw fish to frying food to heavy musky perfumes to the unmistakable cloying odors of marijuana and hash smoke. Eardrums reverberate and heads thump from the blasting of reggae and salsa from powerful amplifiers positioned around an outdoor dance pavilion.

Everywhere are signs proclaiming *Buy Bajan*, *Bajan Pride*, and the more ominous messages from the Barbadian Health Ministry to refrain from drug use and incest. Bajan police officers dressed in plain clothes mingle in the crowds, primarily to protect the smattering of tourists from being pestered, mugged, robbed or assaulted by the criminal drug-user elements. Here the white faces of English, Irish, American, German and French tourists stand out like scattered beacons of light in a sea of black faces.

Stan and George perched atop a wooden picnic table drinking Banks beer from plastic cups. They had eaten flying fish and marlin, grilled corn on the cob and cole slaw at Miss Hattie's Sea Shack and were now watching the backs of a moving sea of young Bajans dancing to the rhythms blasting from the amplifiers. George was particularly fascinated with an ample-bottomed young woman dancing just in front of him. He had no idea people could wiggle their bums that way.

"Quite a show, isn't it?" remarked Stan, noticing George's fixation.

"Bloody hell! No Englishman could keep up with that!" George grinned and then became transfixed again as two other young women joined the one he had been watching, and a young man with dreadlocks and a knit cap came up behind her and placed his hands on either side of her waist. The music picked up speed and so did their bottoms. "Would you look at that? Seems to be a bum wiggling contest!" George laughed.

"You want barbecue? You come to Delilah's. Best fish, best price," said a wrinkled old lady with her head wrapped in a bright blue bandana. She poked Stan's knee.

Stan grinned at her and shook his head. "Sorry, Mama. We already ate. You can bring us two Banks beers, though."

She grinned, and George saw that she was missing two upper front teeth. "I bring you four for price of three," she said, poking his knee again.

"Done," said Stan with a chuckle as he dug in his trousers pocket for three Barbados dollars. "You can drink two more, can't you, George?"

"No need to ask that, as you well know," said George with a laugh. He drained the rest of the beer from his plastic cup and set it down on the table behind him. He brushed crumbs off the front of his Rugby shirt, which then proceeded to fall onto his dark shorts. "This is more to my liking. Had enough of the la-de-da types for a bit."

"Thought you'd enjoy getting out where the locals go," said Stan. "That's always my preference when I come here."

"What happens next?" asked George as the old woman returned with four plastic cups of beer on a red plastic tray.

"Thanks, Mama," said Stan as he and George each picked up two cups from the tray.

"I come back in fifteen minutes. You'll need more by then," said the old lady with a cackle.

"We'll see," said Stan with a laugh as she moved on to the next person sitting atop the table. He raised his cup to George. "Cheers! We'll drink these and watch more of the young ones dance. Then it will be time for the Dance Hut," he said.

"The Dance Hut? What's that?" asked George, raising his cup and taking a sip.

Stan chuckled. "It's where all us older folk go for ballroom style dancing. Lots of older tourist ladies who are on their own easily find partners to dance with. You'll see," he said knowingly. "It opens at ten o'clock."

After sitting there a while longer and finishing their beers, they got up and meandered through the crowd, stopping occasionally to look at local crafts and wares for sale on peddlers' tables set up at various strategic places. Stan led George to the back area to visit the men's toilet before they went to the Dance Hut. They did not notice the young Bajan man with dreadlocks and the oversized balloon-style knit hat trailing along behind them at a distance.

When they got to the Dance Hut, it was already in full swing. As George and Stan entered, the young man with the dreadlocks walked inside and stationed himself in a dark corner near the door. George saw immediately that the Dance Hut was appropriately named. The small crude hut was already packed with bodies. Not a spot remained on the dance floor where couples pranced and swayed to Glenn Miller's "In the Mood" under the crazy patchwork of lights spun off the revolving mirrored dance ball suspended from the ceiling. At the bar, people were standing three and four deep, watching the dancers and attempting to commandeer a bartender's attention for a Banks beer or a rum punch.

Stan and George squeezed their way into a tiny spot at the far end of the bar where another door led into a back room. By standing sideways, George managed to plant an elbow on the bar and carve out a small bit of space for himself. A deeply tanned blonde woman wearing a halter top was standing with her bare back to him on one side, and the back of his shoulder was pressed up against the back of another man who was speaking loudly in German to a large-boned redheaded woman.

"Two Banks, please," yelled George over the din to a Bajan bartender dressed in tank top and shorts. He had come down the bar and was impatiently drumming his hands on the bar waiting for orders. George plunked down two Bajan dollars as the bartender reached below, slammed two bottles on the counter and snapped the lids off.

George passed one of the beers to Stan who was standing in front of him. Stan took the beer and found a spot on the other side of the doorway to the back room, as there was a constant stream of people coming through the door and jostling him.

George turned so that he could lean against the bar and look out at the crowded dance floor. As he did so, he jolted the blonde on his right with an elbow and sloshed a bit of beer on her bare back. She jumped and turned to glare at him angrily. He was shocked to see that she was much older than she had appeared from the back. She must be at least seventy, he thought. "Sorry,love," he apologized.

The blonde's face softened and she gave him a smile. "It's all right. Happens all the time in here. Too crowded, you see," she said in a distinctly Manchester accent. "English, I see. Where are you from?" she asked as she squirmed her way around into a position facing him.

"Wadhurst, about fifty miles south of London, down in Sussex," George shouted in order to be heard over the blaring wah-wah trumpet of Clyde McCoy playing "Sugar Blues."

"Oh, Wadhurst! I had an aunt in Wadhurst. Minnie Ellis," she said.

George grinned. "I remember Minnie Ellis. She used to come out with her broom and shake it at us lads when we passed her cottage on the way to school. We thought she was a witch."

The woman laughed. "Oh, Aunt Minnie was a bit daft. Didn't like boys at all. Thought they were a dirty lot. She wasn't a witch, but she did brew a strong lot of tea."

"Minnie Ellis," said George shaking his head. "She must have died about twenty years ago, or so."

"That's right. Actually, a little less. She went out when the New Year came in at the turn of the century - 2000. What is your name?"

"I'm George Goater. I grew up on a farm just outside Wadhurst. And you?" asked George.

"Annie Brown, formerly Ellis. I grew up in Manchester. Lived there all my life."

"Manchester. I thought as much from the accent," said George. "What brings you to Barbados?"

"Barbados! Isn't it great? I've been coming here on holiday for years, even after my husband Tom died five years ago. Always stay at the Rainbow Reef at the south end of The Gap. Always the same two weeks every year." She smiled broadly as she lifted a plastic cup of rum punch to her lips. "What about you?"

"My first time here," shouted George. Now Gene Kruppa was banging out his famous drum solo from "Sing! Sing! Sing!" over the loudspeakers. "Just came down for a seven-day holiday. I see quite a number of English ladies here. What's the attraction?"

Annie grinned and pointed to the dance floor. "See those two Bajans? The ones dancing with the English women?"

George looked where she was pointing and saw two quite distinguished looking gentlemen in their fifties or sixties. They were dressed in expensive casual wear and were adeptly swinging two older white ladies about the dance floor. George nodded and looked at Annie questioningly.

"That's Marcus and Victor. They are expert ballroom dancers and members of the Barbados Escort Service. Two more numbers and it's my turn to dance with Marcus. Their price is very reasonable," she explained.

George's mouth dropped open. He had no idea women - especially Englishwomen - would pay for such things. Suddenly, a group of huge Bajan men burst through the door of the backroom, and one of them trod heavily on George's sandaled foot. He howled in pain. "Oh, bloody hell! I think my foot is broken!" he cried, hopping about on one leg and jostling everyone around him and drawing attention to himself.

Annie leaned over and nudged him and put her lips close to his ear. "Don't make too much out of it if you know what's good for you," she said urgently. "Those blokes work for the top drug kingpin in Barbados. Very dangerous."

"I don't bloody well care if it's Christ himself. Has no right to crush my foot!" howled George. "Miserable sod!"

The Bajan who stepped on George's foot walked back to him and towered over him. "You talking about me, Mon?" he asked, grabbing the front of George's Rugby shirt.

"That's right, if you're the one who stepped on my foot!" yelled George. "You should bloody well watch where you're going!"

"Who you to be telling me to watch where I'm going? You need to be going back to England!" yelled the man, yanking George up by his shirt collar. "You not wanted here, Mon! You been snooping into things none of your business. If you're not gone by tomorrow, I'll do more than step on your toe!"

As this confrontation was going on, the young Bajan who had followed George and Stan quietly walked up to a man who was wearing a red and yellow tropical print shirt and standing near the entry door.

The man smiled. "Hello, Philip. I like your dreadlocks."

"Hey, Mon. I need a favor," said the young man. He leaned in close to the older man and spoke in a low voice. The older man nodded and motioned to three other men who were standing nearby.

"Who do you think you are to tell me to leave?" yelled George into his captor's face. "I have as much right to be here as you."

"We'll see about that!" The man shoved George back against the bar, and George winced as his back struck the bar rail. By this time, the man's cronies had joined him and the other people standing at the bar had fled.

Four huge Bajans now stood glaring down at George, their hands balled into fists. Through the pain shooting up his leg and the bleariness of drink, George began to comprehend that he was in a bad position. He felt like a rabbit trapped in its hole by four angry foxes.

"This tourist giving you problems, Floyd?" came a voice from behind them, and the four men quickly stepped aside.

"We'll take care of this," said the man in the red and yellow tropical shirt as he walked up to George. Three other men in tropical shirts stood behind him. "Barbados police," said the man showing George a badge. "We're arresting you for being drunk and disorderly and disturbing the peace," he said.

"But it wasn't me," protested George. "That fellow stepped on my foot, and they were the ones who were threatening me."

"That's not the way it appeared to us," said the policeman. "We saw the whole thing. Turn around, hands on the bar."

George started to protest again, but thought better of it. He did as he was ordered. As two of the other police officers came forward and patted him down, the first officer turned back to the four Bajans. "Ok, Floyd. You and your boys can go on with your partying. We'll get this tourist out of your hair."

"Thanks, Mon," said Floyd with a grin. "This one needs to go back to England right away."

The officer nodded. "We'll see what we can do," he said.

The four Bajans left, and the police officer in charge ordered George to place his hands behind his back. He did so meekly, and one of the officers placed handcuffs on him and spun him around. George opened his mouth to speak, but the officer held up a finger in front of his face. "Do not say anything. Just come with us quietly. You are in enough trouble as it is," he warned.

"But I have a friend here who will vouch for me. His name is Stan ..." George said.

"No, I told you not to say anything," said the officer in a harsh tone. "Let's go," he said, and two of the other officers took George by the arms and led him toward the entryway, with one officer going ahead to clear a path, and the officer in charge bringing up the rear.

As George was being led out of the Dance Hut, he saw Stan over by the backroom door talking to a large Bajan man wearing a cream-colored straw hat. It was Ambrose Reynaud.

*   *   *

Chapter 20

"LET"S HAVE A luau!" announced Hank suddenly as Yong Cha braked to a stop in front of their headquarters back at the base. Jane looked at him in surprise. They had all been silent on the drive back from the orphanage after Hank's strange outburst. Hank, himself, had said nothing more, just stared out his side of the jeep, refusing to look at anyone including Jane. Now he was looking at her with a broad grin.

"Are you sure you're up for it?" asked Jane, studying him curiously with a serious look on her face.

"What do you mean? Of course, I'm up for it," said Hank. "Can't come to Hawaii without having a luau. Besides, we have all that mahi mahi and Chih"s *Mai Tais*, not to mention the Jack Daniels and the champagne. What do you say, Chih? Are you and Yong Cha up for a luau?"

The Chinese brothers looked at each other across the short expanse of the front seat and slow grins crept across their faces. Chih looked back at Hank and Jane. "Oh, yes, General Hank. We haven't had luau in years - not since the base was operational. Yong Cha and I prepare it traditional way. You and Doctor Jane relax. I bring *Mai Tais*."

"That's the spirit," said Hank and turned to Jane with a smile. "What do you say, Doctor Jane? Are you up for a luau?"

Jane looked at Hank's face and saw a mix of excitement, warmth and tenderness written there. Her heart melted, and she smiled at him. "Oh, yes, Hank. I've never been to a luau. I'd love to have my first one with you."

"All right then. Why don't you go and change into something luau-ish. I'm going to help Chih and Yong Cha unload the boxes, and then I'm going to have a shower and get out of this damned Mickey Mouse shirt." He glanced at his watch. "I'll meet you on the lanai at precisely sixteen hundred."

Jane laughed and gave him a mock salute. "Yes, Sir! General Kingsman, Sir! I'll be there."

* * *

At ten o'clock the full moon cast its glow through a framework of palm fronds when Hank and Jane walked back to the house from the nearby palm grove where Chih and Yong Cha had held their luau. Hank reached over and took Jane's hand as they walked, and her fingers interlaced with his as if that was their natural state. They paused under a grouping of three palms, and Hank drew her to him so that she stood leaning against his chest. He encircled her with his arms and they stood gazing up at the moon for a moment. After a bit he reached down and brushed the nape of her neck with his lips, a feathery touch that caused her to shiver in ecstasy.

"Sweet Jane," he murmured.

She turned in his arms and put her arms around his neck lifting her face to his. They shared a long, gentle kiss, and when they drew back and stood gazing at each other their eyes were moist with emotion. "How do you feel?" he asked in a low, soft voice.

Her lips curved upward in a tender smile. "Beautiful. Wonderful. Absolutely perfect. What about you?" she murmured in a low husky voice.

"The same, only better. In fact, I don't remember ever feeling quite like this," he said, the smile crinkling the corners of his eyes. "Come. I have a surprise for you back on the lanai."

She sighed with a contented happiness, and they turned and walked hand-in-hand the rest of the way into the house and onto the lanai. As Jane stood looking up at the moon and feeling the gentle warm breeze on her skin, Hank disappeared for a moment and then she felt the warmth of his presence behind her. His arm came around her and in his hand was a large glass of champagne with a tiny orchid floating on top.

She laughed delightedly as she took the glass and turned toward him. He held a glass of champagne also, and they raised their glasses to each other and took a sip, their eyes never leaving each other over the rims of the glasses. He took her free hand and led her over to a large rattan armchair with an ottoman. He placed both their champagne glasses on a cocktail table beside the armchair where there was a huge glass tub containing ice and two bottles of champagne. He sat down in the chair, put his legs on the ottoman and drew her down onto his lap.

Jane nestled into the crook of Hank's arm and lay her cheek on his chest.

They sat this way for a bit, occasionally taking sips of champagne, and then Hank spoke. "Jane, I never expected something like this to happen, especially on a mission, but it has. I never expected to feel this way about anyone, especially at this age, but I do. I'd say I feel like a teenager, but with the exception that I've been around long enough to know that this is far beyond just a physical thing. The moment I saw you at Green Gate, I knew. Even though you were all covered up except for your eyes, I knew. I knew you are the one I've been waiting for all my life, and suddenly there you are popping up at the least expected moment. I hope to hell you feel the same, because I'm afraid you're not going to be getting rid of me."

He stopped and took a gulp of champagne and held his breath, waiting. Jane had not moved. He waited and the thought occurred to him that perhaps she had fallen asleep and hadn't heard a word.

Suddenly she sat up and faced him with a smile and tears in her eyes. "Oh, Hank, I am so glad to hear that," she said. "I felt exactly the same thing when I first met you, but I tried to force it aside. If nothing, I've always been the true professional, you know, and falling in love with your boss is hardly the professional thing to do. But for the first time in my life, in this case I don't care. You're the one I've been looking for and I'm not letting go of you, no matter what, so you'd better just be resigned to the fact that you are stuck with me, period."

They stared into each other's eyes with somber expressions for a moment and then a smile broke over Hank's face. "Good," he said, a mischievous light coming into his eyes. "Now that that's settled, let's get back to business."

Jane swatted him. "Oh, God! You're incorrigible!" she blustered. They both laughed and then kissed again long and deeply as if sealing a pact.

Hank reached over and refilled their glasses. They touched glasses and sipped more champagne in silence for a bit and Jane laid her head back down on his chest. Hank tilted his head back onto the chair and closed his eyes.

"Hank?" asked Jane after a few moments of silence.

"Yes, darling," he murmured without opening his eyes.

"Hank, what do you remember from the time you were stationed here?"

Hank opened his eyes and frowned, but he did not move. "It's strange," he said slowly. "I know I was stationed here for about two years. I was a captain then, and I was flying a new kind of plane - testing, I think, but I don't seem to be able to remember anything about that time."

"There are things you've said that seem to indicate you know what happened here to cause them to cordon off this base ... you don't remember anything about that?" probed Jane gently.

"It seems that I know ... that I should know," he said slowly. "I have flashes of recognition here and there ... sort of like déjà vu, but nothing comes to mind clearly when I try to think about it."

"Today, when we were flying over the orphanage, you had a reaction. Do you remember?"

Hank closed his eyes and winced as if in pain. "Yes ... When I saw the orphanage from the air, an overwhelming feeling of guilt and horror swept over me. I don't know why. I wish I knew ..."

"Do you think it has anything to do with our mission - what happened to the twins, for example?"

Hank was silent for a moment and then his eyes flew open again. He squeezed Jane's shoulder tightly. "Yes," he said in a surprised tone. "Yes, I feel that it does somehow, but I can't think why."

Jane sat up in Hank's lap and looked at him. "I've been observing some things from the perspective of my knowledge of psychiatry, and

I think I know what may be going on - why you can't remember," she said in a soothing voice. "I believe I can help you remember if you want to."

He looked into her eyes without raising his head. "What's your diagnosis, Doctor?"

Jane smiled gently. "Well, this overwhelming sense of guilt you have experienced on several occasions tells me that it's possible that what happened here was so painful to you that you may have suppressed it - buried the memory deep in your subconscious. It's a fairly common - natural - way the psyche has of protecting itself from feelings of pain and guilt brought on by a traumatic event in one's life."

Hank closed his eyes and swallowed. "I've heard of that," he said. "I know it happens to soldiers who've been wounded or captured. They don't remember the events afterwards. I think they call it a kind of amnesia."

"That's right," said Jane quietly. "The body has natural defenses against pain, whether it's physical or emotional or both."

"And you think that's what's going on with me?" asked Hank, opening his eyes and looking at her again.

Jane nodded. "It seems you have all the symptoms."

"And you think you can make me remember? How?" asked Hank.

"It's a technique similar to hypnosis. But it won't work unless you truly want to remember and you trust me. Do you trust me, Hank?"

"Completely," he said without hesitation. "And I definitely want to remember if there's even the slightest possibility it will help solve the puzzle we're working on. Is there a downside?"

Jane nodded. "The downside is that if you remember what happened, it will bring back all the pain that the amnesia is protecting you from. Of course, once I know what the problem is, I will try to help you cope with the pain or be able to let it go, but you will definitely have to live through it again. Do you want to take that chance?"

Hank considered this for a moment. "Yes. It can't be any worse than being shot down behind enemy lines and having to crawl through drainage ditches for three days thinking you were going to be killed any second. I lived through that, and I'll live through this. I truly want to know what happened here, so we can get on with our mission. What do I have to do? Are you going to dangle a watch in front of my face?"

Jane grinned at him. "Boy, are you behind the times! No. All you have to do is drink some more champagne and then we'll go lie down on your bed together."

Hank grinned back at her. "Hey, that's the kind of treatment I can definitely handle. Are you sure you don't have hypnotism confused with seduction?"

Jane looked at him with a solemn expression. "Definitely not. Hypnotism comes first. Then the seduction, but you have to help with that."

"Oohwee! Let's go!" cried Hank with an enthusiastic grin.

"Not so fast, Cowboy," said Jane, poking him on the chest with her finger. "We need to drink the rest of that champagne first. Doctor's orders."

After the champagne was gone, Hank having drunk the lion's share, Jane got up and took Hank by the hand and led him to the door of his bedroom. By this time they were both feeling relaxed and pleasantly tipsy. At the door, Jane turned toward Hank, so that he could open the door and go in first. Instead, he put his arms around her and drew her up to him for a kiss. As the kiss went on and grew deeper and Jane felt one of Hank's hands creeping up to her breast, she reluctantly broke away and held up a finger. "Later," she whispered. They were both breathing heavily.

Hank groaned and opened the door. "You're the doctor," he said. "But now this is starting to seem more like torture than therapy."

Jane grabbed Hank's hand and held it up to her lips. She kissed his palm and rubbed her cheek on it. "Trust me, darling. It will be all right."

She instructed him to take off his shoes and lay on his back on the bed fully clothed. After lighting a candle that sat on the bed stand on one side of the bed, Jane turned out the lights and lay down on her back next to Hank. She reached over and clasped his hand. "Now, then Hank. I want you to just relax and look up at the candlelight flickering on the ceiling, and we're just going to talk for a while. I love you, and I want to know everything about you now that I've finally found you. Tell me about your family and where you grew up."

Hank squeezed Jane's hand, looked up at the ceiling and began to talk. For the most part, Jane listened, reassuring him with a squeeze of the hand, or an occasional question or an "I see," or "How nice," or "Mmmm" in response.

Around midnight, Hank had arrived at that point in his life story where he had been assigned to a special mission on Kahlula Air Force Base on the big island of Hawaii. Jane was careful not to change the pressure of her hand on his, or the tone of her voice, or in any other way convey her heightened interest in this part of his life story.

"I was a captain, just out of the Academy, and it was my first mission in the actual Air Force," said Hank. "It was 1983, and Ronald Reagan was President. That's when I went to Kahlula."

"What was it like at Kahlula?" asked Jane gently.

"Oh, I loved Hawaii. I thought how lucky I was to get assigned to Hawaii first thing out of the chute. Kahlula was a big base, and our headquarters were off in the southwest sector - about ten miles away from the regular personnel. We had our own little base inside the base ... called it Rat Island Express."

"Why did you call it that?" asked Jane casually.

"Because that's where we flew. That was our mission - to fly to Rat Island. It's an uninhabited desolate chunk of dirt in the Aleutians. Well, uninhabited that is, until we flew the goats and sheep in there."

"Sheep and goats?"

"Yeah, to use as guinea pigs for the experiment."

"I see. What experiment was that?"

"Testing the new plane," said Hank. "Oh, that plane was something else - like nothing anyone had ever seen before - black with swept-back wings. Looked like a flying triangle. Had to be careful where we flew it, because if people saw it, they thought it was something from outer space."

"Sounds like the old stealth fighter," commented Jane.

"Exactly right. It was the forerunner. Meant to fly in low undetected by radar, so we could make the drop."

"So you were testing this plane? But why the sheep and goats?"

"Two kinds of testing. We were testing the plane first, and then testing a new weapon that could be dropped using this plane," explained Hank.

"What was it, a new kind of bomb?"

"No," said Hank shaking his head, but still looking at the flickering candlelight on the ceiling. "No, this weapon was much less expensive than building bombs and when used would only affect people, not wipe out the infrastructure that would cost billions to rebuild."

"Do you mean some sort of chemical weapon?" asked Jane, struggling to maintain her composure and not transmit any sense of disapproval or repugnance to Hank.

"Yes. It was some sort of chemical that, in theory, would just put everyone to sleep, giving ground forces time to come in and take over without loss of life or infrastructure. Something similar to what the Russians used when the Chechan terrorists took over that theater in Moscow a number of years ago."

"But they ended up killing a whole bunch of hostages as well as the terrorists in that situation," said Jane.

Hank nodded. "Mainly because the Russians didn't want to tell anyone what they were using. If the doctors had known what it was, they could have saved a bunch of people by giving them the right antidote."

"So you were testing something similar on sheep and goats on this Rat Island in the Aleutians?"

"Yes, and in theory it would have worked except ..." He paused and frowned up at the ceiling.

"Except why?" prodded Jane, not wanting him to have time to block his mind.

"A couple of things, I guess," said Hank slowly. "A combination of the dose being too strong and the inability to control the manner in which it settled on the target. Anyway, the first batch I dropped killed every sheep and goat in sight instantly, so I didn't drop the second load. I turned around and flew back to base, figuring the scientists would have to take the stuff and figure out how to adjust the dosage. Then we'd have to fly in more sheep and goats to Rat Island and try again."

"And did they? Adjust the dosage, I mean?" asked Jane.

"No ..." said Hank slowly. "They had to abandon the project because of what happened ... because of what I did."

He fell silent and Jane squeezed his hand gently. She turned her head slightly and saw that he was still looking at the ceiling. "What did you do, Hank, that made them abandon the project?" she prompted in a low voice.

"It was when I was close to the base and getting ready to land. Couldn't get the landing gear down, so I took her back up and circled to see if I could fix it. I went back to see if I could lower it by hand, thinking that the hydraulic pump had crapped out. Then I saw that wasn't the problem at all. It was the spray gear. Somehow, either it wasn't installed properly or some bolts had come out because it was loose and dangling just below the undercarriage cowling preventing the landing gear from coming down."

He paused for a second, and Jane caught her breath quietly. "What did you do?" she asked.

"Had to think fast. There wasn't much fuel left. I figured I had only one more pass to land before I came down the hard way, so about twenty miles out, I grabbed an axe and cut the pipe to the sprayer. The whole thing fell away, twisting in the air. I got back up front and tried the landing gear - no more problem. That's when I looked down and saw that I was over the ... over the ..."

Jane heard a muffled sob and twisted her head on the pillow to look at Hank. She saw that he was still looking up at the ceiling, but his face was contorted in an expression of agony and a tear was streaking its way down the side of his face.

Suddenly, she knew. "You were over the orphanage, weren't you?" she said quietly, squeezing his hand.

"Oh, God, the orphanage. It was right below me when I cut that load loose," sobbed Hank. "I killed all those people, all the children, the priest, the nuns. Oh, God, Jane, I killed Chih and Yong Cha's parents."

Jane simply lay there squeezing his hand, allowing him to grieve. After a while, his sobbing subsided and she felt the tension decrease in his hand. Slowly she rose to a sitting position and looked down at him. His eyes were squeezed shut. She reached up with her free hand and stroked his forehead, his cheek. He opened his eyes and looked at her.

It wrenched Jane's heart to see the great sadness and pain that lay in the depths of his eyes.

"It's all right, Hank," she said in a calm soothing voice as she continued to stroke his face. "It was an accident. A tragic accident. You must find a way to forgive yourself."

Hank took a great shuddering breath and spoke almost angrily, "Forgive myself? Forgive myself! How can I forgive myself? Do you think any of those people who died or the ones who were confined to this base would forgive me for ruining their lives? What about Chih and Yong Cha? Do you think they would forgive me for killing their parents if they knew? No, Jane, there is no atonement. I cannot bring any of them back or undo what was done. I couldn't at the time. The only thing I could do was rescue the twins ... It was my way of atoning for the contamination and for their mother's death."

Jane sucked in her breath and forced herself to continue speaking in a calm, reassuring way. "The twins ... they were not at the orphanage."

Hank shook his head, and another tear slipped out of the corner of his eye. "No, but like everyone else within a mile of the direct hit, they were exposed. They would have been forced to live out their entire lives as prisoners inside this area, and they were only three months old, Jane. If I had taken responsibility when they were born, their mother wouldn't have been forced to commit suicide and perhaps they wouldn't have been here at all."

"Alicia Kalima? But why do you feel responsible for what happened to her?" asked Jane softly.

"Because it was obvious the twins' father was an American stationed at the base, and I felt guilty," said Hank, looking intently at the ceiling. Jane felt his arm tense again.

"Did you know who the father was?" asked Jane in a voice barely above a whisper.

"No, not for sure, but it could have been me." Hank reached up with his free hand and wiped a tear from his eye. Jane waited. "You see, I was with her right around the time they would have been conceived."

"But according to Chih and Yong Cha, so were many others," said Jane gently.

"That's right," said Hank. "That's why I didn't step up. She had been with so many that she didn't know who the father was, and neither did any of us. Of course, there could have been blood testing - that was really before the days of DNA - but no one, including myself, had the guts to step up and have that done."

Jane lay back down still holding Hank's hand. She stared up at the ceiling for a bit mulling over this new information. "So, somehow you were responsible for getting the twins to the mainland after the incident at the orphanage?" she asked.

"Yes ..." said Hank slowly, still gazing at the ceiling. "I felt so guilty about what I had done to the orphanage that I thought I could atone for it just a little by getting the twins to the mainland where they could be adopted and lead a normal life. When I heard they were bringing in the contamination teams, I knew I had to act fast. I couldn't leave because of the daily debriefings, so I paid Jimmy Wong, a local pilot who used to fly supplies in from Oahu, to fly them to Honolulu and then take them on a commercial airline to San Francisco where he placed them in an orphanage. You know the rest."

"So you managed to get the twins out just before they expanded the base and cordoned it off?"

"Just barely. They brought in the specialists who determined that this all had to be contained, so they cordoned off the whole area, closed down the base and evacuated the military personnel. Then they put a fence around the whole area. Ever since then, there has been an Army unit whose sole purpose is to patrol the perimeter and ensure that no one goes in or out."

"Hmmm ... we know the twins were affected even though they were not at the orphanage. I wonder why Chih and Yong Cha don't have any symptoms," said Jane slowly.

"The actual area of the contamination was centered at the orphanage and only about a mile of the surrounding area," said Hank.

"Then why did they expand the base and cordon off the whole area? Why did they keep all those people who were working on the base fenced in here if they weren't exposed to the contamination?" asked Jane with a puzzled frown.

Hank cleared his throat. "They had to make sure nothing leaked out, that"s why," he said in a disgusted tone. "What we were doing was against international treaty - the ban on chemical weapons. If that leaked out, it would have been bad enough, but can you imagine what would happen if it came out that we killed our own civilians conducting illegal testing? No, the main reason they cordoned off the area and kept people from leaving was not because of exposure to contamination, but because they didn't want them talking about anything that happened here."

Jane frowned. "So, instead we interred our own citizens in a sort-of prison camp, the same way they did Japanese Americans during World War II ..."

"That's what happened, I'm afraid," said Hank sadly.

They were silent for a moment, and then Jane turned to Hank again. "Hank, do you know what the name of this chemical was that you were testing?"

Hank thought for a moment. "I was never told what it was, but I heard it was some new concoction the scientists had come up with."

Jane looked at Hank with concern. "Do you think you might have been exposed to it, especially when you cut the sprayer away from the plane?

Hank shook his head. "No. I always wore contamination protection gear - covered from head to foot - whenever I was flying."

"Well, just in case, I think it's best that I take a sample and test your blood when we get back to Green Gate. I think I'd better do the same for Chih and Yong Cha," said Jane. "If it was some type of nerve agent you were dealing with, even a very small exposure can cause health problems years down the road. Do you mind?"

"No, take all the samples you want, but I've had many physicals and blood tests over the years and nothing has ever shown up."

Jane squeezed Hank's hand. "Just to be safe and set my mind at ease, darling. You know, you may have solved our mystery, Hank. From what you've told me, I feel confident I can go back to Green Gate and develop an antidote for the twins. I'm so glad you were able to remember."

Hank frowned and shook his head. "What I don't understand is why I couldn't remember any of this before. It seems a little extreme that I would block it all out on my own and now suddenly be able to recall all of it. I'm not downgrading your skills as a psychiatrist, you understand."

"Well, the mind can be very strong in its ability to block memory," said Jane. "You'd be surprised. You haven't told me what happened to you when you returned to the base. Do you remember that part? Did you report it? What was the procedure?"

"Oh, sure, I reported it, and I was a basket case of guilt realizing I had dumped the load directly on the orphanage. They brought in the Air Force shrinks to debrief me every day for a month and help me deal with the guilt," said Hank.

"What happened after they evacuated the base? Where did you go?" asked Jane.

"Oh, I was assigned to an entirely different area. I was based out of Frankfurt, Germany for a couple of years."

"Did you think about Kahlula and what happened here?" asked Jane.

Hank frowned up at the ceiling and shook his head slowly. "No, and that is strange now that I think about it. The moment I left Kahlula I seem to have forgotten all about it - never thought about it at all that I remember. Not until we came here and I started having these little déjà vu experiences."

"Not even when you saw the twins and read their file?" asked Jane.

"Nope. Not even then," said Hank in an incredulous tone.

Jane sat up again and looked down at him. She smiled tenderly as she stroked his forehead. "Well, darling, I believe you had some help from the Air Force in blocking out those memories. It's called post-hypnotic suggestion - a sort of induced amnesia technique."

Hank suddenly sat up. "Of course. That's it," he said with a serious look. "It wasn't to protect me from my own feelings of guilt, though, Jane. It was because it was top secret. I'm sure they wiped out our memory so we wouldn't talk about it, so no one would ever know what happened here - that the military was experimenting with chemical warfare. God! Jane, I shouldn't have told anyone about this!" He looked at her in alarm.

Jane grabbed his arm. "It's all right, Hank. It won't go any further than here. I promise. Besides, this would be classified as doctor-client privilege anyway, and I am sworn under oath not to reveal anything said to me in confidence. You trust me, don't you?"

Hank looked at the sincerity in her eyes and relaxed somewhat. He smiled slightly and raised a hand to her cheek. "Oh, yes, Doctor Jane, I do trust you, but just in case I have doubts, I'll just have to keep you with me where I can keep an eye on you, won't I? From now on, I'm afraid you're in a government protection program and will be required to abide by husband-wife privilege as well as doctor-client."

Jane looked at him in alarm for a second and then broke out in a smile. "Yes, I see what you mean. I have to say that I am really looking forward to being in this government protection program. When does it start?"

"As soon as possible when we get back to the mainland," said Hank with a broad grin. "Now, Doctor, what's next?"

"The second part of your therapy," said Jane as she reached up to remove her halter-top.

"Here, let me help," said Hank, drawing her to him.

*　　*　　*

Chapter 21

G EORGE WAS DREAMING of eating flying fish with Sherry Davenport at the Savoy. The fish were flying around their heads and he would reach up and pluck one down and pop it into his mouth. "Good morning, Mr. George," said one of the fish with a broad grin on its face as he reached up to grab it. That didn't make sense, he thought. Flying fish can't talk. Slowly he opened his eyes and saw Philip looking down at him. He was dressed in the blazer and trousers he wore when he had picked them up at the airport.

He squinted and looked about in confusion. He was lying on a cot still dressed in his Rugby shirt, shorts and sandals. Behind Philip was an iron bar door that stood slightly ajar. "Philip," he croaked. His mouth was as dry as the Sahara and even he could smell the foul odor that emanated from it. "What are you doing here?"

"I packed all your things and brought them from the hotel, Mr. George," said Philip smiling at George's confusion. "You will need to get cleaned up and dressed. You have an important appointment at ten o'clock. I will wait outside for you."

Philip set George's carry-on bag on the floor near a small sink and toilet in a corner of the cell. "Be sure to dress up. Wear your blazer and long trousers," he said, pausing at the open door of the cell.

"Appointment? What's going on? Why have you brought my bag? Am I being deported?" asked George in alarm.

Philip smiled. "Don't worry, Mr. George. You have an appointment with someone very important, and you are being provided with new accommodations until your flight back to England on Monday. You'll see."

"New accommodations? Not here in jail, I hope," said George with a frown as he slowly swung his legs over the side of the cot and pulled himself to a sitting position. Every bone in his body seemed to protest.

Philip laughed. "No, not jail, Mr. George. Get dressed now, and I'll be back in a half hour to take you to your appointment."

"Do I have to appear before a magistrate? I still don't know what I did to end up in jail," said George.

"No, you don't have to go before a magistrate. The police put you in jail for your own protection," said Philip. He closed the cell door behind him and walked off out of sight before George could say more. George shook his head sadly. He had known all along that he would be found out over that supposed computer error. He should have insisted on flying economy and staying at the Skeleton Beach Hotel as he had planned.

When Philip returned half an hour later, George was sitting on the edge of the cot feeling much better after getting out of his grimy Rugby shirt and shorts. He had washed, brushed his teeth, shaved and splashed on a bit of after-shave lotion. He had put on his navy blazer and light gray trousers as Philip had instructed.

Philip opened the cell door and picked up George's bag. "Are you ready, Mr. George?"

George nodded and rose to his feet. "Where are we going, Philip?"

"I'm taking you to Bridgetown - Government House," he said. "You have an appointment with the Prime Minister at ten."

"The Prime Minister? Bloody hell, what does he want with me?" asked George fearfully.

Philip smiled at George as he held the cell door open for him to exit. "Do not worry, Mr. George. The Prime Minister is a friend and admirer of your father."

"My father ..." muttered George as he followed Philip down a passageway past other cells. Then he remembered the letter he had found hidden with the vials his father had brought back from Barbados.

"Where is Ms. Peggy? Is she coming to this meeting as well?" asked George as they walked outside the Oistins police station where the

Royal Palms limo was parked.

Philip shook his head as he opened the back door for George. "No,

Mr. George. I took Ms. Peggy to the airport yesterday afternoon. She said her supervisor had called her back on urgent business."

"Peggy's gone back?" asked George in surprise as he climbed into the limo. "Was she with anyone?"

"Yes. She returned on the same flight with Mr. David. I drove them both to the airport."

"That figures," mumbled George disgustedly as he fastened his seat belt.

Twenty minutes later Philip pulled up to the front entrance of the imposing-looking Government House in Bridgetown. He came around and opened the door for George and escorted him up a flight of stone steps and into the grand hall. "Mr. George Goater for a ten o'clock appointment with the Prime Minister," said Philip to the Bajan woman who sat behind the reception desk.

She smiled. "One moment," she said. She punched in a number on a telephone keyboard. "Mr. George Goater is here," she said into the telephone headset she was wearing. "The Prime Minister's secretary will be right down to escort you," she said with a smile.

Philip nodded and turned to George. "When you are finished with your appointment, I will meet you out front to take you to your new accommodations, Mr. George."

"Thank you, Philip," said George. Philip grinned at him and walked back to the entryway.

"Mr. Goater?" asked a mellow male voice.

George spun around and saw a slender Bajan man dressed in a suit approaching him. He wore tortoise-shell glasses. "Yes?" said George.

The man held out his hand. "I am Jeremy Allan, secretary to the Prime Minister. Come with me. The Prime Minister will see you in a few moments. Would you like some tea?"

George shook his hand and then followed him to a set of massive carved wooden doors. "Tea would be nice," said George as he followed him inside the doors. He looked around in awe at the richly furnished room that served as the reception area for the Prime Minister's suite of offices.

George sat in an overstuffed armchair upholstered in a palm tree print. He had just finished his tea and was half-way through an article in the Barbados paper about Thundercloud winning the Gold Cup when Jeremy Allen walked up to him. "The Prime Minister will see you now, Mr. Goater."

George followed the secretary down a hallway to another set of carved doors. The secretary opened the door and stood inside allowing George to enter. "Mr. George Goater, Prime Minister," he said.

"Ah, Mr. Goater, it is good to see you again," said Owen Haynes, walking forward with his hand outstretched.

"Prime Minister," said George, shaking his hand. "I'm honored to see you again."

The Prime Minister clapped him on his shoulder. "No, Mr. George. The honor is all mine. Come, sit, have some tea and biscuits," he said motioning toward a sitting area where comfortable rattan furniture was grouped around a large cocktail table. Atop the table was an elegant silver tea service.

"How is your father, George?" asked the Prime Minister after they were settled in armchairs sipping their tea. "Is he recovering?"

"He is recovering nicely according to the latest reports," said George. Then he looked at the Prime Minister in surprise. "How did you know he had a heart attack?"

"A heart attack?" asked the Prime Minister equally surprised. "Is that what they're saying is wrong with him?"

"Yes," said George. "His doctor said he had a heart attack. They think it was brought on by the shock and stress of seeing his prize cattle destroyed because of Foot and Mouth."

The Prime Minister gave him an odd look and held out a plate of chocolate biscuits. As George selected one he said, "Well, George, I am a doctor by profession, and I can tell you that your father's illness was not caused by a heart attack. I'm also going to share a few things with you that involves your father, and for everyone's safety must be held in utter confidence. Do I have your word?"

George paused with the biscuit halfway to his mouth, and he looked at the Prime Minister with raised eyebrows. "Oh, most certainly. I would never do anything to place Dad in jeopardy. Also, I just retired from the Foreign Office, and I'm used to keeping government secrets."

Seeing George's stunned look, the Prime Minister chuckled. "Fine,

George. First of all, I believe what your father has is our tropical plague known as Dengue. As you probably know by now, your father was here about three weeks ago, and when I saw him right before he left, he was already showing symptoms of it."

"Dengue? What is that?" asked George.

"It's a flu-like virus spread by the bite of infected mosquitoes. Causes severe headache, muscle and joint pain. The joint pain is so severe, it's sometimes called 'breakbone feve'"."

George sat straight up in his chair. "Is this Dengue similar to the Mad Cow virus in humans?"

The Prime Minister looked at him in surprise. "Not at all," he said. "First of all, variant Creutzfeldt-Jacobs Disease, or vCJD - the human variety of Mad Cow - is not a virus."

"Not a virus? I was told that it was ..." said George, remembering Peggy and her analyzer.

"Oh, definitely not. Anyone with basic training would know that. Although we don't know for sure, the most accepted theory is that a modified form of a normal cell surface component known as a prion protein causes Mad Cow. It is definitely not a virus. Who told you that?"

"A woman who is an epidemiologist and works for the Ministries of Agriculture and Health. It all started when I discovered Dad had been to Barbados and found some vials and some documentation that he appears to have brought back to England with him."

The Prime Minister raised his teacup delicately to his mouth. "Describe the things you found, please."

"There were three vials containing liquid, two of human blood and one of horse semen. There was also a receipt from the Veterinarian Association of Barbados and a letter from your office thanking my father for his assistance," said George watching the Prime Minister closely.

The Prime Minister nodded and set down his teacup. "That is correct," he said. "Please go on. Tell me how you learned what was in the vials."

George leaned back in his chair and rubbed his chin. "Well, it was the day after I retired. I got a call that my dad had been taken to hospital with what they said was a heart attack. There was a Foot and

Mouth outbreak at my dad's farm, and after I went to the hospital in Bridgefield, I went to the farm. It was cordoned off, but they let me in, and there was this woman there - Peggy Valentine. She said she was an epidemiologist and that she worked for both the Ministry of Health and the Ministry of Agriculture. She had a computer and an analyzer and said she was there to run tests and find out how the outbreak had occurred.

"Anyway, after I found the vials, she tested the contents in her analyzer to see what they contained. According to her testing, one of the vials contained a blood sample from a woman named Denise Downing who was originally from Barbados. Her analysis showed that this Denise had a variation of Mad Cow virus and that my dad had the same thing. The other blood sample was from Denise Downing's father, but it did not contain the same virus."

"How did this machine determine that Denise Downing and your father both had this supposed variant of Mad Cow, George?" asked the Prime Minister with a curious expression.

"It plotted a graph of what was contained in the blood, and then Peggy cross-referenced it to the DNA and health records data banks on file at Bletchley," said George.

"And what about the horse semen, George?"

"She analyzed that and said it was from the sire of one of Lord Bonderbrook's foals - a filly named Sally Mae out of his mare April Storm. Later, she discovered the sire was Thundercloud, belonging to Lord and Lady Kimberly of Barbados - the very horse that won the Gold Cup on Thursday."

The Prime Minister smiled. "Well, George, the lady was correct about the horse semen, but wrong about the Mad Cow. Let me explain." He shifted in his seat and took another sip of tea. "As I said before, Mad Cow is caused by altered prion proteins. You can think of these as very small pieces of a jigsaw puzzle. They do not have DNA because they multiply by attaching themselves to good cells and converting them to duplicate themselves. The technical term is cloning. When enough normal cells have been altered brain damage occurs. The only way to find out if someone has the disease is to dissect the brain after death."

"No DNA and you have to be dead!" blurted out George. "Seems I've been led up the garden path, but why?"

"But not entirely, George. She identified the owner of the horse semen and identified Denise Downing through her blood sample," pointed out the Prime Minister. "Tell me more of what you discovered about Denise Downing," he said looking intently at George.

"Because of her access to the DNA and Medical Records data banks maintained at Bletchley, Peggy discovered that Denise Downing is from Barbados, but that she and her Uncle Roger Clemens were living in England. Denise was in a private hospital in East Croyden and her uncle lived in West Hamstead. She was correct about that, because I went to visit Denise and got in to see her. She suffers from some sort of disease that causes uncontrolled muscle spasms and dementia. The nurse said it was Genetic Encephalitis inherited from one of the parents. Of course, I didn't believe that because Peggy had told me the analysis had showed that she had a variant of Mad Cow disease. She was also being treated with a special drug that calmed her right down, and I managed to come away with a discarded vial that the nurse had used to give her an injection."

"Quite interesting, George. Now, what did the lady have to say about the other blood sample?"

"She determined that it belonged to Denise's father, but that it didn't contain any of the so-called Mad Cow virus."

"And were you able to find out who Denise's father is?"

George shook his head. "No. The people at the hospital didn't know either. They said her mother had died in a car accident here in Barbados a few years ago and that she had not told anyone who Denise's father was. I went to see her uncle, Roger Clemens, the next day to see if he knew anything, but he had disappeared and the police were looking for him."

"And who decided that you should come to Barbados, George?"

"It was my own idea, really," said George. "I had discovered that my Dad had been here just before his heart attack, even though there was no record of the trip on his passport. I ran into a bloke who took him to the airport - said he'd forgotten and left his passport at home, but just called someone he knew who made arrangements for him to fly in and out of the country without it. I found the vials and the veterinarian receipt and the letter and about Denise Downing. I decided the answers to everything were here in Barbados."

"And this Peggy Valentine came with you?" asked the Prime Minister.

"Yes, I convinced her to come along. She called her supervisor and got permission. In fact, you met her, Prime Minister. She was part of that group with Julian Fleet at the races when I was introduced to you. She was the one in the big floppy hat."

The Prime Minister frowned. "Are you sure? I don't remember being introduced to a Peggy Valentine ... I remember Julian Fleet and Lord and Lady Kimberly and that model Lady Dimshire. I remember Carolyn Braithwaite, the actress, was there, along with her agent, but I don't remember meeting your Ms. Valentine." He paused for a moment, thinking, and then shrugged. "Well, no matter. Perhaps she was there and we just never had the chance to be introduced before the races started. Tell me, George, have you learned anything while you've been in Barbados?"

"Well, thanks to Philip, I found out Denise's grandparents are still living, and I went to visit them hoping that they could tell me who Denise's father is," said George slowly.

"And did they?" asked the Prime Minister looking at him questioningly.

George shook his head. "No. They said their daughter Cecily had always refused to tell anyone because Denise was born out of wedlock and that's why her last name is the same as theirs - Downing. Said no one will ever know because Cecily was killed in a car accident three years ago and took it with her to the grave."

The Prime Minister smiled. "You spoke to Malcolm and Beth Downing?"

"That's right," said George. "You know them?"

"Barbados is a small place," said the Prime Minister nodding. He rose from his chair and held out his hand to George. "Well, Mr. George, I'm afraid I have another appointment in a few moments. It has been a pleasure to meet Bill Goater's son. Please give my regards to him. I hope he recovers from the Dengue soon. I'm sure he will. It usually runs its course in fourteen days to a month."

"It's a pleasure to meet you, also, Sir. I know my father would send his regards to you too if he had been able to speak," said George rising and shaking the Prime Minister's hand.

The Prime Minister walked him to the door with one hand on his shoulder and ushered him through. "Good-bye, George, and enjoy the rest of your stay in Barbados. Be sure to tell your father that thanks to you, we now have proof of the identity of Denise's father, and the assurance of our success in the next election. He will be delighted to hear that."

"We do?" asked George completely at sea. "Who is it?"

"Perhaps you'll come back for another holiday soon. Thank you again, George." The Prime Minister closed the door leaving George with his mouth hanging open.

*　　*　　*

The moment George walked out the entryway to Government House, Philip popped out of the limousine and rushed to open the back door for him. "How was your meeting, Mr. George?" he asked.

"Fine. Your Prime Minister seems a very fine man," said George, pausing at the door that Philip held open for him.

Philip smiled. "Yes, he is. He and his party have done many good things for Barbados. We just want to make sure his party wins the next election so he can continue his plans."

"He said to tell my dad that thanks to me, he now has proof of the identity of Denise Downing's father and assurance of success in the next election. I have no idea what he's talking about, do you?" asked George with a puzzled look.

"I can't say. You will have to ask your father," said Philip with a mysterious smile. "Please get in, Mr. George. I need to take you to your new accommodations. You are expected for lunch."

"That's another thing. Where are you taking me? I don't understand why I am being moved from the Royal Palms," said George, making no move to get into the car.

"I am taking you to Kimberly Plantation, Lord Kimberly's estate. You are being moved for your own safety. It is too dangerous for you to remain at the Royal Palms," said Philip.

George frowned. "Lord Kimberly? Why don't you just take me to Jonkanoo Cottage to stay with Stan? I believe he's returning on the same flight I am on Monday."

"It would be even more dangerous for you there. Besides, Mr. Stan has had a change of plans and will be leaving earlier than he expected," said Philip. He held up a hand when he saw that George was about to ask another question. "I can say no more. Please get in. You do not want to keep Lord Kimberly waiting."

"But I don't understand ..." protested George, as he started to climb in the back seat.

"Trust me, Mon. It's best for you not to know too much for your own good," said Philip with a serious look as he closed the door.

Thirty minutes later after traveling east into the island's interior, the limousine turned into a lane fronted by a massive wrought-iron gateway. On the arch of the gateway were the words *Kimberly Plantation, Est. 1630.* As they drove along the lane, George admired the royal palms that lined the sides of the roadway. On the other side of the palms were acres of white fencing, and inside the fences were dozens of thoroughbreds, ranging from spindly-legged foals to fillies and colts to sleek mature mares, geldings and stallions.

After about a quarter of a mile, the plantation house came into view - a huge rambling two-storied white wooden structure, complete with verandas, balconies, columns and pale green shutters on its many windows. It appeared large enough to be a hotel. A circular drive swept by the front entrance, and in front of the drive and surrounding the house were large expanses of lush green grass dotted with groupings of tropical plants and stone fountains and bougainvillea cascading over walls and arches and trellises.

"My word!" exclaimed George in awe as he climbed out of the car. He put a hand up to shade his eyes and looked around the grounds.

Philip smiled as he retrieved George's bag from the trunk. "Quite something, isn't it? It is the best preserved plantation in Barbados."

"The sign at the gate said 'established in 1630.' This surely isn't the original house?"

Philip pointed at the central part of the house. "The central part is the original. Over the years the other wings were added." He motioned to the left and right sides of the structure.

"Have the Kimberlys always owned it?"

Philip nodded. "James Kimberly was one of the original eighty English settlers who came here with Captain Powell. He built the original house, and until the late 1800s, this was a working sugar cane plantation. James Kimberly served in the House of Assembly, and was given the title by King James I. Lord Lesley is the eighth Lord Kimberly. His great grandfather Lord William turned it into a thoroughbred farm in the 1900s."

George followed Philip to the steps leading up to the veranda, which was covered with groupings of rattan furniture and potted palms. The double doors of the house stood open, and inside George could see highly polished teakwood floors covered here and there with rich tropical print carpets. A palm-frond electric ceiling fan swirled in the circular foyer.

"Ah, there you are, Mr. Goater!" Lord Kimberly, dressed in a light khaki short sleeved shirt and brown riding pants suddenly appeared at the door with a frustrated-looking Bajan man in tropical shirt and tan shorts trailing him. He bounded down the steps and grabbed George's hand in a hearty handshake.

"Lord Kimberly," George managed to croak in surprise as his hand was being enthusiastically pumped up and down.

"Kimberly, Schmimberly. Name's Leslie. Call me Les. Delighted to have you here, old chap!" He gave George a solid smack on the shoulder that jarred his teeth.

"Please call me George," he said still in shock at this enthusiastic greeting.

"George, it is," said Kimberly. "And how are you, Philip?" he asked, turning to Philip with his hand out.

"Excellent, Lord Leslie," he said shaking his hand.

"Right. Just give me that bag and we'll show George to his room. Lunch on the back veranda in fifteen minutes - fish and chips." Kimberly started to reach for the bag that Philip was holding, but the Bajan who had followed him out of the house intervened.

"Allow me, Lord Kimberly," he said with a grimace. He snatched the bag out of Philip''s hand and rolled his eyes upward. Philip grinned.

Kimberly gave a hearty laugh. "Oh, right, Jackson. Forgot about you."

Jackson rolled his eyes again at Philip. "Does this to me all the time," he muttered at Philip and shook his head. "What's the good of having a butler, if you won't let him butle?"

Kimberly laughed heartily again and grinned at Philip. "Stay for lunch, Philip?" He put an arm around George's shoulders to lead him into the house.

"Thank you, Lord Leslie, but I have to get back before the Royal Palms sends out a search party. Good-bye, Mr. George. Enjoy the rest of your stay in Barbados. If you come again, call me and I'll be pleased to pick you up at the airport," said Philip, handing George a card with his private cell phone number written down.

"Thank you for everything, Philip," said George over his shoulder as Kimberly hauled him toward the front door, a disgruntled Jackson bringing up the rear with his bag.

*   *   *

The Barbados sun had completed three-fourths of its journey toward its daily dip in the Caribbean Sea. George in shirtsleeves and a Panama hat on loan from Lord Kimberly climbed out of the Land Rover as Lord Kimberly braked to a stop in front of the vast stables located some distance to the west of the plantation house.

He followed Kimberly to the far end of the stables where there was a paddock enclosed by a whitewashed rail fence. As Kimberly approached the fence, the sole occupant of the paddock raised his head and nickered, his nostrils quivering. Kimberly propped one booted foot on the bottom rail and leaned with his arms draped over the top rail, one hand extended. George followed suit.

"Come, boy," said Kimberly in a low voice, opening the palm of his hand. The sleek black stallion tossed his head up and down and nickered again. "That's right, boy. Come on over for your treat."

The stallion tossed his head again and ambled over to Kimberly in a nonchalant manner. He stretched his neck out and took the sugar cube from the palm of Kimberly's hand. Kimberly reached up with his other hand and grasped the soft lead halter on the stallion's head. "Say hello to George, Thundercloud," said Kimberly in a soothing voice as he stroked the stallion's neck.

Thundercloud stretched out his neck toward George and curled his lips back showing strong white teeth. George quickly pulled his arm back from the rail. "It's all right," said Kimberly with a soft chuckle. "That's his way of saying hello. Give him a pat. He won't bite."

George tentatively reached out his hand and the stallion stood still while he patted his neck. Then he tossed his head up and down again softly blowing through his velvety nostrils. "What a beauty," said George admiringly. "Never spent much time around horses, but if they were all like Thundercloud, I'd be hooked."

"Yes, he is a beauty. A true champion. He's sired many more all around the world and has plenty left in him. His stud fees keep us in oats and entry fees around here," commented Kimberly with a grin. He released his grip on the halter, and the horse tossed his head, kicked up his heels and took a couple of turns around the paddock, his tail arched out behind him. He came to a stop a short distance away.

"Well, George, this is a good place to talk. I'm sure you have many questions that I may be able to answer. I've always found that it's safe to talk in front of Thundercloud. He's quite good at keeping secrets," said Kimberly, glancing over at George with a slight grin.

George looked at him in surprise. He cleared his throat and said somewhat hesitantly, "Well, first of all, I don't understand why I have been moved here from the Royal Palms ..."

"You see that horse out there," said Kimberly looking across the paddock and waving his hand at Thundercloud. "He's very valuable because he possesses certain qualities other horses don't have. There are those who would harm him or try to take what he has, so we keep him in well-guarded quarters to protect him. Remember what happened in the Winner's Circle the day of the Gold Cup?"

George gasped. "You mean that chap that the police hauled away?"

Kimberly nodded.

"I was told he was probably just an overly enthusiastic fan who was high on drugs," said George.

"No, George. He had a needle. He was trying to inject Thundercloud with a fatal substance."

"What! Why would anyone want to do that?" asked George.

"To get at me the same way they wanted to get at your dad and Lord Bonderbrook."

George stared at Lord Kimberly, but Kimberly did not return his look. "I don't understand. Why Dad and why Lord Bonderbrook?"

Kimberly sighed. "It's a long story, George, having to do with British Imports and Exports. You know what I mean?"

George's eyes widened. "You mean the backroom boys ..."

Kimberly put up his hand. "Yes," he said quickly cutting him off. "As you may be aware, BI and E is a huge global enterprise with offices in nearly every country in the world and has many employees."

"Are you an employee?" asked George in a voice just above a whisper.

Kimberly smiled slightly and shook his head. "No, George, but on occasion I do a bit of work for them on a contracted basis."

"What about my dad?" asked George quietly.

"Bill's retired, but he is still on the payroll as a consultant, as they like to call it."

George sucked in his breath and swallowed hard. "What about Lord Bonderbrook, then? He's Britain's representative on the European Commission."

"That he is. Puts him in the perfect position to be BI and E"s General Manager for the Eastern European Division."

"Bloody hell!" exclaimed George. "How did I get sucked up into this?"

"Because of your dad, George, and you must never breath a word of what I've told you. Do you understand?"

George nodded solemnly still trying to digest what he had learned.

"Good," said Lord Kimberly. "Now I'm going to tell you a story for your ears only, understood?"

Again George nodded with a grim look on his face.

Lord Kimberly looked out at Thundercloud grazing in the paddock and began. "Once upon a time in Barbados, a Bajan fisherman and his wife had two sons and a daughter. The oldest son was Martin, the second son was Lucas and the daughter was Cecily." He paused and glanced at George. "Following me so far?"

George sucked in his breath. "Last name of Downing?" he asked.

Lord Kimberly nodded and looked back out at the paddock. "Now, Martin, who was eight years older than the daughter, fell in with bad company and found ways to make lots of money through the drug trade and other illegal means. He had no scruples and when his sister was around ten years old, he began molesting her and then raping her. Because of the threats and guilt he placed on the child, she never told anyone this was going on. When the police were ready to arrest him for drug dealing, Martin disappeared leaving Cecily pregnant at the age of thirteen. Nine months later, Cecily gave birth to a baby girl, and because of her fear of Martin never told her parents or anyone else who the father was."

"And the baby's name was Denise Downing?" whispered George.

"That is correct," said Lord Kimberly. He took a breath and went on. "When Denise was about thirty years old, Martin returned to Barbados. He had changed his name, and because he was much older, he looked entirely different. By this time, he was extremely wealthy and influential and he began buying up property including another plantation south of here and a number of resorts, including the Royal Palms. Then he entered politics and quickly became leader of the Barbados Independent Labor Party - the opposition party at present."

George's eyes widened as he remembered the man he had met at the races. "Is he that Ambrose Reynaud chap? I met him at the races and recall Stan telling me he was the leader of the opposition party and the wealthiest man in Barbados."

"Precisely. But you must never say that you know his real name if you value your life," said Kimberly staring out at Thundercloud. "Do you comprehend?"

George gulped and nodded. "Yes, I see what you mean," he said in a low tone, his voice quavering.

"Good," said Kimberly without looking at George. "Now, on with the story. At first things appeared to be going Martin's way until he discovered that there was someone who did recognize him, and that was Cecily. She went to him and threatened to expose him because of his abuse of her when she was a child and told him he had a daughter out of incest. Now, that's the kind of thing that would write your death sentence in politics. It wasn't long after that Cecily was killed in a strange car accident in Bridgetown."

"Oh, my God! Did he actually kill his own sister?" gasped George.

"At the time, everyone thought it was an accident, although a freakish one. No one knew his link to Cecily, you see. It would have gone undetected if there had not been someone else who knew the whole story."

"Someone else knew?" asked George. "Was it Denise?"

Lord Kimberly shook his head. "No. Denise, as you know, is afflicted with a debilitating illness, and she was in a hospital in Bridgetown. Cecily never told her or anyone else. No. It was her brother Lucas who had seen things all those long years ago and had never said a word to protect his sister's honor. Lucas had always helped take care of Denise, and after Cecily had confronted Martin, she confided in him because she feared for Denise's safety. When Cecily was killed in the car accident, Lucas knew but couldn't prove that Martin was behind it. He feared that Martin would attempt to eliminate Denise as well. Knowing that Martin had his fingers into every local government area, he decided it would be too risky to go to the police. So, he went to British Imports and Exports."

"So, Lucas knew about Denise ... but how did he manage to get in touch with BI and E?" asked George.

"Let's just say Lucas had a very good friend named Philip who knew how to put him in touch. As it turned out, British Imports and Exports already had its eye on this politician, suspecting him of being connected to a huge and dangerous drug cartel in Venezuela run by Jorge Esperanza, known as *El Gato Gordo -The Fat Cat.* They suspected him of trying to take over the leadership of the Barbados government in order to make Barbados the Caribbean base for drug trafficking between South America and Europe.

"British Imports and Exports immediately arranged to transport Denise and her uncle to England where Denise was placed in a secure private hospital, and Lucas's name was changed to Roger Clemens. Then they set about gathering evidence to expose the drug lord, and

That's where your father came in." Lord Kimberly paused and flexed his arms.

"So Dad came to Barbados to bring back blood samples that would show that Martin was the father of his sister's child?" asked George.

"That's correct," said Lord Kimberly.

"But why the vial of semen from Thundercloud?" asked George.

Lord Kimberly grinned. "Oh, that was a little favor to Lord Bonderbrook – Thundercloud's contribution to creating another champion and a sign to Lord Bonderbrook that the package had arrived in England and had been posted."

"Package? Do you mean the parcel Dad posted to West Hamstead when he arrived back at Heathrow?" asked George.

"Exactly!" exclaimed Lord Kimberly, grinning broadly at him. "And through your sleuthing, you also know who received the parcel, don't you?"

"Roger Clemens, who is really Lucas Downing?" asked George.

"Right again," said Kimberly with a smile as if he were a teacher congratulating a student for giving a correct answer.

"And what was in this parcel?" asked George with a frown.

"Something for Denise from Russia with love."

George looked at Kimberly with an even more puzzled expression.

"Think, George. You know what it was," said Kimberly with an enigmatic expression.

"From Russia ..." George thought for a moment and then snapped his fingers. "The drug - *KG9004*, I think it was called."

"Correct again!" exclaimed Kimberly. "When we discovered Denise's condition was not the product of incest as everyone had assumed, BI and E"s Eastern European Division told us Russia had developed a cure for her condition. BI and E managed to quote, unquote import some of it in through Barbados. It is curious what kinds of things tourists bring with them to ease aching muscles from too much wind-surfing."

"Is this *KG9004* a cure for Mad Cow?" asked George.

"Mad Cow? Denise doesn't have Mad Cow, although the symptoms are similar," said Kimberly shaking his head.

"That's curious. I was told both Denise and my dad have a variant strain of Mad Cow disease ..." said George.

"Your dad? Posh! Your dad has Dengue. We didn't want anyone to know that he had been to Barbados, and that is why the doctor said it was a heart attack. Because he was delirious, we didn't know what he had done with the vials, and then the threat on his life made it obvious that Reynaud knew about him. People do die of Dengue, you know."

"Do you mean that incident at the hospital?" asked George fearfully as he remembered the man who had been discovered in his father's hospital room attempting to inject something into his IV.

"Precisely, George," said Kimberly. "That and other events that occurred convinced us that someone inside BI and E was working for our friendly drug lord. You see, several threats were made against the British government and carried out."

"What threats?"

Lord Kimberly turned to George and studied him for a moment with a stern expression. "George, I must remind you that everything that is said here must never pass your lips. If you ever speak of it, you would be putting many lives in danger, including your own, do you understand?"

George returned his gaze with a somber look. He nodded. "Yes, I understand completely. I swear that I will never breathe a word."

"All right, George. I will take you at your word but remember, if you ever break that promise, there will be dire consequences." Kimberly's eyes bored into George. He turned and looked back at the paddock. "To answer your question, I will ask you one. What has been happening in England recently to cause problems for the government?"

George looked down at the fence rail and unconsciously ran a finger along it. "Well, there is the Foot and Mouth outbreak in the south ..." he began.

"And did you discover where this strain of Foot and Mouth originated?" asked Kimberly quietly.

"The papers reported that it had come from a flock of sheep that had been imported from Belgium, but ..."

"Go on," prompted Kimberly.

"But Peggy's analysis showed that it came from South America and was the same strain as in the outbreak two years ago in ... *Venezuela!*"

"Precisely."

"Oh, God! You mean Reynaud caused the Foot and Mouth outbreak?" cried George.

Kimberly nodded. "And what else? Think, George."

"Well, there have been a number of demonstrations that have increasingly become more and more violent ..."

"Right again, George. And what else?"

George concentrated on the top rail, running his finger back and forth. "I can't think ..."

"Think, George. What caused the government to lose its majority?"

"A vote of no confidence in the House of Commons." George was beginning to feel as if a professor at university was grilling him.

"And why was that?" asked Kimberly.

"The article in *The Times*!" George nearly shouted as it dawned on him. "That business about the treaty with Russia. Reynaud was behind that, too?"

"Precisely."

"But what was his motive for doing all that?"

"Because he knew we were gathering proof about his true identity and his connection to the drug cartel and were about to expose him. His intent was to destroy the evidence and silence anyone who knew the truth."

George shook his head, still puzzled. "I don't understand how he could do all that in England while he's in Barbados."

"Remember, I told you it became obvious that he had a BI and E agent working for him? We knew someone had turned rogue because it was obvious Reynaud had identified several of the BI and E agents who were working to expose him. We didn't know who this rogue agent was and were trying to flush him out. At the same time, we had to protect the people he was after. You recall that Denise Downing was taken to America shortly after you went to see her, and that her Uncle Lucas disappeared and ended up coincidentally at Stonehurst where Lord Bonderbrook had been taken after his supposed heart attack?"

"So, they were all moved for protection from the drug lord ..."

"That"s correct, George. And now, I am happy to say that because of your investigations, our rogue agent has exposed himself and will be dealt with."

"Why would an employee of British Imports and Exports be working for a drug lord?" asked George, shaking his head.

"Let's just say he was a disgruntled pensioner that liked to live beyond his means - in fact, it's someone you know quite well," said Kimberly with a mysterious air.

"I do?" asked George totally at sea. The only pensioner he could think of that he knew quite well was his dad.

Lord Kimberly turned to him with a serious expression. "You could probably sort it out if you thought about it long enough, George, but save yourself the agony. You will know soon enough, because the matter is being dealt with as we speak."

"How is it being dealt with?" asked George wide-eyed with fear.

"Now, George, you surely understand that I am not at liberty to

talk about that," said Lord Kimberly. He turned back toward the paddock and whistled. Thundercloud walked over for another treat.

"You know, George," said Kimberly as Thundercloud took the sugar

cube off his palm. "The horse breeding business is sometimes an unpredictable and brutal thing. If a horse goes lame, he's ruined and we have to put him down."

*   *   *

Chapter 22

P RESIDENT GLENN FORBES looked up from the report he was reading and smiled when he saw Prime Minister Alistair Cain's face appear on the teleconference video screen. "Congratulations, Prime Minister, on your victory in the House of Commons yesterday," he said. "I just read the full account in *The Times*."

Prime Minister Cain beamed with pleasure. "Thank you, President Forbes. As you see, there was nothing to worry about regarding our long-standing alliance. *The Times* is quite humble now, as you can imagine."

Forbes laughed. "Yes, I can imagine. It's pretty embarrassing to discover your Foreign Affairs Editor was bought off by a drug lord to run a fictitious article."

"Of course they've sacked him and he'll do a bit of time and never be able to work as a journalist again, but in the end he'll probably get millions for writing his story," said Cain in a disgusted tone. "In any event, everyone now knows there was not a modicum of truth to our supposed treaty with Russia."

"Glad to hear the Hoof and Mouth outbreak is under control too," said Forbes.

Cain grinned. "Yes. We ended up containing it in the South of England after we discovered where it originated. Unfortunately, we did have to slaughter thousands of animals, but not nearly as many as predicted."

"Well, it's good to hear the French have relented so I can send you some good Kansas beef," said Forbes.

"Right. Mrs. Cain and I are really looking forward to that," said Cain.

"Something else I'm curious about," said Forbes. "*The Times* said the Foot and Mouth originated in South America, but didn't say how it got started in England." Forbes cocked an eyebrow.

"Yes, it came from South America. Venezuela to be precise," said Cain with a deadpan expression.

"Venezuela. What a coincidence," said Forbes. "A lot of deadly things seem to originate in Venezuela, these days. Like Esperanza and his cohort Reynaud, for example. Thanks to your boys in Imports and Exports, we got 'em. It'll be a long time before they see the light of day again, if ever. You think they were the cause of all your recent troubles?"

"Without a doubt. In addition to what the public knows about *The Times* article, we also know they were responsible for spreading the Foot and Mouth and inciting hooligans during the public demonstrations. They also tried to do away with some of our MI6 agents."

"My, my," said Forbes clucking his tongue. "Whatever did you do to incite such retaliation?"

"You might say they didn't care for our politics in Barbados," said Cain with a broad grin. "In fact, the only thing they weren't behind is the so-called Mad Cow outbreak, and you know who's responsible for that."

Forbes laughed and Cain joined in. After a bit, Forbes sat forward in his seat with his hands clasped on the top of his desk. "Now, then, Prime Minister, as to that matter at Fordham Down, here's what I'm prepared to do ..."

$$* \quad * \quad *$$

Hank, in full uniform, startled the security guard outside the brick building at Green Gate by giving him a huge grin as he rushed by him into the building where Jane was waiting in the small conference room.

"General Kingsman," she said, rising from her seat at the conference table.

"You got that right!" exclaimed Hank with a huge grin as he rushed over and swept her into his arms and planted a long passionate kiss on her lips.

"Phew!" said Jane breathlessly when he finally released her. "What was that all about? I thought we had to act professional when you're in uniform. You are still a general, aren't you?"

"More a general than ever, Sweet Doctor Jane," said Hank, enthusiastically pointing at his shoulder.

"What does that mean?" asked Jane with a puzzled frown.

"Count 'em," said Hank with a grin, still pointing at his shoulder.

"Oh, the stars ..." said Jane, and then her eyes lit up as she smiled at him. "Why, there are five of them, now. They seem to have multiplied."

"That's right. Just got a promotion, and that's not all ..."

"A five-star general! Wow!" exclaimed Jane.

"How'd you like to live in Hawaii?" asked Hank grinning down at her.

"Hawaii? I'd love Hawaii, but how ..."

"Because you're gonna' marry the Supreme Commander of the Pacific, that's why, and he's stationed in Hawaii," said Hank, his hands on her shoulders.

Jane looked up at him stunned for an instant, and then it sank in. "Oh, Hank, how wonderful! Promoted to a five-star and the Supreme Commander of the Pacific, all in one fell swoop. What great news." She smiled and ran her hand over the stars on his epaulet, and then she looked up at him. "I have good news, too," she said.

"More good news. This must be my lucky day," said Hank. He sat down and drew Jane onto his lap and nuzzled her neck. "Now what is this good news?" he asked, his warm breath sending shivers up and down her spine.

She turned and put her arms around his neck and looked into his eyes. "I ran the DNA," she said.

His smile faded as he continued to look into her eyes expectantly.

"You're a father," she said.

For a moment Hank sat frozen and then he broke out into a broad grin. "Can you beat that? A five-star general and a father of twins all in one day, not to mention the soon-to-be husband of the most wonderful woman in the world!"

Tears came into Jane's eyes to see his ecstatic reaction, and they kissed long and deeply again. When they drew back, Hank looked at her tenderly for a moment, and then a frown crossed his forehead. "Jane?" he said tentatively.

"Yes, darling?" she responded with a loving smile.

"Do you think when Cory and Cody are well enough to hear the truth that they will forgive me?" he asked in a little boy's voice.

Jane smiled and stroked his forehead. "I'm sure they will, darling. Just as Chih and Yong Cha forgave you. I will explain it to them when they are well enough to comprehend."

Hank's face relaxed a bit. "Maybe when they are well, they will come to visit or even live with us in Hawaii. I would like them to meet Chih and Yong Cha ..."

"I'm sure they will," said Jane reassuringly.

After a short pause, Hank asked, "How are the patients today?"

"Much improved. Denise is further along, of course, because she's been receiving the treatment for a longer period of time. She rarely has the muscle spasms now, and her speech is improving. She still sleeps most of the day, but that is to be expected. At the rate of progress she's experiencing, I estimate she will be completely recovered in about a month - the twins in about two months."

"What about the antidote? Will there be enough of it to ship to England by the end of the week?" asked Hank.

"Yes. Fortunately, thanks to the Russians, I didn't have to develop a whole new antidote. The lab's been working night and day on it, and we'll be able to ship fifteen thousand vials by Friday, and another fifteen thousand by the end of next week."

"Great. What is it you're calling this drug? I forgot," said Hank.

"*Antisarilin*," said Jane. "Had to make sure it didn't sound anything like the Russian name, and I also altered the composition slightly so it isn't exactly the same, but still serves as an antidote for the toxin."

"That's right," nodded Hank. "Can't afford to cause a crisis with the Russians, for us or for the Brits."

Jane hesitated. "Hank, I know what happened in Hawaii, but how did Denise in Barbados and all those people in England become contaminated with this same toxin?"

"I know I can trust you. Remember, it's only between you and me,

Jane," said Hank. "You must never let on that you know any of this, understood?"

Jane nodded. "Of course. I promise."

"All right then. As to Denise - back when we were testing the stuff in Hawaii, we'd given some of it to the Brits to test in the Caribbean. We tested it on sheep and goats on Rat Island; they tested it on monkeys that had been placed in rubber dinghies out in the Caribbean Sea near Barbados. Ours was called "Operation Rattlesnake," and theirs was called "Operation Mad Cow." Anyway, the same thing happened with their testing. The stuff killed all the monkeys instantly, and not only that. It killed the fish and caused an economic crisis in Barbados. No one knew about the monkeys, and they blamed Castro for poisoning the fish in retaliation for the invasion of Grenada, so it appeared there was no evidence that they had been engaged in illegal testing of banned chemical weapons. No evidence, that is, until they discovered Denise Downing."

"How on earth did they discover her after all those years?" asked Jane.

"It was a fluke, really," said Hank. "The Brits were trying to prove that Denise was the product of incest, and everyone had assumed her condition was the result of that. When they did the testing in England, they discovered she had been contaminated with the toxin. They put two and two together when her uncle told them that Denise had started showing the symptoms not long after she had been stung by a jellyfish while she was playing in the surf one day when she was just a toddler."

"A jellyfish ... yes, I can see how that would happen with this particular toxin," said Jane thoughtfully. "Who would have thought that a jellyfish would nearly give them away."

"Yeah," agreed Hank. "I guess you could say mad cows come back to bite ... rattlesnakes, in our case."

"What about all those people in England? How did they get contaminated?"

"There's an American air base called Fordham Down near Nottingham. Turns out there was an accident there in 1990 that never made the news," said Hank.

Jane looked at him questioningly. "Do you mean to tell me ... ?"

Hank nodded. "That's right. That's where they stored all the stuff when they abandoned the project. It was never destroyed, as it should have been, and it seems there was an accident involving a forklift truck and the stuff got into the air and was carried down wind. As you know, it disperses fairly rapidly, but because of the wind, it contaminated a larger area than in Hawaii before it dispersed. Of course, the forklift operator was killed instantly when it escaped, and for years they thought he was the only casualty until all those people started showing the symptoms."

"Well, thank God, no one except the forklift operator died from it, and now we can cure them," said Jane.

"Yes, and now the Brits can claim they have a cure for that particular strain of Mad Cow," said Hank. He suddenly snapped his fingers. "Speaking of the Brits ... I nearly forgot with all the other excitement. Another surprise. We're spending our honeymoon in London, what do you think of that?"

"Oh, Hank, really? Wonderful! I've never been to England. Can we stay at the Savoy? I've always wanted to stay there," cried Jane excitedly.

"Sure, the Savoy works fine. In fact, a good British friend of mine wants to give us a reception at the Savoy," said Hank smiling at her.

"When do we leave?" asked Jane.

"This Sunday, the morning after our wedding," said Hank with a grin. "By the way, we're flying on Air Force One."

"What?" asked Jane, her eyes wide with surprise.

"That's right," said Hank. "I have a bit of business to do for the President. He is going over to meet with the Prime Minister, so we'll be flying over with him and the First Lady."

"President and Mrs. Forbes ..." said Jane stunned.

"Oh, yeah, you'll like them. Guess I forgot to tell you Glenn and I grew up together. Been friends since we were little kids. He's gonna' be Best Man at our wedding," said Hank with a playful grin.

*   *   *

Chapter 23

G EORGE'S TANNED FACE stood out amongst the winter-pale complexions of the other diners in the Savoy. He felt resplendent in his new dark charcoal suit and shiny black patent shoes that he had bought for the occasion. He sat at the table he had reserved near the window overlooking the terrace at the back of the Savoy. The wine steward delivered the silver bucket containing two bottles of Dom Perignon and set it on its stand near George's elbow. He placed two champagne flutes in front of George, popped the cork on one of the bottles, wrapped it in a white linen towel and resituated it in the ice bucket. Then he bowed slightly to George and walked off.

George glanced at his watch and looked out the window at the terrace. He felt a stir in the crowd of diners and turned to see that the maitre d'' was approaching his table followed by a tall, slender redhead wearing a black silk cocktail dress. Heads turned as she passed. George smiled and rose to his feet, his heart thumping.

"Hello, George. ''m so pleased to see you again," said Sherry Davenport as the maitre d'' held out a chair to seat her across the table from George.

"Hello, Sherry," said George, actually feeling his face flush with pleasure. "I'm so pleased you accepted my invitation to dinner."

George raised his hand slightly before sitting back down, and the wine steward appeared at his elbow as if by magic. "Champagne?" asked George.

"Oh, yes, please. My, George, this is quite lovely," said Sherry admiring the single long-stemmed white rose that had been placed across her plate.

"Well, we did so well at lunch here that I thought we should move on to the next phase and try the candlelight dinner," said George smiling. He handed her the flute of champagne that the wine steward had poured.

"I had almost given up. Thought you must not have been interested, as I didn't hear from you. It's been three weeks. Where have you been to get a tan like that?" asked Sherry.

"Had to run down to Barbados to take care of a spot of business for my dad," said George. He raised his champagne glass. "But now I'm back and called you as soon as I could. As you can see, I am interested."

"Barbados. They say it's lovely there. I've never been," said Sherry taking a sip of her champagne. "Say, you must have been there at the same time as Stan. Did you see him while you were there?"

George shook his head and picked up the menu and hid his face behind it.

"Quite a scandal at the Foreign Office, as you can imagine. We thought he had gone to Tenerife on holiday and then he turns up drowned in Barbados. Then it comes out he was involved with that drug lord, what's his name, that was arrested by the Americans. You know, the one who was part of that drug cartel in Venezuela. You surely heard about it. It's been top news in *The Times* for the last week."

George shook his head behind the menu. "Yes, I did read about it, but I don't remember the name either," he mumbled.

"And then, all that business with the Foreign Secretary committing suicide. Sir Albert certainly didn't seem to me to be the type to do that, but apparently he was in debt up to his ears. As you can imagine, the Foreign Office is in total disarray," continued Sherry.

She paused. George didn't say anything for a moment, and then he asked, "Would you like an appetizer, Sherry? I fancy the Oysters Rockefeller."

"Yes, an appetizer would be lovely. Order the same thing for me," said Sherry looking curiously at him. He was still hiding behind the menu. "Don't you find it shocking about Stan?" she asked.

"Yes. One never knows about people," said George casually. He lowered the menu and signaled to the waiter who came and took the order for two Oysters Rockefeller.

"Well, let's not talk of gruesome things tonight," he said raising his champagne glass to Sherry after the waiter departed. "Here's to the loveliest lady I know."

Sherry smiled and raised her glass. "Thank you, George. Here's to the funniest and most intriguing man I know."

"How is Lord Bonderbrook? Is he recovered from his heart attack?" asked George.

Sherry set her champagne glass on the table and smiled. "Quite well and back in commission." She leaned forward and said in a low voice, "Between you and me, there was never anything wrong with him. Seems the heart attack was all a put-up in order to take him to Stonehurst for protection from some sort of terrorist threat. What about your father, George?"

George smiled. "Oh, Dad is fine now. He's back at home, making plans. Turns out he didn't have a heart attack either. He had something called Dengue - picked it up the last time he was on holiday in Barbados. It's transmitted by mosquito bites."

"What will your father do now? Is he going to try to rebuild his Angus herd?"

"No. He's making plans to use the government compensation he got for his herd. He's going to move to Barbados and get into the horse breeding business. He has a good friend there who is in the business and has offered to help him get started. He's giving the farm to me," said George.

Sherry raised her eyebrows. "And what will you do with the farm, George? Are you going into the livestock business, too?"

George laughed. "Oh, no, not me. I've had my fill of livestock - too much trouble. I'm going to sell the farm and look for a nice country house with space for gardening. That's what I fancy. I have my eye on a place close to Sissinghurst Castle." He paused and looked over at Sherry. "Do you like the country, Sherry?" he asked shyly.

Sherry took a sip of champagne and looked at him with a slight smile. "Yes, George, I like the country very well, and I've always wanted to try my hand at garden design," she said. "Perhaps you'd allow me to see this place in Sissinghurst?"

A huge smile spread across George's face. "I'd be pleased to take you there - see what you think. How about Friday? I could meet you at the train station in Bridgefield."

"Friday would be fine," said Sherry with a smile.

The waiter arrived with their oysters. Sherry and George sat in silence smiling at each other across the table as the waiter fussed with the placement of the cocktail forks and lemons. As soon as the waiter departed, George raised his champagne glass again. "To Sissinghurst," he said.

"To Sissinghurst," Sherry repeated enthusiastically.

"Is that George Goater?" said a familiar voice at George's elbow just as he had speared an oyster and was about to pop it into his mouth.

He looked up and dropped his fork when he saw Julian Fleet and Peggy Valentine dressed in formal evening attire smiling down at him.

"No, don't get up," said Fleet as George scrambled to rise from his chair. "I don't believe you have met my associate," he said quickly before George had a chance to say anything. "Allow me to introduce Carolyn Braithwaite. Carolyn, this is George Goater."

"Hello, Mr. Goater. I'm pleased to meet you," said Peggy with the hint of a smile. "I see you like oysters. They're my favorite appetizer as well." George was speechless.

"And I don't believe I've met your charming friend," said Fleet smoothly. "I am Julian Fleet and this is my associate Carolyn Braithwaite," he said flashing his well-known smile at Sherry.

"Mr. Fleet, I'd know you anywhere, but I've not had the pleasure of actually meeting you. I am Sherry Davenport," said Sherry extending her hand.

Fleet took her hand and pressed it gently. "Ah, of course. Lord Bonderbrook's niece, are you not?"

Sherry looked at him in surprise. "That's right, but how did you know?"

"Lord Bonderbrook's a close friend. Not much gets by me, Ms. Davenport. Especially when it comes to the ladies."

"So I've heard," said Sherry with a grin.

Fleet laughed good-naturedly and turned back to the still speechless George. "George, it's excellent to run into you. As it happens, I am hosting a reception for a very close American friend of mine. He's a five-star general and Supreme Commander of the Pacific, and he will be very interested to meet you. When you and Ms. Davenport have finished dinner, please join us in the ballroom."

George's tongue was not working. He could only nod.

"Here comes the rest of my troupe, so we'll be off now. We'll see you at the reception," he said. He leaned down to George and said in a low voice, "By the way, you won't need an invitation to get into this reception, George, and your bill has already been paid, the same as it was in Barbados."

Fleet took Peggy's arm and they turned to walk away. As they walked on, another group of people in evening attire passed the table. George gasped as he recognized the two men and the woman. It was David, the sex-change surgeon, and Peter Jones, the private investigator, and Lady Zoë Dimshire. As they passed the table, they looked at George with no hint of recognition.

"Oh, George, how exciting," said Sherry smiling at him across the table. "You never told me you know Julian Fleet."

George shook his head with a puzzled frown. "I don't really know him at all."

He looked down at his plate. "You know, I believe I've lost my appetite for oysters," he said.

The End

B ENSON S. FORBES is the pen name for co-authors and married couple John Benson and Shari S. Forbes. Benson grew up in Tunbridge Wells, England and worked for the Ministry of Defense before immigrating to the U.S. For many years he was head of design engineering for various high tech companies, including several that he established.

Forbes is a native of Rush County, Kansas and is an award-winning writer and editor. A former English and journalism teacher, she wrote, edited and published a nationally-distributed publication aimed at the education community.

The couple currently divides their time between their home in the country near Sherwood, Oregon and their home in Redlands, California where they continue to draw upon their individual experiences and expertise to collaborate on producing works of fiction. *Mad Cows Come Back To Bite* is their second novel, first published in 2004. Other novels include *The Bottom Five*, published in 2003, and Cracking *Heads*, published in 2007.